MW01003978

ATLAS

BOOKS BY ISAAC HOOKE

ATLAS Series

ATLAS

ATLAS 2 (Coming December 2014)

ATLAS 3 (Coming 2015)

Caterpillar Without A Callsign

(A novella about Snakeoil's heroism on his first deployment)

Just Another Day

(A novella about Facehopper's encounter with the infamous privateer Mao Sing Ming)

Forever Gate Serial

Forever Gate 1

Forever Gate 2

Forever Gate 3

Forever Gate 4

Forever Gate 5

Forever Gate Compendium (Parts 1–5)

Other Works

Finding Harmon (Short Story)

ISAAC HOOKE

47NORTH

This is a work of fiction. Names, characters, organizations, places, events, and incidents are either products of the author's imagination or are used fictitiously.

Published by 47North, Seattle

www.apub.com

ISBN-13: 9781477826225
ISBN-10: 147782622X

Cover design by ShooKooBoo

Library of Congress Control Number: 2014910353

Printed in the United States of America

Remember me in the dark nights, when all hope seems lost.

Remember me in the storm, when you think you can't go on.

—Shaw Chopra

CHAPTER ONE

I was standing at the bus stop, minding my own business, when a two-by-four cracked me a good one on the side of the head.

It was my bad luck that it had to happen on the day I'd finally saved up enough to buy myself a ticket out of here.

When I came to, a blurry white-and-black pattern filled my vision. It took a second for my eyes to fully focus, and then I realized that the pattern belonged to the wings of a moth. It was sitting on my nose, just lounging there without a care in the world. I shifted, and the thing fluttered away, quickly vanishing into the hustle and bustle of the city around me.

I took a long inhale of the air. Lots of healthy goodies in it today: ash, dust, industrial smoke, vehicle exhaust, ozone, dried fecal matter. Great stuff. You packed fifty million people into fifteen hundred square kilometers, you were bound to get a few toxins cavorting about. The air filters just couldn't keep up. Not in this city, anyway. Breathing it was like sniffing smelling salts—really jolted you awake in the mornings. It was also useful after getting bashed in the head with a two-by-four.

Besides the throbbing pain on my scalp, the holster at my belt was empty. My augmented-reality goggles were gone. My arm was nicely splayed out too, making the microchip embedded in my wrist easily accessible. That microchip was commonly referred to as an embedded ID, and it contained everything there was to know about me. Everyone had one. Normally, only you yourself could access your ID and authorize such things as bank transfers. Unfortunately, I'd received a notification earlier this morning from CryptoG, the ID manufacturer, that the encryption scheme for my make and model had been cracked again. The notification mentioned that their programmers were diligently working on a patch "at this very moment," but as of this afternoon the corporation still hadn't published one.

I felt fairly certain if I went to a terminal and checked the account linked to my embedded ID, I'd find a zero balance.

Beaten up and robbed of my life savings because governments wanted to encourage commercial software vendors to make their software "exploitable." Well that's fine and dandy for catching criminals, I guess, but not so fine for everyone else.

Not that I was bitter.

Okay. Maybe just a little.

On the bright side, I guess I could take getting beaten up better than most people. I was a Dissuader. Or *Disuasivo* in the local lingo. Used to getting beat up. Usually for other people.

Let me explain. See, when you left home you either carried a sidearm if you looked like you could use it, or you hired a Dissuader. You really had no other choice when the city you lived in was one big ghetto.

Luckily I was off the job today. If I'd let a client get robbed with me, that would've meant the end of my contract. And maybe worse.

Protecting someone, or Dissuading as we called it, was about the only work I could get around here. My skin was too white. I stood out—which is why I'd been robbed today in the first place. Usually the sawed-off at my side was enough of a deterrent, but not today apparently. People always thought I was smart and rich because I was a *gringo*. That I knew something they didn't know. But all I had to do was open my mouth, and when they realized I could speak New Spanish perfectly, I dropped a couple of notches in the respect category. No one spoke New Spanish like that, not unless they grew up here. The barrio residents still put on those fake admiring smiles once they knew, but I could always see the truth in their eyes. *You're just a failure like the rest of us.*

I wasn't planning on living this way forever.

I had a dream, damn it.

This being robbed thing, well, that was just another setback on the road. I could handle it.

At least the robber had left my leather boots and my long black duster, the trademarks of my profession. There were too many bystanders around to rob me of everything, I guess. Speaking of which, a few concerned citizens at the bus stop were hovering over me, all talking at once. One was offering me water while cradling my head, and others were saying something about bringing over a *Guardia*. I took a sip of the proffered water, and ignored everyone else as I struggled to my feet.

A wave of dizziness passed over me. I could feel the blood dripping down the side of my head. I touched it, and flinched at the pain. My fingers came away red. I realized that my trademark Dissuader hat was missing, and in a moment of disorientation I thought it had been stolen as well. But then I remembered I hadn't brought the thing. Never wore it on "off" days.

Good. Those hats were hard to find.

No point staying here. The automated bus wouldn't let me in, not with a zero balance on my embedded ID. Besides, where I needed to go now, no bus would take me.

I began the long walk, knowing that the rest of my day was ruined.

The boxlike buildings around me were one of three base colors: faded orange, faded brown, or faded red. Laundry invariably hung from the balcony railings, or from clotheslines strung between the window grills. There were a few dilapidated shops on the first floors of some buildings. The awnings of street vendors who'd decided to camp out on the sidewalks used up the rest of the space. There was a fold-up cafe serving coffee and tamales on dirty plates. A man selling burnt corn from a hot box. A pastry vendor whose churros looked like dried sticks of beef. There were a few clothes sellers, and the clothing looked relatively decent, I had to admit. For knockoffs.

The streets were packed with the lunch crowd and the vendors were doing brisk business. Cheap fatty food was always a hit with people who made five microcoins a day. You'd think you wouldn't see so many happy faces, but here they were, smiling away as they ate and drank. That's one thing to be said about the people here; they were certainly resilient.

They all carried holsters, either on slings or belts, the stocks of sawed-offs and the grips of pistols readily visible. I felt extremely vulnerable, walking those streets. Everyone seemed to be looking at me. I was white. And I had no gun.

Not that I had anything of value left to rob.

Except my life.

I turned onto a side street, leaving behind the public face of the barrio, and things got more dilapidated. Very few people walked the street here. There were no vendors on the sidewalks. No open shops. Just a bunch of aluminum security doors and grilles rolled down and locked. The uneven sidewalk was littered in plaster that had chipped from the graffiti-covered buildings. One of the abandoned buildings was slathered in posters of *putas* competing for attention. Audio/video loops activated as I passed, and I was bombarded with solicitations: big breasts, little breasts, long hair, short hair, young, old, shaven, hairy, however I wanted them, whenever I wanted them. Just look up the embedded ID and send a message for the time of your life.

I continued on my way. If I felt vulnerable before, now I was positively afraid. Not the best part of town to find oneself in without a gun.

I took off my holster and slid it under my duster. Let any watchers think my weapon was hidden. I raised my double collar. The rim reached past the tip of my nose, making me feel a little like a *bandido*. It was the look I wore when on duty. All Dissuaders did. It would let any who watched me know who I was, and hopefully "dissuade" them from bothering me.

I passed a police robot, one of the *Guardias* as the locals called them. Humanoid in shape, it was made of high-grade polycarbonate. Its blocky arms and legs were colored black and yellow, with grills in the back. The connecting joints—elbows, shoulders, knees, ankles, fingers—were circular. I could hear the subtle whir of servomotors in those joints with every step the thing took.

The head, which was about half the size of a human's, reminded me of the inverted scoop of some excavating machine, complete with serrated bottom. It had antennae and a yellow bar down the middle of its face with two small glass disks stacked one atop the other. A red dot above those disks acted as a laser sight for depth perception. On the very top of the head was a small, inactive emergency light, similar to the ones you found on cop cars. That head didn't contain the silicon brain—the large rectangular box on the chest was for that.

The sight of a police robot wasn't all that reassuring, and I definitely didn't feel any safer. Sometimes the kids liked to lure the *Guardias* into back alleys. When they had one cornered, they'd pound the crap out of it with two-by-fours, pipes, and baseball bats. It was risky, but the kids who survived made good coin selling the fragments. Robot parts went for a small fortune on the black market—3D printers were a rarity around here. And the markup one could expect on the magnesium-ion battery packs was ridiculous. Yeah, I guess it's pretty obvious I'd been one of those pipe-carrying kids.

The police robot swiveled its head toward me, and I blinked as the laser sight flashed into my eyes. The robot was confirming that my face matched the face in my embedded ID, and that I had no outstanding warrants. In moments it moved on.

I wasn't a threat, according to the robot. Just a penniless Dissuader with a fresh scalp wound. Harmless, of course.

Sure.

For a brief moment I considered making a grab for the robot's rifle, which protruded temptingly from the sling around its left shoulder. If I could get it in time to blast the brain case, I might even succeed. If I got that rifle, I wouldn't have to go where I was going. All would be well.

Other than the fact that robbing the robot would be wrong.

Anyway, I'd seen how quick on the draw those robots were. Maybe when I was a kid and felt more invincible (and less moral) I might've made a grab like that. But I wasn't feeling all that invincible today. Besides, I'd heard the designers had added a locking mechanism to the newer models so that only police robots could draw and fire the rifles. I also heard that the things "called home" now before they shut down, transmitting the IDs of any nearby people. If I took that robot out, I'd wake up tomorrow to a whole troop of the things at my door.

Oh well. It was a nice thought.

I watched the police robot retreat. The "*lo mejor coño*" graffiti some kid had sprayed on its backside made my day. That literally meant "the best pussy."

The few locals I passed left me alone. They recognized me for what I was. Good. This was where I grew up after all. I even had a few clients here.

In fact, I saw one of my regulars walking down the barrio right now. Isabella was a graying woman who couldn't afford the rejuvenation treatments. She'd been a seamstress in a former life. These days she subsisted on what little money her daughters could scrape together for her. Sweet as hell. Always gave me extra pay.

I recognized the Dissuader with her immediately. Alejandro Mondego. He wore the black, ankle-length duster that all Dissuaders wore. He had his double collar raised just like I had, and it covered the entire lower half of his face. The rest of him was characteristically Dissuader: Black tricorne hat pulled low, the triangular shape giving the subtle impression of horns. Long black boots shined to a luster. Sawed-off resting comfortably in the holster at his side.

Though most of his face was hidden, I knew it was Alejandro from the way he moved. When he got close, the eyes were the final giveaway. I'd recognize those eyes anywhere. Black, haunted things, the thick set of the brows bent by the weight of unseen troubles. You would have never guessed those eyes belonged to a twenty-four-year-old.

One of the best Dissuaders I knew.

One of the best friends I had.

I nodded at Isabella and bumped fists with Alejandro.

"What happened?" Alejandro said in New Spanish. He was gazing at my scalp with concern. I wondered how big a lump I had.

"Tell you tonight."

"Is that you, Rade?" Isabella said.

I nodded, pulling down the edge of my high collar for a second so that she could see the rest of my face.

"You poor boy." Isabella reached up and I flinched when her palsied fingers touched the blood clot on my scalp. The whole area started throbbing again.

"Get that looked after, understand?" Isabella said.

"*Sí*," I said.

Problem was, there was no one who *would* look after it. Just to get into the hospital emergency ward cost a hundred microcoins. Actual treatment could run upwards of ten thousand microcoins, or ten millicoins. And that was for treatment by a human. If you wanted the best treatment, the *robot* treatment, that would set you back another forty thousand at least.

"Wait." Isabella pulled out a pair of aReal glasses from her purse. The glasses looked like an ordinary pair, complete with lenses. Except aReals were anything but ordinary.

aReal stood for "augmented reality." You could use it to access the Net anywhere, anytime. It was up to you how much of your reality you allowed it to take up. A small postage-stamp area in the lower right, or complete visual overlay. Want to know the weather forecast? Your aReal had it. Stocks? You got it. News. Yup. Want to know the history of some landmark? Pull it up on WikiQwiki. Want to know the price of an item in the grocery story? Look at it and the aReal automatically scanned the barcode and told you not only the price, but the ingredients, the macronutrient breakdown, the product history, gave you its WikiQwiki page and its rotten apples score, the number of verified reviews, and a "most helpful" subset of those reviews—all without you even having to pick it up. Of course, no one really trusted the review section. Too easy to fake.

But anyway, one of the nice things about an aReal was the escape from reality it offered. Let's say you were waiting at a bus stop, and this really annoying dude started chatting you up. You could watch porn, read science fiction, listen to metal, play a multiplayer shoot-em-up—all at the same time. You'd completely forget about the dude. You wouldn't even notice him. Unfortunately, you also gave him the perfect opportunity to rob you. (Note to self: do not watch porn and play video games when an annoying dude starts chatting me up at a bus stop, even if that bus stop is located in a public, high-traffic place.)

Some people had Implants in their brains so they didn't have to wear aReals. Only drug lords and similar types could afford fancy mind gadgetry like that, though I imagine having an aReal in your brain would be quite the trip.

If you were into that sort of thing.

With an aReal you could access the account information tied to the embedded ID staplegunned into your wrist. The thing automatically downloaded the unique codes of any nearby embedded IDs, allowing you to send someone a message, or money, or a video, or whatever the hell you wanted, with just a look. And that's what Isabella was doing now.

She made a few quick bobs of the head. "Three microcoins. That should be enough to tide you over until supper."

It wasn't much, but given how little money she had herself, it may as well have been a fortune.

As I said, sweet woman.

I let them go, then made my way deeper into the barrio without incident. My Dissuader look was working, even without the hat. Good.

I reached a building that was so clean and well kept compared to the others that it was almost an intrusion. It was this sprawling, two-story structure, with thick wooden columns beneath its portico, almost like a manor house. The outer walls were painted white, the window frames blue. Fresh paint, mind you. Not chipped or fading.

At the front door, two muscular toughs stood guard with UZIs.

The home of Mito, my boss.

I lowered my collar, revealing my face, and I was escorted upstairs to Mito's receiving room.

He sat on the floor, revolving two Baoding exercise spheres in each palm with his fingers and thumbs. The spheres, slightly smaller than billiard balls, chimed quietly as they were rotated. I had tried the Baoding once, but the tendons in my wrist started to hurt after about twenty seconds. Seemed a great way to get carpal tunnel syndrome if you asked me, but Mito here could rotate the spheres for hours on end.

He was dressed in a simple gray robe. He was completely bald, and clean shaven. Hell, even his eyebrows were shaved. He was about a hundred years old, but you couldn't tell it by looking at him. He'd bought enough rejuvenation procedures to make his face as smooth and white as a baby's bottom.

Most locals, when they first met him, thought he was some kind of tripped-out addict. What they didn't realize was that he was one of those who had an aReal implanted directly in his brain.

When his eyes focused on mine, that distant look went away completely, and his features hardened. His gaze dropped to my empty holster, and the spheres in both hands stopped rotating. His knuckles turned white—he must have been squeezing the spheres damn hard.

"You lost your gun," he said in English.

"Yeah. About that. I wanted to ask you if I could have another one. You know, as a loan against future—"

"No."

"I got attacked from behind. Wasn't even on duty. No clients were harmed. The robber took everything I had. Took my gun, swiped my bank accounts. You keep up on the news right? The embedded IDs were compromised again. Guess I should have stayed home today. Anyway, Mito, you have to get me a gun. I—"

"No gun for you."

This wasn't going as planned. "Mito, listen—"

"No."

I glanced over my shoulder. The two armed escorts had remained, and were now edging closer to me from the entrance. "Look. It won't happen again. I—"

"You are correct. It will not happen again."

I frowned. I didn't like the sound of that. "Mito, what—"

"Clients do not like you," Mito said.

"What do you mean, clients don't like me? I've always kept them safe, brought them to their destinations on time. Never had a client robbed. And never had a client who didn't tip me. So I'm pretty sure you're wrong on that account."

Mito grinned, bearing his teeth. "*I* do not like you."

"Okay. I get you. No gun. I'll scrounge one on my own, somehow. But if you wouldn't mind, I could use a small advance. As I said, I was robbed. Some guy—"

"No advance."

I regarded him in disbelief. "You owe me this much, Mito. How much money have I made for you?"

"A man is only as good as his gun," Mito said. "How he treats that gun, the care, the attention, shows me how he will live his life. If a man cannot protect his own gun, how can he be expected to protect his client? I have a rule: Lose your gun, and you're done."

Nice of him to tell me about this rule now, of all times.

Mito set the Baoding spheres down. "As of this moment, your services are terminated."

"Wait a second. You can't—"

He smiled, baring his teeth. "Get out of here, little white bread roll. Before I terminate more than just your services."

The armed escorts showed me to the door, none too gently.

I met Alejandro at the local dive that night. Holographic women danced on most of the tables. If you liked what you saw, for a small fee you could meet the living-and-breathing version in a back room. The more upscale bars had the all-too-perfect Skin Musicians—also known as Pleasurers—available in the back. Didn't think that place could afford the robots, though.

"Wish I'd stayed home today," I said. "CryptoG. 'Your Data Security Is Our First Priority.' Right. Well, maybe if you didn't accept billions of government digicoins to bake backdoors into your software, you might actually live up to your slogan. The only people who benefit from those backdoors are the hackers. And the government, of course."

"Mito," Alejandro said, shaking his head. "*Caramba.* I never thought he would fire you." He finished applying the healing ointment to my scalp. Claimed it was the best available. I wasn't sure how much it helped, because I still had a raging headache.

I took a long sip of my Tijuana *cerveza*. "Doesn't matter."

"You going freelance again?" Alejandro said, wiping his hands on his duster. "You know you'll have to seek out clients from scratch. The ones you got through Mito? They're untouchable, if you know what I'm saying."

"I know." Mito would do some pretty nasty things to me if I tried to poach his clients. No, if I wanted Dissuader work, I'd have to post online. That was the only way, really, other than going door-to-door. Which flat-out didn't work, and was a good way to get shot, actually.

"You still want out of this country," Alejandro said. It was a statement, not a question.

"Yeah." I took another sip. "I'm done. I've had it with this place. What happened today only reinforced that. Getting robbed, then fired. I mean look where we live, Alejandro. Take a good, long look. This isn't a good country."

"Maybe the robbery was a sign from above, you know?" Alejandro said. "That you shouldn't be trying to leave."

"Don't give me that."

It was Alejandro's turn to take a long swallow of beer, though he bypassed his glass and drank straight from the pitcher. Classy. "You know, despite all its flaws, the people are happy here. You could be too, if you just let go. Get a nice *mamacita*, a few kids. Maybe try a different line of work."

"That wouldn't make me happy, Alejandro. It would distract me, sure, make me forget about my unhappiness, but in the end I'd still want to leave."

"Rade, the UC isn't the utopia you think it is. Those vids on the Net? All propaganda. Everyone knows that. They make the United Countries look like heaven, make us want to migrate, then as soon as we cross the border, bam! They force us into the army. Courtesy of the EEI Act."

The Enforced Enlistment of Immigrants and Illegals Act.

Alejandro whistled at the bartender and waved our nearly empty pitcher. "José, another." Alejandro wasn't wearing his hat tonight, and he had his double collar down so that his oval face was completely visible. He had a closely trimmed mustache and beard that nicely matched his thick brows. Didn't help his haunted eyes, though.

I emptied my glass and wiped my lips. "What if I like the EEI Act? What if I want to be drafted into the UC army?"

Alejandro nearly choked on the last bit of beer in the pitcher. "Most people sneak across the border because they want to *live* in the UC. Not die for it, you know?"

"Just listen to me for a sec. Joining the UC army isn't so different from what I'm doing now. I'd still get beat up for other people, except I'd get to wear a fancy uniform while doing it. And whenever I lost my gun, I'd get a new one free of charge, no questions asked. I'd get to see the world, and potentially the galaxy. Plus I'd be paid a heck of a lot more."

"Yeah, and get shot at," Alejandro deadpanned.

"As I said, not so different from here. Look. I'm twenty-two years old. I've been in this country far too long. I appreciate everything you've done for me, I really do, but you know what? I'm going to walk all the way to the border if I have to. I've had it with this place."

Alejandro started tapping his fingers against the side of the pitcher. A nervous habit of his. "You really mean that, don't you?"

"I do."

He took another swallow, finishing the pitcher. He stared into the empty container. "I might have . . . I might have paid someone to rob you this morning."

I stood up. "You *what*?" My pounding headache seemed to worsen.

He couldn't meet my eye. "I'm sorry, Rade. I didn't want you to go. I was afraid. *Caramba*. I didn't know how important it was to you."

I held up my thumb and forefinger. "Alejandro, I'm this close to starting a bar fight with you."

"I'll pay the Border Hoppers so you can go," he said softly.

"You'll what?" I wasn't sure I'd heard right.

"I'll pay the Border Hoppers. Because that's how we do it. I did you a wrong, and now I'm making it right."

I sat back down, the fight draining out of me. "I still can't believe you'd do something like that to me in the first place."

"I know. It was a mistake. I guess I hoped it would make you change your mind. But maybe it's better if you go. I don't want to hold you back."

"You're really going to pay the Border Hoppers for me?"

He gave me a cross look. "I said I would, didn't I?"

"But what about the condo you've been saving up to buy with that girl of yours? Your fiancée?"

He stared into the empty pitcher once again. "There is no girl." He sounded ashamed. "I made her up. Brenda is . . . she's a Skin Musician."

"Oh." That explained why he never introduced me. You couldn't marry a bawdy-house sex robot.

Alejandro waved at the bartender. "Damn it, José!"

José finally came and refilled the pitcher.

We portioned out the beer in our glasses, drinking quietly. My headache had faded. Guess the ointment Alejandro had applied was working.

That, or the beer.

"Come with me," I said.

I wasn't sure I could do this myself. Despite my heartfelt, determined words, moving to the UC and joining the army was a frightening prospect. Alejandro had been there for me since I was a child. He'd found me on the streets, guided me, acted like the big brother I'd never had. Sure, sometimes he did a few misguided things, like robbing me, for example, but in the end he was really just looking out for me. In his own way.

Alejandro downed his glass, and refilled it. "I'm not going with you. I'll give you the money, *sí*, but go with you, no."

"Okay." I finished my own drink, looking away. I didn't want him to see the disappointment on my face. I guess I'd have to do this alone after all.

"You don't believe me, do you?" Alejandro said.

"I believe you, Alejandro."

"Then why don't you sound happy? *Caramba*. I just said I'd pay your entire Border Hopper fee!"

I looked at him, and forced a smile. "No. I'm happy."

"Actually, you know what? I'll throw in double what you had in your account."

"Why?"

"Because that's how we do it. I always pay back my debts."

"I don't know what to say. Thanks, bro. I owe you one, I guess."

He smiled, but I could see that his eyes were moist. He looked away. "You don't owe me a thing." I thought he was going to choke up.

I rested a hand on his shoulder. "Seriously, bro, come with me. Leave this sinkhole behind. You know in your heart that the UC isn't all hype and propaganda. You've seen the vids on the Net. And you remember what my Uncle Alek told us, don't you? How the United Countries really is a haven compared to this. Can you imagine, not having to work if you don't want to? Not having to carry a gun around everywhere?"

Alejandro wiped his eyes. "We just agreed that you'd have to join the military. So yes, you'll work. And yes, you'll carry a gun."

"Well sure, but I meant the civilians. They don't have to get jobs. They aren't allowed weapons. Think about what that must be like. To walk the streets and not worry about where your next meal is going to come from. To sit in the park and not worry about getting shot in the back, or hit by a two-by-four. That's living, bro. That's freedom. Not like here." I finished my beer and slammed the glass upside down on the countertop. "Come with me."

"I had someone rob you this morning, and you still want me to come with you." Alejandro laughed, like I'd just told him the funniest joke. "I'm not going with you. And that's that."

CHAPTER TWO

Alejandro came with me.

He said it was because he'd changed his mind, and wanted to ensure he paid back the money above and beyond what he owed me, with full interest. But I didn't believe it. He'd always been there for me, and I think he felt it was his duty to come. And while he wanted to look out for me, I'm sure he also wanted a change just as badly as I did, despite all his fervent declarations to the contrary. Who could resist the promise of a better life? That's what made people emigrate, wasn't it? Or border hop, anyway . . .

I sat in the bed of a pickup truck that was making a run for the UC border. It was pitch black out there: the truck had shut off its headlights for obvious reasons. I was assured the driver wore night-vision goggles, though from the way the truck jolted and swerved, I had my doubts.

The darkness heightened my other senses. I heard the rush of the passing air, which was interrupted by the occasional rustle from a crushed tumbleweed, or the screech as the undercarriage scraped uneven ground. The electric motor itself was soundless, as the driver had disconnected the pedestrian-warning speakers. I smelled dust and fuel and human sweat.

Alejandro sat on my left. In the light of the half-moon I could barely see his face, let alone the faces of the others crowding the truck bed. Men and women appeared as vague outlines against the night sky.

"Scared?" the man sitting on the other side of me said in English.

"Yeah," I said.

"Me too." His accent made me think he was indigenous. Nahua, maybe. Late twenties or early thirties, judging from the timbre of his voice.

"Lucky we're on the same truck then," I said. "Back a scared man into a corner, and you've got a fight on your hands. Back two scared men into a corner, and you've got yourself a war."

The man laughed. "That's a good saying. I like it. I'm Tahoe Eaglehide."

"Rade. And this is Alejandro." I pointed at Alejandro beside me.

"*Hola*," Alejandro said.

"You're Nahua?" I asked him.

"Navajo."

"Interesting." I regarded him in the dim moonlight, but could barely make out his features.

Tahoe was returning the favor. "What's a whitey like you doing on the wrong side of the border?"

"The same question could be asked of you."

"It could." Tahoe sounded amused. "But I'm not a whitey." He fiddled with his jeans and retrieved something. "Here."

I regarded the dark mass in his hand dubiously. "What is it?"

"My wife. *She* is Nahua."

I accepted the item. It was some kind of locket. I opened it, and a backlight illuminated the picture of a wholesome young woman.

"Nice," I said.

"You like her?"

"Sure. Not my type, though."

"She's quite the beauty," Tahoe said. "After four or five *cervezas*."

I smiled, then shut the locket and handed it back.

"She's the reason I'm doing this," Tahoe said.

"What, to get away from her?"

"No," Tahoe said. "I'm going to send everything I make to her and my unborn child."

"Ah. Good man. I guess we all have our reasons."

"We do."

The truck swerved sharply, bouncing and jostling everyone.

"We should've just walked," I complained to Alejandro, switching back to New Spanish. "I don't think these guys have a clue what they're doing."

"No no no." I could barely see Alejandro shake his head. "They're experts, Rade. *Experts*. They come here every night. Know exactly what they're doing."

The bed jerked with a bang as the truck hit what must have been a wide depression.

I gave Alejandro an exasperated look, which he probably couldn't see anyway. "Know what they're doing, huh?"

"Hey," Alejandro said. "We're driving with our headlights turned off in the middle of the night. I think the driver's doing an amazing job under the circumstances. Cut him some slack, okay?"

I crossed my arms, sitting back. This was going to be a long ride.

"You guys looking forward to joining the military?" Tahoe said.

Alejandro leaned over me and answered, in English. "Hey, we only join the military if we get caught."

"You think we're not going to get caught?" I could hear the humor in Tahoe's voice. "Interesting. Tell me, do you agree with the EEI Act?"

"Of course not." Alejandro said. "The UC should open its borders and let people come and go freely. None of this drafting crap."

"But you see why they do it, don't you? Drafting all of-age immigrants and illegals to fight for them, because the majority of their own citizens won't do it?"

"Doesn't make it right," Alejandro said.

"What do you think, Rade?"

I shrugged. "It's a way in for us, isn't it?"

"So you're glad to be fighting for the UC?" Tahoe persisted.

"Well sure. I'll be fighting for my new homeland. And so what if I have to kill a few of the UC's enemies."

"You're forgetting that UC technology won't make you invincible. You may very well die for the UC. Something its own citizens refuse to do."

"Last I heard, no citizen of the UC was ever stopped from volunteering."

Tahoe's head bobbed in the dark. "This is true. But very few citizens volunteer. Immigrants make up the bulk of their army."

I exhaled loudly. "So what's your point?"

"Think about this: How good can a country's military be when its ranks are almost completely made up of soldiers from other countries? Wouldn't actual citizens fight harder? Patriotism and all that?"

"Not necessarily," I said. "Natural-born citizens don't understand just how good they have it. Sure they're patriotic, but not like us. You gotta love a country a whole lot if you're going to give up everything to move there. And when you want nothing more than to be a citizen of that country, and you've wanted it your whole life, you'll fight, even die for that privilege, don't you worry. Because you have way more to lose than any natural born."

"I like that answer," Tahoe said. "And agree with it. I'm looking forward to fighting for the UC too. Though for me, it's all about going into space. I've always dreamed of traveling to the stars. And the UC military is my ticket."

The stars winked out and the truck bed instantly became pitch-black.

"I wonder if the universe is trying to tell you something," I mused. "As soon as you bring up the stars, they vanish."

"Story of my life," Tahoe muttered.

The driver turned on the headlights.

We were traveling inside a tunnel that had walls made of coarse sandstone.

"See?" Alejandro said, the ambient light reflecting off his features. His eyes glinted excitedly and looked like dark gemstones. "Told you these guys were *expertos.* We're going to slip right under the UC border. We're *not* going to be caught, or drafted. I knew I hired the right crew. Did you know, they dig a new tunnel each time the *gringos* sniff out the old one? It's the only way to get past the robot drones and cameras."

"Only way to get caught, you mean," Tahoe said.

Alejandro leaned forward and gave him a dismissive wave. "Will you just shut it?"

I glanced at Tahoe, who raised an eyebrow. I could make out his features now that the headlights were on. I guessed his age at around twenty-five. Both sides of his head were shaved to the skin, and the top was buzzed, very much like the "high and tight" military haircuts I'd seen floating around on the Net. He was clean shaven except for a soul patch just below the lower lip.

I could see the outline of well-defined muscles beneath his white T-shirt, and he had some of the biggest shoulders I'd ever seen.

"So that's what you look like," Tahoe said. "Dissuader?"

I nodded. "You?"

"Construction. Though I'm an astrophysicist by training."

"Nice. How'd you end up in construction?"

He shrugged. "You know what the jobs are like where we're from."

"I do indeed."

As the pickup sped through the tunnel, I saw a flash of metal in the distance.

"Did you see that?" I said quietly.

Tahoe nodded. "And so it begins."

In moments a drone was hovering alongside the truck, police siren blazing. It was a basketball-sized metallic sphere crisscrossed with grooves and grates. There was a small flashing emergency light on top, a miniature version of the one found on the police robots. Multiple exhaust nozzles circled the X- and Y-axis. The rearmost nozzle was constantly firing, while various other nozzles let out occasional bursts so that the drone followed the contour of the cave and remained alongside the truck. Painted in big blue letters on a ring down the middle of the drone were the words: "Customs Patrol System."

The drone matched our speed for a few seconds, then tore past.

I glanced at Alejandro. He wasn't looking very happy.

A few minutes later the CPS drone returned with another. The miniature emergency lights on top of both of them were flashing blue.

The first drone blasted a brief siren yelp, followed by the announcement, "Moderate your speed," in New Spanish. A man's voice. Deep. Authoritative.

The pickup truck surged forward in response.

The drones pursued, emergency lights flashing, sirens wailing.

The truck sloped upward, and the tunnel abruptly fell away. We were back under the stars.

What followed next was rather anticlimactic.

The pickup stalled.

At least, that was the impression I had, because even though I couldn't hear the engine all this time, the pickup started to bleed off speed. It bumped over hollows and tumbleweeds, jostling us around in the back. The wailing CPS drones pursued the whole way.

"You will stop the vehicle immediately," one of the drones blared.

As the pickup slowed to about ten kilometers per hour, people started jumping out of the bed.

One of the drones spun away. "Halt! You are trespassing on UC-controlled territory!" I heard a slight *plunk* come from the general direction of the drone. A fleeing refugee dropped. Another *plunk*. Another runner fell.

The remaining refugees fled the pickup truck in a panic, and the second drone pursued.

Only Alejandro, Tahoe, and I stayed where we were in the truck bed.

Abruptly the driver slammed on the brakes, parked the pickup, and he too jumped out, along with the occupant who rode shotgun.

"That's our cue," Alejandro said.

I blocked him with my arm.

"Rade, we have to go, *hombre*!"

I shook my head. "I'm not in the mood to have twelve million volts pass through my body today."

There was another vehicle out there, something small and fast, and it zoomed along the desert floor, its way lit by high beams. I noticed tiny lights marking where the runners had fallen. The small vehicle pulled up to the first one, and I thought someone jumped out. The light marker vanished, and the vehicle continued on its way, heading toward the pickup truck. Behind it, more light markers vanished as the occupant who had jumped out collected the refugees.

Tahoe began to sing a quiet, traditional indigenous song.

"Rade." Alejandro was getting really antsy now. "Let's go, *hombre*!"

I didn't move. I listened to Tahoe's song. It was calming somehow. Peaceful.

"Remain where you are," a drone blasted beside me.

I hadn't noticed its return to the pickup truck. The other drone was here too, on the other side of Tahoe. Somewhere along the way the drones had stopped flashing their emergency lights and wailing their sirens.

Tahoe had paused his song when the drone interrupted, but he continued now.

The small vehicle stopped beside the pickup truck. A dune buggy of some kind.

"Damn it, Rade," Alejandro said. "I told you to run!"

A dark figure strutted out, and walked in front of the buggy's high beams so that he was silhouetted. I couldn't tell if it was a man or a robot because of that bright light.

"Freeze!" the figure said in English. "Hands behind your heads and out of the truck!"

Tahoe ended his song and carefully raised his hands.

Alejandro and I followed suit.

When we got out, the figure made us lean against the dune buggy. On the side was written: "United Countries Border Patrol."

The figure ordered us to put our hands behind our backs, and then plasticuffed us. Mine were done up a little tight, but what was I supposed to do? The only way to reset plasticuffs was to cut them off and put on a new pair. And I doubted this guy or robot or whatever it was would do that for me.

After cuffing us, the figure walked out to our left, and in the ambient light I could finally see who we were dealing with. He had a tan Stetson pulled low on his forehead, and wore green cargo pants and a white T-shirt. A rifle was slung over his shoulder. About ten more plasticuffs hung from his belt. He seemed human, but I supposed he could've been an Artificial—one of those robots that looked human but wasn't. Those eyes looked real enough, a touch of moisture in each, and when the man opened his mouth he had real-looking teeth.

"Welcome to the UC," the border patrol officer said in English. "Leave your shoes at the door. Don't pass go and head straight to mother-freakin' jail." The officer focused on me. "What are you looking at, huh, chico? Not happy about being de-port-tatoed? You picked the wrong night to border hop."

Great. Just what I needed. A power-tripping border patrol officer. Definitely human, then.

"Bet you thought you wouldn't get caught, huh?" His lips smacked loudly as he chewed gum and surveyed the three of us. "That you were going to make lots of money, huh? That you would hide in our cities, break our laws, and support your *familia* back home off our backs, did ya? Well I got news for you, Hoppers. Ain't no jobs for you. Heck, I'm lucky I got mine. Robots got most of them. Without UC IDs, you illegals will never get the state subsistence you need to survive. You'll resort to robbery and thievery like most aliens. There's a reason, you know, that most crimes are committed by minorities and immigrants."

"I wanted to get caught," I said.

The man focused his glare on me. "You wanted to get caught. We gots ourselves a joker here!" He squinted one eye, and bent closer. "What happened to your face?"

"What do you mean?" I said.

"What do you think I mean?" he said with a snarl. "*Why* are you white?"

"Oh." I grinned widely. "Sailing mishap."

The officer jabbed me in the ribs with the butt of his rifle.

I doubled over.

"No lip from you, buddy." He turned toward the drones, which had shadowed us the whole time. "CPS One and Two, maintain guard."

He went over to investigate the pickup truck while the CPS drones hovered beside us.

"Jeez," I said when I'd caught my breath. "It's like we're in the army already."

"So much for the UC being some wonderful utopia full of white ponies and happy leprechauns," Alejandro said.

Eventually another border patrol officer walked in from the desert. He was dressed in the same cargo pants and white T, with a tan Stetson on his head. He was escorting the escaped refugees. They stood in single file, connected by a long nylon cord that ran between their plasticuffs.

"Is that all of them, Harold?" the newcomer said in a deep voice.

The first officer, Harold, straightened up right away. "It is, boss."

Harold hurried over to him and fiddled with a wristwatch aReal, projecting some sort of holographic display. He turned his wrist toward the second officer, and the holographic display rotated. "Definitely illegals. Most of them have their embedded IDs torn out. As if that would help." He jerked a thumb in my direction. "I think that one got cosmetic surgery done. Probably vocal implants too. His English is too good. But the dumb bastard didn't have the smarts to remove his own embedded ID."

"It wouldn't have helped," the second officer said. "Turn on the Miranda Rights so we can get them processed. And don't forget to pay the drivers their kickback before we leave."

"Yes, boss."

I glanced at Alejandro and commented quietly, "You hired *experts*, huh?"

Harold fiddled with the aReal wristwatch. "Damn it. Speaker's not working." He turned off the holographic display and slid on the pair of aReal glasses he had resting in his pocket. "All right, where the hell is that again . . . Miranda, Miranda, where are you? Ah, here." He glanced at me and the other refugees. "*Hola*."

He waited, like he was expecting an answer or something, and when no one said anything, he read off the rights.

"*Tiene el derecho a guardar silencio* . . ." You have the right to remain silent . . .

When it was done, Harold came up to me with some sort of staple gun. He maneuvered around behind me and held the tip to my bound wrist and I felt a sharp pain.

Harold pulled away. "You've been served," he said with a wink.

"But I already had an embedded ID," I said.

"Well, now you have a proper UC one. All the data from your existing ID has been transferred over, so we know all the crimes you committed in your home country. But the best part is, if you ever get your hands on a UC aReal to check out your public profile, you'll find a special treat: a fresh felony conviction stamped in big red letters beside your photo. That's right, you start off your first day in the UC with the criminal offense of illegal entry."

"What's going to happen to us?" Alejandro said when Harold tagged him.

"What do you think, Border Hopper? You'll be moved to a detention center. There, you'll be questioned, processed, and deported. Thank you for your freakin' cooperation."

The other officer came forward. I hadn't noticed this before in the dim light, but now that the officer was closer, I realized he had no face beneath that Stetson.

I'd thought his voice sounded a little too deep . . .

"These three are of age," the officer said. Like the police robots south of the border, its head was a featureless slab of polycarbonate, serrated at the bottom, with a yellow bar down the middle and two glass disks stacked one atop the other where the forehead would be. The only difference was that this robot didn't have a laser sight—maybe the Stetson covered it. "I'm tagging them for the EEI."

"Yes, boss." Harold gave me a smug look, then chuckled, shook his head, and walked away to staplegun the others. He muttered something about "cannon fodder."

The robot's featureless face rotated to regard me, Alejandro, and Tahoe in turn. Then the officer said, "Rade Galaal, Tahoe Eaglehide,

Alejandro Mondego. I'm proud to inform you that you are now temporary residents of the United Countries. You are granted this temporary residency for twelve years, during which time you will serve the UC in a military capacity. Your active duty commitment is ten years. After you have completed your Military Service Obligation, you may qualify for permanent residency if your record is in good standing. Do you have any questions or objections?"

"Twelve years?" Alejandro said immediately. "*Caramba.* That sounds like a long time."

"Would you prefer to be deported?" There was no emotion in that question. Just cold, machine indifference.

Alejandro glanced at me, then lowered his gaze. "No."

"Good. The three of you are in luck, because the weekly trip from the detention center to the Military Entrance Processing Station is scheduled for 0700 tomorrow morning, allowing you to begin your service term immediately. Welcome to the UC, and have a wonderful evening."

CHAPTER THREE

We spent the night in a detention center, then at 0700 the next morning, two robots that identified themselves as PPAs, or Pacification and Protection Autonomous robots, escorted the three of us into a waiting van. The PPAs looked exactly the same as the robot border patrol officer from the night before, minus the clothing.

The AI-operated van stopped at detention centers along the way, and other draft-age illegals were herded inside so that soon we had a full complement squeezed into the passenger area. No one really said anything. It felt like we were going to prison.

When the vehicle finally ground to a halt and the back door opened, I was more than happy to step outside, but not so pleased with what I saw: I stood within a compound surrounded by a chain-link fence and topped by razor wire.

Prison, indeed.

Three other Immigrations and Customs Enforcement vans were parked nearby. Beyond them, five buses dumped about seventy people each into the courtyard. I noticed that roughly three-fourths of the people seemed to be immigrants. East Indians, South Americans, Africans, Russians, Japanese, and so forth.

The PPAs in the courtyard herded us toward the main building. These robots wore dark-blue blazers and trousers with black shoes. The black letters "MP" were sewn into gray patches on their right shoulders.

As I followed the robots, I looked out beyond the fence of the compound. I saw a paved road, and what looked like residential housing complete with hedges and gated white picket fences. It was the kind of sprawling suburbia I'd seen on Net vids set in the UC.

"Welcome to the Military Entrance Processing Station of New San Antonio," a PPA said by the entrance. "Please store any backpacks or aReals in the marked compartments, then proceed to the scanning stations."

Alejandro, Tahoe, and I had only the clothes we wore, so we headed straight for the full-body scanners. Ahead of us, the alarm went off for one person, and two PPAs escorted him outside. I overheard a few people whispering nearby. Apparently he'd failed the breathalyzer portion of the scan.

"Please exhale," a friendly female voice intoned when I stood inside the glass compartment. I did. "Thank you. You may proceed." The glass slid aside and I walked through.

Beyond the scanners there were long rows of seats, with different kiosks spaced at intervals, and uniformed robots moving to and fro. The whole place had the feel of an airport terminal.

A support robot moved between us, pointing out the kiosks of the different branches. "Navy here. Marine Corps here. Air Force here. Army here."

"So, which branch, *hombres*?" Alejandro said.

I didn't really know which one to pick. As much as I hated to admit it, I hadn't really thought this far ahead. I'd adopted the whole "I'll cross that bridge when I come to it" mindset, I guess, because I never thought I'd actually make it here. Up until now, this was all just some distant, unachievable dream, but here I was, living that dream. I had this vague notion about joining a special forces division, and that's about it.

A girl halfway through one of the lines caught my eye. Long blonde hair, tanned skin, cute as hell.

"Navy." I said, and headed for her line.

I waited with Alejandro and Tahoe as the line slowly moved forward, hoping the girl would look back.

She didn't.

Some of the conversational threads I overheard in line:

"I didn't have a choice. My parents moved here when I was fifteen."

"They drafted me when I tried to board the plane home. How was I supposed to know I'd overstayed my visa?"

"Me?" This from a white dude. "I just wanted to get the hell out of Dodge."

The girl I had my eye on reached the front of the line, exchanged a few words with the robot attendant, then moved off toward a side hall. Before vanishing from view, she finally looked back. She caught my eye and glanced down demurely.

Definitely hot.

The moments passed. Tahoe, Alejandro, and I neared the front of the line.

"Guys, what do you think about the Marines?" I said, having second thoughts. Probably wasn't the best idea to base my branch choice on some girl I'd seen in line.

Tahoe shrugged. "Same difference to me. They still get to go into space."

"No no no," one of the people in front of me said. "If you want to go into space, you join the Navy, not the Marines. We're the ones who control the ships, bro."

Tahoe pursed his lips. "He does have a point."

I shrugged. "All right. Navy it is."

When I reached the front of the line, the metal-faced attendant informed me that new reading material had been installed in my embedded ID.

"How am I supposed to read it without an aReal?" I said.

"You will be given access to an aReal," the robot said. "Enter room number two down the hall on your right. Fill the seats sequentially from the front."

"Don't I get a name tag or something?"

"Enter room number two down the hall on your right," the robot repeated, in the exact tone as before. "Fill the seats sequentially from the front." Damn robotic detachment.

I walked down the hall and eventually found a large auditorium with enough capacity to seat a thousand people. About a quarter of the spaces were occupied, filled from the front on down so that there were no empty seats.

I picked out Ms. Tanned Cutey right away. She was looking back at me—must have been watching the entrance the whole time—and when I met her eyes, she smiled coyly and looked away. There were guys seated on either side of her. Chatting her up. Damn.

Well, I was used to facing hurdles, and I never let some man-made obstacle stop me before.

I'd made it this far, hadn't I?

I walked down the main aisle and crossed the empty seats. When I reached the last empty seat, I continued forward, excusing my way past the recruits toward the girl. I felt my heart rate increase.

She looked up at me questioningly as I came near. The guy just to her right was still talking, telling her a story about how he wrestled alligators or something on his ranch.

"Excuse me," I said loudly. "You're in my seat."

The guy looked up at me. He was a fairly muscular dude, not the type who would ordinarily back down when challenged. But he was on unfamiliar ground now, being given orders left and right by the people and robots around here, and I guess that put him in an obedient mindset because he got up right away.

"Sorry about that," the guy said.

I nodded politely.

As I edged past him, he added, "Didn't know you were together."

"We're not," the girl said right away.

I smiled at the guy. "Yeah, I just had to use the bathroom." I quickly took his seat before he could change his mind.

"Smooth move, big boy," she said.

"Friends call me Rade." I extended my hand, keeping eye contact.

She glanced at my hand, but didn't take it. Her lip curled slightly in amusement. "Sounds like some sort of insect repellent."

I lowered my hand. "Maybe it is. But look on the bright side, insects won't touch you when I'm around."

She smiled—a cute little dimple formed in one cheek—and offered me her hand. "I'm Shaw."

I waited a few seconds before shaking her hand, not wanting to seem too eager. "Nice to meet you, Shaw."

Her grin deepened, as did those dimples. "Pleasure's mine. Us Navy types have to stick together."

"We do."

I glanced to my right and saw Alejandro and Tahoe sit down about seven places away from me, in the empty seats.

"What branch of the Navy are you joining?" I said.

I saw a warm twinkle in her eyes. "What rating, you mean?"

"Yeah."

The twinkle became all-out mischievousness. "Are you sure you want to know? Not everyone can handle it."

I shrugged. "Sure."

She smiled. "Quartermaster. Also known as astrogator."

I nodded as if I knew what that was. "Okay."

"Always been a dream of mine to pilot starships," she continued, a little by rote, as if she'd been repeating that to people all day. "Going to faraway worlds and colonies is just a fun side benefit."

"You know the government would pay you to go into space, right?" I said. "Girl like you? They'd be tripping over themselves to get you to the colonies."

"Was that meant to be a compliment?" she said. "Or an insult?"

Whoops.

"Just making conversation," I said.

She frowned. "Like I'd ever agree to go to some far-flung colony world where there are seven men for every woman."

"Why not? You'd get your pick of the litter."

"Not my cup of tea. No, thanks. I'd have to watch my back wherever I went. Besides, I don't want to be tied down, stuck in one place. As I said, I want to pilot starships, make something out of myself. Anyways, how about you? What rating are you aiming for?"

"Special forces."

She quirked an eyebrow. "MOTH?"

I nodded. "If that's what they're called in the Navy."

"I'm sorry to hear that." She smiled that sexy smile again. Though it was a bit wry this time.

"What do you mean?"

"You're going to be surrounded by men day in and day out. They don't allow women, you know, not like in the Marines. You might as well go to one of the colonies. At least you'll have *some* women there."

"Yeah, I don't know," I said. "It was kind of a last-minute decision. Based on someone I saw in line."

"I hope that someone wasn't me."

"Not at all."

Shaw looked at me appraisingly. "Well, good luck. Navy specops training is supposed to be the hardest there is, bar none. It has the highest washout rate in the entire military."

I nodded slowly. That prospect attracted me, believe it or not, and stoked the competitor in me, the part of myself that wanted to prove I was the best. Meanwhile the slacker in me wanted to take the path of least resistance and just cruise through the military.

I hated that slacker. I really did. He's the one who caused me to stay where I was for so long, in a dead-end city and country, too afraid to move on and change things and strive for something more.

I stoked the competitor. I could handle the hardest training. *I would.*

At that moment, a tall, gray-haired man dressed in camouflage gear entered at the front of the room. The theater hushed as he walked to the podium. "Your aReals, please."

There was an aReal visor connected to my seat by a thin cord. I grabbed the visor and put it on. My vision wasn't obscured, but the lenses were slightly dark, making the background of the real world diminish.

"Welcome to the New San Antonio MEP Station, recruits." He ran his gaze across the room. "I'm Gustav Reyjuk. A retired officer. A civilian. And no, I didn't invent the Carl Gustav." He got a few laughs at that. "The military hires me to come in and give this speech once a week. I'll probably be the last friendly face you see here on out. Other than your fellow recruits of course." The aReal had apparently scanned my embedded ID to determine my ethnic origin, because it was translating every word into New Spanish and displaying subtitles at the bottom of my vision. I navigated through the menus and turned that translation feature off.

"The friendly robotic attendant you met on the way inside installed a short, fifteen-hundred-page document on your embedded IDs," Gustav said. "You can go over it in detail later, using one of the aReal terminals installed in the mess hall. In the meantime, I suggest you follow along."

Using the visor, I navigated to my private offline folder and found the document, labeled *MEPS Guide*. I opened it. I noted that the military had bypassed the usual security protocol—as soon as I turned on the aReal I should have gotten a prompt asking me if I wanted to accept the document download request. They'd rammed this guide down the throat of my embedded ID, using one of those undocumented backdoors no doubt. Guess I'd have to get used to the military messing with my private data.

"I'm going to go over the most important points in the guide," Gustav continued. "You eat lunch from 1100 to 1200. You eat supper from 1730 to 1830. If you don't go to the mess hall during those times, you don't eat. The food is a buffet. Not exactly high-class. If you like all-you-can-eat pancakes and gruel, then you're in the right place. As for your movements, you're restricted to the main lobby, the mess hall, this room, the brain scan hall, the medical examination hall, and the job selection hall. We're aware of your individual locations at all times, and the second you step outside any of the allowed areas, accidental or not, a PPA will escort you all friendly-like from the building and you'll be required to find your own way home. If you're an alien whose residency was granted temporarily on the basis of your draft, you'll be picked up by an Immigrations and Customs Enforcement van and booked for deportation."

He proceeded to go over everything we weren't allowed to do. No smoking. No slouching. No sleeping. No cussing. No looking an officer in the eyes. No disrespecting your fellow recruits. And so on. After a while I began to wonder what we were *allowed* to do. From the sound of it we'd be ejected from MEPS just for holding our breath.

He showed different slides and finally a vid. I heard acronyms and more acronyms. OCS. PT. PST. DOR. LCPO. OIC. XO. BSD/M. Funny thing was, it seemed like we were expected to know what all those acronyms meant. I kept having to jump to the glossary in the guide. I'm sure there was a free app I could download that would subtitle those acronyms for me as they were spoken in real time while I had an aReal on. I made a quick detour to the app store on the Net, and found one.

After a while, I started to browse different sections of the guide, basically ignoring the Gustav guy. Somehow I ended up on the spec-ops section. The more I read about the MOTHs, the more I wanted to be one. These guys were tacticians, corpsmen, astronauts, snipers, and commandos rolled into one. Their specialty was "direct action: short-duration operations of surgical precision conducted in hostile, denied, or diplomatically sensitive environments." If the UC wanted someone seized, recovered, or terminated quietly, and without stirring up a political storm, they called in the MOTHs. They were the special forces of the special forces.

When Gustav was done, a PPA herded us down the corridor to the brain scan hall, where we were given the "vocational aptitude" brain scan. A lot of people had already taken this scan apparently, at local recruiting centers and whatnot, so the waiting room had only about fifty people in it. Shaw had taken it beforehand too, so we exchanged IDs and promised to meet up in the mess hall for lunch later.

When it was done, Tahoe, Alejandro, and I hurried over to the mess hall with ten minutes to spare for lunch. Disappointingly, Shaw wasn't there. After rushing through a ham and cheese sandwich, the three of us made our way to the job selection hall. Before we got there, I managed to convince Tahoe and Alejandro to try out for the MOTHs with me. "It's the hardest training in the world," I told them. "But we'll get to do some crazy missions. Jumping out of starships, sneaking behind enemy lines, capturing privateers."

Tahoe seemed excited by the prospect, Alejandro not so much. I knew he'd join, though, if only for me. I'm not sure that would be enough to get him through the training, which sounded ridiculously difficult. He'd definitely have to dig deep within himself.

We all would.

At the job selection hall, we found ourselves once more at the back of the queue. Again, no sign of Shaw. A computer voice called out whenever a cubicle was free, and eventually I was paired up with a job counselor. He looked to be around fifty-five. His face seemed perpetually locked in a scowl.

Well, at least he wasn't a robot.

His eyes defocused for a moment, and I knew he was accessing my embedded ID. Probably had one of those implanted aReals.

"Morning, son," the counselor said. His voice sounded tired.

"Good morning."

"What's good about it?"

I didn't answer.

"So, you chose the Navy. Two ratings are available to you. Guaranteed Job and Undesignated. Now if—"

"I want to be a MOTH."

"You will speak only when I ask you a question. Do you understand?"

"I want to be a MOTH."

The counselor clenched his jaw.

"You don't understand my role here, do you?" He seemed about ready to give me an epic chewing out, but then his features softened, and he sighed. "You're lucky I'm in a good mood today. So. The MOTHs."

"Yes."

"MObile Tactical Human. Fancy name for a spec-op with a jetpack. They handle operations on air, sea, land, and space. Direct action, mostly."

"I know what they do."

"Do you now? It's all fun and games to you, isn't it?" He took a long, leisurely sip of coffee. "I don't know what we'd do without this stuff. Coffee I mean. It's the ambrosia of the people. The lifeblood.

Nations have fought wars over coffee." He took another sip. "Do you think you could do it? Go to war for your country over coffee?"

"If that's what my country wanted me to do, sir."

"You'd kill people, for coffee?"

I hesitated. "Yes sir."

"Could you kill a man in front of his wife and all his children, for coffee?"

"Yes sir."

"What about a beautiful woman? A model, standing in the middle of the street. Waiting for your convoy to arrive. Bombs strapped to her chest. Could you take her out?"

"Yes sir."

"What about the poor, unknowing child, whose father has given him a grenade to deliver to the men who've just kicked down his front door. Could you take the kid out? All in the name of coffee?"

I swallowed. Hard.

"Not so easy, is it? As a MOTH, you may be expected to do certain things. Things that may not exactly jive with your conscience. And if you can't follow orders without question, good men could die. Still want to be a MOTH?"

"Situations like that are going to happen to any unit that sees street-level combat," I said. "Not just the MOTHs. The Marines, for example."

"Which is why I bring it up. You won't be getting the seaman's or the astronaut's aloof view of war. Spec-ops people get up close and personal with the enemy. You'll experience more of those 'situations' as you call them than any other Navy rating. So answer the question. Do you still want to be a MOTH?"

"I do."

He exhaled heavily, sitting back. "Well. Unfortunately, this is all moot, because you'll never meet the entrance requirements for the training. And even if do, you'll never pass. We're talking the most prestigious spec-ops unit in the entire UC military, here. The training regime is brutal."

"I know all about that. And I'll do whatever it takes."

The counselor straightened up. "Listen, son, you think you know, but you don't. Besides, that's not how the military works. There are qualification requirements. Entry caps."

"Find a way around them."

He leaned forward. "Do you want to be in the Navy or not? You've been given a chance. Don't throw it all away by insisting on a rating you can't pass. Be reasonable. Look, I'll tell you what I can do: you apply for any other rating, I'll give you five thousand digicoins up front."

Five thousand digicoins was awfully tempting. I'd never owned that much money in all my life.

I should have backed down. I really should have. But I didn't.

"No. Sign me up for the spec-ops." I'd made up my mind earlier, after reading about the MOTHs in the guide. Hardest training in the galaxy? Direct action operations? All that was for me. And once I made up my mind, I never changed it.

"I'll be honest with you," the counselor said. "Your physical conditioning is crap. Your brain scan, crap. You wouldn't even make the rating of deck swabber, let alone spec-ops. You can't change your genetics. Well, not without more bitcoins than you'd make in a lifetime."

He tried to stare me down.

I wasn't going to let him.

My brain scan *was not* crap, and neither was my physical conditioning. I was a Dissuader back home, dammit. You couldn't be weak, not in a job like that. He just wanted me to choose a different rating. But I wasn't going to back down, so I just returned his stare, saying nothing.

He blinked, sat back. "Well. If that's the way it's going to be . . . you're actually in luck, because just a few weeks ago we were issued a new mandate: make more MOTHs. I hope you appreciate how extraordinary this is, because otherwise you'd be out of luck. So I'll tell you what I can do. You agree to a fourteen-year service term instead of the usual twelve, and I'll set you up on the spec-ops track. But if you fail to meet the MOTH entry requirements after Basic, or you fail the MOTH training program itself, you'll be banned from spec-ops and you'll have to choose a different rating. You'll still have to complete the fourteen-year term either way. And no five thousand digicoins."

I hesitated only a second. "Sign me up."

CHAPTER FOUR

A short while later I found myself on a vactrain.

Apparently the military had built their own evacuated tubes, forming a continent-wide network of maglev lines capable of transporting trains at up to Mach One. I didn't feel any G forces even at the top speed, though, and during turns I scarcely felt any drag because of the super-gimballed compartments.

I was headed toward New Great Lakes, where I'd begin Basic Training.

Mine was a window seat, and I watched the landscape racing by. It made me feel thoughtful, looking out there. It was hard to believe that only a few days ago I'd been living in another country entirely.

"So what do you see out there, Rade?" Shaw said from where she sat beside me.

I didn't look away from the window. "My old life. My future."

"A bit introspective, are we?"

I turned away from the glass and smiled. "I'm entering a new phase of my life, Shaw. We all are. A better phase. I hope I live up to the high expectations I've set for myself."

"You will, Rade. You have to. We all do. This is serious now."

"Yeah."

"So how's Alejandro holding up?" she said.

"About the fourteen-year service commitment thing?" I glanced at him. He was seated right in front of us, beside Tahoe, but hadn't said a word since we boarded. "Could be better. I think he'll get over hating me in eight weeks or so. Just in time to graduate Basic."

She flashed a quick smile, and lowered her eyes. She seemed a little sad all of a sudden.

"What's wrong?" I said.

"Nothing." She leaned forward slightly and stared out the window past me. "I mean, well, you mentioned graduating, and all I can think is, what about all the new friendships we'll lose at the end of Basic?"

"We'll keep in touch. You know we will."

"Sure." She gazed into my eyes. "But vidmail isn't the same."

"Then we'll just have to make the most of the time we have."

She broke eye contact, and nodded slowly. "I suppose we will."

"But you know," I said. "There's no guarantee we'll even be assigned to the same division in Basic. This might be the last time we get to hang out with each other."

"Actually I think you're wrong," she said. "I have a few friends who've taken Navy boot camp ahead of me, and they said that everyone who arrived on the same train was put in the same division, give or take a few. Besides, we'll have weekends at liberty once in a while. Lots of time to head off base and hang out."

"Or rent a love hotel." I gave her a wink.

She gave me playful punch. "As if."

"Hey, settle down over there," Ace said. He was sitting on the other side of Shaw. She'd introduced me to the natural-born UC citizen when we'd boarded. She'd only just met him that day, and he was trying out for a spec-ops rating, like me, Tahoe, and Alejandro. "By the way, Rade, what part of the UC did you say you were from again? I can't place the accent."

"I'm not from the UC," I said.

"Ah!" He smiled widely. "I would've never pegged you as South American. Not with the pale skin." He had aReal glasses on, and must have been looking at my public profile.

"I'm Caucasian," I said. "Just grew up south of the border, is all."

"Ah. Fancy that." He rubbed his chin. "Well, I don't know what we'd do without you guys. Us natural-borns are some seriously lazy mofos. Staying at home, smoking weed, letting the robos do all our chores, getting the drones to deliver our food. Obesity epidemic? Chalk it up to the robos and the Net. Who wants to live in the real world when the virtual one is so much more fun and the government pays for everything? Did you know the Senate is even passing a bill to consider subsidizing longevity treatments? I shit you not. Don't think it'll pass, though. There has to be at least *some* incentive to work.

"Not that there a lot of jobs available or anything. Robos got a lock on all the blue-collar positions. That said, most companies still employ human managers, but a lot of corporations decided the cost of the more advanced AIs saves bitcoins in the long run, and since the public is becoming more amenable to interacting with robots, a lot of companies have no problem getting rid of humans entirely. White-collar jobs are vanishing left and right. AIs are too advanced these days. Won't be long before you won't be able to get a job even if you want one. Even the creative types are threatened: Did you know someone's developed an experimental AI that writes books? Got about four or five of its novels on the bestseller lists at the same time, written under different pseudonyms. Ridiculous.

"Anyway, the government tried to pass a bill to force all draft-age citizens into the army. Failed. But a bill to enlist immigrants of draft age? A roaring success. You'd think they'd just let the AIs run the military, but they don't trust the machines to fire the weapons. Not completely. Would you? But it's funny. Machines basically run society already. Why not let them kill people too?"

I rubbed my chin. "Got a question for you, Ace."

He grinned. "Shoot."

"Why are *you* joining the military? You're a citizen. You got it made. Like you said, free room and board, robots to do your chores, don't have to work . . ."

"That's the thing. I *want* to work. I looked long and hard at finding a thinker's job. You know, one where I would look far more attractive, paywise, than a machine costing a billion digicoins. I ended up choosing 'theoretical physicist.' Took the free courses on my aReal. The four-year program, you know?"

"Hey, Tahoe," I called to the astrophysicist seated in front of me. "This guy's a theoretical physicist. You should be friends."

Tahoe didn't look back. Didn't want to be friends, I guess.

"Anyway," Ace continued. "When the courses were done, I tried applying for some jobs. Turns out there's no real demand for theoretical physicists after all, not anymore. According to the UC, all the theories we need have already been thought of. There's nothing to discover anymore."

"I don't believe that for a second," I said. "You're telling me that humanity knows every possible thing about the universe? We've only explored one ten-thousandth of our own galaxy, one billionth of the known universe. We haven't even fully explored our own oceans, let alone our own minds. And you're telling me there's nothing more to discover. Have we encountered any extraterrestrial beings? Nope. What about God? Nope."

"Hey, you weren't listening, I said—"

"So don't tell me there are no more theories. That there's nothing more to discover. Because you're dead wrong."

"Hey, you're preaching to the choir, dude," Ace said, a little indignantly. "I did say, *according to the UC*. But I have to give them credit. Apparently the government has a specialized AI working on the theoretical stuff twenty-four/seven. I read a whole article on it at WikiQwiki. A thousand times a second it tests hypotheses and tries things that humans haven't thought of. At least, that's what they think it does all day, though so far all it's done is confirm that Slipstreams are theoretically impossible. And yet, that's how we travel between the stars. Five billion digicoins for a machine that tells us Slipstreams are impossible." He shook his head. "By the way, where you're from, do the robos do all the menial work too?"

"Naw," I said. "Human labor is far too cheap where I'm from. For the cost of buying and maintaining a robot, a business owner can hire a hundred desperate workers. If any of those workers ever gets injured, there's no expensive maintenance costs to repair him or her. You just get rid of the worker and hire another."

"Wow. Glad I wasn't born there."

"It isn't so bad. You learn to make do. The human spirit is resilient, my friend. Not to mention the human body. When you're used to having nothing, nothing becomes your everything, and you never really want for anything. But it's a double-edged sword, because there's the danger of becoming complacent, becoming too happy with that nothing, because you've never known anything better. Complacency is the death of dreams, and freedom. It really is."

We sat in comfortable silence for a time, using the aReal devices connected to the seats to browse the Net, or to peruse the personal collection of books, movies, and music that we had stored offline in our embedded IDs. I was just glad all that data was transferred from my old embedded ID to the new one, because I'd hate to have to seek out and download my stash again.

I thought of something.

"Shaw, everyone has a 3D printer in the UC, right?"

"Sure." She glanced at me from behind her aReal glasses. "Most people do."

"How do they keep people from printing up guns? The Undernet is packed with downloadable blueprints."

"Oh, that's all trackable. If you print up a gun, because of the call-home feature in the printers, you'll get a knock on the door from the local police robot. You'll get a warning the first time, and have it confiscated. Do it again, and you get a mandatory jail term."

"There's an underground market for Net-free printers that come preloaded with gun designs, you know," Ace interjected. "Drop by SilkRoad 5.0 on the Hidden Wiki and you'll find lots of local vendors." He frowned. "What's the matter, Rade? You don't look too happy."

"Nothing. I guess even Utopias have their seedy underbellies."

"Oh you better believe it."

"Honestly, it's not really a problem," Shaw said. "Most people don't even want guns, and those who do just join the military."

The train ride wasn't very long. We reached Recruit Training Command at New Great Lakes in a little under two hours.

The instant I disembarked from the train I realized I was in for a challenge.

A blast of frigid, arctic air swept over me, and my body basically jackhammered. It felt like I'd stepped into one of those cold rooms where they hung slaughtered cattle in the abattoir.

"Thanks, Rade," Alejandro said.

Maybe joining the military wasn't such a good idea after all . . .

I crossed some old tracks that were set up beside the supersonic tube, and made my way, shivering, toward the fenced-off base with the other recruits.

"Looks like a prison," Alejandro muttered.

As we walked through the base, it started to snow lightly. I saw a group of about eighty recruits jogging in perfect formation, completely in sync. One of them called out a cadence. They weren't dressed any warmer than us, but they seemed oblivious to the cold.

A military police robot herded me and the others to the "recruit in-processing" building. I went inside eagerly, glad to get out of the chill air.

The police robot divided us up into Recruit Divisions. I'd expected we'd be divided by alphabetical order or something, but the robot merely separated us based on where we stood. My friends and I were all standing close to each other so we ended up in the same Recruit Division. Shaw had been right after all. All we had to do was arrive at the same time and we ended up together.

The seventy of us were led to a room and the men received a "high and tight" buzz cut from a series of robots. Alejandro's mustache and beard were shaved off, as was Tahoe's soul patch. The women had their hair cut down to the bottom of their collars. A lot of the girls who had longer hair were crying when it was done. Shaw bore it rather well, I thought; although I knew she didn't like it by the way she bit her lip when she glanced at a mirror.

When all seventy of us were barbered, the MP robot had us line up in seven rows of ten people each.

When the Recruit Division Commander showed up a few minutes later, I was almost surprised to see that he was an actual human being dressed in khakis and a matching sailor hat.

"I'm Chief Gunner's Mate Atsu Bowden," the dark-skinned man said. "You may call me RDC Bowden, or sir." He waited. "As in, *yes sir.*"

"Yes sir!" I and the enlistees replied in unison.

"I can't hear you," Bowden said.

"*Yes sir*!"

"Didn't anyone teach you knuckleheads how to stand at attention?" He looked among us as if expecting an answer. More than a few of us tried to straighten up. I know I did. "Well, *stand at attention*!"

He moved among us, shoving his palm into some of our bellies, making others lean forward or backward, forcing the hands of a few recruits to their sides.

"Imagine you're a string puppet," he told one recruit who had particularly bad posture. "And you have a string trailing upward from the top of your head. And the puppeteer gives that string a good hard jerk. Now show me what that would look like, recruit!"

Bowden eventually made his way back to the front.

"Now you're looking more like a division. Remember how you're standing right now because I'm never going to repeat that bull again. If you can't stand at attention, one of the simplest, easiest tasks in the Navy, not to mention the entire history of humankind, you don't deserve to be here. Got that? I can't hear you . . ."

"*Yes sir*!"

"Good. When I ask a question, you answer real loud, because I'm a bit hard of hearing. Got it?"

"*Yes sir*!"

I heard snickering from somewhere behind me.

Bowden got a big smile on his face. "Someone thinks this is funny? You probably expect me to act like all the drill sergeants you've seen on the Net, don't you? Maybe make an example of the knucklehead, make him do some pushups, or maybe take it out on the rest of you, so you all gang up on him later when he's by himself in the showers or lying in bed by his lonesome.

"But I'm not going to do that. That's not the Navy's style. You can laugh all you want, recruits. In fact, it'd tickle me silly if you did that. Laughing at the stench of your collective bodies because you never have time to take proper showers. Laughing at the gruel they call food around here. Laughing through all the Physical Training you're subjected to. Laughing at the pitiful amount of sleep you get every night. Laughing when you're on the second klick of your daily five-K run. Yes. Laugh. Please do."

Bowden waited. No more snickering came from behind me, I noted.

"I can help you or destroy you. You can listen to me or laugh at me. It doesn't matter to me. Respect my authority, do what I say, and you shall pass. Defy me, laugh at me, and you shall fail. With a single one-bit transmission I can have any one of you sent packing. This is my ninth and final push, which means I won't have to lead knuckleheads like you through Basic ever again. So let's just say I've seen a lot of crap, and the crap-I-put-up-with threshold is at the lowest point it's ever been. So try me, I dare you."

When no one tried him, he ordered all the females into the adjacent room and then he had us males strip down. A humanoid robot moved between our ranks and distributed uniforms, using cut-on-demand technology to tailor the clothing to our bodies.

I and everyone else got blue cotton pants, a white T-shirt and underwear, a sweatshirt, and a hat with the word "recruit" on it. Other than the shirt and underwear, each item was a bright blue.

"What happens to our old clothes?" one recruit asked. It was Ace.

RDC Bowden swooped down on him. "You! Did anyone tell you that you could speak?"

Ace looked down. "No sir!"

"Stop staring at the floor and put your freakin' head up."

Ace looked up again.

"Don't look me in the eye, you ingrate! You haven't earned that honor."

Ace snapped his head to the side. He seemed on the verge of panic. "Where should I look, sir?"

"Straight ahead, knucklehead."

"Yes sir!"

"Why is it that UC citizens are always the dumbest of the lot! Thank God for immigrants! Now, in answer to your freakin' question: Your old clothes and any other personal belongings will be sent to the mailing address indicated in your embedded ID. If you don't have a mailing address within this country, all your stuff will be incinerated."

Oh well. Good thing I wasn't attached to my old clothes.

After we'd changed, Bowden had us reintegrate with the female recruits, then he led us all outside. I cringed once more at the blast of frigid air. It was snowing even harder now, and the wind had picked up.

Bowden organized us into a tight square in the courtyard, then he marched us around the base, and we tried our best to stay in line and keep our formation in the cold. A few people slipped in the snow. Bowden swore at us the whole while.

"You worthless pile of snot-eating, toilet-licking knuckleheads! You donkey-humping ingrates! Keep rank! *Keep rank*!"

Bowden led us to our temporary barracks in a nearby building, a room full of bunk beds, with a large partition dividing the room into separate quarters for the males and females. There were lockers at the base of each bunk, with a duffle bag inside.

"You pathetic excuses for recruits will find your spacebags inside the lockers," Bowden said. "Don't you dare let me hear you call those bags anything else. Not a duffle bag. Not a rucksack. Not a barracks bag. And never a backpack. *Spacebag*. Also, you will refer to your sleeping area as racks. They are not beds. They are not bunks. What are they?"

Some people shouted "racks, sir," others "spacebags, sir," and a couple "racks and spacebags, sir!"

Bowden frowned. "Make up your mind you freakin' knuckleheads! Ah, forget it. Turn about and march to the quarterdeck for Physical Training! Actually, belay that. Just drop where you are! Let's see what kind of PT you can do! Burpee pushups. A hundred. Now!"

I and some of the recruits were looking around, not sure what burpee pushups were. I saw someone beside me do a pushup, then launch his feet forward into a squat position, jump up and clap, then squat, touch the ground with both hands, kick his feet back, do a pushup, and repeat.

"That means everyone!" Bowden shouted, his face becoming an even darker shade, an angry vein pulsing on his forehead.

Burpee pushups were surprisingly hard. I found myself becoming exhausted after only five of them.

And I had actually thought I was in shape, just because I was a Dissuader back home.

I may have slightly underestimated my fitness level . . .

"Jump higher when coming out of the squat you insipid weaklings!"

We all jumped as high as we could. But it wasn't the jumping that got most of us: it was the pushups. Around the tenth burpee, my arms started to fail, and by the twelfth I dropped in mid-pushup, panting loudly. Others around me did no better.

"You're all pathetic. I don't know how I ever got stuck with such sorry, mangy asses. Donkeys perform better than you. I'm never going to get you into shape. Never. All right! Enough already. Stop! I can't take it anymore."

The whole class of seventy lay on the ground, facedown, panting.

I think we had a break of maybe ten seconds before he spoke again. Ten seconds of exhausted panting.

"Rest period is o-ver! Now I want to see pushups only! Like a champ, you knuckleheads. Hump the floor. Hump the floor!"

I heard people around me gasp for air as we forced ourselves up. I collapsed after my sixth pushup. I wasn't the only one.

"Pathetic. Utterly so. You're all doomed. We're going to ship you all back to your native countries. And as for you natural-borns, we're going to return you to your hillbilly states and your boring insipid lives. Right back to Mommy and Daddy. Ah! Hell with it! I'm through training you crap-sticks. I give up! I resign! You can go train yourselves!"

Bowden stormed out of the barracks and we were left there, panting, speechless, wondering if we really *were* going to be sent packing.

Bowden came back again five minutes later and, cursing the whole while, made us do PT all over again.

CHAPTER FIVE

The thing I remembered most about the early days of Basic was the smell.

Bowden hadn't been joking about the shower thing. In the first week or so, most of us had maybe two minutes, tops, in the showers. Barely enough time to lather and shampoo. Most people just did their hair and got out. Compounding this was the fact that there was just no time to clean our clothes. We ended up smelling like a bunch of homeless people. Don't even get me talking about how bad Alejandro's feet smelled.

By the way, the showers were *not* co-ed. Guys and gals took separate showers in separate heads (bathrooms). This was hugely disappointing to a lot of us. I'm not sure why anyone expected co-ed showers when we weren't even allowed to dress or undress together. I blame it on all those military sci-fi vids the UC film industry churned out.

After the first few days, RDC Bowden assigned fifteen of us to leadership positions. These "Recruit Petty Officers" held authority over the others, and any orders received from them had the full weight of the RDC behind them. Those positions came and went, depending on Bowden's whim. Bowden made me a Recruit Section Leader, which only meant that I had the pleasure of being punished for the faults of my section as well as my own. Thankfully I only lasted in that position for three days.

Anyway, eventually we got settled in. Processing week went by, we finally found time to properly shower and wash our clothes; we were given our own aReals, granted our division guidon, and assigned to a berth in one of the "starships"—which were really just barrack buildings. My division was barracked in the USS *John F. Kennedy*, which had berths for eleven mixed-gender recruit divisions. It also had classrooms, a library, a galley, a mess hall, and a quarterdeck. The latter was the most sacred part of the starship apparently, and was kept polished and trim. It had naval artifacts like the anchor and rope from the actual USS *Kennedy*—the sailing ship. We did a lot of indoor PT there.

In the berthing compartment, we were assigned to our racks based on our last names. A large partition divided the compartment into two halves, one for males and the other, females. Watches drawn from our own numbers were assigned each night to ensure no one crossed over to the female side and vice versa.

RDC Bowden was happy to explain the terminology. "This is your berthing compartment. These walls are bulkheads. The ceiling is the overhead, or deckhead. The floor is the deck. The washroom is the head. You eat in the mess hall, from food prepared in the galley. This is the forward part of the compartment. Behind you is the aft part. You get me?"

"We get you, sir!"

"Your starship is to be shipshape at all times. You will all be assigned cleaning stations, and are expected to *clean*! You get me?"

"We get you, sir!"

Each morning I and the others awoke to the high-pitched whistle of "General Quarters," followed by a ten-second klaxon. After the klaxon faded, Bowden sometimes ordered us to immediately drop into pushups beside our racks. Other times he had us dress and pile outside to shovel the walkways that led to the starship (the Brass could have had robots do it, but why bother when you had all this free labor lying around). When we finished the pushups or the shoveling, we showered, brushed our teeth, and shaved within the seven minutes of personal grooming allocated us. Thirty-five guys trying to use ten showers and ten sinks at the same time wasn't an environment all that conducive to teamwork—there were constant arguments over things like shampoo and soap, let alone who was using what sink and when. Still, Tahoe, Alejandro, Ace, and I managed to cordon off a sink and shower for ourselves each morning so that we always got ready in a timely fashion.

After integrating with the females, our division trotted in formation to the mess hall. We ate breakfast in ten minutes, then ran 5K around the base in a tight, square formation. We were getting pretty good at that. The first week Bowden had berated us at almost every turn. These days I don't think there were any stragglers among us, and he didn't have to say a word. I guess it helped that we had our running cadence song down pat.

"Everywhere we go-o."

"*Everywhere we go-o.*"

"People wanna know-o."

"*People wanna know-o . . .*"

When the run was done, it was time for a three- or four-hour classroom or hands-on session. Classroom sessions covered everything from ethics to MilNet familiarization to starship basics, while the hands-on sessions ran the gamut from firefighting to weapons training to first aid, and also included specialized Physical Training such as navigating the "confidence" course (an obstacle course where you carried heavy spacebags/sandbags through scuttles and whatnot).

After that we jogged back to the mess hall for lunch, then off to more classroom and hands-on sessions, then to the mess hall once more for dinner, then to the quarterdeck for group PT, then to our berth, where we washed our clothes and shined our shoes, then taps sounded and we went to bed.

And so it went.

RDC Bowden rushed us through each day, keeping up the sense of urgency that was perhaps false, but felt real to me and the other recruits. As astronaut soldiers stationed aboard a ship traveling between star systems, we always had to be on high alert. Space wasn't the safest place. Sure there was the threat from privateers funded by the Sino-Koreans, but a far greater threat came from the starship itself—more vessels were lost due to structural and engine problems than anything else. Running out of fuel apparently was also an issue. A radioactive element known as "Geronium" provided the main fissile fuel. If you ran out of Geronium when you were a billion kilometers from pickup, you had a very big problem.

Anyway, Bowden promised that while the training might let up once we graduated into our respective ratings, it would never cease. The life of a soldier was a life of training and constant readiness.

After the first few weeks we basically got into the rhythm of it all. I was closest with Shaw, Tahoe, Alejandro, and Ace of course, but everyone else was like extended family. After lights out, the recruits assigned as RPOs—Religious Petty Officers—led us in prayer, and sometimes we cracked jokes with our bunkmates. Some used their aReals to browse the Net or catch up on reading for a few minutes before going to sleep. A few people were probably watching porn, though Ricky Boxing (masturbating) in your bunk or the head was frowned upon. Most people were too tired to try anyway. A few people claimed they fed us something that prevented erections. I don't know if that was true or not, but all I know is that whenever I thought of Shaw while lying in bed at night, I had no problems in that department.

Speaking of Shaw, the sexual tension between the two of us was growing by the day.

One time at lunch when she and I were eating alone—Ace and Alejandro had been delayed doing extra PT on the confidence course while Tahoe was off doing some other duty—things got a little out of hand. Our conversation started out innocently enough . . .

"So where'd you grow up?" I asked her.

"On a cider farm," she said. "In the Normandy district of France. My grandparents owned it. Mom's side. Though I spent a lot of summers visiting relatives in Bangalore, India, where my dad was from. Quite the contrast, going from the calm farms of France to the hustle and bustle of India. Anyway, my family eventually moved to the UC when I was sixteen, and here I am five years later."

"How about that. Sweet sixteen and a new country to boot. So your brothers came too?"

"Yup," Shaw said. "My grandparents sold the farm, so my two brothers really had nowhere else to go. They came, and got drafted. One's in the Navy, the other's a Marine. But what about you? You lived south of the border your whole life?"

"I did. My parents owned the biggest orange plantation in the whole country."

"Wow. That sounds like fun. And not so different from my own upbringing."

I sighed. "Yeah. It didn't last too long, though. When we lost the plantation, things kind of spiraled out of control and I found myself on the streets. I was six. Let's just say, I wasn't very street smart. If it weren't for Alejandro, I wouldn't be here today."

Shaw reached out and touched my hand. "He means a lot to you, doesn't he?"

I nodded. "He's like a brother to me. More than a brother."

I noticed that her hand lingered on top of mine. I could almost feel the electricity passing back and forth between us. When she took her hand away, it really felt like something was missing.

"So you're half Desi, and half French," I said.

"*Oui.*" Shaw smiled coyly. "*Comment ça va*?" Her fingers twirled the air beside her neck, right where her long locks used to be. The roots of her short hair were dark, but the tips maintained their dyed blonde color.

"*Très bien*. That's all I know." I didn't break eye contact. I couldn't.

"Well, you have to start somewhere." Her voice seemed a little husky to me.

"I do. I don't suppose you know how to cook French food?"

"*Mais oui*. I can stir up a mean banana crepe."

I leaned forward, just slightly. "Crepes aren't even real French food. That's like a dessert."

"Not so." She smiled that cute-as-pie smile of hers, dimpling her cheeks. "Ever heard of savory crepes?"

"All right. When Basic is over, you're going to make me a savory crepe."

Her eyes hadn't left mine the whole time. "Deal."

"So which half of you is French?"

"The good half," she said.

"And which half is Desi?"

She edged subtly closer. "Guess."

A tray suddenly plunked down between the two of us.

We both sat back, stunned and embarrassed.

It was Ace.

I'd forgotten about everything else. The mess hall. The other recruits.

A dangerous thing to do. If that had been RDC Bowden . . .

"You guys over your little staring contest?" Ace said.

Shaw and I couldn't meet his eyes, or each other's.

I caught a recruit watching us from the far side of the mess hall. Nathan Filberg, aka Dirtbag Nathan. He was one of those lazy dudes who always complained about everything, shirking his duties and doing the least amount of work possible to get by. The kind of guy who you thought wouldn't ever make it through Basic, yet here he was in week six.

He didn't like me very much. The feeling was mutual.

He was smirking.

Bowden took me and Shaw aside that night. "Nothing is going on between you two, yes?"

I shook my head, maybe a little too fast. "No sir!"

"No sir!" Shaw echoed.

Bowden's scowl deepened. "If I catch you two copulating, well, I'm sure you know the meaning of the phrase Big Chicken Dinner?"

I exchanged a glance with Shaw. "Excuse me, sir?"

"Bad Conduct Discharge," Bowden growled. "You get me?"

"We get you, sir!" I said. "But respectfully, it's impossible for Shaw and I to . . . well, copulate. There are cameras everywhere, and recruits stand watch every night."

Bowden studied me through slitted eyes. "Have you ever heard of the Sacred Band of Thebes?"

"No sir," I said.

"They were a band of gay lovers, put together by the ancient Spartans. The theory was, you'd fight better, harder, if not only your life was on the line, but the life of your lover. Good theory, right? And it even seemed to hold some water, for a little while at least. The Sacred Band became the most elite unite in all of Sparta. For a whole three battles. Then they were annihilated by Philip the Second of Macedon. Do you know why?"

Again I shook my head.

"The love bond worked too well," Bowden said. "When one of the two lovers died, the second man went down soon after. When Philip II attacked, he had his soldiers concentrate on the older, weaker man in each pair. When they killed that man, his lover, maddened by revenge or fraught with sadness, invariably fell. Thanks to this strategy, the ranks of the Sacred Band fell apart and Philip the Second's soldiers slaughtered them to the last man." He gave me an appraising look. "This is why we don't allow lovers in the same division. Gay or straight. It's too distracting. How can you concentrate on the battle at hand when all you can think about is the great sex you'll be having with your partner afterward, who just so happens to be crouching beside you, her thigh touching your thigh? How can you focus on your target when your eyes keep drifting toward your lover, out of lust or some need to protect and nurture her? How can you hope to complete the damn mission, let alone retain the will to live, when your partner dies on the battlefield? Do you understand now, recruit? Sex and war don't mix."

I nodded stiffly. "I understand, sir."

"Good. Dismissed."

After that, Shaw and I let things cool off between us. I avoided her, and she avoided me. We still sat with the same group in the mess hall, but I was always careful to sit as many places away from her as possible. She was a distraction, one that could ruin my dreams, and I wasn't ready to give up everything for a girl.

Though she was quite the girl, I had to admit.

A few days into the seventh week, I awoke to a high-pitched whistle in the middle of the night.

"General Quarters!" came the voice over the main circuit. "General Quarters! All hands man your battle stations. Up and forward to starboard, down and aft to port. General Quarters, General Quarters. Incoming rockets, starboard side! Incoming rockets!" The klaxon sounded five times and the message repeated.

My heart was beating fast. It had finally come. Battle Stations. The culmination of Basic training.

Two Petty Officers rushed into our berth.

"RPOC!" one of them said. "Integrate your division and get your soldiers into full battle dress! *You have five minutes*!"

Ace was our RPOC (Recruit Petty Officer in Charge) tonight. He saluted, then turned to us. "You heard the man! Dress and grab the spacebags!"

We dressed and mustered with the women in the compartment outside. I grabbed one of the heavily laden spacebags on the way out. There was one bag for every three recruits. It didn't feel too heavy, but I knew it would feel like an anchor as the evening wore on. I wouldn't have to worry about that, though. Someone would relieve me, right?

Bowden separated us into two teams, Red and Yellow, and assigned two petty officers to each team as facilitators. Alejandro, Tahoe, and I were in Red team. Shaw and Ace ended up in Yellow.

PO1 (Petty Officer First Class) Rao explained the rules. "Everything you've learned in Basic has been building to this. You've been called to arms and it's time to perform! Though the majority of you will move on to your rating schools, in less than a month some of you may be stationed on starships. So while this is a practice run, I want you to treat it like a *real* mission. And you'll be graded as if it were. This is serious business.

"Every tiny mistake you make, that's one strike against you. Three strikes and you're out—you get rolled back to a junior division and have to repeat Battle Stations. If you make any major mistakes, you're rolled back on the spot, regardless of how many previous strikes you have. Stop during any of the runs, or otherwise refuse to train, you're out. Same goes for any gundecking or 'gaming the system' type strategies, which won't be tolerated. You do what's asked of you in the given time allotted, no more, no less. Understood?"

"*Yes sir*!"

He nodded. "Good. Luckily for you, passing is more a matter of avoiding strikes than accumulating any sort of score. Survive the night unscathed, and you're in the Navy."

Ace gave the order to proceed to the first event and we began the half-mile jog to Building 1312. The snow was really blowing around us. Blizzard conditions.

"It's times like this that I really hate you," Alejandro said beside me. "*Caramba.* Why did I ever let you talk me into leaving my sunny country?"

"Who's speaking?" PO1 Rao shouted.

Alejandro quickly clammed up.

Once we reached 1312, Rao explained the first objective. "Sino-Koreans have ambushed your destroyer-class starship and taken out your engines. A boarding party is trying to seize your ship. You're unarmed, so your orders are to extract your injured shipmates and move them to a secure area for treatment. The BEARs are offline." BEAR stood for Battlefield Extraction-Assist Robot. "So it's up to you to perform the extraction of your shipmates. Provide first aid and bring the injured to the designated area as quickly as you can. You are a team, first and foremost, an individual, second. How you function as a cohesive team in times of danger will mean the difference between life and death. Live by the rules of honor, courage, and commitment, and you will do well, not just here in training but in life itself." He picked out three of the taller recruits, including Tahoe. "You, you, and you, you're going to be the casualties."

The "casualties" were led away. The assistant RPOC on our team assigned corpsmen, scouts, and defenders, and then divided the remainder of us into four-person parties. I was teamed up with Jason and Tisha, two recruits I knew peripherally. Unfortunately I also had Dirtbag Nathan in my party.

"Hey, chico," Nathan said to me as we moved toward the stretcher. "Think you're up to being a man?"

I lifted up my end of the stretcher. "That should be easy enough next to a woman like you."

Tisha made a face. "Can we just complete the mission without comparing dick size?" she said.

The four of us were the first to go in after the scouts. We heaved the stretcher past the line of defenders, making our way toward a darkened doorway. Before we went inside I saw the party from Yellow Team enter an alternate doorway nearby.

We ended up in a maze of black-painted walls and metallic floors that echoed our every boot step. Strobe lights flashed from all sides, simulating weapons fire. Screams, gunfire, and explosions echoed from various parts of the maze. I glanced up and caught a glimpse of two petty officers patrolling the catwalks above, observing our every movement. That kind of grounded me, and reminded me that all this was a simulation, which made things a little easier psychologically.

We could barely hear above the simulated screams as the scout from Red Team shouted us forward. We crawled through a scuttle, over pipe barriers, and with difficulty carried the stretcher up a ladder. It was hard enough climbing those ladders with an empty stretcher—I could only imagine how difficult it was going to be when we carried an actual casualty back with us.

We came to a sealed hatch. It wouldn't open.

"What now?" Nathan said. "How the hell are we going to get through?"

Two other stretcher parties from Red Team piled up behind us.

"Tim and I will check the other routes," one of the scouts we'd been following said. "Wait here." The two scouts hurried back and went down the leftmost passage we'd passed on the way.

There was another passage back there, on the right.

"I'll scope out the rightmost passage. Save us some time." I wanted to show my initiative to the watching petty officers. Plus the fire of competition had been lit inside me, and I dearly wanted to beat Yellow Team.

No one said anything as I turned back.

I shoved past the other two Red parties, but before I made it three meters, I heard a voice call down from the observation walkway. "Recruit Galaal," the petty officer said. "Strike one for separating from your extraction party."

Damn it.

I returned to my party.

"Well done, you douche," Nathan said.

The scouts reappeared and led us back to an open hatch. The three Red parties split up in the compartment beyond. My group found the first casualty lying beside some smoking machinery.

It was Tahoe. I was shocked when I saw his face covered in blood.

Then he smiled. "Hey, Rade. What do you think of my new look?"

Tisha went through the process of medically stabilizing him, just like we were supposed to.

Then we loaded him onto the stretcher. Man, Tahoe was heavy.

"This way!" a scout said through the dry-ice fog. Tim.

We followed Tim's voice, and hurried down the scuttle until we came upon the dreaded ladder.

This was going to be tricky. The ladders were wide enough for one person only. I took charge of the front of the stretcher, while Jason gripped the back.

I paused right at the top of the ladder. "Nathan, go down the ladder! We'll need your help at the bottom."

Nathan crossed his arms. "No way, chico. Who made you leader?"

I glanced at Tisha imploringly. She slid down the ladder before I could say a word.

I ignored Nathan and started down the ladder, carrying the front handles of the stretcher. I took each rung one at a time, constantly worried that my knees were going to give out, or that I'd miss a step. Tahoe slid precariously against the straps, but the buckles held.

I felt the solid deck below my feet. Tisha joined my side and grabbed the other handle. Together we lifted the stretcher away from the ladder while Jason climbed down, slowly lowering the opposite side. We could've used another hand holding up the middle of the stretcher from here, though, bearing some of the weight. Damn it, Nathan.

When Jason reached the deck, he lost his grip on one handle and the stretcher tilted to the side. Tahoe banged his side on the bulkhead.

"Gah!" Tahoe said. "Careful, bitches!"

I saw one of the petty officers watching from the catwalk above, and I cringed, expecting to get another strike.

But it wasn't me who got the penalty.

"Recruit Filberg!" the petty officer's voice floated down from above. "Strike for failing to observe proper safety protocols."

"*What*?" Nathan slid down the ladder. "This sucks! I didn't do anything!"

"That's exactly right, you didn't do anything," the petty officer said. "You should have gone down when Astronaut Recruit Galaal asked. They needed you down there."

"Yeah whatever." Nathan shoved a shoulder under the stretcher, finally taking up his share of the burden. "Let's go before that ass-wipe throws some other stupid citation at me." He said that loud enough for the petty officer to hear. Probably not the best idea to insult the officers who were grading you.

When we finally got back, the test was reset—different people were assigned as rescuers, scouts, casualties, corpsmen, and defenders. We repeated the test four times, and at the end of it I'd played nearly every role. The total cumulative extraction times of each team were tallied, and Yellow Team edged us out by about three minutes. As reward, no member of Yellow had to carry a spacebag to the next evolution.

I ended up being saddled with one of the spacebags again, and it was all I could do to concentrate on the man in front of me and listen to the cadence to ensure I kept formation.

"Everywhere we go-o."

"*Everywhere we go-o.*"

"People wanna know-o."

"*People wanna know-o.*"

By the time we arrived at our destination through the blizzard, my vision was filled with floaters and I just wanted to collapse. I staggered inside the building and tossed the spacebag into the pile beside the door.

"Jeez, Rade, you look terrible." Alejandro tossed aside his own spacebag. He had icicles on his eyebrows.

"You know it." I gave him a fist bump.

I paused to take in my surroundings, and I realized where we were: the Weapons Simulator building.

The rangemaster came forward, the stock of a simulated rifle slung over his shoulder. We mustered immediately, and he paced among our front rank. "So. Those darn Sino-Koreans have struck again. Tore a hole in your hull during a surprise attack, they did. And guess what? The goshdarn varmints have boarded. You'll have to wear your SCBAs. Not safe with a hull breach on the ship, it ain't. Artificial gravity is still active, though, and the radiation shielding is still up, so you don't need full hazmat suits. Lucky you. I know, it don't make sense, because if there were an actual hull breach you'd need the full suits. But hey, this is Battle Stations, and they don't want you to use the full suits till later tonight. Shooting with an SCBA on will be tricky enough as it is, don't you worry.

"Anyhoo, you're going to shoot twenty simulated rounds at the target, while observing full safety precautions, you hear? I don't want any mistakes. I'm not in the greatest of moods tonight, so I might just give out three strikes for a minor infraction. Anyway, you've all fired rifles before so this should be a cakewalk: Don't be letting down your teammates by missing targets or failing to observe safety protocols. And don't be letting the sights and sounds of the battle distract you. Show us what you're made of! Show us your mettle! I want you to prove to me that you know what honor, courage, and commitment mean. Red Team shoots first. Go!"

We were given one minute each to don a SCBA (Self-Contained Breathing Apparatus). Miss any step, or fail to complete all steps within the allocated sixty seconds, and we got a strike. We went forward in groups of fifteen.

I was in the group that went first. I approached the SCBA bracket, placed my arms through the shoulder straps, released the SCBA from the bracket, cinched the waist belt, tightened the shoulder straps, opened the main cylinder valve, donned the face plate, slid my protective hood up, pulled on a helmet, secured the chin strap, connected the regulator to my face piece, and finally activated the air flow and Personal Alert Safety System.

The rangemaster and his assistant moved down the line, checking us. A lot of other recruits got strikes for missing a step. Not me. Surprisingly, Nathan completed all the steps perfectly and on time as well.

I grabbed a simulated rifle from the weapons case. These utilized a laser light pointer instead of live rounds, but we still had to observe full safety precautions.

Nathan apparently missed the part about observing safety precautions, because when he grabbed his simulated rifle, three recruits, including myself, were in his line of fire before he lowered it.

"Recruit Filberg!" the rangemaster roared.

Nathan actually jumped.

"Strike for not observing proper safety precautions!"

Nathan slouched, an expression of disgust on his face.

PO1 Rao came forward. "That's what, two, recruit?"

"Yes sir," Nathan said sulkily. He gave me an evil glance, like he was implying it was my fault for not getting out of the way of his rifle.

My turn came, and I aimed at the distant targets fifty feet away. White lights were flashing at random, and artillery simulators were going off. A loudspeaker filled the air with the sounds of gunfire.

Okay. I can do this.

I fired my twenty simulated shots and my targets were scored. I didn't hit them all, but I did pass.

The one thing about SCBAs I didn't really like was how the face mask restricted your peripheral vision: as I walked back toward the weapons case, I tripped on something I didn't see, and fell to the ground. I looked up and saw my rifle was pointed right at RDC Bowden.

"Recruit Galaal!" the RDC roared. "Strike for not observing proper safety precautions!"

I scrambled to my feet, and saw that Nathan was standing right beside me, giggling. I was fairly certain he was the one who'd tripped me.

Thanks to him, I had only one strike left.

The remaining recruits completed the shooting evolution (Yellow beat us), then we mustered and ran back to Building 1312. The cold and the blowing snow were really starting to get to me. Somehow I'd ended up with a spacebag yet *again*. I began missing steps in the march, and I couldn't follow along with the cadence. I was going to mess up the formation.

I was going to fall.

I was going to *fail.*

And then I felt the weight shift. Someone grabbed the bag from me while I jogged, from behind. I glanced back to thank the recruit.

It was Alejandro.

We finally reached 1312.

"There's been a spill in the loading dock," PO1 Rao said. "Some fuel ship broke away before we could untether the line, so now we got Geronium radiation flooding decks three to five, and the anti-rads are down! The berthing quarters are on deck four, and it's your job to go in there and get the casualties the hell out. You'll be going in fully suited, boys and girls. As for those of you chosen to be casualties, well, rad levels in there are enough to mutate your offspring for generations to come. Wouldn't surprise me if some of you grew a third eyeball by this time next year."

"He's joking, right?" Alejandro said.

"Show me honor, recruits!" PO1 Rao said. "Show me commitment. Show me courage!"

We donned hazmat suits with SCBAs on top. I wasn't sure if those flimsy suits would have protected us against actual nuclear agents, but that was Battle Stations for you.

PO1 Rao split us up into six-person extraction parties. *Again* Nathan was assigned to my party.

Rao was going through the line, inspecting our gear. When he got to my group he paused.

"Recruit Filberg!" PO1 Rao said. "Third strike! You're out."

"*What*?" Nathan said. "Why? What the hell did I do?"

PO1 Rao smiled derisively. "You didn't fully open your main cylinder valve. Remove your gear and go see the RDC to talk about your rollback."

"You're wrong," Nathan said. "My HUD shows two green lights! Wait, now it shows a yellow light." He reached back, and touched the valve. "This isn't fair! Someone tightened the valve on me!" He gave me his worst scowl, then he sulkily moved to the side to doff his gear. Honestly, I was glad to see him go.

Alejandro gave me a wicked grin.

"You didn't," I told him.

He winked.

When the evolution was done, the scores were tallied between Red and Yellow Teams. We'd missed two casualties, but the Yellows had missed four.

"What a terrible bunch of recruits you are," PO1 Rao said. "Some of the worst I've ever seen. How would you like it if you were one of the casualties abandoned to the radiation? This is the UC Navy! No one is left behind, you hear me? No one! Where's your honor? Where's your courage? Where's your commitment? None of you deserve to pass Battle Stations. Not a single knucklehead among you! Muster, you maggots."

He made us sprint in formation around the base. I didn't have to carry a spacebag this time around, luckily.

The wind was blowing hard, and I noticed a few of the women were crying. One of them was carrying a spacebag. It was Tisha. I thought she was going to fall any second. Rao's words echoed in my mind. "No one is left behind."

Like Alejandro had done for me, I slid over and took the burden from her. I regretted that instantly, because I was already exhausted and I almost staggered under the weight. But the smile she gave me was priceless.

I scanned the division for Shaw but couldn't see her in the blowing snow. She was on Yellow Team, so I hadn't been able to keep tabs on her. I hoped she was all right. I hoped she hadn't been rolled back.

The evolutions continued all through that night. We had to abandon ship, fight a fire, move heavy magazines from one part of a ship to the other, and carry a one-hundred-fifty-pound dummy through the confidence course while wearing hazmat suits and SCBAs.

When it was finally over, twelve hours later, we were all utterly exhausted.

As we jogged back to Building 1312, the storm abated and the sun came up.

I don't think I'd ever been so happy to see a sunrise in my life.

CHAPTER SIX

A week later our recruit division stood at attention for the graduation ceremony. This was the first time we'd ever worn our tailored uniforms, and it felt good. A lot of us had to pin or tape our uniforms around the belly area, especially the women—most of us had lost an inch around the waist in the four weeks since we were measured. The Brass should've ordered the robots to use their cut-on-demand technology to tailor the clothing for us *now* rather than four weeks ago. Ah well, at least we'd finally exchanged our "recruit" insignia hats for Navy ball caps.

On the whole, the graduation ceremony went well. The stands were full of visiting friends and families, and they all cheered when the band played "Anchors Aweigh."

That song, and those cheering families, made me feel a bit lonely. I didn't have any family to cheer me on.

No. That wasn't true.

I had Tahoe and Alejandro. Ace and Shaw. Who needed a cheering section when I had them?

When it was all over, RDC Bowden had us stand in one final muster backstage, where he gave a speech. I heard several people comment later that it was the most brilliant, inspiring thing they'd ever heard.

Unfortunately I don't remember a word of it.

Well, except for the last bit.

"Bravo Zulu, division zero zero four," Bowden said, his voice thick with grudging respect. "Bravo Zulu. You've demonstrated that you understand the true meaning of honor, courage, and commitment. The UC Navy salutes you. As of this moment, you are all Astronaut Apprentices. You know what that means, don't you? Liberty call."

We cheered.

"That's right," Bowden said. "Now settle down. You only have thirty-six hours on liberty, so don't get all excited for nothing. It's going to go by before you can even blink, trust me. Now you may think 'liberty' means freedom, and going by the strict dictionary definition of the word, that's true. But in the military, we have our own definition for certain words, and liberty, well, its meaning varies with the circumstance. For this particular liberty, you're going to stay within fifty klicks of the base. You're not going to consume alcohol. You're not going to drive any type of motor vehicle or flying craft. And you're going to wear your uniform at all times. You're UC Navy now, goddammit, and you're going to let the world know it. Now get out of here. Dis-missed!"

The RDC raised a halting hand as I walked past him. "I'd like a word with you four, please." He was looking right at me, Ace, Alejandro, and Tahoe.

I glanced at Shaw, but she was already rushing back to the drill deck to visit her friends and family. With a sigh, I followed Bowden.

When we reached his office, Bowden shut the door. He sat down at his desk and put up his feet. His black shoes were polished so well I could almost see my reflection in the faux leather. He slipped a baseball glove onto one palm and tossed a softball into it with the other. The image strangely reminded of Mito, twirling his Baoding spheres, readying himself to pronounce judgment.

"The four of you have signed up for spec-ops," Bowden said nonchalantly.

"*Yes sir!*"

He smirked. "I didn't say you could answer me. Drop, please."

We dropped and did pushups. Ah, Bowden. He just had to show us he still cared.

"Spec-ops." Bowden sounded like he was amused. I didn't dare look up, or pause my pushups. "The Navy MOTHs. Do you have any idea of what you're getting into? Of course you don't. I'll tell you firsthand, I've seen a lot of recruits come through here, hoping they had what it took to join the spec-ops. Dreaming about piloting those newfangled ATLAS mechs. And you know what? Almost all of those dreamy-eyed recruits washed out.

"Some of those failures went on to other postings in the fleet. But most dropped on request. Ended up deported. They were broken, you understand. Right down the middle. Spirits split in half. It's a sorry sight to see an apprentice destroyed like that. A sad, sorry sight.

"I'll tell you what I'm going to do. I'll give you all a chance to say no. A chance to save the Navy, and yourselves, from going through all the trouble. I'm going to offer you a fleet posting to any starship of your choice. You'll be an undesignated astronaut, but at least you won't be broken. Tell me, do you really want to leave the Navy two months from now as a shell of the man you once were? Or do you want to leave on your own two feet at the end of your contract, as a full citizen with a topped-up bank account, and pride swelling in your breast? Don't throw away your Navy careers on some unattainable dream. If you accept my offer, I promise you'll leave this room with your dignity intact. No one will look down on you. Least of all your fellow apprentices."

He remained silent for a few moments, like he was waiting for one of us to capitulate. But none of us said a word. All I heard from my companions were stuttered exhalations as they worked through the pushups.

"Mr. Galaal," Bowden said abruptly. "What do you think?"

I paused, and glanced up. Didn't meet his eyes. I was too well trained for that. "I want to be a MOTH, sir!"

"I was afraid you'd say that." He asked the other three the same question, and got the same answer.

Bowden sighed. "All right, all right. I did my duty. Did everything I was told to do. I tried, I really did. I'll digitally sign the necessary documents. You'll start Pre-BSD/M as soon as the next evolution starts. I wish you luck, I really do. But luck has nothing to do with it. Dismissed."

As soon as we got outside, Ace started chattering away. "Sheesh. That was almost as bad as the session with the job counselor dude back at entrance processing. They really don't want people becoming spec-ops, do they? But I guess we're in now. They couldn't break us, though they tried. Welcome to the most elite spec-ops unit in the galaxy, people!"

"Don't celebrate yet," Tahoe said. "We haven't even started MOTH training."

"Oh I know." Ace was grinning. "And it's gonna be brutal. I can't wait!"

"I can." Alejandro had his arms crossed, and like me and Tahoe, he was shivering in the cold. The sweat from the impromptu PT didn't help. "Not sure how much more of this crap I can take. I watched some spec-ops training vids on the Net. Ace is right, it's brutal."

I glanced at Alejandro. He'd come far these past eight weeks, and I barely recognized him anymore. He'd never really been fat, but his face was definitely leaner now, the hollows of his cheeks and the outline of his jaw clearly visible. His eyes still had that haunted look, though.

The look of a man who had seen his entire family gunned down.

I put my arm around him. The thought of losing him to the training wasn't something I could even contemplate. "You'll do fine, Alejandro. You always make it through."

He sighed. "I don't know, Rade. I'll try, I really will."

"Don't tell me that." I put him in a headlock. "Say you'll make it. Say you'll become a MOTH. Come on, say it!"

The headlock was a mistake. I'd misjudged how strong he'd become these past few weeks, and he easily broke out of it and slammed me against the wall, wrenching my arm behind my back. Though the Navy hadn't given us any hand-to-hand combat training, he knew how to fight. We were still Dissuaders at heart, after all.

I tried to tap out, but he told me, flatly, "There is no tapping out."

When Alejandro finally let me go, I went back inside, looking for Shaw on the drill deck, where the other apprentices were socializing with their families. The band was playing some sappy, upbeat tune.

I saw her right away. She was talking to someone I'd never seen before, a man roughly our age, dressed in civilian clothes.

When I went to the two of them, Shaw stiffened.

"Rade," she said, grinning forcefully. "This is my fiancé." She introduced me to her man, but I forgot his name instantly. I was too dumbfounded. She'd never mentioned him before. Not once.

"Nice to meet you," I said, barely able to function. "Shaw—" I lost my train of thought. I tried again. "Shaw told me all about you. Says you're the man she always dreamed of marrying."

He rested a possessive hand across her lower back. "Sounds like my girl talking! And she's the best woman a man could ever dream of in return, believe me." He planted a juicy kiss on her cheek.

I played at small talk for a while, coercing out the smiles and the laughs as best I could, but I was dying inside. Eventually I managed to excuse myself.

Morale, Welfare, and Recreation provided a few tickets to Saturday's game in New Chicago, and Ace snatched them up. Even though they couldn't get into the game, a lot of other recruits tagged along with us to the city, bringing their family members on the train. Ace gave Shaw and her fiancé two of the game tickets, so I was forced to endure more torture as she tagged along. I almost gave up my tickets so I could sulk on base instead, but I decided I wasn't going to miss out on seeing a UC city for the first time.

New Chicago didn't seem so different at first from the city I'd grown up in. From faraway, it seemed about the same size, with the same layout: a central core of steel-and-glass buildings surrounded by an outer layer of sprawling suburbia. As we got closer, the core of office and condominium towers kept increasing in size until those structures ate up the heavens, quite literally scraping the sky. The goal seemed to be to pack as many people as possible into the tiniest real estate conceivable, while still conserving living and working space, by building upward. Contrast this to my city, where we didn't build upward, or build at all really, and the personal space just dropped as the population rose.

There were at least three distinct roadway levels stacked half a klick above one another, linked every four blocks by spiraling ramps that led up to the different levels. I couldn't see any pillars or other support structures holding up the higher roads, and I guessed they were held aloft by some technology or physics I didn't understand. But when I noticed that all those roadways were in direct contact with the buildings, I realized that the skyscrapers themselves provided the support infrastructure.

Car-sized rotorcraft flew in the clear space between the buildings, seeming to follow preset paths. They moved in orderly lines, with roughly the same amount of space separating each one. No human flew like that—they were definitely controlled by automatic pilots.

When we got off the train, I half expected to catch a whiff of the usual pollutants I'd come to associate with cities, but the air was surprisingly clean. The perfectly straight sidewalk was completely clear of snow—apparently there was some sort of heating and water collection mechanism built right into the pavement.

Ace slid on his aReal glasses and found out the bus route we needed to take to get to the stadium. We left the train station behind and the sidewalk soon became crowded with people bustling to and fro. For a society where work was optional, they sure seemed like they had a lot to do.

"Where is everyone going?" I said to my group.

"Well it's near lunch time, so probably the free food halls," Ace said. "A lot of people just send their robots out to pick up the food. Others order in."

I realized that more than three-fourths of the crowd was composed of humanoid robots, dressed in clothes, betrayed only by their polycarbonate, scoop-shaped heads. Most of the robots were carrying reusable canvas bags full of food, judging by the delectable smells that floated around me. Above the sidewalk, just out of reach, Amazon delivery drones flitted to and fro, carrying various parcels and food containers.

I noticed something else about that crowded street. It was a small thing, I guess, but to me it was the biggest difference between my country and this one: There were no guns. Not a one. Even the few police robots I observed seemed weaponless, though they probably carried hidden electro-stunners of some kind.

For the first time in my life I actually felt safe walking a city street. Like going to my destination wasn't some kind of trek through a warzone.

What a feeling.

Our small party eventually piled into an automated high-speed bus. The AI of the bus scanned our embedded IDs as we stepped in the door and it waived the transport fees because of our enlistment status. One man behind us, he was homeless, I guess, didn't have enough money so the doors automatically closed.

"You have five seconds to step away from the automated doorway before a level two electrical discharge is issued," came a loud, deep voice from the box that stood in place of a driver. "You have four seconds . . ."

The scruffy-looking man stepped away, and the doors folded aside.

I shoved my way through the rest of the people who were coming on board until I was back outside. I wanted to find the homeless man, and transfer some money to his embedded ID. I glanced around, but couldn't see him in the thick crowds.

"Last call," the automated voice of the bus announced.

"Rade, come on!" Alejandro was standing in the entrance, blocking the folding door.

"Please clear the automated doorway," the automated voice said.

I searched the crowded sidewalk a while longer. Nothing. The man had been swept away by the throng.

"Please clear the automated doorway."

"Rade!"

With a sigh I plowed back onto the bus.

"I thought there was no homelessness in the UC?" I asked Ace when we were underway.

"What?" Ace screwed up his face. "Where'd you get that idea?"

"People don't have to work. Food is provided. Rooms."

"Oh. Yeah sure, all that's provided. But some people fall out of the system for whatever reason. Immigrants, usually. Illegals."

"Like me," I said.

"Oh, you don't have to worry anymore," Ace said. "The Navy takes care of its own. They're not going to let you fall through the cracks."

Why didn't I feel all that reassured?

The roads were packed with other vehicles, but they were all going the same speed as the bus, and traveling the same distance apart. When we stopped at a traffic light, I noticed that the drivers didn't even have their hands on the steering wheels.

The day went by in a blur. What I remember most was the level of automation in the city. It was mind-blowing. Robots were everywhere: ticketing the cars, driving the cars, repairing the cars, towing the cars. Robots acted as doormen, hostesses, shopkeepers. The robot errand-runners were ubiquitous in their civilian clothes and reusable canvas bags. Ace explained that in addition to food vouchers, the government guaranteed one robot per family. Public transportation was free on the slower trains and buses, but if you wanted to ride the high-speed buses or own a vehicle, that was something you had to work for. Judging from the busy traffic on the streets, there were a lot of people still working. Either that, or a lot of retirees.

After the game, Shaw went off with her fiancé (good riddance), and the rest of us joined up with some other graduates and spent Saturday night at a Navy-friendly bar, drinking bottled water and flirting with anything that had tits. A fight almost started when some ex-Marines came in, and we had to change venues to another bar, but otherwise the night went well. Most of us spent a good portion of our first month's pay renting hotels in town for the night, and the partying continued into the wee hours.

Back at our hotel, Ace got a civilian to buy us some beer (we were worried our expenses would be tracked), and then most of us got plenty drunk in the room. I was one of the worst offenders. So much for not having alcohol while on liberty. I just hoped the embedded IDs couldn't log blood alcohol levels.

Shaw showed up sometime after midnight. There was no sign of her fiancé. I didn't say anything.

By 0200, I was alone by the fake fireplace, staring at the digital flames. Most everyone else was either asleep on the floor around me, or banging the girls they'd picked up, putting the three-bedroom suite to good use. There was a small group in the kitchen playing some party game—I heard Ace and Alejandro laughing away.

Shaw came out from the kitchen and sat down beside me.

"Hey," she said.

"Hey." I didn't look at her.

"Having a good time?"

"Sure." I pretended to take a long sip of my beer. Truth is, I'd emptied the bottle a few hours ago. It was kind of a reflex, though. Thinking about Shaw, and what she did to me, well, it just made me want to drink.

"Where's the fiancé?" I said, wishing I wasn't so sober.

"Rade, I—"

"It's okay. I understand. I really do. It makes sense actually. Why you've been avoiding me these past few weeks. Brushing me off."

"Rade—"

"No, you don't have to say anything. We're going our separate ways. Today and tomorrow are the last time we'll ever see each other. It's better this way. I only wish you'd told me about him a bit sooner. Might've saved me some heartache." I instinctively tried drinking from the bottle again. Still empty. "You know, what hurts the most is, we could've had something. We really could've. Maybe we'll meet again in another life, you never know. But anyway, you should really go back to your man. I don't know why you're here."

"I'm here because of you," she said.

"Really." I deadpanned. "Well, sorry to disappoint you, but I don't mess with engaged women. Go back to your fiancé."

"Rade. I broke up with him today."

"You . . . *what*?"

She was staring directly into my eyes. "I broke up with him."

"I . . . don't know what to say to that." My hands seemed suddenly clammy, and I felt a drop of sweat trickle down my ribs.

"The whole Navy thing didn't work for us. These past eight weeks were torture for him. You see, him and celibacy, well, let's just say the two of them didn't go well together. He told me, to my face, that he'd slept with three women while I was gone. This after I bought him dinner at the most expensive restaurant in town. So I cut him loose. I had to. Eight weeks . . . can you imagine what he would have done when I was gone for two *years* at a time, out on deployment? I don't know how I could have been so blind. He duped me, Rade. Duped me to the core."

"Like you duped me?"

"I'm sorry, Rade." She leaned closer. Her gaze lingered on my lips. "Let me make it up to you."

Our faces were so close now. "You know what? Hell with it. All is forgiven."

I hoisted her up, led her to the bathroom, and locked the door.

Our group got back to base on Sunday night, and I took my leave of Shaw at the train station. She was moving on to her rating school, while I would stay behind with Tahoe, Alejandro, and Ace. She and I promised to keep in touch.

"Good luck, Astronaut Apprentice," she said, and leaned forward to kiss my cheek. I turned my head at the last minute to meet her lips with my own.

She pulled away. "You're a sly one."

"I am."

She held my hand, her eyes shining with unshed tears. "Remember me in the deepest, darkest hours. When you think you can't go on. When the training is too much. Hold on to the moments we've shared. Hold on to last night."

"I will." My voice was thick with grief. It felt like I'd only just found her, and now I was losing her. "Maybe we can meet again sometime, when we graduate. Arrange some liberty time together."

She beamed. "I'd like that."

When she let go of me and turned to walk away, I couldn't shake the feeling that I'd never see her again. Once she finished training and made it to her posting, she'd probably shack up with someone else. She was far too beautiful to stay single for long. Probably be an officer's wife when we met again.

"Maybe next time we meet you'll be my boss," I called to her back.

She glanced over her shoulder. "You wish. Besides, it won't be so long."

If you say so, Shaw.

I watched her board the vactrain. I waited there, as new recruits emerged from the open doors, recruits both starry-eyed and frightened at the same time, like I had been. I almost wanted to change places with them. To live those eight weeks over again, despite how tedious Basic had been. If only to be with her.

But it was time to move on.

I turned away as the train's last call came, and I didn't look back.

CHAPTER SEVEN

After eight more weeks of intense PT under the tutelage of civilian coaches hired by the Navy, Alejandro, Tahoe, Ace, and I were shipped off to the spec-ops rating school at New Coronado, California, where we would begin MOTH Orientation.

Monday morning found me seated cross-legged on the concrete deck beside the combat training tank (pool). I was dressed in swim trunks and a white T-shirt. Beside me were the other students of Class 1108. I thought it meant we were the one thousandth, one hundredth eighth class to attempt the training.

I heard footsteps echo off the black concrete. I glanced at the clock embedded in the cinder-block wall. It was 0500 on the dot.

Our class leader, Lieutenant Jaeger "Jaguar" Robinson, climbed to his feet. He was the senior officer among us, a Space Warfare Officer with four years experience. We were all equals here—officers trained right alongside enlisted men.

"Feet!" Jaguar yelled.

"*Feet*!" Nearly two hundred voices shouted in unison as the class members clambered upright.

"In-struc-tor Ree-ed!" Jaguar said.

"*Wooyah, Instructor Reed*!" we proudly roared. Sounded like a vactrain in here.

A well-built man ambled into my field of view. His head was completely shaved. I would have pegged him at midforties. He was dressed the way I'd soon learn all enlisted instructors dressed: blue T-shirt, khakis, white socks, black military boots. He wore a pair of wraparound sunglasses—possibly an aReal. His face was almost kindly, but by the way Instructor Reed carried himself, like a tightly wound coil ready to spring into action and pounce at the slightest provocation, I knew he was a warrior.

He glanced at the tank behind him and nodded to himself, apparently satisfied that everything was in good order. Then he turned around and tilted his head, seeming to look at some spot just beyond and above us. He didn't say a word.

Time dragged out. I and everyone else remained at attention, stiff, unmoving.

Waiting was always the worst part of any fight. And I was certain this was about to be one of the biggest fights of my life.

"Drop," Instructor Reed said quietly.

"*Drop*!" the class responded, and we dropped, every one of us assuming the starting position for a pushup, also known as the "plank."

I and everyone else held that position, because we hadn't been given permission to get up again, or to do actual pushups.

The seconds passed. Twenty. Thirty.

My arms were beginning to shake from supporting my body weight.

One minute.

One minute thirty seconds.

Two minutes.

"Push 'em," the instructor said.

"Push 'em!" Jaguar echoed.

"*Wooyah*!" the class said, finally doing the first pushup.

"One!" Jaguar said.

"*One*!" the class responded enthusiastically.

"Two!"

"*Two*!"

After counting out twenty pushups we returned to the plank starting position, and waited once again. My arms were in utter agony, and shaking worse than ever.

There was no command to recover. No command to continue pushups. Nothing. We just held that starting position.

I risked a glance up.

Instructor Reed hadn't moved. He merely stood there, gazing blankly across the ranks from behind those sunglasses.

"Again," he said, finally.

We did another twenty.

"Again," Instructor Reed said.

Twenty more.

"Again."

"Again."

We were up to one hundred pushups in total now. As I held that plank position, sweat dripped down my pecs to pool at the center of my shirt. More perspiration oozed down my forehead, along my cheeks, and dripped from my nose. Along with mucus.

"Again," Instructor Reed said.

Twenty more.

"Again."

I pushed my butt higher into the air, trying to take the pressure off my burning arms. Others around me were doing the same.

"Again."

Men started dropping around me. They just couldn't take it. I was about to collapse, myself. My arms were just jackhammering.

"Recover."

At first I thought I'd imagined the word, because Instructor Reed said it so quietly.

"Feet!" Jaguar said.

"*Feet*!" the class responded. Not a roar anymore. More like a bunch of choked chickens.

I staggered to my feet. Around me, other students fell flat on their faces, their arms too weak even to get up. They managed to stand at attention with help from other students. Alejandro and I had to help Ace up.

"Report, Mr. Robinson," Instructor Reed said.

"Class eleven-oh-eight is formed, sir," Jaguar said. "One hundred eighty-two men assigned, one hundred eighty present. One man on watch, one man at medical. Sick call."

Instructor Reed nodded. "Thank you, Lieutenant." He turned to the rest of us. "Seats."

"*Seats*!" We hit the concrete and sat cross-legged.

"He is best who is trained in the severest school," Instructor Reed intoned. "Who said that?"

"You did, sir!" a trainee near the front answered.

"Drop and push 'em for being an idiot," Instructor Reed said.

The student immediately complied.

"Anyone else?"

I knew the answer. During downtime I'd read *History of the Peloponnesian War*, which was on the recommended reading list, but I didn't say anything, not wanting to draw attention to myself.

"Thucydides, sir!" It was Ace who answered, seated two students down from me.

"Excellent." He glanced at Ace. "Drop and push 'em for being too smart."

Ace's face fell, and he obeyed.

"Thucydides also said, the strength of an army lies in strict discipline and undeviating obedience to its officers." Instructor Reed looked us up and down. "We are here to teach you both these things."

He toured the room, passing between our ranks. He paused beside one man. "Why did you enlist?"

"I enlisted to kill me some SKs!" the trainee said. Sino-Koreans. "Sir!"

"Not good enough. Drop and push 'em."

"Wooyah sir!" The student started his pushups.

The instructor halted beside another man. "You. Why did you enlist?"

"I want to kick some ass in an ATLAS mech, sir!"

"Not good enough. Drop and push 'em."

He went to another student. "I've seen your face here before. What are you doing? Can't you see when something just isn't for you? Can't you look defeat in the face and realize you're a failure?"

"I'm going to make it this time, sir!"

"If you say so. Drop and push 'em."

The student obeyed.

Instructor Reed reached me. I stared straight ahead, at his knees, not daring to meet his eye, hoping he wouldn't say anything to me. I didn't want to stand out. I didn't want extra instructor attention.

"What's your reason, trainee?" Instructor Reed asked me.

I knew he'd mock me no matter what I said, but I decided to give him the most honest answer I could think of. "I want to be a man, sir!"

"You want to be a *man*?" I thought there was a touch of cynicism in his voice.

"Yes sir! I want to see what I'm made of! A chance to be a part of something bigger than myself!"

"Well, that's the best reason I've heard today. But only half right. Drop and push 'em."

So much for not standing out and drawing extra instructor attention.

Instructor Reed returned to the front of the class while I was doing my pushups. "Did everyone hear what that trainee said? He wants to be a man. I find that interesting, do you know why? It's because we're not here to make you into men. Sure, at the end of Trial Week we'll know the difference between the men and the boys, but at that point, we haven't really done anything other than selective culling. After Trial Week, however, that's when the real forging begins. If you make it that far, you'll become something far more than any ordinary man. You'll become a MOTH."

"*Wooyah*!"

"Most of you are immigrants. Patriotism is a big part of what we do here. If you can't fight for your nation, die for it, then you don't belong here, do you understand me?"

"*Wooyah sir*!"

"Well, trainee?" Instructor Reed was addressing someone I couldn't see from where I did pushups on the deck. "Can you fight for your nation, die for it?"

"Yes sir!" I heard Alejandro answer.

"Elaborate."

"The UC is my nation now," Alejandro said. "I'll fight for it. I have to."

"You don't sound too convinced. Drop and push 'em."

Alejandro joined me on the deck.

"You have to really love this country to do what MOTHs do. And you have to really love your teammates. Patriotism to your country is the furnace, and dedication to your team the hammer, that will forge your warrior spirit. Remember that."

"*Wooyah*!"

Instructor Reed paused, then said, "Recover."

Those of us who were doing pushups resumed a cross-legged seated position. I was relieved: my arms were on fire.

Instructor Reed ran his gaze over us. "Some of you know me. Most of you don't. I'm Instructor Reed, and I'll be your proctor while you're in training. Your go-to man. The interface between the other instructors and yourselves. If there's something you need, anything, come to me, and I'll make sure you don't get it." He grinned widely. I knew he was joking, but I didn't dare laugh. None of us did. "Obviously, if you come to me and ask for something that's in my power to grant, it's yours. A chit for some gear, medicine, or just a kick in the pants, come see me and I'll set you straight. Speaking of gear, you are to never, I repeat *never*, steal from your fellow teammates. Your reputation starts right here, and if you become known as a *buddy screwer*, you're not going to get very far at all. None of the Teams want someone like that in their ranks. Would you? You learned about honor, courage, and commitment in Basic. Well it's time to start applying those traits."

Instructor Reed slowly paced back and forth at the front of the class. "So. You all have your own reasons for being here. Most of them are wrong, of course. From a quick glance, I can see we have some gym buffs, a handful of former Olympians, and even a few skinny nerds who think becoming a MOTH will get them more girls. Some of you think you are pretty badass at mixed martial arts. That you're invincible, and during spec-op insertions you'll topple authoritarian regimes single-handedly." He chuckled quietly.

"Then there's the group of you who are here because you think you're pretty good at video games—you want to pilot ATLAS mechs, kill some SKs in Mongolia, and it'll be a grand old time. You bought all the accessories to make your games completely immersive, so you think you're as prepped as can be. But I'll tell you something. Your game designers took out the bad stuff and amped up the fun stuff, leaving you with a poor simulation of what it's like to actually be a spec-ops man. Having to run ten klicks to a rendezvous wearing full kit and carrying a hundred and twenty pounds on your back without a jumpsuit in the mountains of Khentii Province, your beard covered in icicles and your toes so frozen that you can't feel them, *is not fun*. Having to sit motionless for three days in the steaming jungles of the lowlands, waiting for your target to emerge from his mudbrick hole, while fire ants crawl up your every bodily orifice, and you crap your pants and tinkle down your own leg, *is not fun*."

Instructor Reed smiled widely. "But it's not all bad. You do get to do some pretty awesome stuff on the government's coin. Camping out in the wilderness with some of the best outdoorsmen in the world, not to mention using the best gear. Spending a month training with the best marksmen and sharpshooters known to man, with the best weapons. Riding in starships. Visiting new worlds and colonies. And now and then you might actually get to pilot an ATLAS.

"Anyway, right reasons or wrong, you're here. And I have to work with what I'm given. But to succeed you gotta want this more than anything in the world. *More* than anything. This is not a game. This is not a pleasure cruise. You will get hurt. You will get scarred, emotionally and physically.

"Most of you know by now that there's nothing free in this life. Anything of any value is worth fighting for. The more valuable that thing is, the harder the fight. To call yourself a MOTH is one of the most valuable things in the world." He pointed at the door. "The only free thing in the world is right there. You want free, you step through that door, you grab the gavel in the grinder and hit the flint stone three times, and you're done. It's called tapping out. No one will think any less of you. No one will judge you. In fact, you'll be rewarded. We always have fresh cronuts, coffee, and a warm blanket waiting for any student who taps out. And a paid ticket back to your former division, if you have one.

"The Navy Brass has ordered us to make more MOTHs. That means they're letting more of you into our training, but it does *not* mean we're going to pass any more of you. We haven't changed our testing process, not in the least. We're not going to graduate substandard guys. We can't. It defeats the whole purpose of the training. If we did that, you think any of the Teams would want our graduates? They need to know that the man beside them went through the *exact same thing* they did. That the man beside them is reliable. That he's a *brother*.

"BSD/M, Basic Space Demolition/MOTH training, is designed to teach us about you, but it's also designed to teach you about yourself. What are your limitations? What are you truly capable of? When you step out of here, *if* you step out of here, you'll have unshakable confidence, and an unwavering belief in yourself and the guy who stands beside you. You'll know with absolute certainty that he'll cover your back. You'll know without question that he'll die for you if he has to. He'll be more of a brother than a brother by blood. Family is important, don't get me wrong, but what we form here is *tighter* than any family. You'll eat, sleep, and drink together. You'll fight together. You'll die together.

"Still interested? It's a tough school. You can quit at any time. Just come to me or any one of the instructors and say 'I quit,' or grab the gavel and tap out. Three little hits. We don't have a quota. You either make it or you don't. Though if you want the truth, you'll probably wash out. Twenty percent of students make it through to the end of First Phase. You see the guy sitting next to you? And the guy on the other side? Neither of them are going to make it. Statistically, it isn't very likely that you're going to make it either."

He surveyed our ranks, letting his words sink in. "I see a lot of potential here. Some great warriors in the making. Unfortunately, the guys who *look* like they'll make it are usually the first to quit. I'm always surprised by who's left standing in the end. Always. Anyway, do your best, never give in, and you will succeed. How's that for a motivational speech?"

He folded his arms. "All right. Let's get you guys in the tank. It's time to repeat the Physical Screening Test."

And so the real training began.

The next three weeks of Orientation were a blur of activity.

We started off each day with swim lessons in the tank. After that we sprinted a mile to the mess hall and had a seven-minute breakfast (I usually was able to stuff down a few pancakes and sausages and that's about it). Then we ran across the base to the O-Course. A real obstacle course, not like the confidence course we had back in Basic. Parallel bars; tires; low wall; high wall; barbed-wire low crawl; sixty-foot-tall cargo net; balance logs; climbing ropes; the "twiner"—a horizontal set of bars we had to twine our bodies between; a rope bridge; and on and on. Swivel-mounted Visible Spectrum Lasers were placed at strategic points, their beams rotating over the different obstacles. While harmless in and of themselves, if you let one of those rotating beams touch you, then it was back to the start of the O-Course for you.

After the O-Course we sprinted back to the mess hall for lunch, and then it was off to the beach for PT. Instructor Piker usually led us. Beneath his chin, he had this long spade-like goatee. I remember the first day he had us doing pushups and various types of lying kicks right there beside the ocean.

"Put out, you weaklings!" Instructor Piker said. "I can tell when you're not putting out. And I hate that more than anything in the world. Hayward, get those arms up. Hayward! Push! If you can't survive this, there's no way you'll survive First Phase!"

Damage Controlman First Class John "Haywire" Hayward was our leading petty officer because he was the senior enlisted in our ranks. He reported directly to our class leader, Jaguar, and was a frequent target of extra instructor attention because of his rank.

"Push, you bastards! Push!"

I finally couldn't take it, and collapsed to the sand.

Instructor Piker came over and surprised me by sitting down right on my back. "What's wrong with you, sir?" The "sir" came across as completely mocking.

"Nothing, instructor!" I said.

"Name and rank?"

All the instructors had implanted aReals—Instructor Piker could've just accessed my embedded ID. But he wanted me to say my name and rank for everyone to hear.

"Astronaut Apprentice Rade Galaal, instructor!" I said.

"Astronaut *Apprentice* Galaal!" He made his voice sound whiny when he said *apprentice*. "You're not putting out, *Apprentice*! Why is that? Give me a pushup, now!"

"But you're on my back, instructor!"

"I know I am."

I couldn't do it. I tried, I really did.

"Give me a pushup, you worm!" Instructor Piker said. "Or the whole class suffers!"

I pushed. I mean really pushed. I didn't want anyone to suffer because of me.

Amazingly, my upper body started lifting. I managed to get my hips maybe two centimeters off the sand, though it took every last ounce of strength I had.

I thought Instructor Piker would commend me. I thought he'd congratulate me for doing a pushup, minuscule as it was, with all his weight on my back.

Instead Piker got up and said, "See! I knew you weren't putting out, dumbass! You had enough energy left to push me when I was *sitting* on you! Pathetic! All we ask is that you give it your all, that you don't waste our time! *Don't waste our time*! Everyone has to do an extra sixty pushups because Astronaut Apprentice Galaal *wasn't giving it his all*!"

"Thanks, Galaal," trainees muttered nearby. So much for not making anyone suffer because of me . . .

I forced myself to start doing pushups again, though my triceps were basically dead.

"Not you, Galaal," Instructor Piker said. "You're special. You get to run out to the surf, and when you're nice and wet you're going to roll around in the sand. Don't come back here until every square inch of you is covered in sand. I want you to look like a gingerbread man. Actually, belay that. *Everyone* go down to the surf with Galaal and come back looking like a gingerbread man."

I ran into the ocean with everyone else. "Thanks Gay-laal," someone said along the way. I didn't see who, though I thought it sounded like Ace.

I didn't make the mistake of not putting out again, and I promised myself I'd do my best not to stand out and draw attention to myself. Thankfully there were more than enough students to draw Instructor Piker's wrath, and he chewed them out in turn. Unfortunately, he called "Gingerbread Men" each time and we had to run to the beach and come back covered in sand. "If one of you fails to give his all for the team, the whole team pays the price. Remember that when you're in the field."

Whenever someone collapsed from exhaustion, one of the Weavers would take a look at him. If the guy didn't get up after ten minutes of treatment from a Weaver, he would be medically dropped. By the way, "Weaver" was Navy slang for paramedic robot. We called them Weavers because they looked like gurneys with spiders at the back. From the control center protruded twenty jointed, retractable limbs whose cylindrical segments telescoped into one another. Each limb was topped by four spindly, double-jointed fingers. When a paramedic robot was working on someone, those limbs moved around in rapid succession, looking for all the world like a spider spinning its web. Hence the name "Weavers."

When PT was done, Instructor Piker made us do a four-mile run on the soft sand. I was thoroughly exhausted by then, and the wet sand from all the Gingerbread Men sessions was abrading my crotch and armpits. I suspected I was going to have a rash later (and I did).

Running on soft sand was different than on any other surface. The trick, I found, was to make sure my foot hit the sand at a completely flat angle. I passed the tip on to Alejandro and Tahoe, and it was whispered down the ranks.

The laggards got beat for a while, forced to do another set of pushups, while those who made a "decent" time got to stretch out and watch. I was one of the lucky ones.

And so it went for the rest of that week. Soft-sand runs, O-Course, swimming and deep dive practice, underwater knot-tying practice, bay swims, PT, all punctuated by the phrase we had grown resigned to, *Gingerbread Men*. There were about two hours of classroom sessions each day, covering a variety of topics, such as combat swimming, nutrition, naval history, etc. Not even the classrooms were free of PT, though. If you were caught nodding off, you had to drop and push 'em. If you didn't answer the question the way the instructor thought you should, you dropped and pushed 'em. Of course, classes opened with sixty pushups and ended with another sixty. All part of our conditioning, right?

Ace seemed undeterred by it all. I remember one night, when all of us were bitching during supper in the mess hall, he said, "This is what MOTHs do! You have to just brace yourself and plow on through, just like a real MOTH would. If you can't do that, can't dig deep and find the reserves and drive within yourself, well maybe you shouldn't be here, you know?"

Ace quit that first week, before we'd even started First Phase. He didn't even tell me or Alejandro. Too ashamed, I guess. All I remember is waking up at 0400 one morning and he was gone.

Besides Ace we lost fifty other people the first week of Orientation. Most quit during the night. Five left for medical reasons—two of those because of O-Course injuries. One guy lost his grip on the sixty-foot-tall cargo net near the top when he was hurrying away from one of those visible spectrum lasers, and he fell all the way to the ground, fracturing his thigh. I ran to him, but the instructors told me to back off. I still remember his screams, and how merciless the instructors were with him.

"Suffer in your head!" the instructors said. "If you're hurt in the field, are you going to yell your ass off and reveal your position? Endanger the lives of your platoon brothers? Suffer in your head!"

We lost another thirty members the second and third weeks, so that when we finally classed-up to First Phase, we were down to ninety-eight trainees.

That Friday we moved from barracks 618 to 602, the barracks reserved for First Phase students. We berthed with our swim buddies, two students per room. My swim buddy was Alejandro, of course, while Tahoe roomed with leading petty officer Haywire.

"Don't become too invested in your new rooms," Instructor Reed said before dismissing us that night. "Nor your roommates. You're only staying here until you complete Trial Week. Or rather, until you quit. And you *will* quit. There's no ifs or buts about it. As will your swim buddy." Though he addressed the entire class, Reed had the uncanny ability to make it seem like he spoke directly to you. "But I suppose congratulations are in order, Class 1108. You've made it to First Phase. You've done something ninety-eight percent of the population can't even dream of doing. Enjoy the feeling while it lasts. You have the weekend at liberty. The smarter among you will spend the time getting your new berths ready for inspection at 0500 sharp Monday morning, when the real fun begins. Dismissed."

CHAPTER EIGHT

While other students (most of them rollbacks, apparently) went to the city on Friday and Saturday nights for one last bender before First Phase, Alejandro and I spent the whole weekend preparing for Monday's room inspection. We polished the metallic racks of our beds, we shined the insides and the outsides of our lockers, we mopped and waxed the deck, we scrubbed the bulkheads (really just walls, but I blamed Basic for making me call them that). We polished our helmets and stenciled 1108 into the sides in big white letters. We stenciled our names on all our gear. We polished every exposed area of our leather boots, even along the welt line between the uppers and soles, with spare toothbrushes we still had from Basic. We trimmed away any frayed ends on the bootlaces. We ironed every single crease out of our clothes and beds.

All told, we spent about twenty hours preparing. But it was worth it, because we were going to pass the inspection with flying colors. The room, and our clothes, were literally spic-and-span. I wondered if we'd get to sit out the morning PT for doing such a good job.

Alejandro and I slept on the floor in our underwear because we didn't want to ruin the work we'd done.

Monday came. We got up at 0400, shaved, showered, dressed, and did one last check of the room. I found a hair on top of the lockers, and Alejandro found a speck of dust by the windowsill. When we were satisfied that everything was as clean as we could possibly make it, Alejandro and I stood in the hall just outside our doorway, waiting for the inspection.

Two instructors I'd never seen before came in at 0500 sharp. One had a handlebar mustache. The other had a sharp aquiline nose and wore his hair in a fauxhawk. Our room was at the front of the barracks, so we were the first in line for the inspection.

"Wipe that smug expression off your faces," Handlebar roared. He and the other instructor stalked into our room.

Alejandro and I exchanged a worried glance, then followed nervously inside.

"What the *shit*?" Handlebar tore up my perfectly made bed, throwing the entire mattress on the floor. Fauxhawk did the same to Alejandro's bed. Instructor Piker came rushing inside and dumped a pail of wet sand all over our beds and possessions. The other two tramped through the sand and left a gritty trail across our painstakingly polished deck. Handlebar went to the lockers and toppled them. He tipped out the drawers in both our dressers.

"I've never, *never*, in my whole life, seen a messier, dirtier room than this!" Handlebar said. "Fail!" The two instructors stormed outside.

Alejandro and I just stood there, mouths wide, staring at the mess that was our room. I wasn't sure whether to laugh or cry. I was just stunned. We'd spent the whole weekend cleaning that room, putting everything into it. We'd given it our all. I was heartbroken. I looked at Alejandro. He was blinking fast, and his lower lip was quivering.

I gave him a brave smile, and looked away. Nothing I hated worse than seeing a grown man cry. I was about ready to lose it myself. This was an injustice, I knew that. I struggled within myself, trying to understand the point of it all. Why tell us to ready our room for inspection, only to ransack it and tell us we fail?

I went to the hallway and noticed, to my relief, that the students in the room just across from us were receiving the same mistreatment. Beds were thrown out of racks, desks overturned, drawers emptied onto the deck, a pail of sand dumped in the center of the room.

The instructors moved methodically from room to room, enacting the same fervent theatrics, so that when it was done the entire barracks had become a mess of sand and overturned beds and tossed sheets, some of which spilled right out the doors. The names of the instructors were whispered down to us.

Handlebar was Instructor Peterson, and Fauxhawk was Instructor Brown.

Another instructor I hadn't met before appeared at the entrance to the barracks. He had a thick black beard and yellow eyes. A wolf of a man. He loomed there, seeming taller and meaner than any of the others. Definitely wasn't happy.

Someone whispered his name. "Chief Adams."

"What in the hell?" Chief Adams said, finally blowing his top. "You call this sty a barracks? Turn yourselves into Gingerbread Men, now! Double-time!"

We sprinted outside into the predawn twilight, and waded into the freezing ocean, wearing our freshly polished boots, our perfectly ironed white shirts, our sparkly clean swim trunks. I sat down, and doused my head beneath the waves, gasping at the cold, and then hurried back on shore. I rolled in the sand with more than a little regret. When I was sufficiently covered in grit, I stumbled to my feet, my perfect clothes ruined.

Headlamps turned on nearby, and I shielded my eyes. The silhouette of an instructor walked into the light. He moved between us, inspecting. When he came near, I saw that it was Instructor Piker. He had a terrible scowl on his face as he stroked his spade-like goatee.

"What are you trying to pull, Mr. Eaglehide?" He'd stopped beside Tahoe. "You're not properly sandpapered. Your whole right cheek is bare!" He spun around. "All of you, do it again!"

And so we did. This time, when we rolled on the beach, we scooped up the sand in our hands and dumped it on our faces, using the light of the headlamps to make sure we all looked like walking sand castles. My eyes were burning because there was so much grit in them. I even felt sand in my gums, between my teeth, scratching away.

"What the hell are you maggots doing standing around?" Instructor Piker shouted. "To the grinder, you sorry excuses for trainees!"

We rushed to the black asphalt at the center of the compound. The lights were off, so the instructors couldn't see our faces in the twilight, and we couldn't see theirs. But I recognized the voices.

"Take your places, now!" Chief Adams said.

There was enough light to see the outlines painted on the concrete, which indicated where each student should stand. I took the first free place I found and waited while others rushed to find a spot.

When we were finally assembled, Chief Adams said, "I've never seen such a disgraceful display in all my life. That little stunt your class pulled this morning in the barracks cannot be forgiven. Sand everywhere. Beds thrown about. There's only one way to pay for what you've done. You're all going to die. Drop and push 'em!"

What followed was the worst PT beating I'd ever experienced in my life.

Over the next three hours we alternated from pushups to lying kicks to bar dips to pullups. This while being constantly sworn at and accused of being gay. My knuckles became rubbed raw from sitting on my fists for the flutter and scissor kicks. The blood and sweat caused me to slip sometimes on the pullup bar and get a further chewing out from the instructors. Around me, a few students were whimpering. Some were crying. These big, strong men who never cried for anything, weeping like babies.

The flint stone at the far end of the grinder flashed at least once every ten minutes as people quit. Three loud taps. Sometimes it happened several times in a row, as if people were just waiting for someone else to quit first before throwing in the towel themselves.

By the third hour of this beating, with no relief in sight, guys started to urinate and defecate themselves. Some vomited. It started to smell like a mix between a sewer and a pigsty. Instructors moved through the fray with a high-pressure water hose, spraying down whomever they felt like. One instructor sprayed the guy beside me, then doused my face and Alejandro's for good measure. It felt just short of getting slammed in the cheek with an icicle.

All I could think was that this was only day one. And it was going to get a whole lot worse.

I had to force those thoughts away, because I knew such thinking was self-defeating; I knew if I tried to look beyond this moment, I'd get disheartened and just want to quit. And I wasn't going to do that.

I wasn't going to let myself.

I focused on breakfast. I was going to make it to breakfast.

Three hours, thirty-three minutes after we'd begun, the call finally came.

"Breakfast, children!" Chief Adams said. "You have an hour. Go!"

We jogged the mile to the mess hall, and by the time we got there, most of us were too exhausted to even eat. I managed to get down a slice of buttered toast before the announcement came that our time was up.

"I thought we had an hour!" someone whined.

"Since when have you *ever* had an hour for breakfast? Ridiculous, you fecal maggot. Out!"

As we were running back to the grinder I vomited up the toast.

"Rade, you okay?" Alejandro said beside me, panting loudly.

And then it suddenly hit me.

I understood why they were doing this to us.

I started laughing.

"Rade," Alejandro said. "What is it, *hombre*? You aren't going *loco* on me, are you?"

"They want us to quit," I told him. "It's textbook shock and awe. Don't you see? They just want to scare us off. They want us to think it'll be like this every day. But it can't be. Of course it can't. No one would survive. No one would graduate."

Alejandro didn't say anything. I don't know if he believed me. But I was right. I knew I was. I had to be.

Three more guys tapped out the instant we reached the grinder.

"Well, children," Chief Adams said. "It's time to start your next evolution. Get your asses over the sand berm and line up along the high water mark!"

We did as we were told.

"Turn around," Chief Adams said through the megaphone on the beach. We did, so that we faced away from the water. All the instructors were assembled on the berm above us, drinking energy drinks. They had big smiles on their faces. I saw dipping tobacco lining the gums of more than a few of those mouths.

"Shoulder to shoulder," Chief Adams said.

"*Wooyah*!" We pressed ourselves tightly together.

Four Weavers rolled up over the berm. The sight of those medical robots felt somehow ominous.

"Your performance this morning was ridiculous," the Chief said. "Not one of you, *not a one*, deserves to ever call himself a MOTH. You're done for. We're going to get rid of your dumb asses once and for all. Call it a mass extermination." He lowered the megaphone to take a puff on his cigar. His yellow eyes gleamed with a sudden malicious glee. "Turn about!"

"*Turn about*!" we answered, swiveling to stare out across the gray ocean.

"Lock arms!" Chief said.

"*Lock arms*!" I interlocked my arms with Alejandro and the man on my right.

"For-ward mar-ch!"

"*Forward march*!"

We waded into the surf. I winced when a wave splashed my crotch. You'd think the bay water would be warm down here in California, but it felt like it was fed by the arctic. (I learned later that it was—damn ocean currents.)

I kept expecting the Chief to order a halt, but he didn't. Deeper and deeper we marched into the ocean, the freezing bay water coming first to our knees, then our waists.

"Halt."

"*Halt*!"

Finally.

"Sit down."

"*Sit down*!"

Sit down?

We obeyed, and the freezing ocean enveloped us to the armpits. I gasped loudly. I wasn't the only one. I inhaled three or four times, trying to catch my breath through the shock of the cold. Alejandro and Tahoe shivered madly on either side of me.

After about a minute and a half:

"This is *loco*," Alejandro said with his teeth chattering. "I'm not built for this crap."

"Careful, brother," Tahoe said. "Don't think beyond the moment. Therein lies the path to failure. Open yourself to the spirit world."

"The spirit world?" Alejandro said. "You mean the world of the dead? You're telling me I should just accept this and die?"

"No," Tahoe said. "Open yourself to the *spirit* world. Ignore all pain. Ignore all suffering. Transcend it."

"I thought you didn't believe in that crap?" Alejandro said.

Tahoe gripped me tight. "In times like this, I'll believe anything."

I tightened my grip on both their arms, trying to pull him and Tahoe closer to me.

"This is called sea immersion, children," Chief Adams said on the megaphone. "Enjoying it so far?"

"Wooyah," someone responded, weakly.

Around me, the sound of chattering teeth brought an odd image to mind. I thought of a kid, running along a slatted fence with a stick. The chattering I heard was the sound of his stick as it hit each slat. A wolf chased that kid.

I was zoning out. That was bad. I had to stay in the moment. Had to stay aware.

"Everywhere we go-o!" I said, to an imaginary cadence.

No one answered.

"Everywhere we go-o!" I tried again.

Alejandro answered it. "Everywhere we go-o!"

"People wanna know-o."

Three or four others picked it up in addition to Alejandro. "People wanna know-o."

"Who we are-r."

"*Who we are-r*!" More people.

"So we tell them."

"*So we tell them*!" the whole class.

"You're going to get beaten real good if you keep that up!" Chief Adams said through the megaphone.

I didn't care. "We are the Navy!"

No one else seemed to care either. "*We are the Navy*!"

"The motherfucking Navy!"

"*The motherfucking Navy . . .*"

"It's time for your next evolution," Chief Adams said. "ATLAS PT."

Turned out I had been right about the shock and awe. Tuesday morning we had PT for only forty-five minutes, compared to the three and a half hours of the day before, and after breakfast we had classroom sessions until 1000. The instructors *had* been trying to scare us off, and they'd achieved their goal admirably: Thirty guys had quit yesterday. We were down to sixty-eight.

We'd just come from lunch and had mustered at the top of the sand berm. Looking down, I saw several flatbed pickups backing up onto the beach with man-sized robots in the truck beds. The robots were humanoid in shape, with metallic arms and legs and yellow visors lowered over their dented heads. Red chest scars indicated where the power packs had been yanked.

"Some of you native citizens, or fans of old movies, might recognize these," the Chief said. "Old-style ATLAS 1s, relatively ancient precursors to the ATLAS 5s in use today."

I did a double take at the robots in the truck beds again. Yes, I could see the resemblance now. They were miniature versions of the ATLAS 5 mechs I'd seen on the Net.

"These models are obsolete to the extreme of course. Little more than fancy powered exoskeletons. Basically forerunners to the modern jumpsuits. But they make good practice for spec-ops trainees. Don't get all excited on me. You're not actually going to pilot these, or wear a jumpsuit. Not until you've proven that you have at least half a brain. Besides, any parts of value have long since been salvaged. Hell, there's not even a CPU, let alone a battery pack. So what are you geniuses going to do with them?" He grinned widely. "Why, you're going to carry them. ATLAS mechs have one of the highest availability ratios in the fleet, second only to starships.

Unfortunately, they do break down on occasion, due to mechanical failure or battery discharge or, heaven forbid, being shot down in combat. So we do have to portage them from time to time. Look heavy, don't they? Well, they're not that bad, not these ones at least. See, the ATLAS combat mechs are made of some of the most lightweight metallics available, so these ATLAS 1s will set you back only around ninety kilos, or two hundred pounds for you metrically challenged. If these were ATLAS 5s on the other hand, well, then you'd be in trouble. Just be happy you're not qualified to touch an ATLAS 5, because when you have to carry a mech that weighs three tonnes for twenty miles without a jumpsuit, let's just say you gain an appreciation for these early models."

We divvied up into crews, and after turning ourselves into Gingerbread Men, we hurried over to the trucks. I jumped into the bed of the nearest truck, and wrapped one arm firmly around the left knee of the ATLAS 1. Alejandro took the right knee. Haywire took the head, Tahoe took the right shoulder, another guy took the left shoulder, and two others jammed under each hip. Our crew lifted.

The thing was a bitch to carry. The seven of us banged it up pretty good while jumping down from the truck bed.

"You just dented a piece of equipment worth half a billion digicoins, dumbasses!" Instructor Piker said. "Your whole crew, sea immersion. Now!"

A bunch of other crews soon joined us, which didn't really make me feel any better.

When the seven of us were called back from the freezing ocean, we tried again. Eventually we realized that it was all about teamwork. You had to work together if you wanted to move that ATLAS without dropping it. Alejandro started calling out a cadence, and we marched in tempo, taking even steps.

Piker made us dress the suits like Gingerbread Men soon thereafter, which was a *very* gentle process that involved lowering the ATLAS into the ocean, struggling back to the high tide mark, and chucking a ton of sand over the metal. Once that was done, the crews did various PT evolutions while holding up the sandy ATLAS 1s, including squats, lunges, jumping jacks, pushups, and overhead tosses.

"So, how do you like ATLAS PT?" Instructor Piker said. He had a big sarcastic grin on his face. "Beats sitting at home with your feet up on the couch, munching a bag of chips and watching the latest gay porn on your aReal don't it?"

"*Wooyah*!"

As usual, teamwork was essential here. We motivated each other as best we could, but someone inevitably would tire and make a mistake, causing the ATLAS to drop to the sand. The crews were being beat up left and right by the instructors because of that. Some individuals were singled out and forced to become Gingerbread Men while the crews struggled on with one man less. Others just washed out—in fact, one guy on my crew quit while we were doing pushups with the ATLAS balanced on our backs. Not fun.

"You all look like studs," Instructor Piker said while we were struggling through the pushups, one man short. "Especially you, Mr. Galaal. Do you have any tips on getting pussy?"

I was used to this sort of abuse by now and it didn't bother me. "That's a negative, sir!"

"Come on, a stud like you, and you have no tips on getting pussy? Oh. I get it. You're gay. The only tips you can give me are for getting a piece of ass."

"Wooyah sir!"

He focused on Alejandro next. "Mr. Mondego! You are flagging. You're the weakest person in this class. Are you going to make me punish your classmates because you can't keep up? Are you?"

"Wooyah, Instructor!" Alejandro said.

He wasn't flagging. He *was* keeping up. He was one of the hardest workers here. But like I said, I was used to comments like that by now.

Except, for some reason it got to me today.

"Leave him alone," I said.

I don't know why I said it. I should have kept my mouth shut.

Instructor Piker spun toward me like a shark sensing blood. "Why, hello again, Mr. Galaal."

He smashed a handful of sand into my face while I did my pushups. Then another handful. And another. I'd scrunched up my face, but my nostrils were full of sand, and my whole nose was throbbing—he'd hit pretty hard. My cheeks were burning where the grit had dug in. I kept my eyes shut tight, and worked through the pain.

"You really are gay, aren't you, Mr. Galaal?" Piker said.

"Negative, Instructor!" I managed, breath heaving.

"Are you and Mr. Mondego playing with each other's buttholes at night?"

"Negative, Instructor!"

"You're lucky I don't send your whole crew to sea immersion for being gay. In fact, that's an excellent idea. The six of you go cool down in the ocean for a while. For being gay."

And so it went.

The days began to blur together. Morning PT, sea immersion, soft-sand runs, swimming and deep dive practice, bay swims, more PT, Gingerbread Men, O-Course, inflatable boat races, ATLAS PT, pipeline crawls (where we had to crawl in these supertight, super-claustrophobic pipes that had been laid at the bottom of the bay). There were random room inspections, which were really just an excuse for the instructors to ransack our barracks. We were expected to find time at the end of the exhausting day to clean up our rooms again. One time there were two inspections in the same day, the second before anyone had time to clean up after the first one. The instructors gave us an epic beating for that, involving repeated sea immersion and O-Course runs. I tell you there's nothing worse than climbing the cargo net in the O-Course when you can barely move or feel your cold-numbed fingers.

Sometime during the second week I developed pneumonia, but one of the Weavers fixed me up. Not before I was given a chance to quit, of course.

Speaking of quitting, guys washed out left and right, and not just because of the beatings. You have to understand, there were pass-fail qualifications constantly along the way. The instructors thought up all these devious little trials for us. Drown avoidance, where they tied you up and tossed you into the tank and expected you not to panic while you swam and retrieved objects with your teeth. Lifesaving, where you rescued a "drowning" instructor who in actuality tried to drown *you*. Timed O-Course runs. Timed surface swim runs. Timed pipeline crawls. Timed soft-sand sprints. Timed ATLAS portage. And on and on. You were given two chances to pass each test, and if you failed both times you were rolled back on the spot—you moved to barracks 618 and waited for the next class up. A lot of people just quit when they were rolled back. Some stayed. Thing is, you could only be rolled back once. If you failed to make the cut a second time you'd never be back.

Other than the trials, there were four more legendary, three-hour PT beatings like we had the very first day, so that by the time Trial Week rolled around, we were down to forty-five students.

Trial Week. What can I say. The students had been talking about it every day since we started Orientation. The training that would separate the men from the boys. Ninety-eight percent of the students who made it past Trial Week would go on to become MOTHs. But making it through, that was the trick, wasn't it?

Friday night we mustered in the classroom. Chief Adams stood at the front with a bunch of the other instructors, including Reed, Brown, Piker, and Peterson. Basically everyone who had beaten us these past few weeks.

The Chief took the podium. "Excited about Trial Week, children?"

"*Wooyah, Chief*!"

The Chief was just beaming, his yellow eyes glittering in the light. Never a good sign. "I'm glad to hear it. Because next week we're separating the chaff from the wheat. Despite the bone-crushing fatigue, the unending stress and hardship, you'll be expected to demonstrate the core values of the UC Navy: honor, courage, and commitment. We're also expecting a few Team qualities to show through as well, namely self-sacrifice, leadership, and resilience. We expect a winner's attitude from you at all times, no matter how adverse the conditions become. Because you know what? Only the very best of you will prevail. The very best."

He paused, letting his words sink in. "You're all going to have to do a whole lot of soul searching next week. Who are you, deep inside? What do you really want? What are you doing here? How badly do you really want this? That last question is the most important. Every second of every moment you'll be asking yourself that question: How badly do I really want this? Is it worth the sleep deprivation, the pain, the cold? It's all up to you. You've conquered all the timed trials, and every qualification we've thrown at you so far. At this point we're not the ones who decides who passes and who fails. It's all up to you now. Do you want to be ordinary men, and live ordinary lives, or do you want to become more than men? Do you want to become MOTHs?"

"*Wooyah, Chief*!" we roared.

In the barracks, I took Alejandro to see Tahoe and his swim buddy, Haywire, and the four of us made a pact.

"We aren't going to quit," I said. "Not now, not after everything we've been through. We're going to make it through to the end."

I held out my fist, and Tahoe and Alejandro piled their fists on top of mine.

"To the end," Tahoe said.

"To the end," Alejandro said.

Haywire clasped our hands. "To the end," he said.

CHAPTER NINE

The forty-five remaining members of Class 1108 spent the weekend psyching up for Trial Week. We cleaned our rooms and ironed our clothes (minimally of course—enough to pass a real inspection, not enough to feel bad if the instructors tore the place apart). We did PT. We watched movies. We talked about girls, and what we were going to do when we became MOTHs.

Sunday afternoon Instructor Piker ordered us to the classroom and instructed us to bring our gear and a change of clothes for when we quit. I piled everything into my spacebag, hefted it over my shoulder, and when I got to the classroom I saw the usual instructors present plus another ten I didn't recognize, for a total of thirty—almost one instructor for every student. Interesting.

There were five Weavers present, their spiderlike, telescoping fingers sinister reminders that this was going to be a difficult day. Though I wasn't sure why the instructors wanted the medical robots in the classroom environment. Eventually I decided they'd done it just to scare us.

Chief Adams gave the class permission to sit. "Lockdown, children," he said, scratching at his thick beard. "No one goes in or out of the classroom as of now. We're going to get all chummy and watch some movies together. You know, eat some pizza, have some laughs. A good ol' fashioned slumber party. Without the slumber."

The instructors sat down at their desks, which were cordoned off at the front of the room, and put up their legs.

Everyone donned aReals, and we all watched classic movies, instructors and students alike. There was *From the Sino-Koreans, with Love. Superman vs Vampires. Star Wars XXVII.* We were only half-paying attention to the movies, though. Too much on our minds.

I ate a whole large pizza that afternoon, and I wasn't the only one. The instructors had ordered boxes and boxes of the stuff. The Amazon drones were busy dropping them off all afternoon. I had a sneaking suspicion we wouldn't be eating for a long while after this.

As the day wore on, and nothing happened, the tension in the air became almost palpable. I dimmed the movie soundtrack with my aReal, and browsed my personal music archive instead. I tried listening to some soothing tunes. Didn't help. I was too high-strung.

Then finally, when we least expected it, Chief Adams stood up from his desk.

Still facing away from us, he started laughing. Maniacally. "It's time to pay the piper, children! It's time to pay the piper!"

The Chief knelt, then hoisted something up. When he turned around, I saw he was holding an M134D-TH Gatling machine gun in both hands.

He sprayed the classroom with it.

I ducked, frantically kicking down my desk for cover. Others were doing the same around me. There were yelps as people got fingers caught under falling desks. Empty pizza boxes fanned across the floor.

I looked to the exit, searching for an escape route. Two other instructors guarded it. They also carried M134s.

They also opened fire.

I forced myself even lower, and slid my spacebag into one of the gaps between me and the other desks, hoping for at least some protection from the bullets. But who was I kidding? The rounds from an M134 could tear right through desks, spacebags, and students alike.

We were all dead.

But there were no screams above the gunfire. No one begging for morphine, or calling for mother. I hesitantly glanced up. Other than a few sore fingers, none of the students seemed injured. They were damn scared, though.

"Blanks!" someone called above the mayhem. "They're firing blanks!"

The lights abruptly went off. An air raid siren sounded. The bright flashes of the machine guns lit the room like a strobe light, making everything seem to happen in slow motion. The air hung with the smell of cordite.

"Incoming attack! Hit the deck!"

I heard the distant whistle of a dropping bomb. The sound grew in pitch until I heard a tremendous bang.

The room shook and I felt my heart and lungs vibrate from the shockwave.

More bombs fell. The classroom was being shelled.

One shell struck not far from me. Body parts flew into the air. A fine red mist sprayed my upper body.

Alejandro had been beside me. I couldn't see him. I crawled through the carnage, slid his desk aside, and found him.

I felt like I was going to die.

Alejandro was on his back, staring up into space with wide, unblinking eyes. His belly was opened right up like some cadaver straight out of med school, his viscera glistening with cement dust.

I just stared at him.

I couldn't move.

Couldn't look away.

Shells continued to explode all around me.

All I could think was that Alejandro was the closest thing to a brother I ever had.

And now he was gone.

Because of me.

He wouldn't have come here, to the UC, if it hadn't been for me.

He wouldn't have taken spec-ops training, if it hadn't been for me.

What had I done?

I felt like I was going mad.

A part of my mind was still functioning, through the sadness, the guilt. And that part told me that the law of averages wouldn't allow me to survive much longer. I couldn't live, not when the men around me were dying left and right. I was going to get hit by a shell any second, whether I moved or not. I felt utterly helpless and desolate in that moment.

I just stayed where I was, motionless, waiting for the inevitable. The shells dropped. And dropped.

Incredibly, they all missed me.

The classroom didn't fare so well. It was quite literally bombed to hell. The machine gunners had long since stopped firing—they no longer existed. There was no overhead, and through a gaping hole in one bulkhead I saw the beach. It was lit up in the dark by scattered fires, and covered in fresh, sandy craters. Beyond the beach other buildings were destroyed. Plumes of smoke rose from New Coronado in the distance.

How could this be happening? Why were we being attacked?

Who were the attackers?

The air raid siren didn't stop. The shelling didn't cease.

I ducked my head, and covered my ears, just wishing the sound would stop. That the shelling would stop. I was too frightened to move.

Time ticked past.

Still I didn't get hit.

Alejandro was dead, but I lived. And if I wanted to continue living, then I had to overcome this debilitating fear, and push his death from my thoughts. There was nothing I could do for him except grieve, and I could do that later, when I was safe.

Otherwise his death was for nothing.

My mind started going through a dozen different scenarios. I considered making a run for it. If I could somehow escape the shelling, cross the beach, and dive into the ocean . . . or maybe, if I could find out where the ATLAS 5 mechs were stored, I could make a stand. But even if I could find the mechs, I didn't know how to pilot them.

And then I realized something else.

Something that could change everything.

I was still wearing my aReal.

Could it be . . .

I pulled the glasses off.

Sure enough, the classroom remained intact around me. There was no blood. There were no body parts. The students ducked behind their overturned desks, locked inside the hellish world generated by their aReals.

Beside me Alejandro was alive, lying there, still wearing his aReal. He held his face in both hands and wept.

Scattered about the room were ten other students who had torn off their aReals, including Tahoe. They were doing PT under the guidance of the instructors.

Piker stepped forward and angrily pointed at me. "Drop and push 'em where you lie, Mr. Galaal!"

And so I did.

"Better strap yourself in for a long ride!" Piker said. "You buddy screwers are going to keep pushing them until every last one of your dumbass friends realizes the truth and yanks off his aReal! Given the Intelligence Quotient of the average member of Class 1108, that is going to be one very long time. We're going to be here all night."

After about ten minutes of pushups, lying kicks, crunches, and lunges, roughly half the class had unplugged. I finally got sick of waiting and, with a quick glance at the instructors to make sure they weren't watching, I reached over and ripped off Alejandro's aReal.

"I saw that, Galaal!" Instructor Brown came rushing at me. "You think you're pretty smart, don't you?"

"Wooyah, Instructor!"

Alejandro had this confused look on his face. "Rade, you're alive . . ."

Brown turned his attention on him. "Drop and push 'em, dumbass!"

Ignoring the instructor, Alejandro got up and gave me a hug, hopping up and down. "You're alive, you're alive!"

Brown stepped in. "I said—"

"*Sí*, drop and push 'em!" Alejandro dropped. "Dropping and pushing them, sir!" I don't think I've ever seen him so happy to do pushups.

Around me, other unplugged students got the hint and started tearing off the aReals of those closest to them.

"Stop, you disobedient curs!"

But it was too late—in moments everyone had their aReals off.

"You're all going to pay for that!" Instructor Piker roared into the megaphone he'd produced.

One of the students who'd just had his aReal yanked off suddenly jumped to his feet. I recognized him. Markus, a good kid.

He ran to Instructor Piker and fell to his knees, clasping the instructor's pants imploringly.

"I quit," Markus said. "I quit, I quit!"

And so we had the first casualty of Trial Week. It was a little heartbreaking. I knew everyone personally by now. You can't go through three weeks of First Phase and three weeks of Orientation and not make friends with the survivors. But of all of us, Markus was the very definition of a survivor. An Olympic water polo player who'd come back from a terrible injury to win Gold at the Games. He knew how to master his inner self. He knew how to beat the odds. I couldn't understand why he quit. I guess he just panicked. Seeing all his friends die, even in a simulation, was just too much for him.

Another instructor led Markus away. The Olympic medal winner didn't look back.

"On the move, recruits!" Instructor Piker yelled into his megaphone. "I've got some payback to give. Move move move move!"

We hauled ass to the infamous plot of black asphalt at the center of the compound. High intensity spotlights randomly roved the dark, the kind you find in prisons. Artillery simulators blasted away in barrels all around the grinder, whistling and exploding and throwing up gray plumes. There was more gunfire, this time from a mix of rifles and pistols. Instructors fired machine guns up into the night sky. Spent shells poured down into the grinder, scalding those of us unfortunate enough to come into contact with them. Some instructors threw smoke grenades from the sides, others launched flares. I noticed that almost every vertical surface was padded with old life vests—probably a good thing, given that half of us were milling about in confusion.

We knew it wasn't real, but I think we were all still shocked from what we'd seen in the aReals. I know I was.

Finally the instructors got us under control, and we did PT while high-pressure hoses sprayed us down. We did combat drills, low crawling back and forth across the grinder. Then we sprinted out to the beach and did sea immersion.

Fifteen minutes later we were told to crawl out.

My hip flexors were so numb I almost couldn't get up. Somehow I and the others managed, and we began a series of lunges in the dark. Industrial fans were set up all along the beach, and between those fans and the instructors spraying us with their hoses, none of us could get warm. At least I couldn't.

We switched to lying kicks with our heads below the high water line, so that the waves splashed over our faces. We were sputtering and half drowning. Water and sand washed up my nose. I was so cold, my whole body was jackhammering. The people around me weren't doing any better. Alejandro sat on his fists, kicking away, his elbows flapping uncontrollably.

"They're called flutter kicks, not chicken flaps, dumbass!" one of the instructors yelled at him.

I don't think Alejandro heard.

Finally we switched to pushups. It wasn't much better, but at least we were out of the water.

We continued the PT under those brutally freezing conditions for about thirty minutes, then we were ordered to crawl back into the ocean for more immersion.

As I lay there, hanging on to Alejandro on my right and Tahoe on my left, I tried to imagine myself in a hot tub. It didn't work. I was so cold my neck muscles spasmed involuntarily, sending waves of pain flaring through my neck with each seize-up.

Instructor Brown's voice drifted down from shore.

"Why are you doing this to yourself? Why don't you just quit?" Like Reed (and most instructors, actually), he had the unsettling ability to make it sound like he was talking to you and no one else. "Why torture yourself? You don't really want to be a MOTH. You know you don't. It's just not worth it. And you know what? There's no shame in quitting. Come on, we got a nice heater in the truck. And cronuts! Every flavor imaginable. Boston cream. Cherry cheesecake. Orange creamsicle. Vanilla. We also got steak and turkey cooking up too. Hot and juicy. With mashed potatoes and filling so good it'll melt in your mouth. All you gotta do is get up and say the magic words. Come on, we all know this is bull. Just pack her in, and come get your steak and cronuts. You owe it to yourself."

I could smell the greasy good scent of the cronuts on the breeze. And the steak too. Well done, just the way I liked it. With barbecue sauce. I could even hear it sizzling on the grill.

But I didn't get up and quit. To this day I'll never know if there were actually cronuts and steak up there, or if it was only the power of suggestion that had conjured those scents in my desperate, cold-weary mind.

What I did know was that three guys got up and quit right there.

After another fifteen minutes we were ordered out of the ocean and the Weavers moved between us, inspecting us for signs of hypothermia. While the robots did this, the rest of us waited on the beach with our arms out, letting those industrial fans seep away whatever heat our bodies managed to generate, as the instructors decreed.

Haywire was standing right beside me, struggling along just like the rest of us. Abruptly he put his arms down.

"I'm done," he said to no one in particular. "That's it."

"Haywire, wait," I said. "What about the pact? You're our leading petty officer. You can't quit."

"You two!" Instructor Piker said. "What are you doing? Get your arms back up!"

Haywire stepped forward. "I quit, sir."

Piker nodded curtly, and called over another instructor to escort him away.

"No you don't!" I said, stepping between Haywire and Piker. "He doesn't quit. We made a pact. Enough people have quit. Good people."

"Let him go, boss." It was Alejandro. He'd stepped out of line too, and he rested a hand on my shoulder.

Haywire abruptly ran past me to the pickup truck on the beach where the flint stone had conveniently been relocated. Haywire sprinted up the ramp, picked up the gavel, and struck the flint three times, hard. The sparks flew. "I quit! I quit! I quit!"

Haywire slumped. He dropped the gavel and, sobbing and hanging his head, staggered down the ramp and let an instructor escort him away.

I was just stunned. He had sworn to see this through to the end. How could he walk away from it all?

Piker had watched the whole thing unfold with an open mouth, but when he looked back at me, his face screwed up into a snarl. Before he could say anything another instructor intervened.

"Once they get it into their heads that they're quitting, there's nothing you can do to stop them." It was Instructor Reed, our class proctor. I hadn't even noticed his presence until now. He nodded at Piker, who backed off. "Even when you give the student a second chance, he'll always quit in the end. Always." Instructor Reed studied me for a second. He must have seen the heartbreak on my face, because he asked, "Do you want to quit too?"

I staggered over to the truck and stumbled up the ramp. I picked up the gavel, and ran my hands over the flint stone. All I had to do was swing the gavel against the stone three times, cause a few sparks, and I'd be out of here.

"Do you quit, sir?" Instructor Reed had joined me in the truck bed. I glanced at him. Alejandro and Tahoe stood behind him. They'd come too. My faithful companions to the end.

"I ask again," Instructor Reed said. "Do you quit?"

Behind him, Alejandro shook his head. Tahoe frowned.

I stared at the gavel. It would be so easy to give up. To throw it all away. To give in and be released from all pain.

I felt like a man standing on the roof of a building, staring down at the traffic going by, far below. Three small steps . . . three small taps . . .

No.

I wasn't going to even let the *idea* of quitting enter my head. As Instructor Reed said, that was the path to failure.

I refused to give in.

I refused to throw away everything because of some momentary lapse in judgment, some weakness of the moment, because I was experiencing a little pain, discomfort, cold, and humiliation. I could get a juicy steak and cronut any other time of year. But if I quit now, I could never do this again. I'd be rolled back, and have to do this all over again, and I'd probably quit again.

No, I had to continue onward.

I'd once told Shaw and Ace how resilient the human spirit was.

I wouldn't quit. I was stronger than that.

I had to be.

The flint stone reminded me of how easy it was to get out of here. It reminded me that yes, there was an easy way out, but I'd never take it. It reminded me that anything of value in this life was worth fighting for.

I wasn't going to quit.

Not now.

Not ever.

I hurled the gavel so hard that sparks flew when it struck the pickup bed.

I turned toward Instructor Reed. "That's a big fat *negative*, sir!"

Instructor Reed grinned widely. "Then get back to the others, Mr. Galaal!"

"Wooyah In-struc-tor!"

That was my turning point. That's when I knew: I was going to become a MOTH or die trying.

We didn't sleep. All through Sunday evening, to Monday morning, to Monday evening, to Tuesday morning, the instructors hounded us. PT, sea immersion, soft-sand runs PT, bay swims, mud crawls, more PT, Gingerbread Men, O-Course, ATLAS PT, inflatable boat races, pipeline crawls. Did I mention PT? The instructors swapped out in eight-hour shifts that coincided with our meal breaks, so they were always fresh and ready to give a good beating.

Tuesday proceeded much the same. No sleep. Brutal PT.

I focused on getting to the next meal. If I dared look past those meals, at the upcoming days of endless, backbreaking, sleepless work, I'd quickly become dispirited. I had to dismiss those thoughts, and concentrate on the next meal. I'd get to that next meal, dammit.

I'd make it.

I thought of a quote I'd read by Winston Churchill, from one of the books on the recommended reading list. *Never give in—never, never, never, never. If you're going through hell, keep going.*

I thought of Shaw, and remembered what she had told me. *Remember me in the deepest, darkest hours. When you think you can't go on. When the training is too much. Hold on to the moments we've shared. Hold on to last night.* And I did. I held on to that night we'd shared, let me tell you. I held on for dear life.

I heard the gavel striking the flint stone nearly every hour, sometimes twice an hour. I'd hear the sound, see the flash from the sparks, and know that another good man had fallen. No one deserved to be sent home now. But there it was. Men giving up, even though we'd done this all a hundred times before. The exhaustion had finally broken them. I understood now what Bowden had been trying to tell us in Basic. You'll leave MOTH training as a broken man, he promised. Well, those who quit were certainly broken. Maybe irreparably so.

But honestly, for me, hearing that sound of the gavel striking the flint, and seeing those flashes, only strengthened my resolve. I wasn't going to be one of those who tapped out. I wasn't going to be one of the quitters.

Wednesday proceeded much the same as the days before it, though we were finally given permission to sleep around noon. We slept right there, on the beach. I was rudely awakened an hour and a half later, feeling groggier than I'd felt my entire life.

The whole class stumbled all the way back to the grinder, and judging from everyone's sluggish movements, I wasn't the only one who felt far worse than before I'd gone to sleep. We worked through it. We had to.

I noticed something as the day wore on.

People had stopped tapping out. I hadn't heard the gavel ring against the flint stone, seen the flash of a spark, since early morning. This was the homestretch. It had to be. I was training with the people who were going to be MOTHs.

We were all brothers now.

That night Alejandro was sent away in an ambulance and returned a few hours later. He confided in me that the Weavers had treated him for a prolapsed rectum. "I'm going to have stories to tell to my kids, *hombre*! When I was in boot camp, the training was so bad that my intestines fell out. I literally got my ass kicked out of me!"

By Thursday I couldn't keep any food down. I vomited blood too, and couldn't hold my bowel movements worth a damn. I was taken away to the medlab, where a corpsman strapped me down to a Weaver. The robot forced one of its telescoping fingers down my throat.

"Just hold still, let the Weaver apply its laser to your ulcer," the corpsman told me.

When the robot was done, the corpsman jabbed a funnel down my esophagus and force-fed me a concoction he called the Green Goddess. "Just a little gastrointestinal martini I came up with," the corpsman said. "It has an antacid to stop the heartburn, lidocaine to stop the diarrhea, and an anticholinergic to paralyze your peristaltic muscles and prevent you from vomiting. Good stuff." He followed that up with a liquid meal replacement, you know, the kind they force-fed prisoners on hunger strikes. My stomach rumbled and gurgled, but I kept the food down.

Friday morning finally came.

I remember the sun coming up, and Instructor Piker saying, "Well, seeing as it's a bright and shiny Thursday morning, and you got another twenty-four hours of Trial Week ahead of you, might as well let you chow down. After some ATLAS PT first, of course."

Thursday morning? I don't know how I'd come up with Friday. Honestly, I'd completely lost track of the days by then. Monday, Tuesday, Wednesday, it was all a blur of sameness to me.

I just had to last one more day.

Just one more day.

At breakfast, we weren't even allowed to eat. The moment we sat down, the order was given to leave. We all had plates full of bacon, eggs, and toast, and had to throw everything out in the trash. What a waste.

After we ported—or rather, zombied—our ATLAS 1s back to the beach, we found Chief Adams waiting to orchestrate our torture this morning. That was somewhat of a surprise, because he was usually on the afternoon shift.

"Time to begin Thursday's evolutions!" he said cheerily. "We have so much to accomplish today. But first, sea immersion, gentlemen!"

"Wooyah," a few people managed. Not me. All my joints were throbbing, and I hurt all over.

Just one more day.

We marched forward. The waves were coming on strong and I knew we were in for a beating. So cold, so damn cold. I was shivering before even stepping into the water. The sun was well away from the horizon by now, and its rays reflected blindingly from the ocean. It didn't warm me.

Just one more day.

We stepped into the surf and locked arms.

Before we sat down, the Chief said into his megaphone. "Actually, Class 1108, there's no other evolution. Seems I was mistaken. It's Friday after all, not Thursday."

I exchanged a confused glance with Alejandro. Was this another cruel joke?

"I'm serious, gentlemen," the Chief continued. He was calling us *gentlemen*, I noticed for the first time, not *children*. "You made it. Congratulations. Trial Week secure."

I turned around. Ashore, all thirty instructors from the beginning of the week stood on the sand berm.

They started clapping.

I fell to my knees right there in the water. Beside me, Alejandro and Tahoe were weeping openly. I staggered upright and gave them both a hug.

"We made it," I said.

"It's over," Alejandro sobbed. "I can't believe it."

I hugged groups of the other students. It was over.

We'd done it.

We helped each other ashore and over the sand berm. It was like the inner resolve that we'd built up all this time abruptly seeped out, and we dropped the facade of strength we'd put up. Our shoulders slumped. Many of us walked with a limp—I did. More than one man staggered and fell flat on his face.

But another man was always there to pick him up.

Always.

CHAPTER TEN

I have zero recollection of what happened the moment after I crossed that sand berm at the end of Trial Week. All I remember is waking up Saturday morning in the barracks at 1300, with all my joints swollen beyond recognition. There was a box of stale pizza on the floor beside me, untouched.

When I reported in to the Weavers, I found out I'd lost twenty pounds. I also had pneumonia.

A Weaver fixed up my lungs, then drained the fluid from my swollen joints. The robot applied an antibiotic ointment to my knees and elbows (which were scraped raw) and sent me on my way.

They said Trial Week took ten years off your life. I believed it. I guess I'd just have to book a couple of rejuvenation treatments at some point, though I'm not sure if it would help.

I found Alejandro and we walked (very leisurely!) to the mess hall. There we ate, and ate some more. When I got back to the barracks, I ate the stale pizza that was still beside my bed.

The rest of that weekend was spent eating and sleeping.

Twenty-six students were left at the end of Trial Week, out of the forty-five who began it and the one hundred eighty-two who had first reported at Orientation.

I felt privileged to be one of those who had made it.

In the coming days, we had some moderately useful classroom learning sessions. The PT was still pretty brutal, but never quite as intense as Trial Week—most of us were still recovering. It had become more conditioning than elimination at this point. Still, the qualifications themselves remained tough, with a particularly vicious qualification five days after Trial Week.

All of us had gathered on the black asphalt of the grinder in our swim trunks. We knew something was up, because not only was Chief Adams here today, but Captain Lindberg himself, the man in charge of BSD/M training this year. He was the O6 who ran Naval Special Warfare Group One (which oversaw MOTH Teams One, Three, Five, and Seven) at the amphibious base where the spec-ops school was held. His hair was gray at the temples, and his face was all stony planes and hard angles, covered in weather-worn lines. Despite that face, he had the hard body of an athletic twenty-year-old.

Standing beside the Captain were two men dressed in the same blue-and-gray digital camos as him. These men were introduced as Petty Officers First Class Gains and Tavies. They didn't look any different from the average gym-going citizens, but their eyes held a shrewd glint, like they knew something no one else did. Their movements were confident and controlled, as if every action was carried out for a very specific reason. No wasted energy. Like a caiman stalking its prey. I knew they were MOTHs.

Both of them stood before a pile of ominous-looking canisters placed near a six-foot-tall metal bullet catch. The wide surface of the catch was pocked with so many bullet dents that it looked like some lunar landscape gone bad.

A quiet, serious-looking man with a holstered hand pistol watched everything from the sidelines. He was wearing a working uniform with a woodland digital pattern, and he had green camouflage paint on his face. He had a darker complexion, and remained very still, as if used to spending hours motionless in the field. His eyes never moved from the bullet-ridden catch. A whisper passed down our ranks that he was a full-blown MOTH sniper, and a few people joked that he was here to shoot anyone who made a mistake.

With six Weavers and two human corpsmen on standby at the edge of the grinder, I could very well believe it. Other than Trial Week, I'd never seen so many medical robots outside the clinic.

Not a good sign.

"Greetings, sirs," Captain Lindberg said. "Today is a very special occasion. A little over five days ago you secured Trial Week, and that's no easy accomplishment. But that only means we have the real men among us now. And so the qualifications get a little more real. Some of you are still going to wash out, unfortunately. But I hope not today." Smiling widely, he surveyed our ranks. "Today is your Combat Resiliency Qualification. First you're going to get shot. Then you're going to fight. Then you're going to get sprayed with OC-40. Then you're going to fight again."

He let those words hit home before continuing.

"As MOTHs, you are sent on some of the highest-risk operations in the galaxy, into danger zones that make Mongolia look like a cakewalk. It is inevitable that you will be shot in combat. Absolutely inevitable. We always prepare our teams for inevitabilities." The Captain glanced at the MOTH sniper. "We're going to have an expert marksman fire at a non-vital area of your body. Trace here is one of the best we have. He can hit a target five miles away with ninety percent accuracy. But I have to warn you, though you're in the hands of one of the greatest living marksmen, bullets sometimes do strange things. Like when they hit bone. If you're shot in the arm, depending on your body structure and bone placement, that bullet can deflect, and may not travel clean through. Maybe it'll travel lengthwise to other parts of your body, zipping through your intestines, or even your heart. This is why it is imperative that you remain absolutely still when the marksman fires. I say again, it is imperative that you remain absolutely still.

Even so, some of you may suffer severe, life-threatening injuries. If you choose to quit now, no one will think any less of you. Indeed, you've completed Trial Week, come further than most trainees ever dreamed of. You're men. If you want to quit, that's your own personal choice. None of you has a thing to prove at this point, not to me, nor yourselves."

No one quit.

Captain Lindberg nodded slowly. "All right. Good. Now, in the course of the line of duty, you may be exposed to chemical weapons. The most common used in military situations is OC-40. Basically pepper spray with some extra ingredients. That's easy, you're thinking. Just pepper spray. You've all been through the Confidence Chamber in Basic. Petty officer lights a vomit gas tablet, you take off your mask and shout your rank, name, and ID. Well I hate to break it to you, but vomit gas doesn't even come close to the potency of OC-40. The OC concentration is forty percent in this stuff, about triple what's allowed to the local law enforcement agencies. About eight times as potent as the vomit gas tablets you endured in Basic. Think about that for a second."

He casually took one of the canisters from PO1 Gains. Captain Lindberg studied it, pursing his lips. Then he turned the nozzle toward his head and sprayed himself square in the face. He opened his eyes a few seconds later, blinked rapidly, and inhaled.

"Did you know the 'hot' sensation is caused by the capsaicin binding with the pain- and heat-sensing neurons?" His face was starting to turn red. He continued to blink, and his voice sounded strained, but he didn't stop talking. "I'd tell you that the pain was mostly in your mind, an illusion, but that's not true. I'm not going to lie to you poor sons of bitches. OC-40 is an inflammatory agent. It boosts allergic sensitivities, irritates the eyes, bronchial airways, the stomach lining—whatever it touches. Even if you've built up a tolerance to the stuff, like myself, you're going to feel this, trust me.

"We're going to give you a light dose to start with, enough to give you a fighting chance to complete the resiliency part of the qualification, then we're going to spray you until you go down. Don't get up unless you want to get sprayed again." He smiled wryly. "Though I suspect a few of you suckers-for-punishment are going to get up anyway. By the way, if you have any medical conditions the entrance processing scans didn't detect, you better let us know *now*. It's far better to leave the MOTHs because of a medical problem than to leave because you died. We have Weavers with us, but sometimes even Extracorporeal Membrane Oxygenation fails."

He walked in front of our assembled ranks, holding his hands behind his back. His face was a dark crimson by now, but he'd stopped the rapid blinking. "When struck by a bullet, and sprayed with a chemical weapon, you must be able to respond. You must not let anything incapacitate you. Being able to fight back may save your life. So. Who wants to go first?"

The Captain ran his gaze across us. I purposely didn't meet his eye. Don't stand out, don't draw instructor attention. That was one of my rules.

"There's no one among you brave enough to take the challenge? No one with heart?"

That got me.

Despite myself, I raised my hand.

"Mr. Galaal!" Captain Lindberg said, no doubt reading the name on my embedded ID with his Implant. He gave me a fatherly smile. A parent inviting his son inside for a beating.

Lindberg positioned me in front of the metallic bullet catch.

The sniper, Trace, finally moved. He literally flowed forward, taking up a position opposite the bullet catch, about five paces from me.

"Do you have any medical conditions or injuries that would preclude the discharge of a live round into the region just below the mid-ulna of your left forearm?" Trace said.

"No." I had no idea what an ulna was.

"Are you ready to receive a level one ballistic wound?"

Hell no. "Yes."

One of the corpsman came forward, and passed some kind of scan device over my forearm, then he marked an X on the skin with a felt marker before pulling away.

Trace lowered a pair of goggles over his eyes, and he lifted the pistol.

"Rotate your arm outward slightly," Trace said.

I did.

As the sniper aimed, I had the distinct impression he was staring right through my skin to the bone underneath.

"Don't move, Mr. Galaal," Captain Lindberg said. "Don't you move."

I don't think I could have moved if I wanted to. I was petrified with fear, the deer-in-the-headlights kind, as I stared down that tilted gun barrel.

Don't miss. Don't miss.

Then I heard the shot, followed by the ding as the bullet struck the concrete behind me—I didn't actually hear it hit the metallic catch.

It felt like someone had poked me really hard, at first. It took a few seconds for the actual pain to kick in, then I experienced an excruciating, burning sensation in my forearm, in the exact spot where the corpsman had marked the X. Hot blood gushed down both sides of my arm. The rest of my body seemed strangely cold.

The corpsman hurried to my side. He checked my wound, then shouted, "Clean!"

He wrapped my forearm in gauze. A little tight, I thought. The whole area throbbed with every heartbeat.

When he was done, the corpsman retreated. "Secure!"

PO1 Gains stepped forward.

"How many fingers am I holding up?" PO1 Gains said.

I felt faint, but so far I was still relatively lucid. "Three."

"Good."

He held up a padded strike shield. "Punch!"

All I could think was that I'd just been shot. I started to lift my uninjured arm, but a wave of nausea passed over me.

"Punch!" PO1 Gains said.

I squeezed my good hand, and punched the padded shield. Two times.

"Come on, what kind of man are you? Use both hands. Both hands!"

Clenching my teeth, I punched again, this time in sequence. Right, then left. Right, then left. I flinched with each left-arm strike, feeling like the wound was tearing wider each time. I couldn't really form a proper fist with the hand of my injured arm. It just hurt too much.

PO1 Gains lowered the shield slightly. "Knee strikes," he said. "Knee strikes!"

I was feeling quite nauseous now, and had stars floating across my vision, but I grabbed the top of the strike shield with both hands anyway. I raised one leg and kneed the padded shield. Again. Again.

"You're the man, Rade!" Alejandro shouted encouragement. "Keep it up, bro!"

"Done. Back away!" PO1 Gains said.

I released the shield, but lost my balance and tumbled forward. The corpsman rushed to my side, and shined a light in my eyes.

"I'm okay," I said, blinking away the stars. "Just a little dizzy."

"Clear!" the corpsman shouted, retreating.

"Pass part one!" PO1 Gains tossed aside the strike shield, then grabbed a canister from the pile.

He moved me back in front of the bullet catch, then looked me in the eye. His expression was blank. "Do you have any medical conditions or injuries that would preclude the discharge of OC-40 into the facial region?"

Only that I'd just been shot. "No."

"Are you ready to receive level one contamination?"

No. Definitely not. "Yes."

"Close your eyes. Take a deep breath. Close your mouth."

I did all three.

I felt liquid splash my face. It didn't hurt. Not right away.

After a few seconds the burning kicked in and I forgot all about the gunshot wound in my arm. In fact, at first I thought I'd been shot again, because my whole face was *on fire.*

"Open your eyes."

I did, but closed them right away. It felt like there was sandpaper under my eyelids: a thousand little needles pressing into my corneas at the same time. My nose was running. Just plain running, like a waterspout had opened up in my sinuses.

The inside of my nose burned, and my trachea ached too, but that was nothing compared to the intense pain in my eyes. Even the burning in my face didn't compare. The eye pain just took the fight right out of me and all I wanted to do was drop down and die.

My knees started to buckle.

"Blink it out. Blink it out!" PO1 Gains's voice reached me through the darkness and pain.

I opened my eyes but shut them immediately. I squeezed my right fist. And even my left, despite the throbbing pain of the gunshot wound. I jumped up and down. I punched my right hand down against my thigh.

"Come on, Rade, you're tougher than this!" It was Alejandro, shouting encouragement.

"How many fingers am I holding up?" PO1 Gains said.

I tried to force my eyes to open, but they kept wanting to close. The burning was just too much.

"*How many fingers?*"

My vision was all foggy from the tears but eventually I made out the V shape of two blurry fingers.

"Two," I said.

"Good."

PO1 Tavies came forward. He held the padded strike shield. "Punch!"

I squeezed my right fist, and with one eye half-open I punched the padded shield.

"Both hands. Both hands!"

And so I used both. The pain in my left arm returned with a vengeance. But I punched. Right. Left. Right. Left. I managed to block out all pain for three good hits, but then for some reason I couldn't take it anymore and I closed my eyes and doubled over.

"It's all in your head!" Alejandro said.

"Come on!" PO1 Tavies said. "Punch!"

I forced myself upright and punched the strike shield again through slitted lids. After the first strike, I shut my eyes again, and got in three more good strikes.

But then PO1 Gains asked me how many fingers he was holding up.

I'd have to expose my eyes to the burning world again.

Resignedly, I turned toward his voice and raised my lid by the tiniest sliver. Through the pain, I made out his hand. "Three fingers."

"Good!"

Beside me, Tavies lowered the strike shield. "Knee strikes. Knee strikes!"

I kneed the shield just like before, keeping my eye open a crack.

Tavies stepped back, letting Gains come forward. He was holding up fingers again.

"Four," I said.

"Good!" Gains offered me his baton, and I grabbed it with my good hand. "Go get Tavies!"

Though no one touched me, I doubled over again, and it was all I could do to resist rubbing my eyes. Snot and tears flowed down my face and off my chin. My wounded forearm pounded with each heartbeat. The gauze was too tight, too tight.

I didn't realize I was saying it out loud until Alejandro said, "Rade! It's not too tight. Get up! Come on! Don't fail!"

Don't fail.

"I'm going to hit you," Tavies said. "Open your eyes. Open your eyes!"

I felt the padded shield strike my shoulder. With slitted eyes, I got up and used the baton to block the next attack. Tavies was hitting pretty hard with that shield, but I staved off each blow. None of the pain had abated. Not the burning in my face, nor the throbbing in my arm. I wasn't sure how much more of this I could take.

Gains was in my face again. "How many fingers?"

"Five."

I squeezed my eyes shut tight.

"Keep going!" Gains said. "Go get Tavies!"

Tavies was backing away now, holding the strike shield high.

I ran at him and my shoulder collided with the shield. I took a step back and struck the shield repeatedly with my baton.

Gains intervened. "How many fingers?"

"One."

"Good! Now defend yourself. Defend yourself!"

One of the instructors came at me from the side, wielding a baton. I couldn't tell who it was through the tears.

"Defend yourself, dumbass." The baton dug into my ribs hard and I folded in pain.

I recognized the voice. Piker. I'd been wanting to get back at that asshole for a long while now. Anger at all the injustice and mistreatment I'd suffered at his hands drove me on, and I recovered in time to deflect his second baton blow.

Gains shouted as we fought. "Tell him what to do, Mr. Galaal! You're in charge! Tell him what to do!"

"Get down!" I said.

"Sure thing, maggot." Piker's baton struck a glancing blow to my cheek, and the whole area flared up as the OC-40 on my face dug its claws into newly exposed sections of tissue.

"Get down!" I said again. I struck out with the baton. Missed.

"Mr. Galaal, surely you can do better than that." Piker mocked, catching me in the ribs with his baton.

Alejandro hadn't stopped shouting. "Come on, Rade! You can take him!"

I forced myself forward, taking a hit on my wounded forearm. Piker wasn't playing fair, not at all, aiming for my injuries like that.

But all was fair in war.

I bit back the terrible pain, slid my leg behind Piker's ankle, and tripped him. "I said *down*!"

We both fell to the ground.

"Good job, sir!" PO1 Gains said. "Pass!"

"Well done, sir," Instructor Piker said. There was no emotion in his voice. Not hatred or resentment. Not even respect. Like this was something that was just routine to him. And I guess it was, at that.

I staggered to my feet and started toward the open shower on the far side of the courtyard, eager to wash the spray off.

"Not so fast, sir," Gains said. "You still have to pass part three."

My shoulders slumped. I'd forgotten about part three.

I returned to the bullet catch.

"Are you ready to receive level two contamination?"

There was only one option. "Yes."

"Close your eyes. Take a deep breath. Close your mouth."

I did.

Cool liquid splashed my face from both sides in a continuous stream. Gains and Tavies were spraying me at the same time.

All I could think was that the pain was coming.

To calm myself I started a count in my head.

One one thousand.

Two one thousand.

Three one thousand.

The burning came.

Four one thousand.

It felt like twenty people were punching me in the face. Repeatedly. At the same time.

Five one thousand.

The spray didn't stop. The liquid was starting to run down my neck and onto my chest, so that my whole upper body felt inflamed. I was still holding my breath. I had my eyes closed. But it didn't help. I could feel the stings as a hundred hornets tried to stab their way through my eyelids.

Six one thousand.

I staggered backward and fell flat on my butt.

The flow of caustic liquid stopped. I think. It was hard to tell, because my face was throbbing so badly.

I heard Gains's voice. "Stay down stay down stay down!"

Believe me, I thought. *I have no intention of getting up.*

I inhaled, and fire filled my lungs. I had trouble breathing.

"Stay down!" Gains said again.

Incredibly, I got up.

I'm not really sure why I did it.

I guess I wanted to show them that I had what it took to be a MOTH. That I was more than a man.

I guess I wanted to prove it to myself.

Gains and Tavies sprayed me again.

One one thousand.

"Go down!" Gains said.

Two one thousand.

The agony.

The scorching agony.

It felt like the skin of my face was melting right off.

It probably was.

Three one thousand.

I didn't have to do this. What was I trying to prove?

Four one thousand.

It wasn't worth it. There was no point.

Five one thousand.

Finally I fell back.

"Stay down!" Gains said.

I obeyed.

I'd proved what I set out to prove.

I had what it took.

"How many fingers? How many fingers!"

I opened my swollen eyelids as far as they would go, and that was the barest of cracks. I blinked several times before making out the blurry hand in front of me. "Five."

"Pass!"

Gains and Tavies helped me stagger to my feet, and led me over to the open shower to wash the OC-40 spray off. I was wheezing pretty badly at this point.

"Don't let the water run down your lower body." Tavies was beside me. "Wrap the towel around your waist."

He gave me a towel and helped me wrap it around my hips. "Good job," he said quietly. "You're going to make a fine MOTH."

Despite all the pain, hearing those words from a MOTH boosted me right up. I felt like I'd already joined the elite brotherhood. I stood proudly under that shower, momentarily forgetting the pain, and my breathing became almost normal.

"Rub this on." Tavies squeezed some kind of shampoo into my hands, and I rubbed it into my face and torso. It didn't really help—my eyes and skin had already sucked up too much OC-40.

There was nothing I could do but grin and bear it. I caught a look at myself in the swivel-mounted mirror situated nearby as I dried myself off. My face was swollen all over, and it sure wasn't pretty, but at least the skin hadn't melted off like I'd imagined.

"Rade, you okay?" Alejandro called.

I nodded my head, and waved in the general direction of his voice.

Tavies and Gains helped me to one of the Weavers. I lay on the stretcher and let the thing examine and treat me. When it was done, I had fresh stitches in my gunshot wound, anti-inflammatories sprayed over my face and upper chest, and an injection of some kind of analgesic (morphine?) for the pain. I took a seat at the far right, where the "pass" group would sit.

I watched others take their turns. My memories are somewhat fragmented, because I had to watch all this through the lingering pain, with slitted eyes. What I saw wasn't pretty. I do remember Alejandro wailing like a baby the whole time, but he passed. And Tahoe kept rubbing at his eyes, making his hands burn too, but he passed as well.

Most people got up again after the final spray-down, just like me. Some endured the pain better than others. Jaguar stayed on his feet for about fifteen seconds the first time, and when he got up again he endured another fifteen seconds under that caustic spray. His face was a swollen and bruised mess, but he'd set the record so far.

Until Branco came along. Jaguar's swim buddy.

By the time Branco's turn came, the painkillers had kicked in, so I was able to keep my eyes open without too much discomfort. I saw, and remembered, everything that happened to him in vibrant detail.

I'm glad I did.

Branco Cervenko was one of the bigger boys in our bunch, and one of the very few steroid guys who'd made it through Trial Week. His lower legs had been inundated with stress fractures by the end of that week, so the Weavers had him wearing these long, padded boots to give the bones a chance to heal, which gave him quite the bounce to his step.

Anyway, he handled the first two parts of the test admirably. Watching him fight, I would have almost thought that he hadn't been hit by a bullet or sprayed with OC-40 at all—he was just a tank. As far as I could tell, he kept his eyes open the whole time. It was beautiful. Only the redness of his face and the tears streaming down his cheeks gave him away.

"That a boy!" Captain Lindberg cheered him on at one point. "Now this is a warrior, people! Watch and learn!"

We cheered too as Branco took out Instructor Piker in a few hits.

Then the endurance part of the test came.

Gains and Tavies sprayed his face simultaneously.

It took three seconds before he closed his eyes.

"Get down!" Gains said.

Ten seconds passed.

"I said get down!"

Branco refused to drop and the two MOTHs continued to spray him.

Twenty seconds.

Branco lowered his chin so that the majority of the spray hit his forehead. I saw his chest moving in and out. I don't know how he could breathe with that caustic substance pouring down his face, and the fumes seeping into his lungs.

Thirty seconds passed.

"Get down, sir!" Gains said. "Down!"

Branco held his ground.

Forty seconds. The skin of his face was starting to get very puffy.

Fifty seconds.

"Sir!" Gains said. "Please!"

Gains shot Captain Lindberg an urgent look.

"Instructor Piker," Captain Lindberg said.

Piker quickly strode behind Branco and gave him a good kick in the back of the knee.

Branco instantly tumbled forward.

Gains and Tavies stopped the OC-40 spray. They were clearly relieved.

"Stay down! Don't you get up!" Gains said.

Branco remained on the ground, breathing heavily.

Then, unbelievably, Branco got up again.

Gains and Tavies exchanged a glance, then looked at Captain Lindberg.

The Captain hesitated a moment, then nodded his head slowly.

The two MOTHs unleashed the OC-40 spray again.

"Get down, sir!" Gains said. "Get down get down get down!"

But Branco didn't budge. His face had become so swollen that his eyes were permanently sealed shut, and he was having obvious difficulty keeping his swollen lips open. The upper part of his chest and neck were a bright, puffy red where the spray had oozed down.

For another thirty seconds he remained standing, until Lindberg himself came forward and, pushing Piker aside, tackled Branco.

"Stay down, Mr. Cervenko," Captain Lindberg told Branco.

Lindberg held him there for a moment, and when he was sure that Branco had finally given in, he released him and took a step back.

"Stay down!" Gains said.

Branco just lay there. His face was utterly unrecognizable, and he breathed in and out like some wounded beast through a tiny crack between his swollen lips.

"I think he's going to stay down . . ." Tavies said.

But incredibly, Branco got up again. He was wheezing terribly, and obviously couldn't see.

But he got up.

Neither Gains nor Tavies reinitiated the spray. They just stood there, watching in silence as Branco choked on his own swollen trachea. We all did. I knew I was witnessing something of utter horror, yet at the same time sheer, unsurpassable beauty. The strength, courage, and resiliency of the human spirit, stripped back and laid bare for all the world to see in this brave, brave man.

Branco fell to his knees, gurgling. Bubbles of blood spilled from his lips.

"Get him to a Weaver!" Captain Lindberg shouted. "I want an EMO! Now!"

Gains, Tavies, and Lindberg carried Branco to a Weaver and rested him on the stretcher.

The robot used telescoping fingers to inject two tubes into Branco's chest, above and below his heart. I saw blood flow out of Branco from the lower tube, up to the metallic core of the robot, then back out again through the other tube and into Branco's body. A corpsman hurried him and the Weaver away to a waiting ambulance.

The Combat Resiliency Qualifications continued. Thankfully there was no repeat of the Branco incident. The rest of the class stayed down the first time they were sprayed. We'd had enough demonstrations of MOTH courage that day.

Branco died later that night.

I felt guilty because I was the one who started it all. Getting up again, when I should have stayed down. But I knew in my heart that it wasn't my fault, not really. Branco would have gotten up regardless. It was part of his indomitable nature.

But you know what? Branco hadn't died for nothing.

He'd taught us something important.

He'd taught us what it really meant to be more than a man.

When Second Phase commenced, we were given standard-issue MOTH jumpsuits, which were basically strength- and endurance-enhancing exoskeletons. These suits came with burstable jetpacks, used for making tactical elevation adjustments or "jumps." The suits were flexible enough to use in any environment, and were surprisingly tight fitting. The one catch was that if you wanted to use it underwater or at higher altitudes (or in space), you had to wait an hour after sealing the jumpsuit for your body to adapt to the inner environment, or there was a chance you'd experience slight decompression sickness. For the water and space scenarios, the suit utilized a detachable closed-circuit rebreather—a breathing apparatus that scrubbed the carbon dioxide from your exhaled air, recycling the leftover oxygen for reuse. The rebreathers came standard with one canister of pure oxygen, one canister of heliox (ninety percent helium, ten percent oxygen), and a bail-out canister of oxygen.

After six weeks of combat dive training in those jumpsuits, which culminated in my basic combat diver certification, I was sent with the class to NLB (Naval Lunar Base) "Shack" to complete Third Phase. Conveniently located at the edge of Shackleton Crater on the moon's south pole, Shack was bathed in near continuous sunlight year-round. Average temperature negative 83 degrees Celsius, or negative 183 Fahrenheit.

First we learned how to walk on the moon in our jumpsuits. It was tricky. Walking on the lunar surface was like bouncing across a long sheet of ice with your boots dipped in animal fat. I don't know if it was because of all that dust or what, but it was ridiculous how often we fell on the slippery surface. Luckily when you tumbled at one-sixth G you didn't hit very hard.

We got used to moonwalking fairly quickly, and it was actually kind of fun. We were taught this hop-step kind of walk, bouncing forward from one foot to the other. You kind of had to lean forward, keeping your center of mass ahead of you, otherwise you'd just end up hopping up and down. Or slipping.

Once we learned to moonwalk, that meant of course we'd have to pass the Moonwalk Qualification.

The first half was a ninety-meter (hundred-yard) moonwalk away from the base with the rebreather disconnected. I had pretty good lung capacity by then, after all the dive training, so the first part was a breeze. When I reconnected the rebreather and headed back toward the base, that's when things got tough. The instructors kept getting in my way and tripping me. About halfway back, some instructor spray-painted my face mask so I couldn't see a thing. I tried wiping it away. No good. I kept going, relying on the Heads-Up-Display map built into the lens. I tripped again, and an alert sounded in my helmet.

"Suit oxygen level fifty percent," the voice talent in my helmet intoned.

I'd seen others go before me, so I had an idea of what was wrong. I unbuckled the primary life-support subsystem and swung it around to the front, stretching the various tubings that connected it to my suit. I blindly felt my way along the various parts. There—as suspected—one of the instructors had disconnected my airline intake.

When I reconnected the intake, the alarm didn't stop.

"Suit oxygen level twenty-five percent."

I felt my way lower down the tube. A knot was tied in it. Wonderful. I had to disconnect the intake again so I could work on the knot. I did my best to keep calm, knowing that if I panicked I'd only use up the rest of the oxygen in my suit.

Finally I untied the knot, reconnected the intake, and re-secured the life-support subsystem. I had one percent suit oxygen to spare.

I finished the moonwalk, and passed.

Three guys failed that qualification. Actually failed, after everything. Two couldn't get their airlines reconnected, and panicked. The third guy managed to reconnect his line, but he was hyperventilating so much that he used up all his oxygen and blacked out before making it back. (We were purposely given low oxygen levels at the start of the qualification.) The Weavers had to resuscitate him.

It was heartbreaking to lose our brothers so late in the game, but the MOTH instructors took moonwalking very seriously. It might seem harsh to roll someone back at this point, but honestly, I wouldn't want my life in the hands of someone who panicked when things went wrong while the team operated in space.

Next we were taught how to use the jumpjets (very delicately), and performed insertions from shuttles. Manually navigating with jets was surprisingly difficult. AI-assisted insertions were easy of course, but we had to know how to do it by hand. The first few times I hit the lunar surface a bit hard and rebounded too high, and was forced to compensate with the jets. But after six or seven drops I had pretty much mastered it, and landed perfectly almost every time.

We did untethered, zero-G spacewalks, which were somewhat nerve-racking, at least for me, because whenever I went any distance from the shuttle, a part of me always wondered if the jetpack would fail and leave me drifting endlessly through space (until my oxygen tanks ran out). It was a needless worry, because someone in the class would've come out to get me if that happened. No one was left behind and all that. But still.

Learning to fire rounds in low G was interesting. Projectile weapons designed for use in the extreme cold of space came with an adjustable recoil buffer to dampen the effect of the kickback. You could dial the buffer down to zero or leave the weapon at full kick-back. Usually you wanted zero kickback, because obviously in space the slightest momentum could drastically alter your course (or send you flying off the surface of the moon). But depending on the tactical situation, a slight recoil could actually be good, especially when you were low on jetpack fuel.

So anyway, after six weeks of spacewalks and moonwalks I got my basic space EVA (Extravehicular Activity) combat certification.

And then we were flown back to Earth for Fourth Phase and spent ten weeks learning to be the navy commandos we'd all seen in the vids. We practiced on the shooting ranges for hours on end. We were introduced to every military gun available. Submachine guns. Rifles. Handguns. Single shots. Multibarreled. Semiautomatics. Machine pistols.

We had to do jumpsuit training all over again, because the strength-enhancing suits and their jumpjets behaved differently in Earth's gravity. The maximum vertical height we could attain with one full jump spurt was four meters (thirteen feet), but by firing the jets repeatedly and "stacking" the jumps, we could go higher. We had to be careful because the jetpacks had enough fuel for only about twenty full jumps in Earth G, and if we didn't keep track, and stack-jumped too high, we could quite literally fall to our deaths. There were no parachutes, at least not in these models.

With and without the jumpsuits we practiced small unit tactics on the rough terrain, and sometimes inside virtual kill houses and street mock-ups, taking down holographic terrorists and freeing holographic hostages. We practiced raids, ambushes, building searches.

We were taught how to snipe man-sized targets up to five thousand yards away, ten percent of the time. The EXACTO rounds did most of the work, their internal CPUs constantly making micro-adjustments to the flight path, but a certain degree of skill was required. My hit rate as a sniper at targets five klicks away was about fifty percent, near the top of the class.

We used aReals at all times, either in goggle form or helmet form. Augmented Reality in combat was an interesting thing. Imagine a video game where you had a HUD (Heads-Up Display) overlaying your vision. You had a map in your upper right, which you could enlarge at will. Your allies were shown in green, your enemies in red. In your actual field of view, your allies were outlined a slight green, and their names and ranks floated above their heads. Your enemies were outlined in red, with threat levels shown above them as a series of red bars, one being the lowest while five bars meant run like hell. You could do things like tag an enemy to help you launch certain tracking rounds or compute a laser-range find. Great stuff.

In addition to small unit tactics and marksmanship, we also learned patrolling, land navigation, demolitions, and rappelling. We went to a training facility two thousand feet up the Laguna mountain range and learned the art of camouflage and stealth. For one qualification we had to make seven-klick journeys across the mountains in pairs, evading detection the whole way. Alejandro and I managed to come in sixty minutes under the time limit without being discovered—not the fastest time, but definitely not the slowest.

And then amazingly enough it was done. All twenty-five of us had completed Fourth Phase.

No one failed this last phase.

We weren't MOTHs. Not yet. But pretty damn close.

I bumped into Instructor Piker at the phase completion ceremony. He shook my hand and said, "Not bad, Mr. Galaal. Not bad at all. Congratulations. I knew you had it in you."

He offered to buy me a beer.

Surprisingly, I said yes.

CHAPTER ELEVEN

We had two weeks off after Fourth Phase. A few of the guys had gotten together and rented a pimped-out pad in the city, New Coronado, and they invited half of us to stay up there while on liberty. We set up cots and mattresses in the hallways and closets, and the first night up there we basically bought out the local liquor store.

"Damn," I said, seated around the kitchen table, on my eighth or ninth beer. "This is the most I've drank since I signed up." I took a long sip of foamy suds and then belched. Loudly.

"I thought Piker took you for beers," Jaguar said. The lieutenant was one of the few officers who hadn't quit. He was still our class leader, and a co-leaser on the pad.

"Yeah, but he only bought me one drink. Not ten."

Jaguar chugged his bottle. "What did he want anyway? Let me guess. He tried to make a move on you. How about that? For all his anti-gay remarks, he's the one who turns out to be gay."

"No," I said, laughing. "He didn't make a move. Sorry to disappoint you, Jag. I know it would have fulfilled all your deviant fantasies."

"Pfft." Jaguar waved a hand in dismissal. "We're going to have to make a visit to the Gaslamp if you keep this up. Get ourselves cleansed." The Gaslamp was a strip club.

I finished my beer and slammed the empty bottle on the table. "Piker just wanted to congratulate me, okay?" Well, he also told me he expected great things from me in the years to come, but I wasn't about to reveal something like that. It would come off too much like bragging.

"My condolences." Jaguar shot me a mocking grin, then he opened another beer and slid it across the table to me.

I caught it, and lifted it to my lips. "Wooyah."

"Hey," Alejandro said. "Rade's had too much as it is."

Jaguar smirked. "What are you, his mom?"

Alejandro rolled his eyes, then took another bottle for himself. "Just saying."

Jaguar raised his bottle in toast. "Here's to us. The best damn human beings I've ever had the pleasure of serving with."

We clinked our bottles together.

"But we haven't really served together, Jag," I almost called him *sir*. Hard habit to break, him being the class leader and all. "We're still in training."

"Same difference. Some of our qualifications may as well have been missions." His lips pursed, and his eyes twinkled. "Hey, Alejandro, remember when Piker disconnected your rebreather on the moon and you were hopping around like you'd lost your head? Then when the air in your suit ran out, Piker threw you on the ground to reconnect it for you, but you kept flailing around so that he had to tie your hands together. But just when he finished binding you, you kicked him with both feet and sent him flying across the crater. Your way of telling him that you weren't giving up just yet. I thought you were going to black out and fail right there. I'm sure everyone else thought the same thing. But somehow you managed to reconnect the rebreather with your hands tied. Alejandro, you're a regular Houdini."

"Thank you thank you." Alejandro gave a bow.

"How'd you do it, anyway?"

Alejandro folded his arms. "Hey, if I told you all my secrets, I wouldn't be Houdini, now would I?"

Jaguar opened a new beer for himself. "That should be your callsign."

"What? Houdini?" Alejandro didn't sound impressed.

"Yep." Jaguar took a long drink. "If we were on the Teams, you would definitely be a Houdini."

"We're not on the Teams," Tahoc said. That was the first word the Native American had said all evening. He had his aReal glasses on, and was obviously multitasking.

"Not yet, no," Jaguar said. "But we may as well be. The statistics are on our side. No one quits after Fourth Phase. No one washes out. The guys you see here in this room, well, this is it. We're part of the brotherhood now. It won't be long before all of us are the proud recipients of a certain golden badge."

"Now *that's* something I'm looking forward to," Alejandro said. "Finally getting my MOTH badge. What's the first thing you're going to do, Jag?"

"Me?" He smirked. "Bang some MOTH groupie."

I shook my head. "Way to be a class leader."

"Hey, I always believed in leading by example." Jaguar's grin widened. "So what about you, Alejandro? First thing after you get your badge, what are you going to do?"

"Me?" Alejandro sat back and put his hands behind his head. "I'm going to treat myself to a filet mignon buffet at the most expensive restaurant in town, get a massage at the most luxurious spa, rent a loft at the fanciest hotel, and hire ten of the most beautiful *putas* to entertain me the rest of the night. Erectopills all the way, baby."

"Nice," Jaguar said. "Though given our meager pay grade right now, you might want to scale back those plans a bit."

Alejandro pursed his lips. "Maybe I'll hire nine call girls instead of ten."

Jaguar slapped him on the leg. "That's the spirit, bro. Though one question remains: Human or robot?"

"Robot obviously, man. Only the best for me."

Jaguar smiled reminiscently. "There's something to be said about a real woman, though."

"Hey, if you want disease and inexperience, then you rent human. If you want mind-blowing pleasure, you rent robot. Besides, no lives are destroyed when you go robot. It's the safest way to play."

Jaguar shrugged. "I guess it's all the same, when you rent." The disapproval was obvious in his tone, but he didn't say anything more. He glanced at me. "What about you, Rade? What are you going to do to celebrate?"

I frowned. "I don't know. I never really thought about it."

"What do you mean you never thought about it? Graduating is all the rest of us can think about."

I sighed. "Well, I guess I'll take a hot shower, have a nice bottle of wine, read a book. Just relax, really."

"That it?" Jaguar glanced at Alejandro. "He for real? No girls, no partying, just . . . a shower and reading a book?"

I put my elbow on the table and rested my chin in my palm. "Well, there's a certain girl from Basic I'm looking to get back in touch with. Maybe if things work out—"

"Basic?" He cut me off. "Sheesh. How'd you ever find time to bang a girl in Basic?"

"Let's just say things got a little out of control after graduation, during weekend liberty."

Jaguar finished his bottle and gave me a knowing smile. "Don't they always."

I glanced at Tahoe. "You've been pretty quiet, Tahoe."

"Mmm?" he said distractedly, still behind his aReal. "I said something already."

"Are you doing astrophysics crossword puzzles again?"

Tahoe shook his head.

"Come on, take those off and actually spend some time with the people you're spending time with." I reached forward to snatch the aReal from his face, but he swatted my hand away.

Behind those lenses, his eyes finally focused on me. "I'm chatting with my wife, Rade. My child was born today. It's a girl. We named her *Aniidastehdo*. It means, Fresh Start."

"Congratu-freaking-lations!" I stood up and high-fived him. "That's awesome news."

He got high fives and fist bumps all around.

"When are you going to haul your wife and kid up here?"

"I've been talking with Chief Adams," Tahoe said. "He says once I graduate he'll arrange a residency for them both."

"That's fantastic news." I sat back and took a long quaff of my beer. "That's the great thing about the Navy. Everyone looks out for everyone else. No matter the rank, or pay grade. Everyone counts." I surveyed the men here with me in this room. My brothers. "We're almost on the Teams. Phase Four secured. I can't believe it. I never thought I'd see the day. I'm going to miss you guys." I was focusing on Tahoe and Alejandro.

"Maybe we'll be assigned to the same Team," Alejandro suggested.

I shrugged, trying to pretend it didn't matter, when it meant the world to me. "You never know."

Alejandro saw right through me. "To the end," he said, raising his bottle.

Tahoe raised his as well. "To the end."

I raised mine.

"You guys made some kind of pact in First Phase, didn't you?" This was from Costa, a kid from southern Sicily. He looked a little nerdy with those buckteeth of his, but he was the second-best sharpshooter in the class, after me.

"We did." I glanced at Costa. "A pact to see our training through no matter what. To overcome everything the instructors threw at us. But if you think about it, everyone in this room made that same pact, with himself. We're all here after all. We all made it."

Jaguar set down his bottle, a little too hard. He was looking at me with a sad expression. I was about to ask him what was wrong when he spoke.

"Not all of us made it," he said. "I wish Branco were here."

"We all do, Jag." I rested a hand on his knee.

He shoved my hand away and pretended (I thought) to be offended. "Don't go gay on me now, like Instructor Piker."

I smiled sadly. "You can try to hide the hurt but it won't work on us. We're too close to you. We all miss him, Jag. Branco was a good man. The best of us. Braver than all of us combined."

"I can't believe he's dead," Jaguar said.

Tahoe set his beer aside. "You know, my ancestors believed that when a man died in battle, his spirit rose to the heavens and took its rightful place among the stars. They believed that every star in the sky was the spirit of a warrior."

"Is that what you believe?" I said.

"Hell no." Tahoe took off his aReal. "The stars are massive thermonuclear ovens powered by their own gravity. As much as I hate to say it, Branco's gone, and he ain't coming back."

"Way to go and spoil your own platitude, bro," Alejandro punched Tahoe in the upper arm.

"It wasn't a platitude," Tahoe said. "Listen. Branco didn't die for nothing. Don't you forget that, Jaguar. Don't any of you forget that. He taught us the true meaning of courage."

I stared at my beer bottle, not really seeing it. "Branco taught us courage, that's true, but I think your ancestors had it right, Tahoe. There is a place up in the sky for everyone who dies with courage, fighting the good fight. Warriors, true warriors, get their own stars."

I tried to arrange a meet up with Shaw, but she was out in space doing landings on Shack, so I spent the rest of my liberty hanging out on the streets of New Coronado. I was pretty used to the cleanliness and lawfulness of UC cities by now, the profusion of robots and the paucity of guns. Still, it was a strange feeling walking around the city, knowing that I had attained something that 99.99 percent of the population would never attain. That I was superior, somehow.

Yeah, superior.

It was all too easy to get caught up in my own bullshit. I got in a few fights with members of other military branches. I won of course, but got hurt pretty good once or twice, and that was humbling. I guess I was just restless. I needed to resume my training. I was turning into a warrior and fighting was becoming second nature to me. I'd never been this way when I was a Dissuader. All that PT must have boosted my serum testosterone levels through the roof. Or maybe the instructors were just feeding us steroids.

Liberty finally came to an end. I got back to base and the post-BSD/M craziness began.

We got our Implants the first day—at this point, the military considered us at low risk of failure or dropping on request, so the Brass could justify the expense of implanting us with aReals. In combat, if the jumpsuit's aReal failed for whatever reason and you lost contact with your platoon (not to mention all the other tactical benefits the augmented-reality display provided) then you were basically out of the battle. By putting the aReal into our heads, the military had direct access to the Brodmann areas responsible for the visual and auditory cortex. There was still a chance the Implant might fail, but having both the jumpsuit aReal and the Implant break down at the same time was considered an unrealistic probability.

These weren't the ordinary Implants that civilians got either.

These aReals were military grade, and had the technology to interface with the ATLAS mechs and robotic support troops assigned to each platoon.

I remember when I first woke up after the Implant procedure. All the functionality of an aReal was permanently overlaid onto my vision. The little flashing mail icon on the bottom right. The chat box on the bottom left. The friend stream updates (minimizable) on the top right. I could access each option by focusing on it, just like when I wore an actual aReal.

One difference from a normal aReal I noticed right away was the ability to think many common commands, rather than having to say them out loud or utilize eye movements. After I walked the Implant through a quick thought-training session, which involved thinking the words that flashed over my vision, I could issue commands by merely thinking the words. The most useful command, for me, was "HUD off," which deactivated the overlay entirely. That, and the subvocal communication feature: it was kind of fun to make fun of the instructors and have entire conversations with other students in my head during lessons and PT.

After that first day I signed up to take a bunch of core MOTH courses, which involved brain dumps from the top people in the field: tracking with the best woodsmen in the world, combat driving with the best drivers, mountain climbing with three-time Everest conquerors. We learned desert and jungle survival techniques from the Rangers. Hand-to-hand combat techniques from the Marines. Like I said, the best of the best.

I also got to choose two electives. Some of the options included advanced sniping, knife fighting, computer hacking, advanced spacewalking, linguistics, advanced demolitions, base jumping, explosive ordinance disposal, advanced hand-to-hand combat. The list was a few pages long, with many of the electives just advanced versions of the core courses.

For our two electives, Alejandro, Tahoe, and I signed up for the Introductory ATLAS Warfare course and its followup, Advanced ATLAS Warfare. There was a long waiting list to get into both, but that was fine because we chose our electives at the beginning, right after liberty, so the three of us had lots of other courses to occupy our time until the ATLAS warfare class-up.

The months passed in a blur, and then we got shipped out to one of the nearby islands for the ATLAS Warfare course.

The first two weeks were spent in the ATLAS simulator, a pod-shaped cockpit that did a bang-up job of simulating the operation of an actual ATLAS. But you could only do so much in a simulator. There were no G forces when you used the jumpjets, for example. After those two weeks, we were finally allowed to pilot the real things.

I remember standing there on the beach when the bay door opened and the mech stepped outside. It was the first time I'd seen a real-life, modern ATLAS 5 outside of the Net vids, or the simulator. It was this massive version of the ATLAS 1s we'd ported around the base. Three times the height of an ordinary man and ten times wider, it looked like a robot soldier, with arms, legs, and a head. The head was a pinched version of a man's. A red visor with two yellow glows made up the eye area. There was a red circle at the center of the bulky chest where the atomic core resided, beneath the cockpit. That's right, no magnesium-ion batteries in this puppy.

Beneath the red circle someone had spray-painted a maroon-colored moth. I recognized it as the Atlas, the biggest moth in the world. Put your two hands together, palms facing you, and you had the average size of a typical specimen. The Atlas moth also happened to be the symbol of the MOTHs themselves.

I could see my reflection on that burnished armor, and the reflections of the trainees around me, and I saw the awe in all our eyes.

I can't wait to ride this baby, Alejandro transmitted to my Implant.

Our ATLAS Warfare instructor came forward: PO1 Saunier. "Welcome to the Atomic-powered, all-Terrain Land Assault Supersuit you've been dreaming about, gentlemen. Otherwise known as the ATLAS, Model Five. There's a good reason why we've named it after the ancient Greek Titan who held up the world on his shoulders. Let me introduce you. Over a thousand hydraulically actuated joints with closed-loop positions and force control. Onboard hydraulic pump and thermal management. Crash protection. Jumpjets. Head-mounted sensor package with built in LIDAR, night vision, flash vision, zoom, and other augmented-reality perception boosts that smoothly integrate with your Implants. Modular wrists that accept third-party hands—when you're looking to throw a party, put a couple of serpents in one and a twin M2A1 in the other." He grinned widely. "The ATLAS 5. The war machine of your dreams. And your enemy's nightmares. Definitely gives its Titan namesake a run for the money."

Stepping into the big steel suit was extremely disorienting at first, not to mention claustrophobic. When you climbed the steel rungs on the leg and sat in the cockpit, the hatch sealed up and actuators pushed the elastic inner material into your jumpsuit, wrapping you up like a cocoon, ensuring a suit-tight fit (you always wore your standard jumpsuit, in case you had reason to leave the mech). You couldn't see anything except the inside of the cockpit, not until the vision feeds from the mech kicked in—there was no glass in these cockpits, not like in some of the earlier models.

We'd all experienced that "cocooning" in the simulated environment, but it was different being inside an actual ATLAS, with all that steel over your head. I now understood why the BSD/M instructors had made us crawl through cramped pipes on the bottom of the bay—sealing yourself inside three tonnes of metal that might suddenly break down wasn't for the claustrophobic. If power to the suit failed, the skintight inner material was supposed to release you, but that wasn't guaranteed. If you weren't released, you were basically trapped motionless inside a metallic coffin. Claustrophobic indeed. (There was one qualification where the instructors shut off power to the suit and made you sit there, motionless, for two hours. Wasn't fun.)

Operating the ATLAS 5 proved relatively simple. You moved your body, and the mech moved with you. While it was true that the inner elastic material bent and flexed around you, it was the Implant inside your brain that did all the heavy lifting, interpreting your body movements and relaying them instantly to the servomotors of the metallic monster that encased you.

The mech could still be operated in "manual" mode, without an Implant. The encasing material of the cockpit had pressure sensors, so that if your Implant was damaged for whatever reason, you were still in the fight. It was a bit harder than operating with an Implant, though—at first it felt like wading neck-deep through a swamp, with every part of the ATLAS pressing against you, impeding your every movement. But when you got used to it, it wasn't so bad.

The mech had basic weaponry strapped on beneath each forearm: a Gatling gun with three thousand rounds, four serpent rockets, and an incendiary thrower. There was also a deployable ballistic shield on the left forearm, used for protection against armor-piercing bullets. These forearms could be swapped out pre-mission with entirely different appendages for specialized tasks, such as a giant buzz saw, a welding torch, and so forth. Heavier limbs threw the center of gravity of the ATLAS way off, though, and were normally reserved for the more defensive operations.

Operation of the weapons system was relatively straightforward. To cycle between the available weapons, you'd identify the hand first, then the weapon. For example, *right hand, swivel M61* would swivel the Vulcan M61 Gatling into your fully tactile, five-digit right hand, placing the trigger right above the index finger. The actuators inside the mech would apply slight pressure to the inside of your glove, which would then be transmitted to your palm by your jumpsuit, providing further feedback to let you know that, yes, you now held the weapon. *Gun off hand* folded the current weapon out of the way, so you could use your ATLAS fingers to grasp objects, while *gun in hand* brought it back again.

Those first few days were spent mostly walking around and getting comfortable operating actual ATLAS 5s. I hung a "New Driver" sign on the back of my mech, right between the twin jumpjet nozzles. Kind of suited my driving those first few days. All I can say is, it was a good thing we trained in sand because I toppled over more than a few times.

"You damage that ATLAS, it's coming directly out of your paycheck!" Instructor Saunier roared over the platoon circuit one time when I took a pretty bad tumble. "That'll take you the next *four thousand years* to repay at your pay grade, moron!"

When we became comfortable walking, we practiced with the ATLAS jumpjets. Very carefully, I might add. I could almost feel Instructor Saunier and his assistants cringing with every landing. The same rules regarding stack jumps applied to the ATLAS 5, because there were only enough charges for about twenty jumps on a full tank. If you stack-jumped too high and ran out of fuel, not only did you kill yourself but you demolished three billion digicoins worth of equipment.

After a few days practice on the shooting range, the class spent the next five weeks stalking through rocky defiles and across open fields, learning the role of the ATLAS 5 in the platoon and how to integrate with other units.

"You're going to be fighting side by side with the actual units you'll be with on the Teams," Instructor Saunier told us. "None of this Fourth Phase kindergarten playground crap."

He divided us into eight-man squads. Six trainees wore jumpsuits—the usual roles were officer-in-charge and his assistant, two snipers, a heavy-weapons specialist, and a drone operator—while the remaining two trainees were assigned ATLAS mechs. Each squad also had eight robotic support units. A Weaver, the robotic corpsman. An MQ-91 Raptor, for reconnaissance and air support. A K-4 Equestrian, basically a robot tank. Four M-1 Centurions, humanoid foot soldiers capable of fulfilling any role the situation demanded—when dressed in jumpsuits, Centurions were almost indistinguishable from human MOTHs, and only their metallic faces betrayed them. Lastly there was a T-2 Praetor, a humanoid soldier with a more advanced AI that gave it the ability to command other robots. The Praetors helped offload some of the command burden from the drone operator, and were able to react to changing tactical situations on the fly.

Adding in ATLAS 5s and support robots changed the battle space completely, and we had to redo all our small unit tactical training. In each simulated combat mission we rotated to a different role, so that I only got to operate the ATLAS maybe once every five missions. We soon learned that the success or failure of any given mission hinged on the skills of the drone operator more than anyone else. He was the one who controlled the entire cadre of support robots assigned to the squad, and he needed a firm grasp on tactics. I assumed the role on several occasions, and it wasn't the easiest job in the world, I can tell you that, not even with a T-2 Praetor to share some of the command load with. Controlling the drones was sort of like playing one of those real-time strategy games popular on the Net, except your mind was the controller and the battlefield was your game board. I quickly realized drone operation wasn't my forte, but I worked through it, doing my best not to let my squad down. I usually made up for it when I got to pilot an ATLAS again, because riding the mechs was definitely one of my strengths.

Alejandro, Tahoe, and I eventually graduated to the Advanced ATLAS Warfare class, which was pretty much more of the same. The only difference was that we did more training in space. The practice insertions from orbit were particularly tense: we dropped from low Earth orbit in an ATLAS and free-fell all the way to the surface. The ATLAS 5s had a deployable single-use heat shield that burned away on reentry. Air brakes and aerospike thrusters slowed the descent enough for a relatively soft landing. Well, as soft as three tonnes of metal could land, anyway.

There isn't really much more to say about training, because just like the end of Fourth Phase, it all ended abruptly.

A MOTH detailer sent for Alejandro, Tahoe, and I. Detailers were basically the human resources people of the Navy, and he asked us our top picks in regards to the Teams we wanted to be on. Alejandro, Tahoe, and I insisted on staying together, and we chose Team Seven, Six, and Five as our top picks, in that order. The detailer said he'd do his best to make sure we got our top picks, but because each Team had multiple platoons, he couldn't promise we'd be on the same one.

After that meeting I went outside and spent a long time on the beach, watching the sunset.

The sun was setting on the old phase of my life. I was about to join the Teams, the culmination of all my goals and dreams up to this point.

And yet I was probably leaving my friends behind.

When Alejandro, Tahoe, and I went out for drinks that night, it was a bittersweet moment to say the least.

"Even if we're separated, we'll stay in touch on the Net," I told my friends. "And if we're on the same Team, but different platoons, we'll still get to hang out when we're not on deployment. Every night. It'll be just like when we were Dissuaders."

Alejandro and I hadn't been apart since we were kids. This was going to be hard, if we were assigned to different Teams.

Alejandro forced a smile. "Of course. Everything's going to be just like it was." He didn't sound like he believed it. He took a long drink. His eyes looked as haunted as ever. "Rade, when I thought you were dead during Trial Week, when they pulled that crap with the aReals, it was just the worst feeling in the world. It brought me back to the day my family was gunned down. And I realized I did the right thing by joining up. I had to make sure you were all right. No matter what." He finished his drink. "I don't know what I'm going to do if they separate us."

"I don't know either." I met his eyes. "But Alejandro, you're going to have to understand, someday there will come a time when you can't protect me. No matter how much you might want to."

"You're wrong," Alejandro said. "I'll find a way."

I sighed. There wasn't really much I could say to that.

I joined the Navy because I wanted to get a chance at a better life.

I joined the spec-ops because I wanted to see if I had what it took.

Losing my friends to other Teams was just part of the price I'd have to pay, I guess. That was life, after all. You met people at work or play, they joined your social circle or you theirs, and eventually you moved on because of your choices. You had to live your life. No one else could do it for you. As for Alejandro, he'd just have to learn that I wasn't that little kid from the barrio anymore. That I was big enough to protect myself. He'd have to.

Still, I'd miss him and Tahoe. And everyone else.

At least I'd answered the question.

Was I capable of becoming more than a man?

I was.

CHAPTER TWELVE

Incredibly, the next day all three of us were assigned to Alfa Platoon, MOTH Team Seven, Naval Special Warfare Group One. Based right here. I think the powers that be saw what a great team we made and wanted us kept together. Kudos to the Navy for the best decision ever made. And kudos to our detailer for a job well done.

Alejandro, Tahoe, and I received our "moths" that afternoon, golden badges embossed with the broad wings, stout body, and hairlike antennae of the Atlas moth. I'd checked out pictures of the Atlas moth on the Net, and the designers of these badges had gotten the clear "windows" in the forewings and hindwings right, but the snake's head at the tip of the forewings was completely exaggerated. Though I guess the overemphasis was done on purpose, because I had to admit it looked pretty badass.

"Welcome to Alfa Platoon," an officer said when the three of us walked into the barracks lounge carrying our spacebags. He had a slight British accent. His sunburned face was well proportioned, and I thought women probably found him handsome. His blue eyes twinkled with amusement as he stood up from the table to shake our hands. "I'm Facehopper. Your LPO." Leading Petty Officer.

Another MOTH dressed in a gray-and-blue digital camo nodded his head in greeting. He had his feet up on the table and his arms were crossed. He reminded me of Branco a little because of his tanklike build. What stood out the most for me were his forearms, basically these steel girders.

"And this is Big Dog," Facehopper said. "Best heavy gunner this side of the galaxy. The bloke shoots almost like a sniper with that machine gun of his. Plus he can wrestle his way out of a roomful of enemy drones. Definitely don't want to mess with him."

"Uh, what's a bloke?" Alejandro said.

"Means *dude*." Facehopper laughed. "My British accent gets the best of me sometimes."

I shook Big Dog's hand. I don't think I've ever had my hand crushed so readily in a handshake. Big Dog's expression proved unreadable, but I had the definite impression he was judging me and my friends.

"You Colombian?" Big Dog asked Alejandro after they'd shaken hands.

"No, why?" Alejandro said.

Big Dog frowned, but didn't say anything more.

"Big Dog here has a thing for Colombian women," Facehopper interjected. "His next question would have been, 'do you have a sister?' He's Brazilian, by the way."

"I would have never guessed," Tahoe said.

Big Dog glanced at Tahoe and looked him up and down. There was a hint of contempt in his eyes. "What are you trying to say, red man?"

Tahoe looked affronted. "Nothing."

"Easy, Big Dog," Facehopper said. "Now's not the time for hazing the caterpillars."

"Now's always the time for hazing the caterpillars," Big Dog said. "In fact, I think we should duct tape them to the table and start the waterboarding right away. Get it over with."

"Excuse me?" I said, exchanging a nervous glance with Alejandro and Tahoe.

Big Dog erupted in a hearty chuckle. His massive chest moved up and down. "I'm kidding." The humor abruptly fled his face, and his gaze locked with mine. "Mostly."

Facehopper shook his head. "Not in the mess hall, Big Dog. Last time we hazed the caterpillars here we basically destroyed the place. The Lieutenant Commander wasn't very happy about that."

Big Dog shrugged. "Hey, that's why we call it the 'mess' hall, isn't it?"

"All right." Facehopper forced a smile and started walking away. "Moving on . . ."

Big Dog watched us leave the lounge with an evil grin on his face, like he had all these nasty things planned for us.

Alejandro lowered his voice. "Maybe being assigned to Team Seven wasn't the best idea . . ."

Facehopper overheard. "Ah, don't worry about it. Big Dog is just trying to scare you. We haven't waterboarded anyone in, what, two years now."

"Reassuring," I said. "What, uh, other kinds of . . . hazing . . . can the new people expect?"

"Oh, you know, the usual. Random chokeholds, sucker punches, crazy instructions, wild goose chases. You're basically our servants and we can do whatever we want with you."

"I see. And how long is this 'hazing' supposed to last?"

"Not long," Facehopper said. "Usually the first few months. Sometimes into the deployments, depending on your character. Basically it lets us get a feel for who you are, and whether or not we can rely on you when the feces hits the fan."

"What exactly do you mean, depending on our character?"

"You'll get a feel for the Team culture soon enough, mate, don't you worry," Facehopper said. "Come on, let me introduce you caterpillars to the rest of the platoon."

"Caterpillars?"

He smirked. "Baby moths."

Facehopper took us to the berthing area, where most of the team members resided at this hour.

The first room we went to had only one man present, and it was otherwise empty save for a bed with pale sheets and a white desk. It had a very surgical feel to it, almost like a hospital room.

The occupant faced away from us, seated with his shoulders hunched and his chin bowed. I couldn't see his face. His whole posture screamed weakness, and I would've never guessed he was a MOTH, which was odd because every MOTH I'd met up until that point had looked the part.

"This is Skullcracker," Facehopper said. "Like most of us, he doesn't live on base, in case you're wondering at his spartan lifestyle. Come on Skullcracker, don't be shy. Get out of your aReal and say hi to your new platoon mates."

Skullcracker slowly turned around in his swivel chair and looked up.

When I saw his face, I stepped back a pace, and Alejandro actually gasped beside me.

"*Caramba*," Alejandro whispered.

Skullcracker had a very realistic-looking human skull tattooed onto his face. When he met my eyes, he offered me a lopsided grin. "Hey."

I recovered quickly, and went forward to shake his hand.

Despite his looks, his grip actually felt tighter than Big Dog's. I was going to seriously get some broken bones in my hand if this kept up. When he released me, I rubbed my palm with the fingers of my good hand and didn't take my eyes off him. This was one dangerous man.

"You wouldn't guess it by looking at him, but Skullcracker is our second heavy-weapons operator," Facehopper said. "You should ask him to tell you why we call him Skullcracker sometime."

"No, don't ever ask me that," Skullcracker said. He sounded extremely weary all of a sudden.

Facehopper looked the three of us over. "Actually, probably best if you don't ask him, mates. I'll give you a hint, it's not because of the tattoo."

"Wooyah," I said.

Skullcracker lowered his eyes and turned his swivel chair away from us, signaling that this meeting was done.

When we left the room, Facehopper turned to me. "One thing. Don't say *wooyah* anymore, okay, mate? No one says *wooyah* anymore, and doing so will just further hammer your caterpillar status into everyone's head, and may instigate a hazing on the spot. Also, we don't call those spacebags anymore either." He nodded at my spacebag. "They're just plain ol' rucksacks now, like they should be. Got it?"

"Yes sir. But I didn't say anything about the space . . . er, rucksacks."

"Exactly."

Facehopper brought us down the hall to another spartan berth. A vertical pile of metallic spheres (inactive drones, I believed) rested in one corner, while two men were seated at a desk between perfectly made beds. Both wore mirrored sunglasses, hiding their eyes. They manipulated invisible objects with their hands.

The first MOTH was olive-skinned (Italian, I thought) and wore a tight V-neck T-shirt; the sleeves barely constrained his bulging biceps, and his low V collar showcased the deep grooves in his pecs. His entire left arm was tattooed with what looked like the rivets and servomotors of an ATLAS mech. His right arm was inked with renditions of other military robots including the Centurion, Raptor, and Equestrian. The tattoo of an Atlas moth decorated his neck, the dark ink of its wings reaching down his chest.

The second MOTH was a black man with several gold chains around his neck and big hoops hanging from each ear. He had gold piercings on the outer tip of each eyebrow, a gold labret stud beneath his lips, and several gold rings on each finger. He was even more muscled than the first guy.

As soon as we entered, a miniature Rottweiler I hadn't noticed started barking softly on the table. Obviously a robot, judging from the size of the thing.

Both men froze and looked up.

"TJ and Bender are our drone operators," Facehopper said. "TJ is the one who looks like the tattooed son of a fashion model and a football player. Bender is the muscular dude who looks like a rapper. And though they may not seem it, they're also leaders in the AI field. They've helped improve the combat algorithms used by the T-2 Praetors, for example. Probably were working on their latest neural designs when we came in." Facehopper picked up the miniature dog from the table. It started growling at him. "Did I mention they're in love with their machines? But I have to give them some credit—given the choice between five women and five drones, they'd take the women every time. Though I wonder sometimes, given the five drones they have stacked up in the corner."

Neither TJ nor Bender said a word. They didn't offer to shake our hands. They just sat behind their sunglasses, scowling.

"I like your tattoos," Alejandro tried.

TJ's scowl deepened.

"As I said, love their machines." Facehopper leaned into me and added, "Don't worry, they'll warm to you once you've seen some action. They just don't like caterpillars, is all."

I shook my head. "I wish you wouldn't call us that."

He gave me a brotherly squeeze on the shoulder. "Don't take it personally. Until you've proven yourself, all you really are is a CWC. So get used to it."

"CWC?"

"Caterpillar Without a Callsign."

"I ain't ever warming to these dudes," Bender said suddenly, revealing a flash of gold teeth. "Look like they're from the Army. And you know I hate Army."

"They're not Army, Bender," Facehopper said, soothingly. "I guarantee you."

"Then why are they looking at me like that? Like they think they know something I don't? Looking at me like *Army*."

"Stop looking at him like that," Facehopper said to me.

"Like what?" I had no idea what he was talking about.

Bender pursed his lips, and tutted. "Giving lip already. Look at that. Can we haze them, sir?"

Facehopper actually laughed. "All in good time, Bender."

"Dammit. Why'd you bring them in here then? Just to bother us?"

Facehopper sighed. "I figured I'd introduce you guys, you know, so that when you passed them in the hall you'd know they weren't Army?"

Bender shrugged. "Not going to stop us from hazing them."

Facehopper glanced at me, and smiled. "No it's not. TJ and Bender do love a good hazing. They got it pretty good themselves when they first joined up."

"Damn right we did," Bender said, shaking his head enthusiastically. "And I swore when my turn came, I was going to give as bad as I got. Baby, was I gonna get my hazing done. I was gonna make those caterpillars sorry they ever joined the military. Sorry they decided to pick the Teams. Sorry they were ever born!" He was standing now, and repeatedly jabbing his finger in the air, toward me.

"All right, Bender," Facehopper extended his arms around us in a protective gesture, and backed us out of the room. "We'll see you at PT."

Next we were introduced to Manic, Bomb, and Lui, our resident ATLAS operators. These were the guys I wanted to be hanging out with, in and off the field.

"Yo, what's happening?" Bomb said. Instead of a handshake, he gave me a fist bump. He was black, like Bender, but didn't wear a single item of jewelry. He had his head shaved on both flanks, and down the top of his head he'd dyed the remaining hair blond.

Lui was an Asian American with an easy smile that belied the dangerous MOTH glint in his eye. He moved like a dancer, and I knew right away he was an expert ATLAS pilot. "Nice to meet you." Very mild mannered too.

Manic was lanky, and, like Skullcracker, lacked the usual muscular definition I'd come to associate with MOTHs. Too much time spent in the ATLAS mechs, maybe. The most distinguishing feature on his face was a small port-wine stain above his eye, vaguely reminiscent of a moth (the insect). "So you guys are the new caterpillars, eh?"

I answered. "We are."

"Got your first hazing yet?"

Alejandro threw up his hands. "Hazing hazing hazing, that's all anyone ever talks about! *Caramba*. I wish you'd just haze us and get it over with!"

"Where's the fun in that?" Manic said. "It's all about the buildup. When you least expect it, you know?" Manic cracked an abrupt smile. "Just kidding. I love psyching out the newbies. So what's your name again?" He was looking right at me.

"Rade."

"Oh yeah. Rade." Manic nodded. "Rade's an interesting name. Galaal, I see. Ah, you immigrated. Illegally."

"Come on, Manic, you know it's rude to read someone's personnel file when they're in the same room as you," Facehopper said. "Better to do it in private." He winked at me.

That was one feature of these military aReals we had in our heads. You could go beyond the public profile associated with a given embedded ID and get someone's full governmental record, assuming you had the necessary rank and security classification. I pulled up the list of IDs in the room, and focused on the one associated with Manic. His public record appeared before my eyes. I delved deeper.

Entered MOTH training at age 17.

Mediocre PT scores.

Mediocre swim scores.

Mediocre spacewalking scores.

Outstanding ATLAS scores.

I compared his ATLAS aptitude scores with mine, and I edged him out, but just barely. Out of curiosity I checked Lui's and Bomb's. Again, my scores were slightly higher.

"Uh uh ah," Manic said. "I've set up a trigger, so I know when someone accesses my full record. You see this?" He tapped the moth-shaped port-wine stain on his temple. "That's right, I'm a MOTH. Knew I'd be one since I was a kid. You can't pull a fast one on me." He leaned forward with a sour look on his face, and I thought he was going to stand up and hit me.

Then he was all smiles again. "But I actually don't mind. I scope out the full record of every caterpillar who comes my way, to see how they measure up and all, so feel free to scope me right back. Though I prefer when chicks scope me out, if you catch my drift. Speaking of chicks, you coming out for beers later? We know this place, got the best hops in town. And chicks too. You're going to love it. Oh, unless you have a squeeze already? Well if you do, bring her. We don't mind. We love girls. Especially strippers. We wouldn't touch your girl if you brought her along of course. Well, unless she was hot. But even then we'd ask for permission first. From her. And what about you guys?" He spun toward Alejandro and Tahoe. "You got some chicks to bring? If you don't, I'll introduce you to some tonight. I'm big at opening chicks. I'm the one who gets half the guys laid around here. Did you know most of the guys on the platoon are really shy? Why, I once—"

"All right, mate," Facehopper rested a hand on his shoulder. "I want to introduce the caterpillars to the rest of the platoon sometime this year." He turned toward me. "I guess you can see why his callsign is *Manic*. His frenetic energy translates really well on the battlefield, though."

Next up were Snakeoil and Fret.

"Meet our commos. These guys carry rucksacks full of communications equipment into battle. This in addition to the usual weapon and ammunition loadout. Each pack contains the equivalent of an InterPlaNet node, so we'll always be in touch with HQ no matter if we're in the heart of the jungle or the farthest reaches of space. Fret's the tall guy who looks like a giraffe."

I reached up to shake his hand. Fret towered over me, at six feet five inches. His forearms weren't big, but they were definitely corded.

"Snakeoil's the shorter guy," Facehopper said. "Kind of looks like a cross between a midget and a bear."

Snakeoil shook my hand. Though his arms were the biggest I'd seen on a MOTH so far, his grip was also the gentlest. "Hey," Snakeoil said.

I noticed a small puckered scar beneath his right cheek.

"Snakeoil took a bullet in the face on his first deployment. Came out just under his ear. He got up again and kept right on fighting. He ended up commandeering an ATLAS mech, and fought off an entire company of insurgents to save the rest of us. Most heroic thing I've ever seen. He's not wearing it now, but he was awarded the Navy Cross for combat heroism by the Commander-in-Chief."

Snakeoil seemed embarrassed. "Shucks. Only doing my job. Y'all would have done the same thing for me any day of the week. Definitely not something worth a medal. All I can say is I'm proud to have you as my commanding officer, Facehopper."

The leading petty officer nodded. "Not as proud as I and the Teams are to have you."

In the next berth, we met Trace and Ghost. "These guys are our snipers. Ghost is the one who looks like a pale demon, and Trace is the mean-looking East Indian. Trace can take out a target at five klicks with ninety percent accuracy. What do you think of that?"

I nodded my head. "Impressive."

"You may or may not remember him from training. He often helps out with the Combat Resiliency Qualification."

"I do," I said. "He was the one who shot me."

Trace broke into a grin. "I shoot only the best."

His movements were as calm and self-assured as ever. Facehopper had said he was East Indian, and I believed it from his darker complexion. I checked his profile and saw that he hailed from Bengal.

Trace pursed his lips. "You got fifty percent accuracy at a range of five klicks in training?" he said, obviously viewing my own profile. "That's nothing to scoff at. I bet you're going to be platoon sniper for your first few deployments."

"Thank you, sir." Though I really wanted to be an ATLAS pilot.

"Ghost here, in addition to sniping, is our Interrogator. I'm sure you can guess why."

Ghost bowed his head and touched the tip of his navy cap in greeting. He was a tall, warrior albino, and with his white hair, red eyes, and pale face, he reminded me of an elf from some fantasy or science fiction novel. An evil elf at that. I definitely wouldn't want to be interrogated by him.

Facehopper led us on, and when we entered an office area, I knew we'd moved on to the upper echelon of the platoon. I felt a surge of trepidation, as I always did when I met the people who were ultimately responsible for the direction my life took.

We entered one of the smaller offices. The UC flag hung limply in the background. On the far bulkhead, between several framed certificates and degrees, was the portrait of a sailor from old times, dressed in a bright-blue uniform and white navy cap. An empty bottle of whiskey sat on the desk. There was a starship model inside the bottle, dreadnought class. Beside the bottle were three figurines. The first figurine was obviously old, judging from the faded paint, and it depicted a sailor with ridiculously huge forearms crushing a can labeled "spinach." The second figurine was of a panting dog in an orange life vest. The last figurine depicted a realistic-looking MOTH, complete with jumpsuit, jetpack, and combat rifle.

Behind the desk sat a grizzled man, his dark, tilted eyes seeming to judge my every movement. The skin of his face was weatherworn, and he had a hooked beak of a nose above his thick, gray-specked mustache.

"This is Chief Bourbonjack," Facehopper said. "Our fearless leader. Got more body parts shot off than anyone I've ever met, and he's been awarded more medals than most admirals. He should be a Navy Captain by now, but the Chief has forever refused advancement. Didn't want to go back to school, I guess. Or just likes to fight."

The serious expression left the Chief's face, and he broke into a grin. "Right on both accounts!" Chief Bourbonjack got up and gave me a combination handshake and one-armed hug. "Greetings!" He shook my palm warmly. A good, solid grip. The hand felt almost real, but the texture was slightly off, a little like corrugated cardboard. The Chief must've seen the expression on my face, because he shrugged. "That's right. 3D bio-printed! Weren't you listening? I've had more body parts shot off than most admirals. I'm almost an Artificial. Ha!"

"If they could build an Artificial with the character of this man, we'd be out of a job," Facehopper said.

"Well thank you, Leading Brown-nose Officer!" He gave Facehopper a mocking nod. "Anyway, glad to have you boys joining Alfa. The detailer sent your profiles a few weeks ago and I just knew we had to keep you three together. When I find a group of men that work well with each other, I don't see the point in separating them. Makes them less effective, in my experience."

"Thank you, sir," I said.

Chief Bourbonjack's gaze snapped to my face. "So you're the spokesman?"

"Uh, I guess so, sir."

"Good. Every group has a spokesman. Lets me know who I should talk to when I need something, and who I should chew out when that something doesn't get done. I'm not sure if Facehopper here has gone over any of the rules, but all I care about is that you do your time, *on time*. While not on deployment, you'll be expected to show up at 0600 each morning, and stay until 1800 at night. Most of us go home at the end of the day. The three of you have no dependents living in the country, so it's up to you if you want to live in the barracks or not. If you live off base, you'll collect BAH." Basic Allowance for Housing. "You'll still have a barracks berth of course, but you just won't stay overnight. Anyway, Facehopper here is hopping on his toes, so I can see he's eager to introduce you to the Lieutenant Commander."

"Among other things," Facehopper said.

"All right then, get on with it." The Chief folded his hands on his chest. "I'm sure I'll be seeing you boys real soon!"

Facehopper led the three of us into an adjacent office. "And finally, I present to you Lieutenant Commander Braggs, the officer responsible for Alfa and Bravo Platoons."

The Lieutenant Commander reminded me of a younger version of Chief Bourbonjack. He was about fifteen years older than me, but there wasn't an inkling of gray in his brown hair. His face was all hard planes, and though he wore a long-sleeved service jacket, I could tell from the way he moved that he still had the body of an athlete despite his rank.

The Lieutenant Commander stood up and towered over all of us. He was just as tall as Fret. He reached over the desk and shook my hand. His grip was in the medium range of the MOTHs I'd met so far today, not overly hard, but just enough to give the bones of my fingers a good grinding.

When he had shaken each of our hands, he sat back down. "Have a seat."

We sat down in the three empty chairs that were conveniently arrayed in front of the desk.

The Commander's office was positively spartan compared to Chief Bourbonjack's. Other than the UC flag situated near the far bulkhead, all the Lieutenant Commander had on his desk was a portrait, facing outward, presumably of his wife and son. People who spent a lot of time in their Implants didn't really have much use for material objects, I supposed. Or maybe he just didn't use his office very much.

"Mr. Galaal, Mr. Eaglehide, Mr. Mondego. The Teams are an elite unit, the best the Navy or even the entire military has to offer. Sure, other branches have ATLAS mechs and support robots and all the other wonderful assets that go along with a platoon of course, but their training doesn't hold a stick to our own. Which is why my expectations for you three run so very high. However, don't let those expectations interfere with your duty. I'm all for a little friendly competition, but remember, we're brothers here. Most of us have been through hell and back together. The life of your brothers comes first, above everything else, except maybe the mission objective. We'd all fall on a grenade to save the man beside us. Heck, *I'd* fall on a grenade. That sense of brotherhood makes us who we are.

"We've got an almost insanely competitive drive within us, a drive tempered with the care we feel for our brothers, a drive honed by the endless hours of training. We've taken that drive, and used it to forge ourselves into some of the most ferocious, unstoppable fighters in the galaxy. Most of us have, anyway. Whether or not you display that drive remains to be seen."

He glanced at Facehopper. “Could you grab the utility tape, LPO? And tell the Chief to bring in some of that excellent bourbon of his.”

“Now, sir?”

“Well, why not? I figured I might as well get my turn in while I have some time.”

“Yes sir.” Facehopper left.

Smiling widely, Chief Bourbonjack came in and set down three shot glasses on the desk. He filled them with bourbon.

“Drink up, boys,” the Chief said. “This here is the best whiskey Bourbon County has to offer.”

“What about you guys?” I said, feeling a tad guilty. Not to mention suspicious.

“Ha!” Chief Bourbonjack said. “We’re on duty!”

“But aren’t we—”

“Drink!” The Chief got in my face. “Before I ram the drink, shot glass and all, down your freakin’ throat!”

All three of us took the shots.

“What’s this?” the Chief said to Tahoe. “You’re sipping your shot? *Sipping*?”

Tahoe quickly downed the rest of his glass.

I had this queasy feeling in my stomach, and not just from the liquor. It felt like I’d dropped back in time and was in First Phase all over again.

The Chief refilled our glasses. “Again.”

We ended up having six rounds each, and by then I was really plastered. Never could hold my liquor.

Facehopper finally came back and proceeded to tape the three of us to the chairs.

“What’s going on, sir?” I said, my voice slurring.

But I knew.

We were being hazed.

Facehopper unbuttoned my shirt.

"Did you bring ice?" Lieutenant Commander Braggs said.

"Roger that," Facehopper said, grinning. He handed the bucket to the Lieutenant Commander.

"Uh, I thought you said you'd fall on a grenade for us, sir?" I said.

"And I would." Lieutenant Commander Braggs smirked. "But this isn't a grenade." He shoved a handful of ice down my pants.

I started shivering right away. Damn, it was cold. I had flashbacks to sea immersion.

"You're not some kind of substandard graduate, are you, Mr. Galaal?" Lieutenant Commander Braggs said.

"No sir!"

"Well, good. You can never tell these days, what with the duds they've been sending us."

He stuffed ice down Alejandro's and Tahoe's pants next.

"Welcome to the brotherhood," the Lieutenant Commander said. He, Chief Bourbonjack, and Facehopper grabbed felt markers and proceeded to draw graffiti of a highly sexual nature across our faces and chests.

CHAPTER THIRTEEN

"Go go go!" Facehopper shouted over the comm line.

In my rifle's scope, I kept an eye on the building Facehopper was leading his fire team into. I was on overwatch position on the third floor of an apartment across the street. I lay by the window, on an overturned nightstand. I'd put a bedroll from an adjacent room on top, making the setup semicomfortable.

Outside, the buildings were made of either stucco or bricks. Two to four stories tall, the rows of boxlike, squat houses were broken only by the occasional colorful monastery or school. Two- or three-story apartment buildings stood at every street corner. A towering statue of Buddha covered in a green patina dominated the center of town; the statue had one palm upraised as if it were trying to stop the war that swept the country.

I heard gunshots on the comm, then "clear!" I kept scanning the two different exits from the building. No targets came out.

I moved on to the next house in my range, and watched a Marine fire team sweep the building. Still no targets. I moved on to the next house. A division of Centurion robots dressed in Army camos emerged. I saw a basketball-shaped drone hover down from an open upper-floor window—an HS3 (Hover Squad Support System) drone. We'd been using the things to help us map out the city, and to sweep through buildings we'd already cleared. Unfortunately, the insurgents had been shooting them down constantly. Either this was one lucky HS3, or we'd received a fresh supply of the things. Anyway, still no targets for me.

Too big for the buildings, a couple of ATLAS mechs roved unopposed between houses. The fanatics had figured out a while ago that four or five rockets launched from behind were the best attack against the mechs, so our platoons often used the ATLAS 5s as bait to draw out the rocketmen for our snipers. It wasn't a tactic that was approved of by the Brass, and if the Lieutenant Commander had known we were using the multibillion digicoin mechs as bait, he would've probably shat his pants. Nevertheless, the ATLAS boys sure seemed to be having fun down there.

A gunship strafed a smoking target in the distance. Far above, a Raptor circled unchallenged, ready to provide heavy air support. Both aircraft sent a clear message to would-be attackers: We rule your skies.

My platoon was working with the Marines in the contested zone in Khentii Province, Mongolia. The Russians, our allies, were trying to take back New Baganuur City. Most of the fanatics who had taken over the city weren't even Mongolian. Sure, there were the small groups of Mongolian guerrillas who didn't want to return to Russian rule, but for the most part the fighters were foreigners. Basically anyone who wanted to kill Russians or members of the UC had come to this city. You had your Chechen rebels, your mujahadeen, your kashmiri separatists. And while Sino-Korea wasn't directly involved, there were a fair share of Sino-Korean fighters who'd joined in, just because. Ex-military, judging from the armaments and equipment they'd brought along with them.

Why the big deal with Mongolia? This small country that sat smack-dab between Russia and China was home to thirty percent of the world's Geronium-275, precursor to Geronium. Starship fuel.

You'd think with all the colonies we had out there on other planets that this wouldn't matter.

It did.

So far, in all the systems and planets we'd gone to, no other form of Geronium or its isotopes had been discovered, save for the deposits detected beneath the metallic hydrogen core of a gas giant in Gliese 581—of which there was no economical means of harvesting.

So Mongolia was just a little important to us.

Alejandro turned over, stifling a yawn. He was taking a rest on the floor beside me, while Tahoe was guarding our backs with his heavy gun. Like everyone else on this deployment, we were wearing trimmed-down, planet-side jumpsuits, with ordinary helmets. No face masks, but we still had SCBAs we could don in case the enemy decided to launch chemical weapons.

The suit exoskeletons were still strength enhancing and had jetpacks of course, and provided protection against shrapnel and lesser bullets. Didn't really help all that much when half of your opponents used thermobaric grenades and armor-piercing rounds, though.

I waited a few more minutes, passing my scope from house to house, until finally the frustration of having no targets got to me.

I turned to Alejandro. "Well, it's been about three hours. Your turn, big boy."

Alejandro rubbed his eyes. "How many did you get?" he said.

"Nada. Haven't seen an engageable target the entire watch."

"Mmm." Alejandro took my place, and relaxed into a sniping position on the bedroll, eye on his scope.

I lay back on the floor and closed my eyes. After about ten seconds I heard him fire.

"I hate your guts," I said.

Irritated, I scratched my beard with my free hand. It was getting pretty itchy. Everyone on the team had a thick beard by now. Only spec-op soldiers were allowed facial hair, mostly because we were the ones given the hardest operations, the ones where you had to sit motionless in the field for days at a time and where it was physically impossible to shave, or the missions where shaving would give away the fact you weren't a native. Anyway, the guys considered beards a badge of honor. We grew them mostly because we could.

Alejandro and I had pretty fancy beards by that time, but Tahoe unfortunately was incapable of growing anything more than a thin mustache and a soul patch beneath his lower lip. Anyway, we made fun of his lack of beard quite often.

Speaking of which . . .

"Hey, Tahoe," I said, sitting up. "I've been thinking about your beard. Or rather, lack thereof. Maybe I should snip off a piece of mine for you? What do you think? With some glue and a little creativity we could get you a decent facial rug. You'd look very manly."

Tahoe didn't say a word, not looking back from his defensive position by the doorway. I should probably leave him alone, let him do his job. I laid back and closed my eyes.

"You know, I'm kind of glad this deployment is on Earth," Tahoe said suddenly.

I glanced at him. His back was still to me, his eyes on the hallway, his rifle pointed out the doorway. Good.

Alejandro fired off another shot.

"Lucky *puto*," I told Alejandro.

"What was that, Tahoe?" Alejandro said. "I couldn't hear over Rade's whining."

"I said I'm glad we're still on Earth."

"Why, *hombre*?" Alejandro sounded tense, as he usually did when he was concentrating on finding something to kill. "I thought a big reason you crossed the border and joined up was for the chance to go into space? Mr. Astrophysicist and all . . ."

"That was part of why I joined up, yes," Tahoe said. "But you know what? Being a father changes everything. I don't want to be away from my wife and kids for more than eight months at a time. If we go into space, it could be up to two years. Or longer. It's just not worth it anymore, for me."

"You know it's inevitable that we're going into space, right?" I said. "This is just the beginning. This is our training ground. You better get used to the idea, Tahoe. You're going to be away from your wife and kids for long stretches of time."

He didn't answer.

"Straight up, I'm not looking forward to space deployments all that much either," Alejandro said. "I kind of like my planet."

Alejandro let off another shot.

"Damn you," I said. "I think I want to go on overwatch again."

"No way, José."

"That's already, what, two? And you only just started."

"Three," Alejandro said. "I don't know what the big deal is anyway. See those ATLAS mechs down there? I'd rather be piloting those."

"At least you're getting kills," I said.

He wasn't the only one who wanted to pilot an ATLAS. Most of the platoon did, but there just weren't enough mechs to go around. At first I had thought it a little unfair. My ATLAS aptitude scores were the highest on the team. But I had to give our designated pilots Manic, Lui, and Bomb some credit: they had actual field experience. Eventually I decided to accept whatever role the Chief gave me. If he wanted me to be a sniper, I was going to be a sniper. If he wanted me to be a corpsman, I was going to be a corpsman. And not just any sniper or corpsman, but the best this team had ever seen. Which is why it pissed me off so much that Alejandro was getting all the kills.

Again I heard him fire.

"Bitch," I muttered.

"Hey," Alejandro said, not looking from his scope. "Not my fault if the bad guys decide to show themselves on my watch."

"Maybe they just find Alejandro more attractive than you, Rade," Tahoe said from his position by the door.

"What?" I said. "With his ugly face? Right."

"You never know," Tahoe said. "The insurgents might have a thing for ugly. You've heard of the similarity theory of personal attraction? You know, ugly attracts ugly?"

"Now you're talking."

"Well, if that were true," Alejandro said. "Then Tahoe would be getting all the baddies. Because he is one ugleee bastard."

"Hey, I'm married," Tahoe said.

"So?" Alejandro pressed. "What does that have to do with anything? You think *mamacitas* marry only handsome dudes?"

"In my case, yes. Besides, I'm an artist in bed."

Alejandro chuckled. "That's fine, mighty fine. But it's not going to help you in the end. You do know that the divorce rate for MOTHs is ninety percent, right? Artist in bed." He shook his head. "That only makes it worse when you're away. She gets used to that constant pleasuring, and comes to *expect* it. What do you think your *mamacita*'s doing back home right now? When the cat's away . . ."

"Hey." Tahoe turned away from his position for the first time. "Don't you be talking about my wife like that."

Alejandro shifted beside me, but he still hadn't looked from his scope. "Relax, *hombre*. I was kidding. Of course she's keeping all alone and to herself right now, raising those kids of yours. Of course she's not giving the plumber a special bonus payment involving handcuffs and bed poles and—"

"That's it!" Tahoe locked his heavy machine gun and sloughed it off his shoulder.

I sat up. "Get back to your position, Tahoe. Get right back. Now! Do your job."

"Well tell him to quit provoking me," Tahoe said petulantly, though he did pick up his heavy gun again.

"He's just mad because I'm getting all the baddies," Alejandro said.

I made my voice as stern as possible. "Stop provoking him, Alejandro."

"Yes sir." He looked away from the scope for the first time, and glanced back at Tahoe. "Rade here thinks he's Junior Chief or something."

"Every second you take your eyes away from that scope is a second one of our guys could die," I told Alejandro. "Remember that."

He shook his head. "*Caramba.* Two seconds. I look away for two seconds." He put his eye back on the rifle site. "How long do you think Tahoe looked away from the hallway he was supposed to be watching?"

Normally the two of them were way easier to get along with, but we'd been out here for about eighteen hours straight now and we were getting on each other's nerves. That was nothing compared to the five days we stayed awake during Trial Week, of course. But still, the lack of sleep didn't have the greatest impact on our moods.

"How's it look up there, mate?" Facehopper transmitted over our fire-team frequency, in that slight British accent of his.

"Great view, great view, Facehopper," Alejandro replied. "All is well. Just took over from Rade. Got four kills so far." He just had to rub it in, didn't he?

"Well, let me know when you need to find a new hide," Facehopper sent.

"Roger that," Alejandro said. "We should be good for the next half hour or so, sir."

I shook my head. "Why does Facehopper still think he needs to babysit us? We've been on deployment for two months, you'd think we'd know our way around by now."

"I heard that, Rade," Facehopper sent.

"Oh." I felt my face flush. "Sorry, sir, I thought my comm was off."

"It was," Facehopper sent. "But your mate kept his turned on."

Alejandro winked at me.

"Anyway, as always, be sure to let me know when you switch hides," Facehopper sent.

"Affirmative," Alejandro returned. "By the way, sir, any openings for ATLAS 5 pilots coming up soon?"

"Negative," Facehopper answered.

Alejandro shrugged. "Had to ask."

Behind me, I heard a muted thud as the far door to the apartment burst open.

"Fuck." Tahoe opened fire.

"Sir sir taking fire sir sir!" I sent to Facehopper, ducking beside the doorway of our room.

Alejandro rolled from the window and took up a position on the other side of the doorway, beside Tahoe.

"Sit tight," Facehopper transmitted. "We're coming up."

I glanced at the situation map overlaid on the upper right of my vision. Seven red dots had appeared on the far side of the hallway, the last known positions of the targets Tahoe's Implant had flagged and transmitted to the rest of us. Meanwhile, on the street outside, two green dots were quickly converging on our building.

"Where did they come from?" I asked Tahoe.

"Dunno," he said from where he was crouched behind the doorway opposite me.

"Cover me," I told him.

Tahoe rammed the barrel of his heavy machine gun past the doorway and laid down suppressive fire.

I peered past the edge of the doorway. My Implant was supposed to outline the bodies of positively identified attackers in red, but I saw only one outline at that moment. Actually, only part of an outline—the target was ducked inside one of the side rooms, leaning against the doorway, waiting for the suppressive fire to stop.

I only had a thin sliver of a man to aim at, but I did, and shot. The red outline darkened as the target toppled, as did the dot on the map. Speaking of which, the other red dots blinked out because I couldn't see any of the other targets and my Implant had decided to make an update.

My target's weapon flopped out the doorway, and when I saw the make and model I realized we were in serious trouble.

I immediately ducked back behind cover.

"Only got one?" Tahoe said, pulling back as well.

"One." I agreed. "They got armor piercers."

"Shit."

We dropped to the floor as gunshots echoed from the hall. Pieces of plaster and dust rained down on us as holes appeared in the wall above.

"Facehopper, now would be a good time," I sent on my comm.

"Bender and Big Dog are almost there," Facehopper sent back.

I glanced at the friendlies on the HUD. Two greens were right on our position.

"I don't see . . ."

Big Dog came leaping through the window, courtesy of his jumpjets. Shooting the whole while, he unleashed a hail of machine-gun fire down the hall.

Bender appeared right on his heels, a Carl Gustav on his shoulder.

On cue, Big Dog stopped firing and dropped.

"Wait," I said. "Don't fire that in—"

Bender launched the rocket from the recoilless rifle.

The explosion from the hallway sent me flying across the room and I rammed against the far wall.

I lay there on the floor, coughing up plaster dust, my hearing filled with a high-pitched keening sourced by my own eardrum.

The four other members of the platoon were piled against the wall beside me. Well, except for Big Dog, who still lay where he had dropped on the floor.

Bender crawled to his feet, caked in gray dust. "Yeah baby!

Yeah!" I couldn't see his gold chains because of the jumpsuit, but that didn't mean he wasn't wearing them. He still had those loop earrings on after all, swinging away. "Threat neutralized," he said, flashing his gold teeth in a grin. Those teeth seemed exceptionally bright with the rest of his face covered in dust like that.

Big Dog and Tahoe went into the hall to confirm that the threat was indeed neutralized.

We waited a few tense moments.

"Clear," Big Dog said.

Alejandro sighed heavily, and slumped against the wall. "You crazy, man?" he told Bender. "You could have killed us."

"Not a chance," Bender said. "Come on, live a little, dudes."

Big Dog returned from the hall. "Blew half the apartment clean away."

"That's what I'm talking about!" Bender high-fived him.

I glanced past Big Dog. The middle of the hallway ended in a precarious ledge that dangled off into empty space. The whole back side of the two-story building was just gone.

"He's crazy," Alejandro said. "*Loco*."

"We're all a bit crazy," Bender said. "Why do you think we're here?"

"Suck it up," Big Dog patted Alejandro on the shoulder.

Tahoe shook his head. "Now I know why they call him Bender."

We got only that proud, golden smile in return.

"By the way, you might want to find a new hide," Bender said. He gave us a mock salute, then leaped out the window.

"None of you were ever in any danger," Big Dog said. "The guy's got custom line-of-sight software installed in his Implant. Lets him calculate the explosive radius of his rockets down to the micrometer. What I'm saying is, we got your back. You just have to trust us, like how we're trusting you by giving you overwatch. So don't call him *loco*. Especially not after he saved your life. Now come on. Let's go find you a new hide."

Big Dog jumped out the window. I glanced at Alejandro, shrugged, and followed.

When the platoon finally got back to the makeshift camp later that night, I made a beeline for the sack. I was pretty much a zombie by then, but managed to place an empty bottle beside my bed to use as a chamber pot—I did *not* want to have to get up in the middle of the night just to relieve myself.

Wake up call came a measly six hours later, and we did our own physical training on the floor beside our racks before hurrying off to breakfast (organized PT wasn't allowed—if you ran around outside doing PT you were liable to get shot by an enemy sniper).

Most of us kept to ourselves at breakfast, since we were still exhausted from the day before, and maybe a little sick of talking to the same people we'd be hanging out with for the rest of the day. So we buried ourselves in our Implants, reading, playing games, or calling friends and family while we ate.

Myself, I used the time to make a quick call to Shaw. She was graduating this week. It had been two years since I'd last met with her in person, back when I watched her depart in the vactrain after Basic. We just hadn't been able to arrange our hectic schedules. Twice when she was on leave, I just so happened to be on the moon for training. One time when I had a week off after finishing Advanced ATLAS Warfare school, she sent me a note explaining that she was on liberty, and would be visiting family. We agreed to meet. I bought a train ticket to visit her, but before I boarded she sent me another note telling me that she was really sorry but her liberty ended early. To this day I'm not sure if she really had been recalled, or just got cold feet and canceled.

That one night we'd shared together after Basic was a distant memory by now, and it may as well have never happened. I'd been with other girls since then of course but no one really compared to her. I wished things could have worked out differently, but I knew we'd never be together, not while the two of us were both on active duty. Even though we worked for the same branch of the military, our different ratings ensured we'd very likely never see each other again in person, not until our terms were up.

Unfortunately, I couldn't forget her.

"How's my favorite astronaut?" I said to the image floating in front of my eyes that morning. I was trying very hard to keep the regret out of my voice. She looked beautiful as always. She'd grown her hair out after that fiasco in Basic, and it was her dark, natural color. I liked it.

"Hey," Shaw said. She seemed a bit distant, which wasn't unusual. "How's the war going?"

"Not bad. But tell me, are you looking forward to graduating next week?"

"You remembered." She smiled. I really dug that smile, because her eyes always crinkled up, and her face just glowed with life. Plus she had those cute dimples. Abruptly she got this mischievous look about her, like she was up to something. "And, you'll be happy to know, this astronaut already has her first assignment!"

"Oh yeah? Do tell."

"It's all hush-hush, you understand. But I can tell you that I'm going to be the *lead astrogator on a starship*!"

I must have had the biggest smile in the world right then. "Shut up! Congratulations are in order! I'm so proud of you. I mean come on, lead astrogator for your first assignment? That's pretty sick."

"I know, right?" She bit her lower lip, and rocked her shoulders from side to side, almost like she was dancing. "I'm so excited."

"Yeah, I bet. You must have had some amazing qualification scores." Or maybe just slept with the right people. No. She wasn't like that.

"Yup. So." She was twirling her hair coyly with one finger. "Do you have any leave time coming up?"

I shook my head emphatically. "No. We're only seven weeks into the deployment. Got another six months to go. Course I don't have any leave. Nor do I want any. To be pulled out of action, *now*? This is why I immigrated to the UC in the first place. To make my mark. To fight." Maybe I was being a bit harsh with her, but hey, this was how I felt about it. I crossed my arms. "Why would you even bring up leave time? You've avoided meeting me for the past two years. Why pretend you want to meet me now all of a sudden, when you know I can't? Trying to lead me on for all I'm worth?"

She seemed taken aback by my outburst. Good. "Rade, I haven't avoided you. It's just that, well, our schedules haven't meshed. You're completely misinterpreting—"

"I'm misinterpreting?" I said in disbelief. "Okay. Tell me something. If I said I had leave time, right now, at this moment, would you want to meet?"

"Of course."

"Would you really? Are you sure you wouldn't just cancel, like last time?"

She frowned, and finally sighed. "You're right. I'd probably cancel."

"There you go. Doesn't surprise me in the least. Look, I'm going to ask you something serious, and I want an ultra-serious answer. Do you even want to keep in touch anymore?"

Her frown deepened. "Why would you ask me something like that? Of course I do. We're friends."

I nodded slowly. "Friends. Yeah." Though I wanted more. So much more. But that's life, always wanting something you couldn't have.

An uncomfortable silence followed.

"So how are Tahoe and Alejandro?" she said finally, pretending that everything was just fine and dandy between us.

I rubbed my chin, glad for a change of subject. "Oh, you know, holding out. Alejandro's been keeping in touch with a stripper he met, and Tahoe—"

"Wait, what? A stripper?"

"Yeah. He met her back in California, at a strip club called Gaslamp."

"Ah, that's what you meant. I thought you were saying he'd met some Mongolian stripper or something!"

I had to laugh. "No, she's definitely not Mongolian. Though some of the chicks are pretty hot here, I have to say. A few of them wear these really interesting dresses . . ."

"Yeah, I've heard about those traditional 'dresses' of yours. They wouldn't be so bad if they weren't see-through!"

"Hey, who are we to judge the dress code of another society? Just because our own culture is full of prudes doesn't mean we have to look down upon an enlightened nation. I'm all for white, see-through dresses worn without underwear. I think women the world over should adopt the fashion."

"You would." She rubbed her eyes, and laughed quietly. It felt almost like old times. "So. Alejandro's dating a stripper. Is she real at least?"

"Yeah. Not a robot, if that's what you mean."

"I seem to remember he had a certain . . . predilection . . . for pleasure robots."

I chuckled. "Yeah, but he got over that."

"Good for him. So what about Tahoe? How is he doing?"

"He's good, but misses his wife and kids like crazy. I'm sure he's vid-chatting with her right now. Did I tell you the Chief finally cut through all the bureaucratic crap to get Tahoe's family moved up to California?"

"No you didn't. And that's great." She glanced over her shoulder and nodded to someone behind her. I couldn't see who it was because only her face, neck, and shoulders were illuminated, and everything else was dark. "Rade, I gotta go. Time to rack out."

"Oh yeah. I'm always forgetting the time-zone difference."

"G'night, Rade."

"Shaw, wait."

"*What*?" The irritation in her voice caught me off guard, and kind of stung, especially since I was about to tell her something important, or so I thought.

"Well, I wanted to—" I hesitated. I should've probably let her go right then. Telling her how I felt about her would only mess things up between us. Not that things weren't messed up as it was. "It's just, you mean a lot to me, Shaw."

She smiled. "That's sweet, Rade. Now I'm sorry, but I really have to go."

"No. I mean it. Remember when you told me to think about you in the deepest, darkest hours, when I thought I couldn't go on? Well I did, Shaw. I did. Thinking about you has gotten me through some very dark places."

She was quiet for a few seconds. And then:

"Look, Rade, you and I . . . it was just a dream. That one night we had, it didn't happen. Not really. And as for that corny line about the deepest, darkest hours? I probably got it from some science fiction novel I was into at the time. Don't read too much into it. I care about you, I do, but we've grown apart. You know it. I know it. Even if we could arrange some time together, it would only be for a few nights, and then we'd have to be apart again. I can't live like that. Long-distant relationships, they just don't work for me. I tried that already with my fiancé, and you know what happened there. I'm sorry."

"So am I."

"I have to go," Shaw said. "Something else. I won't be in touch for a while. This new starship I'm assigned to? Well there's kind of a mandatory communications blackout, so I'm going to be incommunicado for the next few months. I'm not sure when I'll be able to check my messages, let alone answer them. Definitely no vid chats."

I just stared at her, not sure if she was telling the truth or just making up some excuse to avoid future uncomfortable vid chats with me.

"Rade, did you hear what I said?"

"Yeah, I heard. That's fine, Shaw. Completely fine. Have fun on your deployment. Bye."

I disconnected.

Ten days later, the Brass pulled Alfa and Bravo Platoons out of Mongolia a good six months before the deployment was due to end.

That left a lot of hard feelings and pissed-off platoon members, let me tell you.

The Chief assembled us, and calmed us as only he could.

"You're big boys now, aren't ya?" Chief Bourbonjack said. "Settle down. You know Brass wouldn't have pulled you without a good reason. Look, I'll deal it to you straight up. You're going from one deployment smack-dab into another. And your new mission is far more important."

He combed down the tips of his mustache with his index fingers, like he did when he was about to say something he considered momentous.

"The Teams go where they are needed," Chief Bourbonjack said. "And we are needed in space."

CHAPTER FOURTEEN

We were assigned to the battlecruiser *Leaping Matilda* and launched into orbit the next day. The Chief didn't tell us anything else, other than that the mission was Special Reconnaissance on one of the colonies. He promised that the Lieutenant Commander would explain more before we made the jump through Sol Gate I.

The shuttle trip to the cruiser was uneventful, if not reflective. I sat by the window the whole time. Shuttling back and forth between the Earth and moon had become almost routine in training, so I was used to the sights. Still, I gave the Earth a good, long look through the tri-paned portal along the way, because this was the last time I'd be seeing my favorite blue planet for a while. Far below me I could see one of the agro ships that produced most of the planet's food, the dome-shaped glass surface perpetually bombarded by sunlight.

The shuttle reached medium Earth orbit and approached Space Station Nine. There were a lot of military ships up here, queuing for a refueling spot or simply waiting for their crews. Most of the ships were little more than dots in the distance, but the shuttle did pass near a hulking battleship. Its midship had large superstructures containing numerous LIDARs and electronic warfare antennae and sensors, while the forward portion was reserved for the heavy-caliber gun turrets and swivel-mounted torpedo tubes.

Not a ship to be messed with.

When the hangar doors opened, I realized this battleship was the *Leaping Matilda.*

Our ride. Nice.

I glanced one last time at my receding homeworld.

Ah, Earth. I don't know when I'll see you again. I'll miss you, that's for sure. Despite your faults. And your wars.

I felt like I was only just getting to know that planet of mine, and here I was leaving it.

I didn't really regret it.

I was far too excited for that.

At standard speed it would take fifty-eight absolute Standays (Standard Earth Days) to reach Sol Gate I.

We didn't get that time on liberty. The G dampeners and the artificial gravity ensured that we kept in tiptop shape: PT in the mornings, classroom and virtual reality-based training in the afternoon. The builders of the *Leaping Matilda* had been kind enough to install a virtual kill house to accommodate us commando types, so we got lots of practice against the contingent of MAs (master-at-arms) who served as part of the ship's permanent security force, not to mention a handful of Marines who were hitching a ride. There was also a room with no artificial gravity where we could practice spacewalks. They even had a couple of ATLAS simulators, which Alejandro and I used to rack up our simulation hours. Manic, Lui, and Bomb often joined in.

The *Leaping Matilda* was escorting three civilian ships to the Gate. While the UC and the SKs kept up a tenuous peace on Earth, as part of a policy of military and economic competition, the SK government gave "letters of marque" to privateers, sanctioning the takedown of UC ships for salvage purposes in certain regions of space.

This was great for the SKs, who were a smaller naval power—it gave them armed ships and crews at no cost. Not so great for the UC, because it meant we had to deploy warships to protect civilian assets.

The weeks passed, and finally, about three hours before reaching Sol Gate I, Lieutenant Commander Braggs assembled Alfa and Bravo Platoons for the promised pre-Gate briefing.

I took a seat and observed my platoon mates. They were antsy as they waited for the Lieutenant Commander to arrive, which could be expected. But mostly eager to get to work.

Tahoe sat down beside me.

"Hey," I said. "Looking forward to the jump?"

"I was made for this." Tahoe gave me the standard tough-guy-on-the-teams response, but when he palmed his chin I saw a momentary flash of grief in his eyes.

"Missing the wife and kids, huh?"

Tahoe hesitated, as if debating whether to speak his mind. "More than ever, Rade."

"I hear ya," I said. "It's hard, being separated from those you love. But you'll still be in touch, right?"

"Sure. But the lag's only going to get worse."

I tapped my lips. "You talking about the InterPlaNet lag between solar systems?"

"I am. There will be an eight- to ten-hour lag no matter which system we end up in. And that's just for text chat."

I hadn't really chatted with anyone from Earth via my Implant since we left, so I wasn't sure what the in-system lag was like. There was no lag for voice or text messages sent between people on the same ship, of course. Earlier I did try watching some Net vids, though, which were sourced out of Earth. Playback was instantaneous for the more popular vids (which were probably cached locally on the warship's servers), while the less popular vids took about ten minutes to buffer for every minute of play time.

"How's that all work again, anyway?" I said, hoping to distract him from thinking about his family, if only for a short time. Tahoe always liked talking about how things worked. "Why is the lag so bad between systems?"

"You weren't paying attention during the InterPlaNet course, were you?"

"I must have slept through that one."

Tahoe sat up a little straighter. "Each star system has an InterPlaNet, which is comprised of network nodes on bases and starships. These nodes sync with the interplanetary network every few days. When a military ship Gates from one system to the next, its onboard computer carries with it all the archived bundles of data it has received from the InterPlaNet while in that system. When it arrives in a new system, it transmits those packets, which are picked up by the interplanetary nodes in that system. The bundles slowly disperse throughout our little section of the galaxy as the starships move from solar system to solar system, syncing up their bundles. Of course, we also have Node Probes, small drones whose sole purpose is to pass in and out of Gates all day, transferring data bundles. Taken altogether, all those individual InterPlaNets form the InterGalNet. Obviously that's a simplified description, but you get the idea. Delay-tolerant networking at its finest."

"Well," I said. "Just be glad you can send a message at all. And come on, quit your complaining: At least you got someone back home to send a message *to*. I have no one."

Tahoe frowned. "You know that's not true, Rade. You have us."

He was right.

My family was here, now.

Lieutenant Commander Braggs entered the room and took the podium.

Everyone quieted.

This better be good, Alejandro transmitted on his Implant.

Shut up, I sent back.

You shut up, Alejandro transmitted. *Think you're pretty hot stuff right now, don't you, just because you won the ATLAS simulation this morning? Rematch time*, hombre. *When this briefing is over, you and me are heading to the sims. I'm gonna crush your ATLAS and eat your metal arms for breakfast. I'm gonna rip you out of that cockpit and—*

I put his ID on a two-minute block.

"I have to apologize once again for pulling all of you off your previous deployment," the Lieutenant Commander began. "But trust me when I tell you that this mission is far more important. You guys are getting to do the fun, hard-core stuff. Not like the rest of Team Seven, stranded back on Earth, battling tooth and nail for every square meter of Mongolia."

"Sounds fun and hard-core to me," Bender said.

Lieutenant Commander Braggs gave him a polite smile. "I won't use up too much of your time, Bender. This briefing is going to be quick. And I mean real quick, because, unfortunately, I can't go into too much detail on the overall mission, Operational Security and whatnot."

Not this OPSEC bull again, Bender transmitted on the platoon-level comm line via his Implant, which included everyone on Alfa Platoon except the Lieutenant Commander.

Quiet, Facehopper warned. *We don't need attitude right now.*

"All I can tell you is that we're headed into the heart of Sino-Korean territory," the Lieutenant Commander continued. "After passing through Sol Gate I to Sirius, we'll take the next Gate to Gliese 581, where we'll rendezvous with an SK bulk carrier in Franco-Italian space. Once we've docked with the carrier, the plan is to pass through the SK-owned Gate in Gliese 581 to Tau Ceti."

"Tau Ceti?" Fret frowned. "The solar system the SKs use as their space operations center?"

"The very same. As I said, we're headed to the heart of SK space."

The lanky communicator pursed his lips. "I like this mission."

Lieutenant Commander Braggs smiled. "I can see you're trying to puzzle out just how we're going to sneak two spec-op platoons past SK Gate Customs. Well, feel free to speculate all you want, because as I said, at this time I'm not at liberty to divulge that information." He ran his gaze over everyone. "I only really have one other thing to say. Due to the sensitive nature of this mission, all public profile data associated with your embedded IDs has been wiped. If you're captured, the enemy will have no idea who you are. Furthermore, I am restricting all inbound and outbound Net and Milnet transmissions once we pass Sol Gate I. You can communicate with the people on this ship by ID number, and this ship alone. If you absolutely need to send a message to the outside, you'll have to come see me first. Don't worry, your full Net access and profiles will be reinstated when we return. Until then, you're all ghosts."

There was silence in the room. We all knew that this would happen, eventually. We were special forces operators. Being out of touch with our friends and families for months at a time was expected. Though it would be harder for some than others of course. Like Tahoe.

I glanced at him. He was staring at his feet, his lips pressed tight together.

Ghost finally broke the ice. "We're all ghosts?" the albino said. "But I'm supposed to be the only *Ghost* here."

He got a few polite chuckles at that.

Lieutenant Commander Braggs forced a smile. "If there are no questions, return to the berthing area and prepare to enter Sol Gate I. Send your final messages to your families. Dismissed."

The barracks were located on the forward side of the ship, giving us a front-row-seat view of the Slipstream jump. Through the portal in the berth, I watched the *Leaping Matilda* near Sol Gate I, which was this massive circular frame of metal that spanned ten klicks of otherwise empty space. Beyond the Gate, space seemed perfectly normal. The constellations weren't distorted, as one might expect from an object that projected a hole through the very fabric of spacetime.

There was a line of about twenty ships queued up in front of the Gate, offset to the right from the absolute center. Incoming ships always entered on the right, which ensured that outgoing ships always emerged on the left. Sure enough, as I watched, a starship appeared seemingly from nowhere to the left of the queue, and thrusted away.

The *Leaping Matilda* took her place at the back of the line and waited her turn as the queued ships accelerated and vanished through the Gate one at a time.

Our turn came.

I braced myself. In all my training, I'd never once left the solar system. My heart was beating with excitement, and the fear of the unknown.

I glanced at Alejandro. His eyes were wide. I saw a bead of sweat drip down his forehead.

"Look at them," Bender said, nodding at me and Alejandro. "They're like frightened girls. You'd think they'd never set foot in space before."

I ignored Bender's words, and TJ's guffaws. Their behavior brought me right back to the first few weeks after I'd joined Alfa Platoon, to the daily hazings forced upon Alejandro, Tahoe, and I. While everyone had hazed us, Bender and TJ had given us the worst of it. Random knockout punches. Choke-outs from behind. Ice bucket wake-up calls. Hair remover mixed in with shampoo. Definitely not fun. But we'd taken it in stride, and endured whatever punishments those two dished out. When we finally deployed to Mongolia, the hazings had stopped, but those two never really respected us, and it showed.

It didn't help that the three of us hadn't been given callsigns yet. That was at the discretion of the leading petty officer, and I guess Facehopper thought we hadn't seen enough action yet. So as far as Bender and TJ were concerned, we were still caterpillars.

The actual passage through the Gate was a bit anticlimactic. I was staring at the vast rim of the Gate the whole time, and the moment we flew underneath, the stars shifted. I couldn't tell if those points of light moved a few centimeters, or a few meters: they seemed entirely different to my eyes. After a few seconds I reoriented myself and was able to pick out some of the constellations. They'd shifted slightly to the left.

That was it. No sensation of having my molecules ripped apart and reassembled. No tingly feeling.

No nothing.

Just a shifting of the stars.

We had been catapulted eight lightyears to the binary star system Sirius and hadn't felt a thing.

The discovery of the Slipstreams and the invention of the Gates had kicked off the era of colonial expansion, effectively short-circuiting the distance between star systems. According to the course I had taken, Slipstreams were quantum disturbances that tunneled through the fabric of the galaxy. A given Slipstream had specific entry and exit points in spacetime, usually around fifteen to twenty lightyears apart. Exit points also served as entry points, and vice versa.

Slipstreams couldn't be entered by themselves—the gravitational forces tore a starship apart. However, since Slipstreams followed a known, calculable trajectory between entry and exit points, it was possible to build special "Jump Gates" along the path of the

Slipstream to stabilize those sheer forces. A spacecraft entered the Slipstream via a Gate, and would drop out again when it reached the next Gate along the Slipstream's trajectory, or the natural exit point, whichever came first. However, if you came out and no Gate was there, you were SOL until the Builder ships decided to pop through the Slipstream and build you a return Gate.

The ability to create Gates anywhere along a Slipstream's trajectory allowed starships to enter and exit at convenient points in spacetime, such as solar systems. Funny thing was, most Slipstreams already had natural entry and exit points inside or near solar systems, which caused some people to postulate that the Slipstreams were created by extraterrestrial life. Others, mostly the ET detractors, believed that the Slipstreams formed as a natural byproduct of massive gravity wells, such as stars.

Whatever the case, most of the explored solar systems had at least two Slipstreams passing through them. This allowed a starship to enter a system from one Gate, travel to the second Gate, and jump to the next system. In our own solar system, Sol Gate I led to Sirius and was regulated by the UC, while Sol Gate II on the opposite side of the system belonged to the Sino-Koreans and led to their space. The SK ships weren't allowed through our Gate and our ships weren't allowed through theirs, under threat of war.

I watched the rim of the Gate quickly recede behind our ship, and I knew the *Leaping Matilda* had increased its thrust. We'd be accelerating to standard speed as soon as the three civilian ships we escorted came through.

Alejandro shook his head. "That it?" He laughed nervously. "I've been on roller coasters that were worse than this."

"The roller-coaster ride has only just begun, bro," I said.

CHAPTER FIFTEEN

Sirius A was damn bright, and caused the photochromic glass portals on the starboard side to become opaque, completely blocking all direct-eye views of space on that side. As for Sirius B, well, the star map said it was there, and I guess I'd just have to believe it. I'd been taught all about binary systems in the astrophysics class I took. Perhaps the most interesting fact, and about the only thing I could remember from that course, was that as binary stars orbited one another, the habitable zone in the system fluctuated. That meant Sirius I, "Albuquerque," the only terraformed planet in the system, had its seasons run the gamut from spring, summer, fall, winter, and back again over a period of weeks.

The *Leaping Matilda* secured two of the civilian ships at the spaceport above Albuquerque, where they would queue up for the next military escort. The third civilian ship stayed with us, and we also took on another vessel, a massive colony ship filled with seventy thousand pioneers.

Thirty-five days later saw us reach Sirius Gate II. We queued and took the jump to Gliese 581, a neutral system controlled by the Franco-Italians.

Gliese 581 was kind of a transport crossroads, and was unique in that it had six Slipstreams passing through it. Gates had been built upon all six. It was too bad the Franco-Italians had control of the area—it was a very strategically important system. That said, the

Franco-Italians had signed treaty agreements that basically handed over two of the Gates to the UC, and two others to the SKs, keeping both sides happy. FI space was considered neutral, so merchants from all three sides could trade here without violating extra-solar sanctions.

SK privateers weren't allowed to operate here, so we cut the two civilian ships loose.

A few weeks later our battlecruiser reached a secret base just within the Gliese 581 comet belt. Once there, our team shuttled over to a massive, boxlike bulk carrier. My teammates and I gathered around the portal and watched the approach to her docking bays.

The rough-hewn shape of SK design was evident throughout that metallic hull, and the dragonhead logo of the SK manufacturer was stamped in red on one side. I saw the ship's name, written in Sino-Korean characters: *Fàn Shāngrén*. That meant Rice Merchant, according to the translator built into my Implant.

The shuttle passed right by the docking bay.

"Hey, I think the pilot missed a turn," Manic commented.

The shuttle continued onward, heading for the cargo hatch on top of the bulk carrier instead.

"Holy *madre*—" Alejandro said.

I leaned forward, following his gaze.

An entire ship was moored inside that cargo hold. The triangular hull barely fit within the confines, and though it was about the size of a frigate, the ship didn't have the sleek design of a military vessel—its boxy aft section bore more of a resemblance to a merchant craft than anything else. SK make too, I'd venture.

"Ladies and gentlemen," Lieutenant Commander Braggs announced. "Meet the *Royal Fortune*, your home for the next few months. Also known as *Róng Fù*. It's a little SK privateer we captured a while back. Really just a merchant vessel retrofitted with turrets, but that suits our needs well enough. It's been modified with a few UC enhancements of course, but I won't get into that.

Crew complement is forty, with berths for an extra thirty-five mission crew."

"Looks a little stuffy," Fret said. He, like the Lieutenant Commander, had trouble just fitting inside the confines of this shuttle, and both of them had to slouch.

"I think it looks cozy, personally," Snakeoil said. "But I like my ships small."

"You would," Fret said to the short strongman. "Myself, I'm not looking forward to ducking under every hatch and bulkhead for the next two months."

"Come on, it'll be good for you," Snakeoil said. "Extra PT."

The instant we flew within the cargo hold, the bulk carrier started sealing its outer hatch.

Ahead, the *Royal Fortune* had opened her own, smaller hangar bay, and our shuttle landed inside. A ship within a ship within a ship.

When the privateer's hangar doors closed and the bay depressurized, our team stepped out.

Most of the crew of the *Fortune* had come to welcome us aboard. They stood outside the airlock in a long file and saluted as one: eight officers, thirty-two enlisted.

Shaw was one of the enlisted.

Of all the ships to be assigned to . . . the universe sure had a way of messing with me.

As the Lieutenant Commander and the Captain exchanged formalities, Shaw stared straight ahead. I knew she'd seen me. I was positive. But she refused to acknowledge me.

I sent a message to her embedded ID via my Implant. *So this is the secret ship you couldn't tell me about.*

We were on the same network node, so I didn't have to worry about my message reaching her or not. I knew she got it.

But she didn't answer.

I looked right at her as I walked past, but she kept her gaze focused straight ahead.

Ridiculous.

Some ensign led us through the warren of passageways and ladders to deck four, where the mission-crew berthing compartment awaited.

"Wasn't that Shaw?" Alejandro said along the way.

"Mmm? I don't know. I didn't see her." I tried to sound nonchalant, but the crack in my voice betrayed me.

"Yeahhhh, you saw her." He grinned. "A *mamacita* like that? Pretty hard to miss. She sure got hot in the past few years."

"You talking about that showpiece who was standing three down from the Captain?" Big Dog said. "Now there's a woman. Definitely Officer Bait, that's for sure." He shot a significant glance at Facehopper, who ignored the comment.

"She's not some showpiece." I was getting riled now.

Big Dog shrugged. "Relax, Rade. What, you know this chick or something?"

"Yeah. I mean, well, I used to."

Big Dog nodded thoughtfully. "Girl like that in the Navy? The way she looks? Definitely has to be strong."

"She is," I said. More than he knew.

There were six racks in the mission berthing area, stacked three high. Since Alejandro, Tahoe, and I were the newest members of the team, none of us got the prime real estate of the lower racks. Manic took the bottom bunk on my rack, and I let Alejandro take the middle one, so that left me the top. Tahoe got the top one beside us.

Manic stuffed his gear into the vertical locker beside the rack, leaving Alejandro and me the locker beneath the bottom bunk.

When I finished unloading my gear, I saw the new message icon appear on my HUD. It was from Shaw.

I hopped onto the topmost bunk and opened the message up.

Well look who showed up, it read.

I smiled, and sent a message right back. *Great gig you got for yourself here. Enjoying the life of a quartermaster?*

I prefer the title "astrogator," she answered. *Nice beard by the way.* That last comment was in reference to the new profile photo I was using.

You've seen it before.

Yup, came the immediate reply. *But you've grown it out.*

Let's switch to vid.

I initiated a vid call. She didn't pick up. I waited, and eventually the call canceled.

There was a long pause before her next message. *Look, Rade, I'm kind of seeing someone.*

Suddenly my hands were shaking. She was *seeing* someone? I tried my best to keep calm. What did I care, anyway? *That's okay. We're a zillion klicks from Earth. He'll never find out. Can we switch to vid?*

No we can't. And he's on this ship.

It was my turn to pause. *Oh. Didn't know you had your own Cruise boo.*

Whatever. He's kind of the jealous type, so we can't really hang out.

My vision became slightly blurry at that comment. *What, you're not allowed to have friends now? Sounds like he's more the possessive type to me.*

There was no answer.

Good luck avoiding me on a ship this size, I sent stubbornly. *Unless you plan on eating in your berth and never going to the gym.*

I waited for her to say something more, but the message box didn't update.

"Rade," Alejandro was saying. "Alejandro to Rade, do you read me, over?" He waved sarcastically.

Rade, what up, bro? he transmitted. *Get out of your Implant.*

"What," I said. "I'm here."

He jerked a thumb toward Tahoe, who was waiting by the door. "We're going to get some chow. Coming?"

"In a bit. Just, uh, checking my mail."

Alejandro snorted. "Yeahhhh. We don't get mail anymore, remember? But I know exactly what you're checking up on, if you know what I'm saying." He winked at me, then ducked outside. The rest of the platoon had already gone.

I lay back and closed my eyes.

I thought again on the universe's twisted sense of humor. I just had to find Shaw here, didn't I?

Shaw. The girl I had a thing for.

And she refused to hang out.

Unbelievable.

I heard the knock on the door a few seconds later.

"Come in," I said. I couldn't help a smile.

She'd come.

I put my hands behind my head and didn't look down from where I lay on the upper bunk.

"Well hello there, QM Shaw Chopra," I said, using the abbreviation for her quartermaster rating. I looked at my Heads-Up-Display map, double-checking that it was indeed her.

"Don't give me that QM bullcrap, PO3 Galaal."

"Hey, we *are* in the Navy, ma'am. It's only proper to be proper."

I finally glanced down at her. She had her arms crossed under her breasts and she was wearing her worst scowl. She certainly looked mighty fine in uniform, though.

"So you don't want to be friends anymore, huh?" I lay back again.

I heard one of the mattresses below bounce and, taking a peek, I saw she was sitting on the bottom bunk of the rack opposite mine. Facehopper's. I'd have to straighten out the leading petty officer's sheets when she got up.

"You've changed," Shaw said.

"So have you."

"You look older, more mature," she said. "And that's good, I suppose. I never really noticed while talking over vid. But here, in person, I can definitely see it. And it's not just the beard. There's something else. The way you move. The look you have in your eye. Like you know some secret no one else knows. Like you've seen things. Bad things. I suppose . . . I suppose it's the look of a killer."

I shook my head. "You're priceless as usual, Shaw."

"Isn't that what they train you to be in spec-ops? You're all killers, aren't you?"

I sat up and dangled my legs over the edge of the bunk. "Look, sure, I've made a few kills in the war, but I'm not a killer. You're jumping to conclusions. I'm a warrior. And there's a difference."

"Is there?" She didn't sound convinced. Not at all.

I'd have to fix that. "A killer is someone who kills the weak and the innocent. A warrior is someone who removes those killers from society. He fights for justice, and the safety of his country. He's a protector of the innocent."

"Now you're just spouting propaganda."

"It's not propaganda. It's what I believe, Shaw."

"You know how to kill someone in a hundred different ways, and the way you move shows that you're well aware of that fact. You can't tell me you're not a killer."

"Who have you been talking to? A *hundred different ways*?" I shook my head. "Sure, maybe I'm more confident now, but listen, Shaw, trust me: The Rules of Engagement won't let us target innocents. We'd all go to jail if we did that. Everything that happens on a battlefield is recorded by our weapons. We have thousands of military lawyers reviewing battle footage day in and day out from multiple angles, with the help of AIs. If I shot down someone who wasn't a baddie, I wouldn't be here with you today. I'd be in jail. All right?"

She didn't have anything to say to that.

"I take it you're not a big fan of the war in Mongolia?" I said.

"No. Not a big fan of wars in general."

I sat up on the bunk. "I was a warrior when you first met me. A Dissuader. A protector of the innocent. I just wasn't trained up. Just hadn't gone to war. I've come so far since then, but you know what? I'm the same now, even after everything. Maybe a little more confident, maybe a bit rougher around the edges, but I'm the same man inside. Shaw, look at me. Look at me." She did. "I'm the same."

She couldn't hold my gaze for long.

When she answered, her voice sounded so far away: "I can't believe it's been two years. Feels like a lifetime."

"It didn't have to be this way. We had so many chances to meet up. Maybe we should have taken them."

"But you know how I feel about long-distance relationships . . ."

I felt my face flush as I remembered our last chat session on Earth, when I'd told her how I felt about her. A strange mix of emotions bubbled up inside me. Anger, embarrassment, disappointment. "We're not long distance anymore, are we?" I said, a little bitterly.

She didn't answer.

"Tell me about this officer dude you're seeing," I said into the uncomfortable silence that followed.

"Um, he's not an officer." Shaw fidgeted with her utility belt. "That would be fraternization."

"Oh, then how did you get assigned to the *Royal Fortune* then?"

She looked up at me, the shock clearly evident on her face. "Is that what you think? That I slept my way into this post?"

I remained quiet.

"Well, if you ever bothered to look at my profile, you'd find out that I graduated top of the class. I got the highest grade possible in every course I took. I got to where I am today because of my determination, not my sexual activity, or my looks."

"You're right," I said. "I don't know what I was thinking. I didn't mean that, not at all. I know you better than that." I paused, reflecting on what she just said, and then I gave her a mischievous smile. "But your looks helped, you have to admit."

Her scowled deepened for a moment, but then she let out a small laugh. "I suppose my charm helped sway a few people, yes."

"Well, who is this mystery dude of yours, then?"

She hesitated.

And then suddenly I knew. "There's no one, is there?"

She sighed, staring at her fingers. "Not now, no."

"Why say there was, then? Why throw away everything we had? Everything we *could have* had?"

She didn't meet my gaze. Just stared at her hands, twining and untwining her fingers. "No one could ever measure up."

"To what? Your breathtaking, put-me-on-a-pedestal beauty? Or maybe your awe-inspiring personality?"

She didn't look at me.

"Well, maybe it's about time you got over yourself and came back down to live with the rest of us mortals."

She shook her head. "You don't understand." I couldn't believe it. She sounded like she was crying. "My expectations are high because of you." She finally met my eyes. Definitely tears. "No one could ever measure up to *you*."

I stared at her, openmouthed. "I'm such a jerk, Shaw."

I leaped down from my rack, led her to a storage closet, and took her right there.

The bulk carrier that held the *Royal Fortune* headed straight for the SK-owned Gate, *Tiàoyuè De Kǒng*, which led to Tau Ceti. The Gate name roughly meant "Leaping Hole." The transport time to the Gate was estimated at fifty-five days.

A whole lot of time for me and Shaw to get reacquainted. It was almost like old times. In the enlisted mess hall, Tahoe, Alejandro, and I normally ate with Snakeoil, Fret, Manic, Lui, and Bomb, and we folded Shaw and her friend Benjamin "from engineering" into our group readily enough. Benjamin didn't like me too much—I was pretty sure he'd been angling to bang her before I came on board, despite Shaw's insistence that he was "just a friend." Or maybe he was a previous flame of hers. I didn't know, and I didn't ask. I was the one who was banging Shaw now, and that's all that really mattered. Who was I to hold any ill will against the dude? I don't think he even knew what was going on between us, but I'm sure he suspected. Just as my closest friends suspected, though so far I hadn't admitted to a thing.

"So what's it like banging the hottest girl on the ship?" Manic said one time after Shaw and Benjamin left early. He scratched the moth-shaped port-wine stain on his temple with one finger. "Bet she does some amazing things between the sheets. Speaking of which, man, that reminds me of this one stripper back home, what's her name, RPG Tipper, that's it. You guys remember her? The one who poses with the rockets on her animated poster? She has this special bra she wears, looks like gun barrels on the tips of her nipples. Anyway, she sure could give it. Mmm. Sometimes I wish I could just lie with her every moment of every day and just bang the crap out of her, the service be damned. But it wasn't meant to be. I'd probably get bored after a few weeks anyway. So what was I talking about again? Oh yeah, Rade, you and that girl. Man!"

"Yeah baby!" Bomb interjected quickly, before Manic could say more. "Lucky bastard. What I wouldn't give for a piece of that right now." Bomb's short mohawk was dyed red these days, which, combined with his dark skin, gave him kind of a punk look.

"Stick to your virtual women, guys," Alejandro said. "You touch his *mamacita* and Rade will castrate you both, I guarantee it. This one time in the barrio—"

"Not another barrio story!" Lui threw up his hands. "I've had it up to here with those." He raised his hand far above his head. "To here!"

Tahoe was wolfing down his fifth serving of ham. "They're actually right, Alejandro," he said calmly. "Rade is a very lucky man. I know if Tepin were here, I'd be rushing back to meet her at the end of each day. But there's a warning in that. Back on Earth, when Tepin had finally come to live near the base, I found myself constantly distracted. It was hard to focus on the training, because I'd be thinking about her all day, and my kids. For all I whine about not seeing my wife when we're on deployment, it's probably better for the mission, for the *team*, that she is very far away."

I nodded. "Point taken, Tahoe. I'd never put any of you in danger because of her." His words reminded me of the admonishment RDC Bowden had given me way back in Basic, about love and war not mixing.

"So you *are* banging her!" Manic said. "I knew it!"

"I never said that."

And so it went.

To be honest, I was training as hard as ever, and didn't think my performance had declined. In fact, I felt more alive than ever because of her, and excelled at everything I did as far as I was concerned. I'm sure my friends saw it. I worked out harder. I trained harder. I did everything to the best of my ability. It was like I wanted to be the best possible man for her.

She made me want to be my best self.

Still, she kind of ruined the little dream life I was living a few weeks into our fling. Shaw, she was good at that.

"You know there's no future for us," she said, after we'd had our fun in one of the supply compartments during a mutual break. "You know how I feel about long-distance relationships."

"Yeah, I know." I pretended not to care, but it felt like she'd slapped me.

She must have sensed my lie, because her face softened, and she said, "Maybe when our terms are up . . ."

But my term wasn't up until twelve years from now. Hers ended in ten.

No, after this mission we'd go our separate ways.

Again.

"I wish I could say that this was more than just fun," she continued. "But I can't."

"I know."

"See, right here, right now, this is why I didn't meet up with you these past two years. This feeling, right now, knowing that it would all have to end."

I smiled sadly. "Okay, Shaw."

"What I'm trying to say, Rade, is . . . don't get your hopes up."

I exhaled. "Shaw. You've already fulfilled my every hope. If the mission ended today, if I died now, I could say I lived full. I'd die a very happy man."

"Good," she murmured softly. "Good." I saw her eyes move to the upper right as she accessed her Implant.

"What, looking for a quote more suitable to the moment?" I said.

"No." She smiled sadly. "I'm archiving what you said. So I can replay it in the deepest, darkest hours."

"There won't be any deep, dark hours again, not while I'm around."

But not even I believed that.

Eventually the starship reached *Tiàoyuè De Kōng* Gate. The "Leaping Hole."

The ship was on Condition Zebra, which was the highest possible state of readiness. The *Royal Fortune*, like most starships, was subdivided into many smaller airtight compartments, and Condition Zebra ensured that all hatches and scuttles were sealed tight so that in a breach scenario (i.e., combat) the entire ship wouldn't implode. The spread of fires and fumes was prevented as well, because valves in the pipes and ventilation systems would activate in damaged sections, completely sealing off those compartments from the rest of the ship. The bulk carrier that harbored us was set up the same way.

Condition Zebra also meant that almost everyone was at their duty stations, or in the case of my platoon mates and I, locked down in the berthing area. No portals to the outside were available in that compartment, so all of us tapped into the hauler's main viewscreen courtesy of our Implants.

There was a lengthy line of starships queued before the Gate, but my eyes were drawn to the long, sleek SK Customs vessels hovering alongside. Black, triangular-shaped corvettes. Definitely fast. Definitely deadly. I counted at least twenty gun turrets on each of them.

The customs vessels moved forward in pairs, pausing beside each ship, probably sending over a slew of questions to the respective Captain. "What's the purpose of your journey?" "When was the last time you visited Sino-Korean space?" And so forth, topped off with an invasive scan of the cargo holds.

I was surprised at the number of merchant ships of Franco-Italian design that were turned away, those bright, polished hulls limping away from the Gate like dogs with their tails between their legs. Other ships, SK and Franco-Italian alike, were pulled to the side for further inspection via boarding.

I had a bad feeling about this.

I felt like I did two years ago when I was an illegal trying to sneak across the border into the UC. Except back then I wanted to get caught.

Today I definitely didn't want that.

"Is the LC going to give us an in on the back and forth?" Facehopper asked Chief Bourbonjack.

The comm system of the bulk carrier had been diverted to the bridge of the *Royal Fortune.* Our Captain would be doing the talking when SK Customs opened up communications, rather than the bulk carrier Captain. Lieutenant Commander Braggs was on the bridge, and would hear every word.

The Chief held up a hand as if to say, "Let me check," then he shook his head. "That's a negative. The LC will give us an update on his return."

I called up Shaw on my Implant. *Hey, girl.*

Hey, she sent. *Kinda busy now.*

Figured that. Can I get a cochlear feed on the bridge today? Pretty please?

In answer, I heard the characteristic beep as she switched me to speaker, and the ambient noise of the bridge flooded into my head as perceived from her perspective. I heard the shuffle of feet on the deck, the persistent beep of some soft alert.

Shaw could have given me a retinal view too, but I thought if I asked for that, I'd be pushing my luck.

I merged the call with the platoon circuit. "We have an in," I announced.

On the viewscreen already overlaid atop my vision, I watched the two SK vessels pull up alongside our own.

"Stay calm, people," I heard Captain Drake say. "We're just a bunch of SK merchants off to sell our batch of legally procured Flame." That was the cover story. There was a huge demand for Flame in SK colonies these days. It was a type of perfume manufactured from a rare strain of bacteria that flourished in zero G.

"Tap in," the Captain said.

I heard static for a second, then silence. A voice came over the comm, speaking Korean-Chinese. "Captain and vessel name?"

"If it pleases you," Captain Drake answered in perfect Korean-Chinese. "This is Captain Chan Sung of the *Fàn Shāngrén*, devout and forever the servant of the Great Empire." A speaker of the language always said "if it pleases you" when addressing someone considered a superior. I learned that in my Korean-Chinese course, though I'd forgotten almost everything else. Luckily my Implant was subtitling the conversation for me.

"Destination and purpose?"

"If it pleases you, we head for Orbital Outpost Yue-Lao V, Tau Ceti III. We have a haul of Flame to drop off."

"Switch to vid, please."

I heard a bump as Shaw shifted, then a small beep. I knew that she or someone else had switched on the broadcast overlay system: the live feed from the bridge would be adjusted by the computer in real time to make it appear that the broadcast originated from a typical bulk carrier bridge. Captain Drake and the bridge crew would be "adjusted" too, their clothing and features transformed to match SK expectations.

"If it pleases you, is there a problem?" the Captain said.

"Transmit your crew profiles."

"Transmitting," the Captain said. A unique profile had been prepared for every member of the bulk carrier crew, in SK format.

"What do you think, Lui?" Alejandro said. "You're Korean. Is it going to work?"

"Korean American, bro," Lui said. "And yes, it's going to work."

Silence. And then: "Prepare for cargo scan."

On the viewscreen I saw blue beams issue from the two SK Customs vessels on either side of us.

"Keep your fingers crossed, mates," Facehopper said.

I held my breath.

Intelligence had apparently done a sweet number on the bulk carrier that harbored our ship, lining the hull with lead plates of differing thicknesses arranged in just the right pattern so that when invasive scans hit, the reflections that bounced back would make the cargo bay appear to be full of crates, rather than one barely fitting privateer. The technology was similar to what was used in holographic data storage devices, apparently.

The blue beam abruptly shut off.

"Proceed to the designated area for boarding and further inspection," the SK voice said matter-of-factly.

I glanced at Alejandro. He was just as wide-eyed as I probably was. I felt my heart pounding.

It was over.

"If it pleases you, one moment," Captain Drake said. "It would seem that a previously unnoticed one million *won* has appeared in our company log. In the interest of preserving the goodwill between my company and the revered custom officials who guard our Great Empire, I would like to donate this extra money to further enhance the security of the Empire, paying homage to the magnificent officials he has chosen to guard our great borders. If it pleases you, you who bask in the glory of the Paramount Leader, relay the ID number of the individual to whom these credits should be transferred."

Silence. Then the SK voice came back. "Transmitting account information. Bitcoins, please."

Ah. The subtleties of dealing with SK border guards.

"Received," Captain Drake said. "Transferring funds now . . . if it pleases you, transfer complete."

When the SK spoke again, he sounded friendly for the first time: "You are free to go, Captain. May the Paramount Leader guide you."

"May the Paramount Leader guide you," the Captain echoed.

And so the bulk carrier successfully traversed the "Leaping Hole" Gate, sneaking two highly trained spec-op platoons right into the heart of SK space.

CHAPTER SIXTEEN

Roughly six hours after entering Tau Ceti, the bulk carrier made a slight directional change, moving closer to the system's debris field. The *Royal Fortune* undocked, and hid behind a small planetoid as the carrier continued on its way toward the third planet in the system, keeping to the trade lanes.

"I don't really understand the logic," Tahoe said, during PT. "Why bother to hide inside a bulk carrier at all? Why not just take the *Royal Fortune* directly through? The ship is of SK make after all."

"Privateer ships are far more likely to be physically searched at Gate crossings than bulk carriers," Facehopper explained, not stopping his lunges. "Once the customs officials are aboard, they start doing a bunch of nasty stuff: planting contraband, arresting crew members, and so forth. Gives them an excuse to ask for a bigger bribe."

Tahoe rubbed his chin. "Okay, I guess I'll buy that. But why not stay in the bulk carrier now that we've reached Tau Ceti? What's the point of undocking the privateer?"

"Other than the fact that the privateer is more maneuverable and better equipped if it should come to ship-to-ship combat?"

"Sure."

"Well, if we continued in the system as a bulk carrier," Facehopper said, "moving away from the expected trade lanes, we'd draw unwanted attention. Privateers, however, can go wherever they want, and don't have to answer to a soul once they've crossed the Gate."

"But this isn't privateer-sanctioned space," Tahoe said. "We're in SK territory. No UC targets here. A privateer doesn't have any reason to be here, other than passing through."

"Passing through is a very good reason, mate," Facehopper said. "Besides, there are privateer bases scattered throughout Tau Ceti. You'll find fortified stashes and private refueling bases system-wide. We have every reason to be here. We'll fit right in as privateers. Trust me."

"You say it like you've been here before."

There was a knowing gleam in Facehopper's eye. "Maybe I have."

Despite Facehopper's reassuring words, the Captain seemed to be doing his best to avoid other ships. He kept the *Royal Fortune* in hiding behind that planetoid for three days, until two SK patrol ships flew past on an apparent scheduled sweep of the system. If there was anything to be said about Captain Drake, it was that he was certainly a man of caution.

At the end of the third day, the *Royal Fortune* set an extra-solar course and accelerated to standard speed.

A hundred days later, the *Royal Fortune* reached the dwarf planet Tau Ceti 582, near the outskirts of the system. The vessel navigated to the dark side of said planet, sheltering in high orbit behind a massive half dome made of black plates. I almost didn't see it at first, and the only reason I knew it was there was because the stars were entirely blotted out behind it. Fret said it was some kind of big LIDAR absorber/background-rad pass-through, which would mask whatever was behind it from the remote scans of patrols.

Other than our ship, there were two objects stashed between the stealth dome and the planet.

The first was a space station, with all its navigational lights turned off so that it looked like a darker blotch against the blackness of the planet.

The second object was a Gate, of all things. Again, unlit. I hadn't even realized it was there until Alejandro pointed out the dark bands, slightly lighter than the planet behind it. And it was massive, by the way—about a third as big as the dwarf itself.

After we docked with the station to refuel, Shaw joined me in the *Royal Fortune*'s mess hall. As we downed the galley's specialty, "reconstituted" beef, I gazed out the portal.

"Is it just me," I said, "or does this Gate seem bigger than the last two we've gone through? As in, a hell of a lot bigger?"

"It's not just you," Shaw said.

"Any explanations? You've taken a Slipstream physics elective, right?"

Shaw rubbed her chin. "I think it has to do with the magnitude of the Slipstream. The farther through space the rip travels, the bigger the Gate needs to be."

"Then this Gate is going to take us pretty far then."

Shaw seemed distant. "Yeah."

"What aren't you telling me?"

Shaw eyes defocused, then she squeezed my hand. "Have to go. I'm needed on the bridge. We're undocking." She shoved her plate forward. "Feel free to have as much as you want."

I regarded the gooey beef hesitantly. I was having enough trouble finishing my own.

On the way back to the berthing area I received a message from Facehopper, ordering me to the briefing room.

Finally, we were going to learn the mission.

When I got there, the other members of Alfa and Bravo Platoons were already present. I took a seat beside Alejandro and gave him and Tahoe the usual fist bump.

When we had all assembled, Lieutenant Commander Braggs approached the podium. "I just wanted to say, thank you all for your patience. I know you've been waiting a long time for this. Just what the hell are we doing here, deep in SK territory, hiding behind some dwarf planet, beside a Gate of all things? To answer that question, I'll have to start at the beginning."

A map of the Tau Ceti solar system overlaid my vision, with a flashing dot indicated between the first planet and the G-class star.

"Approximately one year ago a new Gate became operational in the heart of Sino-Korean territory, right here in Tau Ceti. A Gate we code-named Anesidora."

Anesidora is Pandora's other name, Tahoe transmitted on the platoon-level frequency of our Implants, which excluded Braggs.

Shh! Facehopper sent.

"A few weeks after its official activation, our intelligence boys at the Special Collection Service reported massive numbers of SK fuel tankers making jumps through Anesidora. Those tankers invariably returned a few days later, every last one of them laden to the brim with Geronium-275."

Geronium-275. The expensive radioactive element that served as the precursor to Geronium, the main fission fuel for starships.

"At the time, our theorists had two opinions on where the SKs were getting this Geronium," Lieutenant Commander Braggs continued. "One, they somehow used the Gate itself to mass-produce the element. Two, they'd found a natural source at the other end of the Slipstream. Option one seemed less likely. That left option two. A second natural source of Geronium-275, other than Earth." He paused, letting us digest that fact.

The number of ships the fleet operated at any given time was directly proportional to the current stores of Geronium, and how fast the factories could manufacture said element from the supply of

Geronium-275. If the SKs had discovered another natural source of Geronium-275, the balance of naval power could shift in their favor.

You think it's true? Manic transmitted on the platoon line, interrupting my thoughts.

No, Lui sent. *It's impossible. There are no other mineable sources of Geronium-275. Earth is the only place.*

"I can see you're all jumping to conclusions in those smart little minds of yours," Lieutenant Commander Braggs said. "But please, quiet the chatter."

How did he know? Alejandro said.

Shh!

"About eight months ago the SKs stopped using the Gate entirely. We thought at first they'd exhausted whatever natural supply of Geronium-275 they'd discovered. But then they dismantled the Gate and closed up shop completely. We detected heavy nuke mining spinward of Tau Ceti, in a location Fleet believes marks the natural exit point of the Slipstream."

Remember, you dropped out of a Slipstream whenever you reached the natural exit point, regardless of whether there was a Gate there or not. So by dismantling the Anesidora Gate and mining the natural exit with nukes, the SKs effectively ensured the destruction of any starships coming through. But why they'd want to destroy their own returning vessels was the question.

"Our analysts didn't quite know what to make of the whole thing," Braggs said. "Our best guess was that they had accidentally unleashed some sort of bioweapon or contagion. We captured and interrogated a couple of high-ranking SK officials. Useless. All they could tell us was incomprehensible gibberish like 'we reached too far' or 'we offended nature.' Fact is, the officials didn't know squat. The SK President, or Paramount Leader as they call him, probably mind-wiped most of his cabinet. That, or he had the people in-the-know executed. I wouldn't put it past him. The guy's one nasty dude. Though I have to admit if it were legal in the UC, there's a few people I might mind-wipe or execute myself. But I digress.

"Anyway, at that point we'd exhausted the intelligence route. The only SKs who could have given us a straight answer were Paramount Leader Guoping Qiu and his top staff, and good luck interrogating any member of that group without causing a war. So Fleet decided it was time for a change in tactics, because if there was a threat that merited a fifty-thousand-megaton load of nuclear mines, you can bet your sweet behind we weren't going to turn a blind eye. Nor were we going to abandon a potential natural source of Geronium-275 until we could properly assess the threat level.

"So, Fleet called in the Teams, and here we are. We're going in through the Gate, boys, and we're going to find out what exactly the SKs are hiding. Questions?"

I cleared my throat. "Sir, you said the Anesidora Gate was dismantled. I'm assuming the Gate floating outside our ship right now is not Anesidora?"

Lieutenant Commander Braggs flashed a grin. "That would be a correct assumption, Mr. Galaal. The handy fellows at Fleet built us another one. Anesidora II."

Facehopper spoke up. "Respectfully, sir, would you mind telling us how Fleet pulled that off? Building a Gate in the heart of SK territory without igniting a political shitstorm. That's quite the feat."

Braggs laughed. "Wasn't easy, I tell you that. The robot-manned Builder ships had to be hauled into the system in parts and assembled in secret. You know the dwarf we're orbiting? The trajectory of the Slipstream follows its orbit, and passes almost right through the planetoid. The perfect spot for Anesidora II. It's almost too convenient, and for the longest time Brass suspected some sort of trap. But we built it, and so far, we've gotten away with it."

On the map of Tau Ceti a dotted line moved away from the

flashing icon that represented the original Anesidora, and progressed outward until it reached the dwarf planet. A new flashing icon appeared there, labeled Anesidora II.

"The dwarf hid most of the construction, giving the Builders time to pad the whole area in LIDAR absorbers and background-rad pass-throughs to mask what they were doing. I don't know if you noticed, but there's also an SK base on the far side of the planet. Manned by robots. The good boys of Team Six went in and reprogrammed the lot of them, allowing us to sneak our Builders right by. Remember to treat Charlie Platoon to a few rounds of beer when you get home.

"Anyway, the point is that, yes, we have ourselves a Gate, and it took a hell of a lot of work to make sure the SKs don't know it's here. We'd like to keep it that way. Igniting a political shitstorm is right: We risk war with the SKs if Anesidora II is found out. We've violated SK space, created a Gate to an unknown part of the galaxy. If there really is some contagion or bioweapon out there, their Paramount Leader could accuse us of building the Gate as some form of stealth attack, even if his own army engineered said bioweapon. Not the best scenario to say the least.

"Moving on: Unmanned probes sent through Anesidora II didn't come back, and we realized the SKs probably dismantled the return Gate too. Fleet ordered the Builder ships through 'in the blind,' and assembled us another one. Subsequent probes mapped out a G-class main-sequence star system. Three planets."

A different solar system overlaid my vision now. A bright yellow star dominated the center, surrounded by ellipses representing planetary orbits. The map zoomed in on the second planet. The rotating surface was gray and brown, with no visible water masses. A smattering of clouds sprinkled the atmosphere. "Here we have the second planet, a terrestrial, rough Mars analog. Turns out the planet's entire mantle is rich in Geronium-275. As in, ninety-five percent of the surface. That's right, a massive, naturally occurring source of starship fuel just waiting for us to dig up. We've nicknamed the planet Geronimo. The SKs had already started terraforming it: See the little cloud specks in the picture? That's from Forma pipes driven into the surface. Even though the planet is abandoned, those pipes are still functioning. Don't get too excited, though: The atmosphere isn't breathable, not yet. Nor is the pressure conducive to human life. The radiation doesn't help much either. You're going to need full jumpsuits down there."

My attention was drawn to a beacon that now flashed on and off in the planet's uppermost hemisphere.

"Here we have what appears to be an abandoned SK outpost. Your target. Your job is to go in, land on Geronimo, scout the outpost, find out what spooked the SKs, potentially secure the planet for the UC, then get out."

The graphical overlay faded from my vision.

Sounds easy enough, Alejandro transmitted.

Always sounds easy, Ghost sent. *Never is.*

"There are no other ships in the system. No hostiles that we can detect. No signs of bioweapons. As I said, it's been eight months since the SKs abandoned the system. So it should be a cakewalk. But, there is one small thing I should mention."

Here it comes . . . Lui sent.

"Normally Slipstream jumps transport a ship between fifteen to forty lightyears. The longest jump we know of is ninety lightyears. Well, the Gate to Geronimo? When the probe returned and dumped its data, the telemetry told us it had traveled *eight thousand* lightyears."

That statement was met with stunned silence.

"We're going to travel eight thousand lightyears?" Big Dog finally said. The disbelief was obvious in his voice.

"We are. Geronimo is located in NGC 3372, right inside the nebula known on Earth as 'God's Birdie.'" A nebula shaped like a hand flipping the bird overlaid my vision. "This is the farthest anyone has ever gone, other than the SKs. Before now, we as a species have never traveled more than ninety lightyears away from our cozy little planet. We've barely scratched the surface of our own galaxy, let alone our own interstellar neighborhood. We would've reached NGC 3372 eventually, of course—in about five centuries, given the current rate of Slipstream discovery and colonial expansion. But we have ourselves a shortcut now, a chance to establish a foothold in a part of the galaxy entirely unknown to us."

He paused, reflecting for a moment. "I'm excited, but hesitant at the same time. Probes can be wrong. There's only so much data that can be read from orbit. Which is why we need the Teams in there. Alfa and Bravo Platoons are among the best we have, which is why Brass chose you. When the feces hits the fan, you're the ones we want at the forefront, wiping that feces off and lobbing it right back in the face of whoever threw it in the first place." He glanced at the portal in the briefing hall, toward the Gate. "That said, we do have a contingency plan in place, if something goes wrong. A plan most of you won't like. Some of you may have noticed we're sending a probe back and forth through the Gate multiple times a day. Well, that probe is returning telemetry data, and once we're through, if the *Royal Fortune* drops off the map for more than an hour, Fleet has orders to blow the Gate on this side." He paused, letting the ramifications sink in. "We also have the full authority to destroy the return Gate, if deemed necessary. So." He gave us his biggest fake smile. "Any more questions?"

"Other than the obligatory one about how we plan on sneaking a planet's worth of Geronium-275 through SK space if we're successful?" Fret said, smiling ironically.

Braggs smiled patiently. "That's a bridge for the Brass to cross, if we ever come to it. Though I'm pretty sure you all know the answer to that."

All-out war between the UC and the SKs.

Crossing Anesidora II was just as anticlimactic as passing through all the previous Gates, except we didn't have to queue up.

I had my Implant linked to the external viewscreen so I could watch the crossing in real time. When the *Royal Fortune* went through, as usual I couldn't tell how far the stars had moved, and they seemed completely different to my eyes. Normally I'd be able to orient myself after a few seconds, but not this time. The constellations hadn't merely shifted a few centimeters—they actually *were* completely different.

Well, what did I expect? The *Royal Fortune* had just leapfrogged eight thousand lightyears. Of course the stars were going to be different out here. All our telemetry, and everything we knew about this place from Earth, was eight thousand years old—discounting the most recent data obtained from the probes of course.

"Rade, you gonna get your girlfriend to give us a feed?" Bender said, toying with one of his gold chains.

"She's not my girlfriend," I said, maybe a bit more defensively than I intended. He was just trying to bother me. Only a few people in the platoon knew what was going on between me and Shaw, and he wasn't one of them.

Or so I hoped.

"Just get us the damn feed," Bender said.

Even if he knew about Shaw, he'd never bring it up with the Chief or the Lieutenant Commander. It was an unwritten rule: No one ratted out a member of the Teams. No one. Not even if that member was a caterpillar.

"Fine." I keyed Shaw. She gave me access to her cochlear feed without a word. She knew what I wanted.

I linked the feed through to the platoon comm line for my brothers.

"Telemetry report," the Captain said.

"Everything is consistent with what the probes sent." I didn't recognize the voice, but I supposed it belonged to one of the officers, or maybe one of the Fleet scientists we had on board. "G-class main-sequence star.

Three planets. Mining outpost detected on the second planet, along with partial atmospheric terraforming. I'm not detecting any other vessels, nor any signs of life on the planets. The star field patterns are consistent with NGC 3372, taking into account the time dilation from our previous frame of reference. There's still something I can't figure out,though."

"What's that?" Captain Drake said.

"Why the nebula NGC 3372 isn't here."

"Well, as the Brass said, things are going to change in the time it takes the light to travel eight thousand years back to Earth," the Captain said.

"That's true, Captain, but according to my latest readings from the trace gases I'm picking up, that nebula should have stuck around for at least another twenty thousand years."

The bridge crew was silent for a moment. All I heard was the gentle whirring of various ships systems, and the occasional soft beep as someone accessed a bridge control.

"Well," Captain Drake said. "We're the farthest anyone from the UC has ever gone. We're treading unmarked ground here. Expect things to be a little strange. Maybe this is some new attribute of nebulae that we haven't discovered yet, and our physics model needs some updating. I'll let you work on figuring that out. In the meantime, I'm going to call the stand down."

Captain Drake's voice came over the main circuit.

"Secure from General Quarters! All hands stand down. Return to normal duties. The time is 0800."

"All right mates, time for the gym," Facehopper said. "We have forty days to Geronimo. I don't want to waste a single one of them."

"Do you think we'll find aliens?" Alejandro said after PT later that day, when we were showering in the hydro-recycle containers.

Facehopper laughed. "Bro, *we're* the aliens now."

"Okay okay," Alejandro said. "But you know what I mean. Come on, you heard all that bridge chatter about the nebula being gone. What do you think? Gotta be an alien's work. If we meet one, do I have permission to blow it up?"

Facehopper gave him a look of mock seriousness. "No you do not. You are to leave all alien life alone, for later tagging and bagging."

"Stop talking about aliens," Lui said. "Like the Captain said, our physics model just needs some updating."

"Aliens? Did someone say aliens?" Tahoe came into the showers. "Did I ever mention the Rare Earth Hypothesis?"

Alejandro glanced at me, and I shook my head. "Nope."

"For the benefit of those who haven't heard it, the hypothesis states that alien life is not possible, because the conditions required for life to develop naturally are far too rare. Earth is the only inhabited planet in the entire galaxy. And possibly the entire universe. Hence the name, Rare Earth."

"You're discounting the colony worlds," Facehopper said.

"That's true. But I did say *alien* life. We're basically just creating more Rare Earths by terraforming and colonizing. And actually, that brings up an interesting point. Can you imagine ten thousand years from now when the colonies we've populated come to fruition? Or how about fifty thousand years. Or a hundred. The genetic differences between humans on each colony world will be immense. We'll have created our own aliens."

"A hundred thousand years," Alejandro mused. "*Caramba.* I can't even think past next week, and you expect me to imagine what life will be like a hundred thousand years from now?"

"And I haven't even touched on biologics," Tahoe said. "We've already recreated the woolly mammoth. The Tyrannosaurus Rex. When are the custom bioweapons coming? An army of face-sucking creatures straight out of a vid. We're creating our own aliens, boys."

It was a sobering thought. "That's not something any of us will have to deal with in our lifetimes," I said.

"You keep up on the news, don't you, Rade?" Tahoe said. "The SKs have been performing bioweapons research for decades now, mixing and matching DNA from multiple species—insectoid, mammalian, fish—customizing the brains to provide easy access for implantable circuitry, with the goal being, of course, to create the ultimate biological weapon. You heard about the Ghengis Blast?"

"Yeah." The Ghengis Blast was a planet-scale thermobaric test the SKs had conducted a few years ago. They'd launched it against one of their own minor colonies, Alpha Centauri 2. The planet's surface had been obliterated.

"Well," Tahoe continued. "The conspiracy theorists think Alpha Centauri 2 had been overrun by some of the SKs' own creations. They nuked the planet to hide the evidence, and prevent it from spreading."

"The conspiracy nuts are wrong," Lui interjected. "Alpha Centauri 2 had a nitrogen atmosphere. Couldn't support any animal life, genetically engineered or not."

Tahoe turned toward him. "Who says genetically engineered life needs an O_2 atmosphere?"

"Yeah, well, all this bioweapon stuff is overrated," Lui said. "You mentioned the Tyrannosaurus Rex. What about the Rex the SKs crossed with a Brontosaurus a few years back?"

"Didn't work out too well for them," Tahoe said.

"Exactly. Sure, the thing had the head of a Tyrannosaurus, but its Brontosaurus body made it far too slow for any kind of predation. Couldn't even catch food for itself, let alone function as a real weapon. Though I suppose it would have been a great unit for tanking. Anyway, the SK government got its money back by setting up an exhibit in one of its twisted Bioengineering Zoos. They feed the thing fattened sheep, political prisoners, and disgruntled citizens."

"The SK justice system at its finest." Facehopper dried himself off.

"You're missing the point," Tahoe said. "The Tyrannosaurus Rex is perfectly capable of being a bioweapon on its own."

Lui shook his head. "Give me an ATLAS mech and put me in a room with a Rex, and I guarantee you the Rex will be coming out of that room in pieces. As for my mech, won't have a scratch."

"I hope you're right," Fret said. The supertall, superskinny MOTH had the odd habit of scrubbing himself with a brush whose stiff fibers ordinarily were used to clean torpedo shafts. He was working on his privates right now, which always made me cringe. I think he did it to show that although he wasn't as muscular as everyone else, he was tough. Or maybe he just liked the fresh feeling you got when you scoured your balls with a torpedo brush.

"Well of course I'm right," Lui said.

"You heard what the LC said during the briefing?" Fret persisted.

Lui dried off under an air outlet. "What?"

"Intel's best guess is that the SKs unleashed some sort of bioweapon on Geronimo. I tell you, I got a bad premonition about this one, people."

"You always have a bad premonition." Facehopper patted Fret on the shoulder before leaving the hydro-recycle area. "Take a happy pill, mate."

I had to agree with Fret on this one.

In the coming weeks, the dread I felt only increased the closer we got to our destination, and the farther we traveled from the Gate. It felt to me like the thin thread that connected us to our homeworld was stretching, becoming thinner by the moment, like it was going to snap any day now and trap us here forever.

Only when I was with Shaw did I forget that dread, losing myself in her. But the moment I left her presence, the sense of foreboding always returned.

I had no reason to feel this way. Everything was quiet out there in the system. No sign of any hostiles. Or anything amiss.

Maybe that was the problem.

It was a little too quiet out there.

The PT and training helped distract me, as did the camaraderie and competition among my teammates. If I didn't have them, and Shaw, I probably would have gone insane. I don't know how people could travel solo in space, especially on a dangerous mission. That was a recipe for mental disaster.

We were about ten days out from Geronimo when I awoke to the klaxon.

"General Quarters!" came the voice over the main circuit. "General Quarters! All hands man your battle stations. Up and forward to starboard, down and aft to port. General Quarters, General Quarters. Torpedo strike, starboard side! Torpedo strike!"

There was a fire in the berthing hall. I leaped down from my rack. Everyone had already made it out. Except Alejandro and me.

I forced him awake.

"What's going on?" Alejandro said.

"We're under attack! Torpedo strike!"

We hurried to the door. It wouldn't open. Lockdown.

I checked my HUD map. Most of the crew seemed to be congregated on the bridge and outlying corridors.

I heard a distant explosion, and the ship rocked. I lost my balance but Alejandro caught me.

"What are we going to do, Rade?" he said.

I coughed. The smoke was getting to me. The entire far bulkhead was on fire.

"Gotta get suited up!" I told him.

The two of us retreated to the armory, and we put on the spare jumpsuits.

I just finished securing my helmet when the bulkhead failed.

The explosive decompression sucked the two of us into space.

I was still facing the ship, and watched it recede. I instinctively reached a hand toward it, grasping at the empty space in front of me as if I could somehow clutch the privateer. I hadn't had time to attach a jetpack.

"Alejandro. Did you get a jetpack? Alejandro?"

The hull of the ship was blackened in several areas, and one exposed region was sparking repeatedly. That was the bridge.

Shaw.

I tried a message to her Implant. *Shaw, can you read? Shaw!*

The ship drifted away. Or rather, I did.

I had to get back to the bridge, somehow. Find Shaw. I hadn't seen any of the lifeboats launch. She was still aboard. She needed me. "Alejandro, where the hell are you? We have to get back to the ship. Alejandro?"

No answer.

"Alejandro?" I was starting to get a sinking feeling in my stomach.

If he hadn't secured his helmet in time . . .

A torpedo struck the *Royal Fortune* and the privateer split in two.

"No."

Another torpedo. Another.

Each strike felt like a physical blow to my own body.

"Alejandro. Shaw. Anyone. Do you read?"

No answer.

I was alone. Trapped, immobile in a jumpsuit, waiting for my oxygen to run out.

My ship gone.

My friends, probably dead.

And then I had a 9-mm pistol in my hand.

I was standing at the edge of some sort of obsidian cliff, in the heart of a volcano. A stream of lava geysered beside me.

Alejandro was on his knees before me. He was looking up at me, his eyes entreating.

"Please, Rade, don't kill me," he said.

My 9-mil was pointed right at his head.

Of its own volition, my finger applied pressure to the trigger . . .

I woke up drenched in sweat.

The end of the forty days finally came.

I was doing PT in the gym with the rest of my platoon when Facehopper, who was leading us in a series of body-weight squats, abruptly froze. His eyes seemed to defocus, then he nodded.

When he glanced at us, his expression was grim.

"It's time."

CHAPTER SEVENTEEN

Every member of Alfa Platoon stood in the *Royal Fortune*'s launch bay, which had been retrofitted with long magnetic tracks for the upcoming drop. All of us were in jumpsuits, jetpacks fully fueled, rebreathers charged. The only thing left was to wait the designated hour for our bodies to adapt to the suits.

"This is the worst part," Ghost said. "The time before the drop. Being on the drop is fine. You know, taking fire. Dishing it out. Performing your mission. But right here, right now, this is the worst. The waiting."

"Sure, mate," Facehopper said. "But it always ends quick."

"Not always," Ghost said.

Beside him, I started tapping out a staccato rhythm on my jumpsuit leg assembly.

"Stop fidgeting," Manic said. "You're making me nervous."

"Definitely don't want that," Fret said. "When Manic's nervous, he shoots his mouth off. Better stop, Rade."

"Man, he shoots his mouth off anyway," TJ said. Beyond his face mask, I could only see a small part of the Atlas moth inked to his neck. He didn't seem so tough when he was cocooned like that inside the suit. The same was true of everybody else. Inside the bulk you couldn't tell the strong from the weak, and it didn't really matter because the jumpsuits boosted everyone's strength to near identical levels. Jumpsuits, the great equalizer.

"I've never shot my mouth off," Manic said. "Well sure, sometimes when the fighting gets heavy, maybe I have a tendency to flap my lips, but that's only because I'm trying to distract the enemy."

TJ snorted. "What, you think the enemy can hear you?"

"Well sure, not every target is far off you know."

"Dude, if you've let them get that close, then something is very wrong," TJ said.

Manic folded his arms. "I'm taking a nap now. Good-bye." He inclined his head and closed his eyes.

"Don't know about you guys, but I sure hope I don't get stuck babysitting Fleet," Bender said.

I glanced at the two Fleet scientists who stood off to one side in jumpsuits. They'd be coming with us.

"What do you think we'll find down there, Chief?" Snakeoil said.

Chief Bourbonjack shrugged. "Couple of empty whiskey bottles. Couple of uneaten MREs. Maybe a few bodies. Who knows? We land, insert the scientists, look around, take the scientists home. Back before dinner."

"I like the sound of that," Skullcracker said. He had a detailed picture of a screaming skull spray-painted on his jumpsuit. It complemented the tattoo on his face quite nicely. "Speaking of dinner, I've already placed my order with the galley. Got a steak in line. Mashed potatoes. Gravy. The works."

"You know that stuff's all reconstituted, right?" Lui said, a look of disgust on his face.

Skullcracker shrugged. "Tastes good to me."

The airlock of the hangar bay irised open and Lieutenant Commander Braggs entered. He was wearing his service khaki and nothing more—he obviously wasn't coming down with us. Alfa Platoon immediately mustered in front of him.

"All right, boys," Lieutenant Commander Braggs said. "Listen up. Operation Dead Cat Bounce is a go. The HS3s report no occupants in the SK base, living or dead. I repeat, no occupants." HS3s were those basketball-sized, Hover Squad Support System drones we always sent ahead for scouting purposes.

"Maybe the SKs truly abandoned the place," Braggs continued. "Or maybe they're just out for lunch and will return with a couple of ATLAS mechs in a few hours. As of this moment, we have a bunch of Centurions performing a sweep of the base and the immediate area, but I want Alfa Platoon to follow up. Chief?"

"Thank you, sir." Chief Bourbonjack stepped forward to address us from inside his jumpsuit. "Alfa Platoon will touch down in the relative center of the outpost." An overhead map overlaid my vision. I saw the outline of the different buildings in the outpost. A flashing dot in the middle indicated where we would land. Looked like some kind of courtyard. "We're going to augment the Centurions down there, do a building-by-building search until we've secured the entire outpost. Big Dog, Skullcracker, and Tahoe, you're on the heavies. Ghost, Trace, Rade, Alejandro, you're our snipers. TJ and Bender, drone ops. Snakeoil and Fret, commos. We're going in without Weavers to make room for the scientists and their survey equipment, so we're going to need a couple of you to double as corpsmen. Since Trace and Rade are the fastest runners in the platoon, they win that role by default. As for the ATLAS 5s, I'm giving Manic and Lui the authorization to ride Ladybug and Aphid down."

"Thank you, sir!" Lui said.

I still got a bit jealous whenever someone else got assigned to the mechs, but I'd assume whatever role my Chief needed me to. If he wanted me to be a sniper first and a corpsman second, I'd do it without question. Someone had to assume those roles. And if he thought I was the best man for the job, that was a compliment.

"Bomb," Chief said. "No mech for you this time round. I want you to be grenadier."

I could tell Bomb wasn't too happy about that—he was one of the platoon's official ATLAS pilots after all—but he took it in stride. "Yes sir!"

"This will be a hot drop," Chief Bourbonjack said. "We're treating it like a warzone. Any questions?"

There were none.

"Well," Lieutenant Commander Braggs said. "You heard the man. Get yourselves equipped!"

I hurried to the loadout area and grabbed a Mark 12 rifle from the rack, as did the other snipers. The heavy gunners took the general-purpose machine guns, and everyone else picked up the SI (standard-issue) rifles. One thing I did was swap out the lower receiver of the Mark 12 for one from the SI.

I collapsed the stock and slung the Mark 12's strap over my shoulder, then stowed a 9-mil pistol in my belt, stocking up on armor-piercing rounds for both. I also loaded up on grenades.

"Enough grenades there for you, Rade?" Facehopper said. "I thought the Chief assigned Bomb the role of grenadier?"

I glanced at Facehopper's belt. He'd only taken two.

I shrugged. "Figured I have the room, so why not."

"If you accidentally blow yourself up, don't say I didn't warn you, mate."

I considered putting some of my grenades back, but pride wouldn't let me.

Fret piled on the grenades just like me. Grinning widely, he said, "You can never have too many grenades."

I grabbed a bunch of extra magazines, maybe more than I should have, filling up almost every available pouch in my jumpsuit. Since I was also corpsman this time out, I grabbed a full medbag off the rack and tossed it over my shoulders—it fit easily over my jetpack. The bag had various medical supplies including four one-liter IVs filled with blood substitutes, SAM splints, all-purpose tape, pressure dressings, jumpsuit seals, etc. You'd think a lot of it would be difficult to apply to a man in a jumpsuit, but not so: there were injection slots above the gloves where you could attach a vial or IV tube, and inside the suit a needle would extend directly into the dorsal venous network of the hand. There was no breaching of the suit, no chance of depressurization. There were also SealWraps, these self-sealing, translucent funnels I could wrap around one wrist to form a seal between my glove and the suit of a patient. Using the surgical laser in the index finger of my glove, I could then cut a hole in the patient's suit without depressurizing the whole thing. When I was done, I just left the funnel on the suit until the patient could get back to a safer environment.

Everyone carried a smaller medkit, affectionately called a suitrep (suit repair) kit, because it had mostly jumpsuit seals and patches, though it also had a few bandages, one IV, a SealWrap, and some clotting agents. This went into the left-hand cargo pocket on the jumpsuit leg assembly. You always used someone else's suitrep kit if they were wounded in the field and you got there before the corpsman or Weaver, because if you used your own kit, how would you help the next guy, or yourself?

I hesitated beside the Carl Gustavs. Officially known as the M7 Multi-Role Anti-armor Anti-tank Weapon System, those recoilless rifles packed a mighty powerful punch. I still remember what happened when Bender fired one of those in the apartment back at Mongolia. Took out the entire side of the building.

What the hell. Never hurt to have a portable rocket launcher with you. I grabbed one of the Gustavs and looped its strap over my shoulder, then clipped two high-explosive dual purpose rounds to my belt—the kind that fragmented on impact, useful when you wanted to shred a lot of soft targets at once.

"You're acting like you've never been on a drop before," TJ said, rather snarkily. "A bit nervous today, caterpillar?"

"I'm not a caterpillar," I said.

"Facehopper ain't given you a callsign. You're a caterpillar."

I ignored him and went over to Fret, who was struggling to fit the heavy communications rucksack down over his jetpack. I told the tall man to bend over, then I helped him secure it, making sure no part of the sack blocked his jumpjet nozzles.

I approached the MDV (MOTH Delivery Vehicle). Basically a shuttle on steroids, the MDV was made of a variety of heat resistant materials, including reinforced carbon-carbon, toughened fibrous insulation tiles, felt reusable surface insulators, and so on. Design-wise, it had wide parabolic wings on either side and a stabilizing fin on top. There were small windows lining the left and right sides. Near the center of the fuselage a small hook allowed the drop arm to latch on. Black nozzles on the rear provided forward thrust, and similar nozzles on the underside added lift. Thrust outlets on the left and right of the fuselage allowed the MDV to make lateral adjustments during flight. A swivel-mounted Gatling turret hung beneath the cockpit.

"Warning," a female voice echoed in the hangar. "Depressurization commencing. Hangar atmosphere venting overboard. Warning."

Robotic arms were loading the scientists' survey equipment into the MDV storage compartment. I sidestepped those arms and hurried up the ramp, heading straight to my designated drop space. Clamps automatically wrapped around my shoulders and my waist.

I received a message from Shaw just then.

Come back in one piece, you hear?

Yes ma'am, I sent back. *Keep the ship safe for me while I'm gone.*

You know I will.

Alejandro clamped in across from me. He was grinning. "See you planetside, *puta*!"

By then everyone else was onboard, except Manic and Lui, who would drop directly in their ATLAS mechs.

The ramp closed. I felt the compartment shake as the drop arm latched onto the MDV (though I couldn't see the arm, of course) and the craft slid forward on the magnetic rails, which now extended out from the hangar and into space.

I watched through the small window across from me, between the shoulders of Big Dog and Alejandro, as the MDV passed the open doors at the end of the bay. The metal bulkheads of the hangar slipped away, replaced by the stars of open space.

I felt the weightlessness instantly. It was like my stomach jumped. I had no sense of balance or direction at all. I was upside-down. No, I was sideways. No, rightside up. I'd experienced this sensation many times before in training, and I concentrated on ignoring the confused feelings my inner ear was sending to my brain.

The rails supported the weight of the MDV as we slid forward. When we were three meters from the ship, the advance ceased. I knew that the rails were withdrawing right now. The craft abruptly shifted, which meant the robotic arm alone held us in place.

That arm must have opened, because through the window the *Royal Fortune* shot skyward.

I could see the planet nearing below, this spherical object that quickly became planar and swallowed the horizon. I started to feel some Gs—when I moved my head my inner ear reacted, reinforcing my sense of balance and of up and down. The forces increased to around two Gs as the atmosphere of the planet abruptly (and temporarily) slowed our descent.

The sky outside the window changed colors, going from light pink to red and orange in a matter of seconds, as I looked out from the fireball that the outer surface of the MDV had become. I always got this slight panicky feeling here, like I was inside a box at the center of a raging bonfire. You'd think there would be some shaking, or some vibrations, but I felt nothing.

Thankfully the compression shockwave of reentry never lasted very long, and the sky soon turned gray as the MDV fell into the upper atmosphere.

The G forces picked up, pulling me left, then right, then left again, locking my facial muscles in fixed positions each time. This was new and unexpected. It was like the MDV had flown directly into a hurricane and we were being battered in all directions.

"Hang on, people," Mordecai said. "Some strong winds in the upper atmosphere." He was our MDV pilot today. A Special Warfare Combat Crewman. Basically someone who failed BSD/M. I remembered him actually. He had been one of the overly muscular dudes whose weight had worked against him in training. Still, Mordecai was one of the best pilots out there, and if anyone could land us in a hurricane it was him.

The Gs picked up again, and the impromptu roller-coaster ride of tight turns, corkscrew inversions, and steep loops got so bad that I almost passed out.

When things calmed down a bit, I noticed that the two scientists had their heads bowed inside their helmets. I checked their vitals on my HUD (Heads-Up Display). They were unconscious.

"Sir, the scientists," I told Chief Bourbonjack.

"I see it," the Chief said. "Take care of them after we secure the site."

The turbulence increased for a few moments, then finally ceased entirely. "We're through," Mordecai said. "It's all smooth sailing here on in, folks. Heading for the outpost."

Through the window, the sun illumed a jagged landscape of shiny obsidian. The black rock ranged as far as the eye could see.

"Looks homey," Trace said from beside me.

A few minutes later the MDV did a quick pass-over of the outpost and I caught a glimpse of the mirrorlike domes and the can-shaped passageways that connected them.

Mordecai landed us in the relative center of the outpost. Through the window I recognized the courtyard from the earlier briefing: domes and connecting passageways surrounded the MDV on all sides.

Chief Bourbonjack straightened up. "TJ, report."

"HS3's report all clear, Chief," TJ said.

Chief Bourbonjack looked down the ranks. "Prepare to deploy to the alleyway indicated on your six."

I pulled up the map on my HUD and saw the alleyway highlighted in blue.

The MDV's ramp folded down and my shoulder and waist latches clicked open.

"Trace, Fret, Bender, Big Dog, give me a defensive perimeter on the MDV!" Chief Bourbonjack said.

The designated troops sprinted outside.

"Everyone else deploy to the alleyway! Deploy deploy deploy!"

I was the second-to-last out. I ran forward at a crouch, staying close to Alejandro, my "buddy" for the mission. I kept a watchful eye on the nearest dome, slightly distracted by the platoon's reflection on its surface. I was looking for any sign of enemy fire. I saw movement on my three: one of the spherical HS3 drones, acting as a scout.

I ducked into the alley—a small space between two of the domes—and dropped, taking my place near the back of the group. Crouched at the entrance to the alleyway, Ghost and Facehopper covered the MDV.

I heard a sonic boom, then a cloud of dust erupted from behind one of the domes on the left. Another sonic boom, another cloud, this time farther off in the distance, on the right. The HS3 scout spun off toward the nearest cloud, and I switched to its viewpoint.

The two-meter tall form of an ATLAS 5 emerged from the cloud. Gatling guns mechanically swung into the armed position on either hand. The augmented-reality label "Lui-Aphid" floated in green above the mech.

I switched back to my own view, glad to have the mechs on *our* side.

Each of us reported "all clear" over the comm line. I saw two more streaks in the sky then, which marked the payload elements that were launched after the ATLAS 5s. These contained the jet-packs the mechs would need to return to the ship. Nothing I need concern myself with. That was the domain of Lui and Manic.

"Site secure," Facehopper said.

I hurried to the MDV to check on the scientists. They were awake, and responded well to the brief mental status exam I gave them. Satisfied that they didn't need any further attention, I returned outside.

All the men were gathered around Chief Bourbonjack, though most of them kept their eyes on the domes and interconnecting passageways of the outpost.

"Report, Rade," Chief Bourbonjack said.

"The scientists are a bit shaken up, but otherwise ready to go."

"Good." He glanced at TJ. "Have all the Centurions checked in?"

TJ nodded. "They've done three random sweeps of every single compartment. Place is as abandoned as you can get."

"I want all the buildings checked again," Chief Bourbonjack said, glancing at Facehopper. "I'll be damned if I trust some robot."

"Got it, Chief." Facehopper turned toward the rest of the platoon. "Ghost, Trace, and Big Dog, provide moving overwatch of the sweep. You pick the hide. Rade, Alejandro, and Tahoe, you provide overwatch on the scientists and the MDV. Your hide is the roof of that silo over there."

I looked at the building indicated. A cylindrical structure. It might have been a silo of some kind, maybe for grain.

"Yes sir!" I ran at top speed toward the smaller dome beside the silo. When I came close, I leaped, activating my jumpjets with a mental command. The boost from the jet sent me to the roof of the dome. As my foot made contact, I bent my knees and pushed off, activating the jets again. I landed on top of the silo and dropped.

Alejandro and Tahoe were right behind me. They scaled the silo just as expertly (Tahoe took a more direct route by firing his jumpjets twice in a row, straight up, while Alejandro followed my path) and settled in beside me. Alejandro and I kept watch on the MDV through our scopes while Tahoe guarded our backs.

I watched my teammates fan across the square in two groups. The nearest fire team converged beside an airlock. The lead man activated the release, and returned to his position against the wall as the hatch opened. He "pied" the entrance, slowly stepping away from the wall, keeping his gun trained inside the airlock and moving in a semicircle, or "pie" pattern, increasing his angle of view. Then he gave the all clear and all four piled in, closing the airlock behind them. If things got hot past that inner airlock, they'd be piling out of there just as fast.

I saw a glint of metal in the distance, and backtracked on my scope.

It was just one of the Centurion robots, on patrol over on the west side of the outpost. A spheroidal HS3 drone joined it.

"Anything?" Alejandro said.

"Negative. You?"

"Nada."

Movement drew my eye skyward, and I saw the Raptor drone fly past at fifteen thousand meters. It was operating in full stealth mode, and made no sound at all. If I hadn't seen it, I wouldn't have even known it was there.

Nearby, the white-hot globe of the alien sun shone its yellow light down upon us. It was about the size of my fist, and whenever

I looked at it, the photochromic polycarbonate in my face mask instantly darkened.

I waited with Alejandro, prostrate on the rooftop, keeping watch on the MDV as the scientists started to set up their survey equipment.

"Chief," I sent directly to Chief Bourbonjack on a private line. "Do the scientists have permission to set up?"

My words were met with silence, and I knew that the Chief was checking with the Lieutenant Commander. Or maybe arguing with him, given how long it was taking him to respond. Finally: "Roger that, Mr. Galaal."

Mordecai, our pilot, was sitting down on the ramp of the MDV, standard-issue rifle in one gloved hand. In front of him, both of the scientists were bending far forward to unfold some sort of retractable antennae on their equipment.

"How's the view from down there, Mordecai?" I subvocalized to the pilot. "Bet you wish you passed BSD/M."

He gave me the finger.

"What did you say?" Tahoe said.

I chuckled. "Nothing. Just asking him if he liked the view. I might have teased him about failing MOTH training."

"Oh you're a bad man," Alejandro said, voice dripping with irony. "A bad, bad man. Though actually I wouldn't mind being down there right now. That scientist on the right? Bet she has a sweet behind. Even suited up, you know what I'm saying?"

About an hour later Facehopper ordered us down and we reconvened with the rest of the team.

"Well, the SKs sure left this place in a hurry," Facehopper said. "Meals half-eaten in the mess hall, beds left unmade, closets fully stocked with gear and clothes."

Chief Bourbonjack was rubbing the lower part of his face mask. "Any leads? Rad trails?"

Fret pointed to the east, beyond the mirrorlike silo where I'd perched with Tahoe and Alejandro. "Found a strong rad trail at the edge of the outpost. SK signature. About eight months old." Atomic-powered machines always left a radiation signature, and unless it was cleaned, anyone with the proper equipment could track it. "TJ had an HS3 follow the trail. Looks like it leads to one of their Geronium excavation sites. TJ has the Raptor patrolling the area now."

Chief Bourbonjack glanced at TJ.

Our drone operator shrugged. "Looks clear, Chief."

"How far?"

"Two klicks," TJ said.

The Chief nodded. "We should really take the MDV." He glanced at the scientists. "You two. How easy is it to move all that equipment you've set up?"

The first scientist shook her head. "Not easy at all. We've already started drilling. It would take at least an hour to pack everything up again. That's an hour we could spend getting core samples. The sooner we finish, the sooner everyone goes home." There were tubes and wires running from the survey equipment back to the MDV. It was pretty obvious that you couldn't move one without packing up the other.

"Damn." The Chief gazed longingly at the MDV, then bit his lip. "Guess we'll go on foot." He surveyed the rest of the platoon. "We move out in five. Facehopper, get 'em ready. I'll be on the comm with the Commander." He walked up the ramp and into the MDV.

Facehopper had us all recharge our oxygen tanks and jetpacks, courtesy of the MDV's inventory. Neither scientist had a jetpack, but Facehopper had them refill their O_2 supplies too.

When the five minutes were up, Chief Bourbonjack wasted no time in organizing the platoon.

"Bomb and Fret, you're staying behind with Mordecai to guard the MDV and scientists."

"Yes sir."

"The rest of you are coming on our little walk. Facehopper, if you would?"

"Traveling overwatch formation," Facehopper said. "Two squads, seven men each. ATLAS 5s on point. Heavy gunners on drag."

He proceeded to divide the platoon into two squads. I was in the lead squad, whose members, from front to back, included: Manic, Snakeoil, Facehopper, Bender, Alejandro, me, and Big Dog. In the second squad were Lui, Tahoe, Chief Bourbonjack, Trace, TJ, Ghost, and Skullcracker.

The labels above each member of the platoon updated to reflect the new squad level designations, prefixing the letters S1 or S2 to the front of each name, depending on which squad we were part of. We also had a new squad-level comm assigned, so we could send messages only to those in squad one or two if we wanted.

Before leaving, I considered dropping off most of my gear at the MDV, but decided to keep it. I just hoped all those extra grenades and magazines didn't slow me down, but I figured the strength boost from the jumpsuit would more than compensate for the extra weight.

We used our jetpacks to quickly travel over the domes to the outer section of the outpost, where the buildings were set farther apart, and then we started the eastward march into the barren landscape.

The entire area sat on the shoulders of a mountain range, and the digital coloration on my jumpsuit darkened to match the loose, rocky shale at my feet—it wasn't obsidian, as I had thought during the descent, but those rocks were still ink black.

I heard the unified trod of five polycarbonate feet as the Centurions sprinted past, led by a Praetor command unit. My finger involuntarily reached for the trigger on my rifle.

"Rest tight, people," Facehopper sent over the S1 line. "Chief had TJ deploy the bots in a scouting capacity, is all."

A few seconds later an Equestrian tank rolled by in hot pursuit, its treads crushing the shale. Five HS3s hovered alongside.

I saw Alejandro start in front of me. "Where the hell did that come from?" he said.

"It dropped with the Centurions," Facehopper said. "Keep the comm chatter to a minimum, please, people."

Approximately three hundred meters ahead the robots slowed to match our pace and then spread out. The hull of the Equestrian, and the clothing of the Centurions, had changed coloration to match the terrain. The robots were damn hard to make out. I hoped the platoon melded into the background just as well.

In each squad, every person was situated five meters from the next in a zigzag line. Twenty-five meters separated the dragman of the first squad, Big Dog, from the pointman of the second squad, Lui (in Aphid). The separation ensured that an enemy would have difficulty attacking the entire platoon at once, and limited the effectiveness of mass-casualty weapons such as grenades or rockets that might be launched against us. Plus the formation allowed one squad to "overwatch" the other, hence the name.

Like the jumpsuits, the metallic skins of Aphid and Ladybug had changed colors to match the terrain. Both ATLAS 5s had also deployed their ballistic shields, which were these long translucent shells in the left hands that ran from the base of the mechs to just above their heads and protected against armor-piercing rounds. The shields used up a weapon slot, effectively taking away half the firepower of each mech.

You know that feeling of dread I had before on the ship, deep down inside me? It was completely gone. I guess all I needed to do was get into action, and finally deploy. It helped that I was surrounded by men who knew how to kill, and weren't afraid to do it.

I felt extremely safe with Manic at our point, in Ladybug. The mechanical hum of those large servomotors punctuated the mech's every movement, and I felt the ground shake with each step it took, even though I was twelve meters away.

Everyone else looked just as confident as I felt. Snakeoil with his communication rucksack, walking with his belt-fed machine gun. Facehopper and Bender with their standard-issue rifles. Alejandro and me with our sniper rifles (and my extra grenades and the Carl Gustav thrown in for good measure). Big Dog bringing up the rear with another heavy machine gun.

We were practically invincible.

None of us had been wounded during our earlier deployment in Mongolia. I figured that this was going to be just as easy. Even if there were SKs here, I knew we'd easily take them. It didn't even matter if they were better equipped. You know why? Because we were better trained.

I wondered if I could access Shaw from here. Snakeoil was carrying around an InterPlaNet node on his back, so it was entirely feasible. However, sending any unnecessary communications while in a traveling overwatch was strictly prohibited. If there was an enemy somewhere on these mountains, we didn't want to do anything that might compromise our position.

Shaw. I glanced involuntarily at the sky. She was up there now, somewhere, maybe looking down on the planet at this moment. I couldn't wait to see her when I got back tonight. In that moment I remembered the warning Tahoe had given me, and I quickly forced her to the back of my mind.

Ahead, I caught sight of the Raptor in the permanently gray sky. The unmanned aerial vehicle circled our distant target, reminding me of a vulture.

I pulled up the map on my HUD. The excavation site sat inside a crater approximately two klicks ahead.

The land sloped upward, becoming a narrow escarpment with a high cliff on one side and a steep drop on the other. We managed to keep our zigzag formation, even though the path had tightened considerably.

"How the hell did that Equestrian tank get up here?" Alejandro said.

"With difficulty," Facehopper answered.

I could see tread marks on the cliff beside us, as well as on the path at my feet. The automated tank had had to drive at a forty-five degree angle to traverse the area, with half its treads on the wall, the other half on the path.

Ahead, Ladybug moved on, this impenetrable bastion of unstoppable steel not slowed in the least by the terrain.

Behind Ladybug, Snakeoil abruptly lost his footing and plummeted over the ledge.

He reappeared a few seconds later, his jumpjets on full burn, and returned to the path.

Snakeoil smiled sheepishly. "Lost my footing. Sorry to scare y'all."

Facehopper didn't find it funny. "Please, mates, for the love of God, watch—where—you—tread."

He'd only just stopped talking when a spine-tingling laugh pierced the air.

I spun, training my rifle on an evil-looking thing at the top of a distant outcrop opposite our own. It just stood there, yapping away, looking like a cross between a hyena and a bear. It had an elongated, wolflike head. Its bulky body was covered in thick black fur, and tufts of green hair tipped its knees, shoulders, and ears.

Four more of the things ran up onto the outcrop, cackling away like demons.

"HQ," Chief Bourbonjack sent over the troop line (which included Lieutenant Commander Braggs). "We got something.

South-southeast of our position. One hundred and fifty meters. Over." His voice was the epitome of calm.

"Aliens!" Alejandro said. "I knew it! Friggin aliens!"

"Weapons hold. Confirm element. Over," Lieutenant Commander Braggs sent down from his cozy compartment on the *Royal Fortune*.

"TJ," Chief Bourbonjack sent to the platoon line, keeping us all in the loop. "Are these SK bioweapons?"

One of the HS3 drones with us hovered over to the strange animals. The lead beast stepped back and growled, lips curling to reveal a row of sharp teeth. The HS3 launched some kind of dart, and the animal yelped, but held its ground, growling even more fervently.

"Receiving prelim data from Arnold," TJ replied. Arnold was the callsign of the HS3 drone, apparently. "Definitely bioengineered from Earth stock. They seem to be contributing to the terraforming. Inhale the CO_2 and H_2O, exhale O_2. Body uses up the extra glucose. Those green marks on their body? Chlorophyll. Got some incredible adaptations going on, genetic-wise, to let them withstand the low pressure. Our scientists are going to have a field day with this data. Maybe we should bring a specimen back with us."

"HQ," Chief Bourbonjack sent to the troop line. "Confirmed bioengineered elements. Earth DNA. Possible contributors to the terraforming. Over."

I glanced at Alejandro. "Aliens, huh?"

Alejandro shrugged. "Hey, they look like aliens, okay?"

"The bioengineered elements are extraneous to the mission," Lieutenant Commander Braggs sent. "However, if you want to engage, it's your call. Over."

"They're not actually producing enough glucose from the sun to survive," TJ sent on the platoon line.

Facehopper glanced at Big Dog. "That means they've been getting the bulk of their nutrients from somewhere else . . ."

Big Dog pursed his lips behind his face mask. "I suppose if there were any surviving SKs left behind, now we know what happened to them."

Those snarling jaws took on a whole new dimension.

"*Puto*!" Alejandro cursed.

"Facehopper, has your squad come to the same conclusion we have?" Chief Bourbonjack sent on the platoon line.

"We have, sir," Facehopper sent. "Ghost, Trace, Alejandro, Rade. Take them out."

The creatures didn't have a chance. We picked our targets and downed the bioengineered animals at the same time. Four gurgled yelps echoed across to us as we shot, and the creatures went flying back. When the dead animals came to rest, greenish steam wafted from their wounds.

"What is that?" Alejandro said, the disgust evident in his voice.

"Their blood," Big Dog said, rather dispassionately. "The boiling point of a liquid is dependent on pressure. The higher the pressure, the higher the boiling point. The lower the pressure, the lower the boiling point. You bleed out here, your blood's gonna boil."

"Then why don't their eyes bug out, or boil away or something?" Alejandro said, lowering his rifle.

"Dunno," Big Dog said. "Ask TJ. He's the one with the sensor drones."

"You know what? Forget it. I don't want to know. Bioengineering. *Caramba*. It's just as bad as encountering an alien." Alejandro stared at the bodies a moment longer. Then he glanced at me. "What if we were wrong about them?"

I couldn't meet his eyes. "We weren't."

The escarpment leveled out, and we proceeded across a short plateau, keeping our zigzag formation. Manic's ATLAS 5 crunched eagerly ahead, an unstoppable war machine ready to go into action.

The rad trail eventually led to a relatively wide, V-shaped defile. Cover was limited, though if we were attacked in there, I could probably burrow into the shale that was a prevalent feature of the landscape.

According to the green dots marking the map on my HUD, the Centurions and the Equestrian were about three hundred meters ahead, roughly halfway through the defile. There were two green dots on both my left and right, and looking up, I saw the corresponding HS3s hovering along the peaks of the bordering slopes.

"How's it look, TJ?" Facehopper sent over the platoon line.

"All support troops report clear."

"I don't like it," Facehopper transmitted. "Chief, recommend we turn back and find another route."

I glanced at squad two, twenty-five meters behind us. The Chief seemed to be looking up at the rocky escarpments. "I'm with you, Facehopper. We double back, find another route. TJ, recall the scouts."

"Recalling . . . wait." TJ jerked his gaze upward. "Just lost contact with the HS3s!"

I turned around in time to watch a barrage of rockets launch from the tops of both escarpments.

CHAPTER EIGHTEEN

My training took over.

I could almost hear the instructor's voice in my head, guiding me through each step of the Contact Response protocol.

"Drop!" the imaginary instructor said.

I dropped immediately. The shale scratched the bottom of my face mask.

I never saw where those rockets struck, but I heard the explosion and felt the shockwaves.

There was little to no cover here. I tried to burrow as far as I could into the loose, rocky shale, and keep my head down, hoping the black-and-gray digital pattern of my jumpsuit would hide me. I heard the familiar belt-whip sound of bullets flying past and narrowly missing. The shale exploded all around me as the rounds struck. Black dust kicked up.

"Find your buddy!" the instructor said.

I glanced to my left. Alejandro was there, dug into the shale about five meters away. He nodded, then looked into his scope, aiming up the escarpment.

I glanced over my shoulder. The other members of the platoon were dispersed behind me, wherever they could find cover. In a tiny depression here. Behind a pile of rocks there. Or just on the open ground like me, burrowed into the shale.

"Complement your buddy's field of fire!" the instructor said.

I gazed into my scope. The range wasn't great enough for the processors in the EXACTO rounds to kick in—any hits I made would be all me. A target in a jumpsuit decided that now was a good time to lift his head from where he was hiding behind a rock.

I took him out.

There was a bright flash overhead. With a quick glance skyward, I saw that the Raptor drone was on an exponentially decaying flight path, a plume of smoke streaming from its engine.

We'd just lost our air support.

I forced myself to peer into the scope again.

Another target presented himself. He was close enough that I could make out his features through the lens of his jumpsuit.

Definitely SK.

Got him.

"Ladybug down!" Manic sent on the comm. "Hydraulics are blown to shit! Can't lift my arms or legs!"

What, how could that be possible? An ATLAS 5 already out of action?

"Aphid down!" Lui said on the platoon comm.

The *second* ATLAS 5?

I couldn't believe it.

Both mechs, gone.

It must have been dumb luck on the part of the attackers.

The ATLAS 5s were invincible.

We were invincible.

Our training had taught us that.

Our deployment in Mongolia had taught us that.

This shouldn't be happening.

Yet here it was.

We were going down, one by one.

Well at least I knew what the targets of those initial rockets had been. The ballistic shields each ATLAS carried were meant to protect against armor-piercing *bullets*, not rockets. The first strikes would have crumpled the shields away, leaving the mechs defenseless for the second and third strikes. The ATLAS 5s had something called a "Trench Coat" countermeasure, which used 360-degree radar to send out seventeen pieces of metal, one of which was bound to hit any incoming rocket. However, it didn't work too well when four or five rockets locked onto a mech at once.

On my HUD map, a bunch of red dots appeared on the escarpments, about three hundred meters into the defile, to the left and right of the green dots that marked the robot friendlies—our support troops were identifying and transmitting the positions of the enemy units farther in. I gazed through my scope, down into the defile. I saw the Centurions pinned behind the Equestrian tank. The tank was firing repeatedly up the slope on one side, taking out huge chunks of the escarpment.

I observed a barrage of rockets launch from the slope behind the Equestrian. I'm not sure where those rockets hit, but the Equestrian hurtled straight up into the air and landed upside down. The displaced Centurions took cover behind the damaged shell of the tank, taking heavy fire. The command unit of the Centurions, the Praetor, fell in a shower of sparks.

We weren't going to be getting any help from that quarter.

The hail of bullets continued around me. Shards of rock and dust were flying into the air. Along with the communications equipment in Snakeoil's rucksack was a newly developed Node-jammer, which was supposed to scramble SK wireless frequencies and prevent the enemy adhoc network nodes (i.e., their Implants) from exchanging information. In theory that meant if an SK identified one of us, our positions wouldn't be broadcast to all the other SKs. It was a recent technology, and I dearly hoped the SKs hadn't yet developed a countermeasure.

On my HUD, everyone's vitals were bright green: No one had been injured. Yet. Apparently the SKs were firing based on sight alone, so I guess the jamming technology was working.

Suddenly the gunfire around me began to pick up.

I'd been spotted. I searched for cover, any cover. My eyes focused on Ladybug, Manic's crumpled mech.

"Going for Ladybug!" I sent on the squad one line.

I got up, and somehow managed to make it behind the mech without getting hit. Facehopper, Bender, and Snakeoil were already there, and had given me covering fire. Manic was there too—he'd ejected from the mech and was now firing a pistol. His jumpsuit was blackened in several places, and one side of his face mask was smashed in, but so far the glass had held and he seemed to be maintaining suit pressure.

I took up a position on the right flank of the fallen mech and threw a few grenades, then switched to full-auto to give Alejandro and Big Dog a chance to join up with us.

We were in a defensible position, but I kept waiting for another barrage of rockets to come in. For every target we took down, another replaced him. I'm not sure how long we kept firing there from behind the mech; all I know is the gunfire never abated on either side. We were using up our magazines at a frightening rate. Big Dog had already exhausted his machine gun rounds, and he'd switched over to a standard-issue rifle.

Behind us, about twenty meters away, squad two was firing from behind a small, waist-high boulder, giving us support. Lui's mech lay crumpled on the ground not far from the boulder.

You'd think we could just use our jetpacks and get to the higher ground. But that was the worst strategy in a situation like this. You used your jetpack, you exposed yourself to attacks from all sorts of projectile weapons. In the heat of combat, an airborne soldier was, more often than not, a dead soldier. The jetpacks were more useful in urban warfare scenarios, where you could flit between buildings for cover.

The enemy continued to advance down either slope, and I realized that they were trying to outflank us. It was classic military strategy: get 360-degree coverage on your target and you will take it out. The kind of strategy we would have employed.

"Guys, you really need to get over here!" Chief Bourbonjack said over the comm.

Just then the inevitable barrage of rockets came in, and we dropped behind the damaged mech. Clouds of shale and dust filled the air. I had visions of that Equestrian flying up and turning over, and I hoped that wouldn't happen here.

A shard of shale embedded in my helmet lens, causing tiny cracks to spider along the surface of my face mask. When the dust settled, my mask seemed foggy. I wiped my gloved fingers across it, clearing away soot.

"You guy's good?" Facehopper said. He was covered in black dust like the rest of us.

"Never better," Big Dog said. "You worry about your fine English ass instead, how about that?"

A rocket struck the right side of the mech and the explosion sent the seven of us hurtling backward.

I landed, and the bullets immediately came in around me. I was out in the open.

I picked up my rifle and scrambled back to cover. Other members of squad one did the same.

I heard a whir behind me.

Thirty meters away, Aphid was getting up, the servomotors in its legs revving wildly. The whole front side of Lui's ATLAS had been bashed in, the charred ballistic shield welded to its chest. Must be cramped as hell in the cockpit. The right leg was dented all around the knee area, but the mech was able to walk.

The gunfire shifted away from squad one, toward Aphid instead.

Go Lui! I sent his Implant. I probably wasn't the only one sending him messages of encouragement right about now.

The Gatling gun on the mech's right hand locked into place, and Lui aimed it at the men coming down the closest escarpment and fired.

The roar of the Gatling filled the air. Lui immediately stopped taking gunfire from the closest slope of the defile. He rammed his left fist into the ground, breaking off the useless remnants of the ballistic shield, then he swiveled the second Gatling into place on his left arm and aimed it up the other slope.

Each Gat was capable of firing one hundred rounds per second, or six thousand per minute. The fire rate was so incredibly fast that it was like a thread of light connected the Gats to their distant target, a thread that alternately dimmed and brightened at various points along its path. Those bullets almost seemed to be traveling in reverse, away from the target: the effect was similar to a hubcap spinning at high speeds and seeming to rotate backward.

Anyway, the enemy positions were positively battered.

I hadn't been paying much attention to the comm chatter up until this point, but I tuned in now.

"I want that mech covered!" Chief Bourbonjack was saying.

Lui raced Aphid up the nearest slope.

I turned my rifle toward the top of the defile and started taking out fleeing SKs, keeping my other eye open as I shot so as not to diminish my battlefield awareness.

A rocket fired down at Lui.

Lui darted sideways and launched the Trench Coat countermeasure: seventeen pieces of metal flew toward the rocket. Incredibly, the rocket got through. Lui spiraled his body as the rocket came in, and the missile tore by just in front of his torso, exploding farther down the slope.

Unscathed, Lui landed, then clambered the final steps to the top of the leftmost peak. Red dots instantly appeared on my map around his position as men in SK jumpsuits were identified. Lui swept his massive arm to the left and right, swatting them from the escarpment like bugs. As fast as those red dots appeared, they vanished.

I was scanning those slopes, looking for the rocket operators. I was distracted by the sound of several rockets firing, and when I swung my scope toward Lui, I saw that he'd swapped out one of the Gatlings for a rocket tube and was unleashing a barrage of serpents at the peak on the opposite side of the defile. The deadly payloads took out good chunks of the slope. Rock shards and SK body parts rained down. More red dots appeared and vanished.

Aphid leaped across the defile to the opposite peak. That action flushed fifty SKs down the escarpment, conveniently outlined in red on my Implant. Those men scrambled over and down the rockface toward my position.

Lui didn't dare unload his Gatling at the fleeing men—we'd be caught in the crossfire.

But Lui didn't have to do the killing now.

We were perfectly capable.

I peered into my sniper scope and picked off SKs one after another. I was like a killing machine. Coldhearted, relentless. Shaw had been right about me after all.

I was a killer.

But right now all that mattered was that I kill, or be killed.

Alejandro, the other sniper in squad one, was firing almost constantly, as were Big Dog, Bender, and Facehopper with their standard-issues. Snakeoil was using up the last of his own machine gun ammo.

I decided I wanted to do some more damage.

I lowered my sniper rifle and slid the strap of the Carl Gustav off. I loaded a round, mounted the Gustav against my shoulder, held the grips near the front, aimed through the optical sight, and fired from my prone position. Where it struck thirty meters above me, a huge chunk of rock fell away from the slope. The fragments from the warhead took down five SKs.

On autopilot, my body automatically slid the hinged breech aside to reload the Gustav. I popped in the second round, and fired. Another huge chunk of rock fell away. That was my last round so I had to toss the Gustav away.

I grabbed my rifle and started picking off men again.

The SKs continued to run into our meat grinder. They didn't have a choice, not with Lui behind them in Aphid.

For a second I thought we might actually win this.

For a second I thought the tide of battle was shifting our way.

That we were invincible after all.

But then three more rockets streamed toward Lui's position from the opposite slope. He'd missed a group of enemies.

Actually no, that wasn't true. I was the one who had missed that group of enemies. I should have taken them down. I should have kept scanning that opposite slope. But I'd been too tempted by the easy targets.

And now Lui would pay.

Lui launched his Trench Coat again. One of the three rockets went down.

Lui tried to jump, but it was too late—

Aphid took the full brunt of the two remaining rockets. I saw the mech fly forward then roll down the hill.

It was a long, painful roll.

Lui's mech tumbled past the fleeing SKs, then continued another twenty meters, finally coming to a stop at the bottom of the defile.

Alejandro and I rushed forward to help him. We weren't going to abandon our brother there, on the slope. No MOTH ever left another MOTH behind.

The mech was a crumpled wreck, and I knew right away that it wasn't going to get up again. Not this time. As for Lui, his vitals were still being transmitted, but they were weak.

The hail of gunfire resumed, pinning Alejandro and me behind Aphid.

I heard Chief Bourbonjack on the comm now. Troop level. "We don't have a few minutes! I need a CASEVAC immediately! And where's my QRF? Goddamn it!"

"Just took out two of the rocketeers," Ghost said on the comm. "No sign of the third."

I wasn't sure that meant anything. Take out a rocketeer, and someone else would just pick up the rocket launcher.

Lui managed to pull the manual release inside Aphid, and the cockpit opened up. Thankfully the mech was facing away from the enemy, and the open cockpit provided us additional cover.

Alejandro and I hauled Lui out. Gunfire whipped past on all sides, beyond the ATLAS.

Lui was shaken, but alive. I couldn't see any bulletholes in his jumpsuit, or signs of blood, but it was possible he was suffering from crush injuries beneath the suit. That was something I couldn't treat out here. We'd have to get him to the Weavers on the *Royal Fortune.*

Lui shook his head, apparently trying to clear it. "What happened?"

"Can you walk?"

He nodded.

As the rest of squad one lay down suppressive fire, we hurried Lui to Manic's disabled mech and took cover. The SKs were coming down both slopes again, reattempting their flanking maneuver.

"Guys, I want you to fall back to our position!" Chief Bourbonjack said on the comm line.

"Roger that, Chief," Facehopper said. He looked at us. "Well, you heard the man. Two at a time. Go!"

Big Dog and Bender went first, while the rest of us lay down suppressive fire. I hurled a few grenades.

Facehopper and Manic went next.

Then finally Snakeoil and a limping Lui.

That left me and Alejandro.

I hurled the rest of my grenade loadout and without waiting for them to explode I took off with Alejandro across the open ground.

Gunfire rained down all around us. It didn't stop, not even when my grenades went off.

Alejandro was ahead of me, and I saw a burst of steam erupt from one of his jetpack fuel canisters. It had taken a bullet. The contents quickly steamed out, leaving behind a charred puncture hole.

Somehow Alejandro and I made it to the waist-high boulder where the rest of the platoon sheltered, without getting shot. I took cover behind the crowded rock and aimed my rifle out along the rightmost flank. The SKs had started to flow onto the plateau now, and some of them were already taking cover behind Aphid, Lui's mech.

It must have been about twenty minutes into the gunfight by now. I was picking off the SKs as fast as I could. I just kept firing and reloading, firing and reloading. I was glad I'd taken along so many magazines now, despite all the teasing. The barrel of my rifle was burning hot. My ears were throbbing from the sounds of gunfire. Around me, the heavy gunners had all run out of ammo and had switched to rifles or pistols.

I glanced quickly at the health indicators on my HUD. As corpsman, it was my job to make sure everyone was all right. Everyone seemed fine. No, wait. The green bar representing Bender's vitals was dim, with a hint of red in it.

I glanced at him.

Bender was slumped up against the boulder, firing his standard-issue rifle at the left flank.

"Bender is your suit compromised? Are you—"

Bender's attention never left the enemy. "Don't move, caterpillar. Blood sealed the puncture. My suit's fine."

I leaned back to get a better look at him. I could see red steam erupting from his jumpsuit, near the small of his back beneath the jetpack. The steam pulsed from the bullet hole, probably in time to his heartbeat. His insides in the immediate area had obviously been pulled toward the puncture, sealing the outlying area and preventing suit decompression. But he was at serious risk of bleeding to death.

I made my way over to him.

"I said my suit's fine!" Bender hissed when he saw me approach.

"Your suit's not fine, and neither are you." I reached for my medbag.

"No." Bender grabbed the wrist of my jumpsuit, rather forcefully. "Shit. If you're going to do this, use my suitrep kit, man. Patch my suit. There's no time for anything else."

I stared into his eyes and saw the determination there.

"Caterpillar," he said, almost pleading. "I can hold till we reach the MDV. Come on!"

I nodded. "Okay."

I fetched his suitrep kit from the pouch in his leg, and I patched the back of his suit while he continued firing his standard-issue rifle.

"Now get back to your position," Bender said. "We need your rifle."

I had sealed the breach in his suit, but that wouldn't help with his actual wound. He'd bleed out unless we got that looked after soon.

"Go!" he said.

I turned away.

"And Rade." That was the first time he'd ever said my name.

"What?"

"Thanks, bro."

I nodded slowly, then loaded a fresh magazine and returned to my place on the outer edge of the boulder, scanning the area through my scope.

The SKs had taken cover positions behind both Lui's fallen mech and Manic's now. Just then I saw an SK peer out from behind the closer mech. He held a rocket launcher over his shoulder.

My HUD displayed four bars above his head. High threat level.

Got you, bastard.

I took him out.

"Watch the flanks!" Facehopper said.

I glanced at the far left side of the plateau. Then the right. Groups of SKs were creeping forward on either side. *Again* they were trying the outflanking maneuver.

And they were succeeding.

The rest of us started to take them out, but then rockets came in from the forward direction, from behind the mechs, and we were forced to go down. Shale erupted all around us, and the shockwaves of the explosions caused vibrations to run right through my torso. None of us got hurt during that barrage, as far as I could tell. The whole point of the rocket fire was to allow the two groups on the far left and right sides to move forward unmolested.

"Squad one fall back!" Chief Bourbonjack said. "Rally at the edge of the plateau. Move move move!"

As Chief Bourbonjack and the rest of squad two laid down suppressive fire, the members of squad one raced along the open ground toward the edge of the plateau. I heard the belt-whip sound of near-miss gunfire. Shards of rock burst into the air around me. I fired off a few random, unaimed shots into the SKs on my rear flank.

Ahead of me, other members of the platoon were using quick horizontal bursts of their jumpjets to increase their speed. I did the same, careful to thrust only horizontally—remember, an airborne soldier in a situation like this was a dead soldier. It was a tricky business, firing off the jets over rocky terrain and not losing my footing, but I managed to get in two good spurts. On the third spurt I actually tripped, and ended up diving over the edge of the plateau and onto the downslope beyond.

Facehopper was already in position to provide covering fire beyond the lip, with a few other members of squad one arrayed behind him. My momentum carried me over him and the others, toward the edge, and I slipped right off the escarpment. I saw someone's hand reach out to grab me, but it was too late.

I slid down the slope. Fast. It must have been at least a seventy-degree angle.

I tried firing my jumpjets, but a bunch of shale had jammed up the nozzle. I clawed at the rock, but I couldn't get a grip. Nothing worked. The shale was chewing up my jumpsuit. I expected to lose suit integrity any second.

Miraculously, my suit remained intact, and somehow I managed to check my momentum. I'd ended up sliding about thirty meters—halfway down the slope.

I spun around, lying flat, breathing hard, and I aimed my rifle upward. The sound of gunfire had been swapped out for the staccato of my beating heart.

I tried activating my jumpjets again to get back to my squad.

Still jammed.

I was about to call for help when I heard a transmission from the Chief on the platoon line.

"Squad two, fall back!"

I wasn't going to call for help now: squad one needed all the rifles it had to cover squad two. Besides, I was safe. For now.

Some moments later:

"You see Mr. Galaal down there? He's got the right idea! Take cover on the hillside!"

And so my teammates slid down the shale, using their jetpacks to control the slide, stopping at various points around me and taking shelter along the side of that steep escarpment. We all aimed our weapons at the plateau above, waiting for the inevitable appearance of the enemy. Alejandro was the closest, about three meters away on my right.

As I lay there waiting for the enemy to attack, my breath coming in spurts, my heart pounding, I was still convinced of our invincibility. *My* invincibility. The thought that we might actually lose never even crossed my mind.

Then the hail of bullets began.

I peered into my scope and picked out the face mask of an SK, peering over the edge of the plateau, his rifle aimed down at me.

I got him in the temple.

I got another SK in the chest just as the man got up to help his buddy.

I didn't feel any remorse. Couldn't. This was war. It was either those two, or two of my brothers.

I kept firing, taking down targets mercilessly. For a moment I truly believed my own bullshit. That we were unstoppable.

Then I felt a sharp, poking sensation in my lower abdomen.

I knew from my training that I'd been shot. I also knew that the skin of my gut would be sucked outward because of the pressure differential, and would partially seal the bullet hole, while my coagulating blood would complete the seal.

At least, that's how it was supposed to work.

For two glorious seconds I felt no further pain.

Then it returned.

Tenfold.

This excruciating, burning sensation.

At first I thought I'd been hit with a certain illegal bullet called a helo-round: after it embedded in your flesh, the bullet sprouted six blades and started rotating lengthwise, chewing up your insides.

I bit down a scream.

Suffer in your head. Suffer in your head. Don't put your teammates in danger.

Though it probably wouldn't have mattered if I screamed: the SKs seemed to have a pretty good fix on us.

The pain increased, and I bit harder, feeling blood trickle down my chin.

I glanced down at the wound, and I realized why the pain was so bad.

It wasn't a helo-round. At least I didn't think so, because I could see this small, bubbling red mound protruding from my jumpsuit where the bullet had pierced. Pulses of red steam erupted from the bullet hole in time to my heartbeat, just like what happened to Bender.

My insides were literally being sucked out and boiled away.

I had to fix myself up.

Fast.

I started shrugging off the medbag.

That's when I saw Alejandro's vitals take a dip.

I glanced at him. He'd been hit too.

Worse than me.

He had a red spot on the far left side of his back, a little behind the armpit. He wouldn't even be able to reach the area to apply a suit patch. The wound was too high up on his back. He needed more than a suit patch, though: between the pulses of red steam coming from the perforation in his jumpsuit, I could see a part of what I guessed was his lung bulging through. I'm not sure how he was even breathing.

Maybe he wasn't.

I didn't have time to properly stitch my gut. I had to repair my suit and go help Alejandro.

I slung the rifle over my shoulder and fumbled the suitrep kit out of my leg pouch, flinching at the terrible pain in my belly. I opened the kit up and haphazardly applied the patch to the tear in my suit, right over a fresh plume of red steam.

The pain didn't go away, but at least now I was just merely bleeding internally rather than having my insides sucked out. I could feel the hot blood pouring down my hip.

Not a pleasant sensation at all, but I'd finish patching myself up after I helped Alejandro.

I turned toward him, and it felt like someone took a sledgehammer to my belly.

"I'm coming over there," I sputtered. "Alejandro."

He answered subvocally with his Implant. *Negative, Rade.*

As I suspected, he probably couldn't breathe very well.

I started for him, biting down the agony.

I said negative! he sent. *I'm serious. You make a move toward me, I'll shoot you*, hombre.

I punched the shale, partly in frustration, partly because of the sheer agony of my wound.

That's when I made my choice.

"If you have to shoot me," I said through gritted teeth, "then shoot me. But I'm coming either way."

I crawled along the shale toward Alejandro, doing my best not to slip farther down the slope, my jaw clenched against the waves of agony that throbbed through my abdomen.

Around me, my platoon brothers were firing for all they were worth from where they lay along that slope. Not a one of us would surrender, I knew. No one would ever give up. We'd fire to the last bullet, and when the bullets ran out, we'd fight hand to hand to the last man. Though a few of us might have our differences, we'd be here for each other to the end.

I reached Alejandro. He didn't shoot me.

I slid my medbag off my back, feeling utterly drained because of the pain.

That's when I realized I couldn't do this.

Sure I was tough. Manly. I could endure pain. But if it endangered my ability to help my friends, then pain was something I could do without.

I fetched the vial of morphine from my medbag and slid it into the injection slot above my glove. Inside my suit, a needle extended into my hand's dorsal vein network, feeding me the morphine intravenously.

The pain magically receded.

I knew it would be about three minutes before the effects of the morphine peaked. That meant three minutes of relatively pain-free work before the drowsiness kicked in.

I left the morphine slotted in place and retrieved a chest seal for Alejandro's body, along with a SealWrap, one of those funnel-shaped patches that I'd use to form a seal while I lasered into his suit. I started closing up the bag but my fingers slipped and half the contents spilled out, strewed over the slope below. Oh well, nothing I could do about that now.

I carefully set the medbag down on the shale beside me.

Alejandro was still gazing through his scope, firing off rounds at the enemy. I had no idea how he could do it. Maybe his injury wasn't as bad as it looked.

But then I saw his vitals momentarily flatline.

Yup, it was bad.

I felt a wave of drowsiness, and I blinked it off. I couldn't go to sleep, not until Alejandro was safe.

The bullets continued to come in.

I gripped the occlusive chest seal between two gloved fingers, then secured the SealWrap around the wrist area of the same hand so that the wider portion of the funnel went out past my fingers. I pressed the rim down tightly over the puncture area of Alejandro's suit, timing the movement so that I wouldn't get caught by the pulses of red steam from the bullet hole, and then I activated the sealant.

I felt the edges of the funnel tighten. Immediately the pressure within his suit equalized and the entire area sank in.

Alejandro's vitals fluctuated, and his head dipped. His insides were no longer being sucked out but he was still grievously wounded.

I bit down on my lip to stave off another bout of drowsiness. I could still feel some pain. That was good. Kept me awake.

I was vaguely aware as the bullets continued to whiz past, and my platoon brothers returned fire.

The funnel that sealed my hand to Alejandro's suit was translucent, allowing me to use the laser add-on in my gloves to cut away the punctured portion of his suit by sight. When I had revealed the bubbling wound underneath, I positioned the chest seal I still held over it, and then I slid the adhesive dial on the chest seal to the far right.

Done.

I'd sutured his chest lesion.

Battlefield medicine at its finest.

I could finally hear Alejandro panting in his helmet. His vitals seemed to stabilize.

He'd been shooting at the SKs the entire time. A true warrior.

Feeling really sleepy now, I pulled my glove away from his suit, stretching the flexible funnel that connected us. I groggily wrapped the fingers of my other hand around the neck of that funnel, crimping it just below my fingers. I carefully extracted my wrist out of the funnel, then turned the adhesive dial, completing the seal. The SealWrap would stay on Alejandro, a permanent fixture of his suit, at least until we could return to the ship.

I decided his blood pressure was too low, so I slotted one of the IV tubes into the injection slot on his glove, and hooked him up to a bag of plasma volume expander. I secured the bag to his belt with tape.

Alejandro glanced at me. "Owe you one." He sounded short of breath.

"Boy do you ever," I said.

Now I could sleep.

I lay back on the slope and closed my eyes.

I knew I needed to work on my own wound. And I probably could use a bag of plasma volume expander myself. I'd bled out. A lot. Problem was, the other plasma IVs were strewn along the slope farther down because of that little fumble with the medbag I'd had earlier.

Well, I'd just have to go get one, wouldn't I?

I wasn't a quitter.

That's when I felt someone press down really hard on my shoulder. I glanced at my suit, expecting to find Facehopper or Alejandro or someone, but instead I saw a small puncture wound.

That's when I realized I'd been shot.

Again.

The morphine prevented me from feeling much pain, thankfully.

Unfortunately, my vision was starting to grow dark.

But I wasn't going to quit.

My brothers needed me.

With eyes half-open, I took a step down the slope. Slipped a little. But that was good. It got me closer to the medical supplies.

But what was it I wanted to get from those supplies again?

And why were my supplies strewn out like that anyway, when I had the medbag on my back?

None of it made any sense.

Shale exploded around me as bullets honed in.

"Rade, where you going, bro?" came a voice inside my helmet. "Rade?"

I glanced at my HUD map for a second, trying to figure out where I was.

On that map I saw a bunch of green dots near me, with a bunch of red dots at the top of the slope.

I saw another green dot moving in from the left. Very fast.

An MDV abruptly roared past overhead, strafing the plateau with Gatling guns and rockets.

At first I thought it was our own MDV, but when the craft halted over the plateau, sixteen more green dots piled out onto the map.

"Bravo Platoon!" said a voice over the comm.

I blacked out.

CHAPTER NINETEEN

When I woke up, I lay in a bed. There were rails on the side to keep me from falling out. I tried sitting up but winced at the pain in my lower abdomen. Actually, it wasn't really pain, more discomfort. Mostly I felt dizzy.

I glanced down. A light-blue patient gown draped my body. I ran my hand over my abdomen and beneath the gown I felt a large bandage. It seemed to be wrapped around my entire midsection.

There was a needle connected to the top of my right hand, in the dorsal venous network. Connected to the needle was a tube that led up to an IV drip. Beside me was the *beep*, *beep* of a wireless EKG. I also heard the distant ambiance of the ventilation system, a subtle hum that indicated I was on the ship.

Convalescence Ward, then.

I glanced at the bed beside me. Alejandro was there, unconscious. I could see a slight bulge beneath his gown where gauze wrapped his chest.

Besides Alejandro and me, there were four other beds I could see, and each one was occupied. Lui, Manic, Big Dog, Facehopper. All asleep. I was expecting Bender as well, but he wasn't here.

I fumbled with the switches on the rails, looking for something to call the doc or nurse or whoever was in attendance.

A dark man dressed in blue scrubs came over. With his wild

hair, disheveled beard, and ingratiating smile, he looked like a cross between a Fakir and the Cheshire Cat. "Welcome back, Mr. Galaal."

"And you are?"

"Doctor Banye. GMO." General Medical Officer.

I glanced at his rank device. "You're a captain."

"I am. But not *the* captain, of course."

"No. If the captain looked like you, I'd jump ship."

That ingratiating smile never slipped.

I nodded at Alejandro. "How is he?"

"He is fine."

I glanced at my platoon brothers. "What about them?"

"They are fine."

"And Bender?"

"He is fine too."

I stared at this *doctor.* "Care to elaborate?"

"In what way?"

I sighed. "Is everyone all right in Alfa Platoon?"

"Everyone is all right in Alfa Platoon."

"No one is dead?"

"No one is dead."

I screwed up my face. "What kind of doc did you say you were again?"

"GMO."

"Yeah. GMO." I rubbed my bandage. Damn thing itched. "Straight up, doc, what did you do to me?"

He steepled his fingers. "Me? Nothing. The machines did all the work. The 3D bio printers re-created half your large intestine, and the Weavers put it in. Most I did was diagnose, help with the bandaging, and set up the IV. Doctors these days are more glorified nurses than anything else, you must understand. It's a shame what the profession has come to, really. A shame. Or maybe *sham* is the better word. And they said the machines would never replace us . . ."

"Help me sit up," I said.

Doctor Banye grinned widely. "I can do better than that."

The doctor eagerly showed me how to use the controls on the rightmost rail to tilt the bed up and down. "Give a man a fish, feed him for a day. Teach him how to fish, and feed him for life."

"What is that, a proverb?"

The corners of Doctor Banye's eyes crinkled. "It's from the Bible."

"I guess I should read that sometime."

"I highly recommend it."

I felt a jab of pain in my right shoulder and rubbed the muscle. "I thought I got shot in the *left* shoulder."

"You did. Your left shoulder was an exploded mess. We had to replace your rotator cuff, 3D print some bone, and so on and so forth. You made quite the engaging task for the Weavers. I'm sure they enjoyed it. I wish I could have."

"Well, then why is my *right* shoulder sore?"

"Oh." That smile wavered for the first time. "Due to the morphologic characteristics of your acromia, you were genetically predisposed to developing a torn rotator cuff. So I had the Weavers replace your right rotator cuff too. With an elastic bio-substitute. You'll never develop shoulder problems, thanks to me."

I looked at the doc dubiously. I noticed he'd sprinkled in far more medical jargon than he had while describing my abdomen or left shoulder injuries, like he was justifying what he'd done. Overly justifying. "You replaced my uninjured shoulder?"

"Why, yes. I just said that." He definitely seemed a bit nervous.

"Leave it to a doctor to find something wrong with someone perfectly healthy."

The doctor frowned. Good-bye Cheshire Cat. "It's called preventative medicine. You should be grateful."

"Ah, you're one of those, are you? Maybe you should cut off my hands too, because they're predisposed to choking you out!" I leaned forward and snatched at him, but the doc wisely stepped out of reach. "I can't afford to have my shoulders replaced on some doctor's whim like this. You better not have my pay docked."

The smile came back. "You're a valuable piece of property now, Mr. Galaal. The Navy is footing your entire medical bill."

"The Navy is footing your experiments you mean," I muttered.

He bowed slightly, smiling away, steepling his hands in front of him.

I glanced at Alejandro. "Are you going to tell me what you did to Alejandro?"

Doctor Banye followed my gaze. "Mr. Alejandro Mondego. Yes. Left lung was completely unsalvageable. I had to bio-print up a new lung for him, and the Weavers put it in. He now has the left lung of an endurance athlete. He'll be able to climb Everest without an oxygen mask. The wonders of medical science."

"Yes, the wonders." I forced a smile. "Did you do anything 'special' to him too? You know, to boost your professional sense of self-worth?"

The doc took a step backward. "Well, now that you ask, I noticed in the records that he had suffered from a prolapsed rectum in training. So I had the final three inches of his intestine replaced with an appropriate bio-substitute. Preventive medicine, you understand."

That actually made me laugh. I was imagining what Alejandro would do to the doc when he found out. "Let me guess, he'll be able to take a shit on Everest without toilet paper."

"Something like that."

"I'm sure he'll be glad to hear it."

I glanced at the far bulkhead. Seemed a bit abrupt, given the design of the rest of the room. Too close to the beds.

I examined the map of the ship on my HUD. Yup. The Convalescence Ward was actually twice as big. A breach seal had been activated to cut the room in half.

I pointed at the bulkhead that blocked off the rest of the ward. "What's the deal with that?"

"Mmm?" Doctor Banye followed my gaze. "Oh. SKs, Mr. Galaal. A wardful of wounded SKs."

Many people might assume I'd feel angry about the SKs being here. Angry that we were healing those who were trying to kill us.

I didn't feel that way at all.

And I knew none of my teammates did either.

The SKs were human beings with families, just like us, who had the misfortune of being in the wrong place at the wrong time. They were just following orders, however wrong and against our interests those orders might have been. We were all taught in training that when you're told to do something, you did it without question because if you didn't, your teammates might lose their lives. So I couldn't hold it against the SKs for following orders and doing their best to protect their own brothers.

When the battle was done and the guns were lowered, we didn't have any hard feelings.

I didn't, at least.

If any member of my platoon had been killed, I may have felt differently. I don't know. I was just glad everyone on my team was all right. I could imagine there must be a lot of anger and resentment coming from the other side of the bulkhead right about now, though. By my reckoning, we'd wiped out at least a hundred SKs.

I put my head back, and the doc left me alone.

I sent a message to Shaw. *Hey, babe.*

She sent me a message right back. *Rade! I'm coming down to the Convalescence Ward right away.*

Okay . . .

"Hey again," I said when she arrived.

Her eyes were red. Obviously she'd just been crying.

She threw herself at me and gave me a hug.

"Whoa, careful, you're hugging an injured man here," I said, feeling a little dizzy.

She pulled away, the concern written all over her face. "The doc told me you were fine!"

"Yeah. He says that about everyone."

"What's wrong then? You're going to be okay, right?"

"Shaw, yes I'm fine. Maybe a bit worse for the wear, but otherwise just dandy. Look, new shoulders." I lifted both arms, doing my best not to flinch. "Now I can climb Everest without toilet paper apparently. Or wait, that's Alejandro."

Her lower lip was trembling and I thought she was going to start crying.

"What is it?" I said.

"Nothing." She turned around, unable to look at me. Or maybe she was just ashamed because she almost teared up. "I was so worried about you, Rade. You almost got killed down there. And now you're just making light of everything. Acting like it's some kind of joke."

"Shaw . . ."

She spun around to face me. "Next time you're down there on the surface, try not to be so selfish. Try to remember there are people up here who care about you. Who want you to return in one piece."

I was completely taken aback, maybe even a little offended. "Selfish? You're calling *me* selfish? You really don't understand, do you? In a gun battle, all that's keeping the enemy from killing you is your Mark 12 and your platoon mates. I'd die for any one of them,

Shaw. Any one of them. And they'd die for me. Selfish." I nearly spat the word.

"Didn't you just hear what I said about the people who care about you? You say you'd die for your platoon mates. Well that's wonderful. But what about me? Would you live for me, Rade? Would you?"

I forced a laugh. "You care about me, do you? What happened to being just friends who bang? Why the sudden concern for my well-being? I know I'm a great screw and all, but come on . . ."

That did it. The tears I'd seen welling in her eyes spilled over.

"I see I've made a mistake." She turned to go.

"Shaw, wait, I'm sorry. I didn't mean it. Shaw—"

She hurried from the ward in a huff.

I could be such an insensitive jerk sometimes.

Shaw, I'm sorry—

She blocked me.

Great.

Well, at least Alejandro was in good spirits when he woke up.

"Well looky here," Alejandro said. "Someone's all bright and shiny this morning."

"Hey, Alejandro," I said grumpily.

"Man, it feels like someone stuffed a rag down my windpipe," he said. "Like all the way down." He struggled to sit up. "*Caramba*, I'm dizzier than a *mamacita* on a stripper pole." He lay back down.

Doctor Banye hurried in from his office in full, wild-haired glory, and attended to Alejandro, eventually telling him the same details he'd told me. When I mentioned the "upgrade" Banye had done on his lower intestine, Alejandro actually made it up off the bed and almost got the doc in a chokehold, but he ended up tripping on his IV tubes.

Banye sedated him and helped him back up on the bed, then hurried away.

"That doc freaks me out," Alejandro said, heavy-lidded from the sedative. He shook his head. "I got a whole new set of pipes. And new guts, like you. I guess that makes us gut brothers. Like blood brothers, but without the blood. Hey, bro, we got guts."

"Har har."

Alejandro frowned sleepily. "I'd never be able to afford something like this back on Earth. I can't even imagine how much money they spent on us today."

"Like the doc says, we're valuable assets now. It'd cost the military way more to replace us than to fix us up."

"God I hope so," Alejandro said. "Because the moment that's not true, we're dead men. Thanks for what you did back there, by the way. When I said I owed you one, I meant it."

"You don't owe me a thing. You've saved my life countless times over the years."

"If you say so. But I do owe you for this one, Rade. And I'm going to pay you back. Because that's how we do it."

"Seriously, it was nothing. You'd have done the same for me. Besides, I was the corpsman. It was my duty to get you fixed up."

Alejandro nodded, closing his eyes. "Yeah, but you patched me up before properly taking care of yourself. I won't forget that."

"I know you won't, Alejandro." I got up and started wheeling my IV toward the head. Over my shoulder I added, "Buy me a beer when we're back home or something."

He was already snoring.

I spent the rest of that day, and half the next morning, resting in the ward. At least I was in good company. Lui, Manic, Big Dog, and Facehopper woke up in turn.

Big Dog had taken a bullet in the abdominal sac too, and like he had for me, the doc had to print him up a new large intestine.

Facehopper was being treated for multiple shrapnel injuries obtained during one of the rocket strikes. The shrapnel had formed a seal with the jumpsuit, sparing him from decompression, which is why he was able to fight on throughout the gunfight.

But what was the most eye-opening for me were the injuries sustained by Lui and Manic. Because their ATLAS mechs suffered such grievous blows, Lui and Manic had broken bones throughout their bodies, along with several punctured organs. Luckily none of those punctured organs included the heart or brain. Manic had to have half his face reconstructed where his helmet had caved in. Lui lost his right leg below the knee. (The Weavers had already installed a new one, but he'd walk with a limp for a while until his body acclimated to the new tissue.)

I'd always thought that riding an ATLAS was the safest, most powerful position in the platoon. I mean, come on, we're talking an ATLAS here, this superpowerful mech, this one-man army. Invincible? The ATLAS mechs gave new meaning to the term. It was a revelation, that's for sure, to see that the ATLAS pilots were some of the most badly injured among us. I guess it made sense, though—in an ambush situation, because of their size and threat level, of course the ATLAS mechs would be the first targets.

The only people worse off than Lui and Manic were Bender and Fret. Neither had awakened—they were both in a medically induced coma in the ICU (Intensive Care Unit), just past doc's office. Both had suffered head shots, Fret while he defended the MOTH Delivery Vehicle, and Bender while we made our desperate stand on the slope. (Bender's earlier wound in the lower back was a joke in comparison, and the doc had already taken care of it.) Their damaged neural tissues had been replaced, but extreme swelling and intracranial pressure required that the fluid be drained from their skulls every six hours. The doc warned us that when they woke up, their personalities would probably be different.

So much for being invincible. So much for our training making us unstoppable.

I should back up a bit regarding Fret. Facehopper explained that while we were busy in the firefight on the plateau, another group of SKs had ambushed the MDV back at the outpost and had attempted to flee the planet. Mordecai and the scientists were taken hostage, while Fret, who was in charge of guarding the MDV with Bomb, took a hit in the face. The strands of hair and globules of coagulating blood sealed the puncture hole in his suit, saving his life; however his helmet quickly filled with blood. Bomb managed to drain the blood with careful positioning of Fret's body, stabilizing him until Bravo Platoon arrived.

As for the hijacked MDV, the *Royal Fortune* easily overrode the command codes and steered the craft back to the launch bay. The SK renegades surrendered when the doors of the MDV opened to three masters-at-arms carrying belt-fed machine guns.

The brig of the *Royal Fortune* could only fit nine people with its triple-racked bunks, so the rest of the captured SKs, including those who survived the firefight, were locked in the gym. All the gym equipment had been moved to one side of the room and sealed off—I guessed we wouldn't be working out there for a while. The badly injured prisoners were stuffed into the Convalescence Ward here with us, beyond the sealed bulkhead. The doc told me that there weren't enough beds for everyone, so mattresses with restraining buckles had been put on the floors and in the outer hall on that side of the bulkhead. Navy masters-at-arms worked alongside Pacification and Protection robots to safeguard the gym, the brig, and the SK side of the Convalescence Ward at all hours.

During the next two days, other members of Alfa Platoon visited us here in the ward, as did members of Bravo Platoon, or the Black Panthers as we called them. (They called us the Artists in turn.)

Tahoe, Snakeoil, Bomb, Ghost, and Trace became relatively permanent fixtures in the ward. They stayed pretty much the whole time during those two days, except during mess breaks. They talked with us, played co-op games on our aReals, and generally helped pass the time.

One talk we had stands out for me, because it helped me cope with what happened.

We'd just finished playing a game of Drone Wars, an interactive strategy game that mimicked the techniques and strategies involved in drone warfare. Everyone started the game with one Raptor, five Centurions, and two Equestrians. You could build more, but that required resources, which had to be mined by worker robots. You had to protect those worker robots, because they had no defenses, so you had to either build defense towers or assign Centurions to the workers. Anyway, the last game, I'd just devastated the other players, Alejandro in particular, who I'd wiped out in a mad rush in the first thirty seconds, taking out all his worker robots before he could assign any defenses.

"Good game," Facehopper said. "Who's up for a rematch?"

"Not me," Tahoe said. "I'm getting hungry. Gonna be supper time soon."

"All right, mate," Facehopper said. "Have a good supper."

Tahoe shrugged. "In ten minutes."

The others started talking about the game, and the strategies they'd used. How Ghost had nearly missed Tahoe's mine, or how Facehopper's Raptor had taken down Lui's Centurions just in time, and so forth.

I lay back, put my hands behind my head, and stared at the ceiling.

"You're pretty quiet, Rade," Tahoe said. "Normally you'd be gloating your ass off right about now. What's up?"

I smiled briefly. "I don't know. Guess I'm not really in the gloating mood."

Facehopper sat up in his bed. "What's on your mind, Rade?"

I hesitated. These were my brothers. I could tell them anything, especially this group. Might as well open up.

"I'd been dreading coming to this planet," I said. "But once we got here, I was sure everything would go well. I guess because, well, together I always thought we were invincible. But what happened out there, I just . . . it took me by surprise, to say the least. Seeing my teammates fall like that. Seeing my best friends, my *brothers*, go down. We're supposed to be the most elite spec-ops unit in the galaxy. *We do not fall.* Our training hammered that into our heads. And throughout our entire deployment in Mongolia, not one of us got hurt. And yet here we are. Seeing my platoon brothers fall was like having pieces of my heart torn out."

Tahoe nodded. "When I saw Lui go down in Aphid, and then watched you guys get shot up, that was just gut-wrenching. All I could think was that I was next. That I'd never get to see another sunset on Earth. Never get to hold my wife in my arms or make love to her again, or watch my kids grow up. But somehow I fought through it. Somehow I managed to block out those thoughts and stay focused on the battle. My training, I guess. The discipline that we force ourselves through each and every day. When I was lying out there on the mountainside, I kept telling myself I'd been through worse in training. That I could take this. But like Rade, I definitely felt humbled. I wasn't a superman. Not anymore. None of us were."

Tahoe was seated beside Facehopper's bed, and was close enough for the leading petty officer to rest a hand on his shoulder.

"That's a feeling all MOTHs get," Facehopper said. "Both caterpillars and veterans. It's a rude awakening, that's for sure, and it happens to us all, one way or another. The first deployment is usually easy. The second one, not so much. You soon learn that, no, you're not invincible, despite what your training, or your distance from the last deployment, might have led you to believe. All you can do is compartmentalize those feelings. Block them out and fight on. Sure, when someone falls, you save them if you can, and if you can't you have to deal with it later, because now, right now, you have to fight on for those of your brothers who you still can fight for."

I stared at my hands. I'd killed so many men with these hands. First in Mongolia. Now here. I wondered why I never felt any remorse for what I'd done. I guess it was because of my training. It had desensitized me. Pointing a rifle and shooting at someone in a simulation felt no different than doing it in real life: my brain couldn't draw the distinction between simulated rounds and live ones.

I was kind of glad about that actually.

I didn't think I could handle regret and guilt right about now.

"You three have finally been blooded," Facehopper said. "It's time for your callsigns."

I didn't look up from my hands. "You know, it's funny. I've been waiting for this day for so long, the day of my naming, but now that it's finally arrived, for some reason I don't really care. I don't even want a callsign anymore."

"That's how you know you're ready," Facehopper said. "When you finally realize that teamwork and brotherhood are more important than mere names. By giving you a callsign, we acknowledge this fact, and show you that we recognize this trait in you, and trust you with our lives. You're one of us now."

"Yeah, but—"

"No buts," Facehopper said. "Today is your naming day."

"Okay . . . what's my callsign then?" I said, resignedly.

Facehopper mulled it over. "Well, what I remember most about you from back there was how you fought when the SKs had us pinned behind Manic's mech. You were one pissed-off MOTH. Definitely wouldn't sell your life cheaply. You just waled on the SK positions. Threw a full complement of grenades. Even launched a Gustav a couple of times. You were just pure, raw rage. There, that's your callsign. *Rage*."

"Rage," Alejandro said. "I like it."

Tahoe nodded thoughtfully.

I shrugged. I didn't really see it, nor did I care. "Okay."

"And you, Alejandro." Facehopper scratched his chin. "From the way you kept fighting through to the end, protecting your fellow team members even though you had a punctured lung and could hardly breathe, your callsign is Houdini. Because you escaped death and kept battling on."

Alejandro chuckled.

"What is it?" Facehopper said. He glanced at me and Tahoe.

Tahoe grinned widely. "Houdini was what we called him in training."

"We have ourselves a synchronicity then. All the more reason to choose that name. The universe is trying to tell you something." Facehopper gazed at Tahoe next. "As for you, Tahoe, I've been talking with the Chief. He was definitely impressed by what he saw, and he had a couple of suggestions."

"Oh yeah?" Tahoe leaned forwardly eagerly. "Like what?"

"Hell-On-Wheels."

"Pfffft," Big Dog said. "Hell-On-Wheels! Ridiculous. That's the name of a platoon, or an Equestrian. Not a teammate. Never let the Chief name people. Look what he calls himself. Chief Bourbonjack. Come on."

"Well okay then." Facehopper tapped his lips. "The Chief's other suggestion was Cyclone."

Big Dog considered that for a moment. "Better, but still kind of corny."

"And none of our callsigns are corny?" Facehopper said, sitting back.

"What about Fearless?" Alejandro suggested.

"That's even worse," Big Dog said.

Tahoe shrugged. "Call me whatever you want, I'll do my job to the best of my abilities either way. But I'm definitely not fearless. I almost wet myself out there, I'm ashamed to say. Yes, a big guy like me, surprising isn't it? But being outgunned and pinned down by SKs on a planet eight thousand lightyears from home isn't exactly what I'd call a pleasurable experience, not at all."

"You're not the only one who was afraid," Big Dog said quietly.

Facehopper nodded gravely. "Cyclone it is."

The nice thing about being in the ward with Facehopper was that I got to hear his briefings with Chief Bourbonjack.

"Gives me the creeps having those SKs so close." The Chief nodded at the sealed bulkhead.

"They can't hear, don't worry," Facehopper said.

"I know they can't, but still . . ." He shook his head. "Suppose the doc's got most of them sedated anyway."

My eyelids were only open a crack, but it was enough to see Facehopper give me a significant look. I closed my eyelids entirely. "We can switch to subvocals if you prefer."

"No," Chief said. "I trust wireless communication even less. Anyway, okay . . . here's the deal. The Lieutenant Commander had our boy Ghost do some interrogations in the Box. He'd take an SK officer or enlisted and bring him in for a little session, all one-on-one like. Ghost would feed a good dose of truth serum to the subject, then ask the same questions, and get the same answers."

Facehopper arched an eyebrow. "Let me guess, those answers were just short of useless."

"Bingo," the Chief said. He sat down, sitting in one of the empty chairs that our visiting platoon mates had vacated when the Chief had ordered out all "non-essentials." He shook his head as if to clear it. "You're going to love this. Guess why they were abandoned on the planet? No idea. Guess why they destroyed the Gate? They didn't know the Gate was destroyed. Oh, but this is where it gets good. Guess why they stopped mining the Geronium? Death. Yup. The 'Great Death' swept in and scared them off."

Facehopper frowned. "Any elaborations on that point?"

"None. And get a load of this. You know those hyena-bear things we encountered? Turns out the SKs *did* bioengineer them. Why? Not so much for terraforming, but for protection. Against what? They won't say. Well, let me rephrase that. They don't know. The mysterious Great Death again. Keep in mind all of this is taking place after the truth serum has been injected right into their medial prefrontal cortexes. We asked where their support robots were. Their ATLAS mechs and walkers. No idea. All they could tell us was that their company was the last surviving group of SKs on the planet.

"So anyway, the doc looked at their blood work. Turns out the whole lot of them had traces of scopolamine in their systems. It's what the SKs use as a truth serum. Illegal in the UC. Makes the victim extremely susceptible to suggestion while the drug is active. Plus has the pleasant side effect of numbing the recall neurons, so that anything they do under the influence of the drug is forgotten. Thing is, scopolamine is basically a one-shot drug, you don't want to be using it too often—too many side effects. By itself, it doesn't last more than twenty-four hours. So that doesn't explain why they can't remember anything before the scopolamine was administered."

"You think they've been mindwiped," Facehopper said.

The Chief stroked his thick mustache. "That's exactly what I think."

"As for the scopolamine, the SKs drugged their own soldiers to make them do something they didn't want to do," Facehopper continued.

"Yup," the Chief agreed. "Though what it was they were supposed to do, I'm not sure we'll ever find out."

"What about the Implants? Have we broken the SK encryption on the units?"

"We got three AIs on it, under the guidance of two Fleet cryptologists, doing brute force attacks. None of the backdoors are working, so it could be a while. I'm not sure it'll matter, though."

"Why not?" Facehopper said. "The Implants maintain an archive of everything that a given person sees and hears."

"Sure," Chief Bourbonjack agreed. "But their Implants were deactivated when we found them. To the last man."

"Oh."

Their Implants were deactivated? So much for the Node-jammer in Snakeoil's rucksack protecting our positions out there. The SKs wouldn't have had even a Heads-Up Display during the battle.

"Why the bloody hell would they deactivate their Implants?" Facehopper said.

The Chief chuckled, and deep laugh lines appeared on his weatherworn face. "Besides the obvious reason of preventing anyone from viewing a recording of what happened? Doesn't seem worth it, does it? To lose all the tactical advantages granted by an Implant just to cover up whatever it was you were doing."

"I don't like it," Facehopper said. "Not one bit."

"No one does. Commander Braggs was yelling at Ghost and Banye when they brought him the news. And he never yells."

Chief Bourbonjack glanced at me with his dark, tilted eyes, and I quickly relaxed my eyelids, pretending I was asleep. I know Alejandro, Big Dog, Lui, and Manic were doing the same thing.

"You boys can stop pretending you're asleep now," the Chief said.

I opened my eyes, grinning sheepishly.

The Chief turned back to Facehopper. "Anyway, everything seems to revolve around that Geronium excavation site. Don't go there, all the SKs say. Don't go. No explanation other than 'the Great

Death awaits.' I don't have to tell you that the excavation site is now the focal point of our investigation. We've had the HS3s and a handful of Centurions scouting the area, but so far it seems quiet. There's a deep mineshaft that leads to an underground cavern of some kind, and the Commander has ordered Bravo Platoon down to join the robots for a recon. He gave them four ATLAS 5s. The scientists have gone too. At the first sign of trouble they're to evac immediately."

"Great," Facehopper said. "You saw how well that went with our platoon."

The Chief scratched his hooked nose. "I know. Never said I liked it. But the Commander wants to get to the bottom of this, if you'll excuse the pun. Initial reports from the HS3s indicate that the cavern is safe. No flammable gases. No hostiles or lifeforms of any kind. Just walls and walls of Geronium-275."

"No sign of hostiles. Where have I heard that before?" Facehopper crossed his arms. "Maybe we should just leave now while we're still ahead? Cut our losses, destroy the Gate, and never come back."

"Not going to happen. You know that." He patted Facehopper on the shoulder. "Have a good, long rest, my friend. Save up your energy. I have a feeling you're going to need it."

Several hours later the Chief returned.

This time with Lieutenant Commander Braggs.

"Bravo Platoon missed their scheduled check-in," the Lieutenant Commander said.

CHAPTER TWENTY

It could be nothing," the Lieutenant Commander continued.

"But if it were nothing, you wouldn't be coming down here to tell me." Facehopper lowered the side rail of his bed and stood up immediately. He winced painfully, but only for a second. "I'm going in." His voice was firm.

I was the next person standing. I felt dizzy a moment, but blamed it on lying down for thirty-six hours. Alejandro, Big Dog, Lui, and Manic rose in turn.

"You'll have to cuff us and throw us in the brig if you want us to stay behind," I said. "Sir."

Chief Bourbonjack nodded stiffly. He was blinking rapidly, and his chin quivered slightly so that for a second I thought he was going to choke up. But the moment passed and he became all hard scowls once more.

I was surprised when the Lieutenant Commander got suited up with us. He shouldn't have come. He shouldn't have put himself in danger like that. But no one said anything. We all understood why he did it. He was a MOTH, like all of us. He'd gone through the exact same training. All officers and enlisteds did. We were brothers. And he'd be damned if he left one of his platoons alone on some harsh planet without making every attempt to help them.

He was a warrior first, a Lieutenant Commander second.

Almost everyone from Alfa Platoon was coming along, except for Bender and Fret, who were still unconscious in the ICU.

In the prep room an SK was sitting cross-legged on the deck in one corner. His hands were bound. The way he looked at us reminded me of the prisoners of war we'd captured in Mongolia: there wasn't just anger and resentment in those eyes, but undisguised hatred. I knew he would've shot us all without hesitation, given the chance.

Chief Bourbonjack introduced him while we donned the jumpsuits. "This is Mao. One of their officers. Friendly chap, as Facehopper would say." His voice oozed sarcasm.

Facehopper paused. "You say Mao?"

"Yeah. What about it?"

Facehopper slid on his left arm assembly. "I met a Mao once, if you remember."

"Oh yes. The privateer. You didn't get along too well."

"Not at all."

"What happened?" I said.

"Oh, nothing." Facehopper fastened the right arm enclosure to his torso assembly. "Just that he tried to shoot a hole in me."

Mao wasn't paying attention. He had gone very pale, and his eyes were latched on to Ghost.

The albino gave him a mock salute. "Nice to see you again, Lieutenant. No hard feelings, huh?"

Mao leaned back, saying nothing to our interrogator.

"I don't think he likes you, Ghost," Lui said.

Mao shot Lui an evil glare. "You are a traitor to your race," Mao said in English, practically spitting the words. "You are the one who should be rotting on the planet, along with all your White Devils. Not my men. My good men."

"What race are you talking about, bro?" Lui said with a sigh. "We're all human here."

"You are less than human." Mao wrinkled his face in disgust and spat a glob of phlegm at the deck. "When I die in the *Yaoguai Dòngxué*, I will go down laughing, knowing that you and your men, you who slaughtered your own, die with me. You will get your, how do you say, just desserts."

Lui gave him a disgusted look. "Whatever."

"What's *Yaoguai Dòngxué*?" Trace said, zipping up the liquid-cooling-and-ventilation undergarment that went on beneath the jumpsuit. He was one of the slower dressers.

"Use your Implant," Big Dog growled.

"It's what the SKs call the Geronium mineshaft," Lieutenant Commander Braggs said. "*Yaoguai* is a demon from the underworld. Likes to eat the souls of men, apparently. And *Dòngxué* means cave."

Trace pulled on the lower torso assembly of his jumpsuit. "So we're going into a demon cave." The swarthy East Indian chuckled softly. "Nice." He glanced at the Lieutenant Commander. "And let me guess, the drones are still giving us the all clear, right?"

Lieutenant Commander Braggs nodded gravely. "So far. But the place is huge. A damn labyrinth. The second wave of HS3s and Centurions we sent down have mapped out maybe one-fifth of it. We're going down to speed that process along."

"Didn't we get any telemetry of the cave from Bravo?"

"Some. Problem is, we can't get a signal out from the underground cave network. That one-fifth of the cave we've mapped so far? We're getting it by sending the HS3s and Centurions in a ways, then ordering them back to the surface so the robots can transmit what they've found to us."

"What about the ATLAS mechs, and the robot support troops sent down with Bravo?" I said. "Have we found those yet?"

"No." Lieutenant Commander Braggs secured the helmet of his jumpsuit. He seemed bothered by what I'd just said.

"You will find only death," Mao said in broken English. "The Great Death."

Skullcracker stepped forward. "Howdy."

Mao flinched backward. The sight of that skull tattoo was enough to shut him up.

We all finished suiting up. The doc injected Mao with a sedative, then Facehopper and Skullcracker unbound him and dressed him in a trimmed-down version of our jumpsuits, basically just an environmental suit minus the strength-enhancing exoskeleton—the same type of suit the scientists wore on our first drop. When Mao was suited up, Facehopper and Skullcracker strapped metallic anklets around the outer assembly of each of his feet and bound his wrists with fibroin cords.

We waited the necessary hour for our bodies to adapt to the lower pressure in the jumpsuits. Well actually that's not true: we cut the adaption period short by about fifteen minutes. We were too wound up.

I tried to say good-bye to Shaw. She still had me blocked. Too bad. I didn't know if I'd come back, and I didn't want to leave things just hanging like this between us.

I proceeded to the weapons rack in the hangar bay with the others.

Facehopper had made fun of me the first time around for bringing so many grenades. Well, he packed on more than a dozen this time. The whole team did. My brothers loaded up on the magazines, slung Carl Gustavs over their shoulders, tucked two pistols each into their belts.

I loaded up on magazines too, but as for actual weaponry, I grabbed only a couple of grenades and a 9-mil.

Why?

Because before we had gone over to the weapons rack, Lieutenant Commander Braggs took me aside.

"Mr. Galaal, most of the remaining ATLAS 5s are down there with Bravo Platoon. We salvaged Ladybug, Manic's ATLAS, but it's going to take a lot of work to repair her. That leaves only one working mech aboard. You understand me?"

"Uh, yes sir." I glanced over my shoulder, toward the mech storage alcoves on the far side of the hangar, behind the drop vessel. Those alcoves were all empty, save one. Hornet moored there, brooding in silence, a behemoth waiting to awaken, a deathdealing avenger ready to unleash its wrath upon the world below. "Uh, not really, sir."

"I want you to pilot Hornet. Our last ATLAS."

"You're shitting me." When it finally sunk in that he wasn't joking, I just stood there with a stupid grin on my face. Finally I was getting a chance to prove myself. A chance to pilot an ATLAS 5 in an actual combat situation.

Braggs didn't say why. He had full access to my qualification results of course. He obviously knew how high my ATLAS aptitude scores were. I guess he was just waiting until I had my callsign before he assigned me to a mech. Or maybe he wanted to punish Lui and Manic for losing theirs.

"Thank you, sir," I said. "But I have to refuse."

"Excuse me, Mr. Galaal?"

I glanced at Lui, Manic, and Bomb. All three were eavesdropping attentively nearby.

"I have to refuse. Bomb is really the one you should pick, sir. He has more actual experience in combat. And he hasn't had a chance to drop—"

"You're going to drop in that mech, do you hear me, Galaal?" Lieutenant Commander Braggs said. "Don't give me that I'm-sacrificing-myself-for-my-friends bull. We need the best out there on the ATLAS 5 today, and you're the best."

"The best in training maybe—"

He gripped my jumpsuit by the chest handle and actually lifted me up. I could hear the servomotors in his suit's exoskeleton revving. "I've never had to force anyone into a mech in my life. Are you actually going to make me regret my decision? Do I have to kick your sorry ass into that steel cockpit myself?"

I swallowed, taking very good care not to look at anyone else. "No sir. I won't let you down, sir."

"Damn right you won't, Mr. Galaal. Damn right. We're all distraught because of what's happened with Bravo Platoon, so I'll forgive your insubordination. This time."

I realized I'd made a big mistake questioning the orders of the Lieutenant Commander in front of everyone like that. Of course he wouldn't be able to rescind an order once he gave it, even if I was right. It would only make him look bad. If we survived this, I'd probably never get assigned an ATLAS mech again.

Damn it.

Even so, as I approached the mech alcove, I felt a sudden buoyancy in my step.

I was doing this.

I was really doing this.

I climbed the support rungs on Hornet's right leg, and swung myself into the cockpit. The hatch sealed, and the elastic inner material pressed into my body from all sides. I felt the usual moment of claustrophobia inside that windowless cockpit, but it passed when the mech overlaid what it saw onto my vision and I looked down on the hangar bay from the height of an ATLAS 5.

When everyone was onboard the MDV, and the ramp closed, I watched the magnetic rails gradually extend beyond the opening of the hangar. Secured to the overhead was a long robotic arm, and it latched onto the top of the MDV.

The craft slid forward on the rails. When the MDV was outside the launch bay, the rails demagnetized and slowly slid back inside.

The MDV, supported now only by the robotic arm, wobbled back and forth ever so slightly. The pincers of the arm opened up and the MDV fell from view.

The arm retracted and the metallic rails extended beyond the doors once more. The rails flattened, widening, and moved closer together, forming a bridge of sorts. I walked Hornet onto that bridge, feeling the power in every step. I passed beyond the opening of the hangar bay and out into space.

There was no artificial gravity out here, and the weightlessness of space took over immediately, playing havoc with my inner ear. There was no up or down, no left or right. It felt for all the world like I was walking upside down and sideways. At the same time.

I concentrated, ignored the feeling. Right foot forward. Then left foot. Right. Left. The magnetized metal below ensured I wouldn't float away with each step. I could feel the resistance as each foot lifted away, and the suction as that foot lowered again.

I heard no sound except my own tense breathing.

I told myself this wasn't a big deal. I'd dropped in a mech before, in training. "Walking the plank," we called it.

I reached the edge. The world floated below me, filling up the sky from horizon to horizon. I could see the curvature at the far edges.

I always loved this part. Perched here like this, I was literally on top of the world.

The next part, I didn't like so much.

I stepped off.

The ship sped away and in an instant was a tiny dot above me. Below, the world didn't seem to get any bigger.

Not at first anyway.

On my HUD, I saw indicators showing that the gyroscopic thrusters were firing regularly, keeping me stable during the descent. The single-use aeroshell heat shield deployed, forming a giant inverted mushroom about ten meters in diameter beneath Hornet.

Soon my vision was filled with orange flames as that shell deflected the heat of entry. I always got this panicky feeling of being trapped in a burning casket in a crematory right about then, even though I knew the physics of it all. Or perhaps *because* I knew the physics: The compression shockwave below the mech heated the air molecules to several thousand Kelvins, and the blunt shape of the shield caused the air right underneath to act as a cushion, pushing the heated shock layer away from the ATLAS. If the silicon-coated Kevlar shield sprung a leak and the nitrogen gas leaked out, both the shield and the mech would disintegrate into so much molten slag.

Even with that shield, it still got a little hot. Well, more than a little. I was sweating in profusion. Hornet's aerogel insulation (not to mention the liquid-cooling undergarment I wore in the jumpsuit) was supposed to regulate the internal temperature to a decent level, but it always got a bit too warm for my tastes. I checked the internal temperature. Fifty degrees Celsius, 122 Fahrenheit. Way over human body temperature.

Yup, a bit too warm.

Then there were the G forces. I'd felt them the moment the mech decelerated as it passed into the thicker air. An ATLAS weighed three tonnes, so it didn't slow down a whole lot, but the negative Gs were still noticeable. I practiced doing the muscle contractions we'd been taught. The forces topped out at three Gs according to the indicator. Not as bad as doing a drop in a jumpsuit. That was the worst. Because of the light drop weight, the negative and positive forces could reach up to eight Gs. Not fun. I'd fallen unconscious one time in training during a jumpsuit-only drop, and the autopilot had saved my neck.

I concentrated on the real-time data that overlaid my vision, trying to distract myself. I saw my current altitude, elevation, acceleration, internal and external temperature, my body temperature, my heart and breathing rates. The latter two were pretty high.

Stay calm, Rade, I told myself. *Stay calm. You've done this a hundred times.* Well, more like three, but I didn't think any exaggeration would hurt right about now.

I just wanted it to end. The Gs, the heat. Still, I knew it would be over soon. I concentrated on this moment, just like I'd done in training, and didn't look past it. I just had to get through this. Just had to get to the next meal.

And then I was through.

The flames receded and the internal temperature dropped. Rapidly. Now I was freezing. All that sweat I had over my body might as well have been ice. I had flashbacks to sea immersion all over again, and I half expected an instructor to yell at me to go and turn myself into a Gingerbread Man.

The heat shield broke away.

I could see a large, black landmass below.

The internal heaters kicked in, stabilizing the interior temperature, and I stopped shivering.

After about twenty seconds, the autopilot engaged the air brakes, increasing drag and my angle of approach. Both legs swung forward, and the aerospike thrusters built into the feet of the mech activated at full bore. Even so, the ground came up fast and I hit the rocky surface extremely hard. On impact my body curled up—my knees were forced way up, and my thighs nearly touched my chest, while my calves brushed my hamstrings, mirroring the posture of the mech. A shockwave of shale and dust spread outward from the ATLAS.

I stood up to my full height, swiveling a Gatling into my right hand and a serpent launcher into my left hand. I took two steps forward, emerging from the dust cloud, leaving behind two molten footprints where I'd landed.

I felt invincible. I almost dared more SKs to come leaping out at me. None did.

Too bad.

I stood on a bleak, gently sloping plateau of black rock. On my

HUD, I saw the green outlines of my teammates in the distance. I had landed about a quarter of a klick from the MDV, which had touched down close to the Geronium excavation site. Far to the west I could see the hilly defile where we'd been ambushed earlier.

I saw smoke streak across the sky and watched a fiery object smash into the ground about one klick away, farther up the slope. That was the payload element, which dropped right after me. A flashing blue dot appeared on my HUD. Inside that payload were the external rocket boosters I'd have to attach to Hornet when I wanted to return to the ship, along with charges for my mech's O_2 tanks and jumpjets.

Other than the sun, and the streak of my payload element, there was nothing else in the sky. No clouds. No Raptors to offer air support—we'd lost our only one during the SK attack. Not that we needed air support where we were going.

"Site secure," Facehopper sent over the platoon line.

I hurried forward, just springing along with my two-meter-long legs. This was great. This was how man was meant to travel. Everyone should have one of these. The Brass needed to tighten their spending and focus on getting us more of the assets that could really make a difference in combat. So what if these things cost three billion digicoins each? Make it work.

I joined up with Alfa Platoon in no time. They'd landed beside Bravo Platoon's MDV, which was empty. No sign of the platoon, the pilot, the support robots, or the ATLAS 5s.

Facehopper ordered Mordecai to stay behind with both MDVs, and assigned Manic to guard him, then he broke us up into traveling overwatch formation. I was in the lead squad and took point. Big Dog was right behind me, dragging Mao along.

I followed the map on my HUD toward the flashing dot that was our destination. As usual, the coloration and patterning of the jumpsuits had changed to match the terrain—as had the surface of my mech, thanks to the array of paper-thin LEDs coating the metal.

I made good time, and in a few minutes I reached the edge of the site, which was this huge, man-made open excavation. There were giant, deactivated machines everywhere. I saw towering dump trucks that looked like they could carry four hundred tonnes each, the wheels as tall as Hornet, the dump bodies probably capable of holding the *Royal Fortune*. Between the trucks were huge hydraulic power shovels, just as dead.

On the western side, toward the outpost, there was some kind of rock crusher perched at the edge, with a conveyor belt that led away to a grimy, dome-shaped factory, where three lifeless chimneys poked at the sky.

The flashing dot indicating our target, the mineshaft, lay in the center of the excavation. I spotted three Centurions dressed in gray-and-black digital camos, waiting beside the shaft.

I signaled the all clear, and waited as the rest of the platoon approached the edge.

"Looks like a big cairn," Ghost said.

"I hope not." I glanced at him from my mech. The albino seemed like a little kid, standing there beside me.

"No," Ghost said. "I meant in memory of the Geronium operation the SKs ran. Not a cairn for our guys. Never our guys."

"Good," Facehopper said. "For a second there you sounded like that Mao character."

"Notice how half the dump trucks are still loaded with rock?" Snakeoil said. "And look at the conveyor belt. Covered in crushed fragments. They sure closed up shop quick."

"Closed up shop?" TJ said. "No, man. The SKs downright fled. Something spooked 'em."

Facehopper turned to Mao.

"Death," Mao said.

Facehopper nodded. "Figured you'd say that."

Something else was a bit odd. There were shell casings all over the place, leading up the slopes of the excavation, right to here.

Skullcracker held one of the casings to eye level.

"Bravo Platoon?" Facehopper said.

Skullcracker shook his head. "Naw. SK make."

"It was like this when Bravo Platoon got here," Lieutenant Commander Braggs said.

"What were the SKs shooting at?" Alejandro said.

Facehopper was grim. "That's the question, isn't it?" He glanced at Mao. "Let me guess. Death, right?"

Mao shrugged noncommittally.

"How are the radiation levels?" Facehopper said.

Snakeoil stepped to the edge and waved a gloved hand slowly back and forth. "The millisieverts are off the scale. The suits are capturing about half of it, but we're still going to have to be on the juice when we get back."

"Lead the way, mechman," Facehopper said, slapping his strength-enhanced hand against my right leg. The thud echoed through the metal and I felt the reverberation in my cockpit.

I started down the slope, the loose rock crunching underneath my massive feet. On my map, the green dots of squad one followed me in the zigzag pattern of traveling overwatch.

I reached the Centurions, and they gave way before me. I was the biggest robot, after all. The rest of squad one froze in place behind me.

I stood before a shaft that seemed to have been cut into the rock. A pole had been strung across, and ropes led downward into the darkness. It reminded me of a well, somewhat. A square shaft about two meters wide by two across. Too small for my mech.

I know it might sound clichéd to say this, but that hole looked evil somehow, like it led to the abyss itself. Just looking at it, and the darkness inside, gave me chills. Alarms went off inside my very being, and some sixth sense told me that it was a very bad idea to go down there.

But I had to. Bravo Platoon was inside, and needed our help. I wasn't going to abandon them. None of us were.

I just wish I could've brought Hornet.

"Rage, did you dispatch the probe?" Chief Bourbonjack said on the comm.

"Dispatching, sir." I launched the shoulder-mounted ASS (the ATLAS Support System—yes, whoever named it was being a smart-ass), kind of a miniature version of an HS3 probe, and it traveled down the shaft, its revolving cones of light illuminating the walls in a plummeting corkscrew. On my HUD I viewed the video feed, which cut in and out every few seconds.

"The support probe just reached the bottom of the shaft," I sent on the platoon line. "Looks like some kind of natural cavern. The walls are smooth, with none of the signs of drill bore. Going deeper."

As the probe advanced, the feed progressively worsened—the pixelization became so bad that I couldn't tell what anything was, and the vid frame froze constantly. I sent a quick command to the probe, telling it to return after sixty seconds of scouting. I wasn't sure if the command got through because the feed abruptly cut out.

"Just lost contact with the support probe," I sent on the platoon line. "Giving it a minute to return."

I waited one minute, then two. Just when I was about to give up and declare the probe lost, the video feed kicked in again. The probe was ascending the shaft. I rewound the video.

"Looks clear all the way to the first HS3 sentry, which is waiting near some interesting rock formations. I think we're good, Chief."

"Roger that," Chief Bourbonjack said. "Squads, approach."

I recalled the support probe and waited as the rest of the platoon approached. Four HS3s remained behind, taking up positions along the rim of the excavation.

When everyone had convened beside the shaft, Lieutenant Commander Braggs glanced at Snakeoil. "Even though we won't be able to contact the ship while we're in there, I want you to bring the comm equipment along, got that, Snakeoil?"

Snakeoil nodded. "Roger that. Don't think I'd leave it behind even if you told me."

"Good. We'll send an HS3 probe back up every fifteen minutes or so to keep the *Royal Fortune* apprised of our status." Braggs glanced at the Chief. "Let's get started."

Chief Bourbonjack nodded at the drone operator. "TJ? Send Lucy, Larry, and Lucky in."

TJ's eyes defocused. The three Centurions that were waiting for us vaulted gracefully onto the ropes and slid into the shaft one after the other. One of the HS3s hovered past and vanished down after them. The HS3 returned thirty seconds later.

"Looks clear," TJ said. "Like our mechman said, I see an empty chamber. Seems naturally carved into the Geronium. Erosion, maybe. I'm reading a high concentration of methane gas down there, but as long as none of you develops an O_2 leak, shouldn't be an issue. One thing though: rad levels are through the roof down there. When we get back, we're definitely going on the juice. Probably for a week or more."

"Wait a second, a high concentration of methane?" Alejandro said. "As in, how high? I'm a little more concerned about the methane than the radiation."

"Look, bro," Snakeoil said. "Without an oxidizer, we're fine. Heat from our jumpjets, or gunshot sparks, or even grenades won't ignite the methane. Like TJ said, as long as none of us starts spewing oxygen into the cave, we don't have to worry."

"Yeah well, I'm going to worry," Alejandro said. "What if one of us takes a bullet in the life support system?"

"You assume we'll even face bullets down there . . ." Snakeoil said.

Lieutenant Commander Braggs stepped forward, and stared

down into the darkness. "I'm not going to order anyone to come. If any of you wants to stay behind and be our rear guard, you're welcome to it. But if you do come, save your jumpjets till we really need them."

Without a word, Skullcracker approached the evil shaft. He turned on his helmet light, secured his heavy gun, leaped onto the rope, and slid down.

The rest of the squad followed, one by one.

When about half of us had gone down, Mao abruptly broke away from Big Dog and started running back the way we'd come.

Big Dog rolled his eyes. A ring of threaded fibroin darts launched from Mao's left anklet and embedded in the shale, instantly tripping him.

"Remind me why we're bringing him along?" Big Dog said.

"Maybe the Chief hopes to use him as a canary," Trace said.

"A canary," Big Dog deadpanned.

"Sure, you know, early warning system. Ever heard the phrase 'canary in a coal mine?'"

"Yeah well, your early warning system just activated." Big Dog made his way toward Mao.

The Lieutenant Commander secured his rifle and leaped onto the rope.

"Wait, sir," I took a massive step forward, crunching the rock underfoot. "There's no way I'm fitting Hornet down there."

"You can't bring the mech, obviously," Braggs said dryly. He slid down into the darkness.

I stepped away to give the others room, then I knelt and activated the hatch. The cockpit folded open and the internal actuators pulled apart my cocoon. I was momentarily disoriented as the vision feed from Hornet cut out, then I climbed down from the mech's chest.

I stared at the shaft before me. I was merely moving from one claustrophobic environment to another. Except in one I was powerful, the other, powerless.

"Don't worry, Rage," Snakeoil said. "You're not the only one who has a bad feeling about this. But we gotta find Bravo Platoon. They wouldn't leave us behind."

"I know, Snakeoil." I glanced at Hornet. "Guard," I instructed the mech.

The chest of the ATLAS sealed up and Hornet stood. Its weapons armed as the AI within took over.

Without warning it spun toward Mao, who was in Big Dog's custody once more.

"Target acquired," Hornet said in its authoritative male voice. "Preparing to terminate."

"Stand down," I said. "Stand down!" The mech had read Mao's embedded ID, no doubt, and since the mission profile had all SKs tagged as enemies, Mao was definitely a target.

The ATLAS lowered its weapons.

"He is a friendly," I said.

"He is a friendly," Hornet repeated.

"But if he tries to run, you have my full permission to gun him down." I grabbed a Mark 12 from a storage rack behind the mech and went to the shaft.

Only Big Dog, Alejandro, and I were still here. And Mao.

Big Dog tossed the SK officer into the shaft. "In you go!"

I saw the rope swing and I knew that Mao had grabbed it. Lucky for him—his trimmed-down jumpsuit didn't include jumpjets.

Big Dog ignored the stunned look I gave him, and leaped onto the rope.

"See you in hell!" he said cheerfully, and slid down.

I was the last one to go in. I secured my rifle, activated my helmet light, and hesitated.

That sixth sense was just going crazy.

I ignored it, and jumped onto the rope, lowering myself into the bowels of this planet that was eight thousand lightyears away from everything I had ever known.

CHAPTER TWENTY-ONE

I had traveled maybe ten meters down when the walls abruptly fell away. I lowered myself to the floor of an eerily circular tunnel, about five meters in diameter. The polished black walls looked like obsidian.

My platoon brothers had already deployed in a zigzag pattern down the chamber.

"Creepy how smooth the walls are down here," Trace was saying on the comm. "What do you think made this? Laser cut? Or burrowed by giant alien slugs?"

I could just imagine the disturbed look on Alejandro's face.

"Cut the chatter," Facehopper sent. "Rage, in case you missed the order: Single squad, zigzag formation. You get to be dragman."

"Any luck on the ship comms, Snakeoil?" Chief said.

"No sir. I'm still getting static. That goes for the MDV too."

"All right," Chief said. "TJ, send Hummingbird back up. Let the Captain know we're in."

An HS3 hovered past me and flew up the shaft.

I started forward, assuming my position as dragman. Everyone had their helmet lights on, so I could see quite a ways down that long obsidian tunnel.

A moment later the HS3, Hummingbird, hovered into place behind me, maintaining a constant drag position five meters back.

"Captain sends his regards," TJ said over the comm.

It wasn't long before the tunnel opened into a broad, underground cavern of astounding size. This seemed more of a natural cave, versus the artificial, too-round tunnel we'd just traversed. Immense formations of stone thrust from the floor, veritable pillars, wider at the bases than at the tops. Similar formations bit down from above. Stalactites and stalagmites. I could never remember which was which, though. I resisted the urge to look it up in the dictionary on my Implant, because as I strode forward, I had the unnerving feeling that I was passing between a mouthful of teeth.

Still, there was beauty here, I had to admit. The black jagged walls yielded in places to sparkling crystals, radiant translucent hexagons that jutted forth at different heights. Above, entire portions of the ceiling twinkled with color.

"Ever do any spelunking?" Bomb asked me. His mohawk was back to its original, black color, not that I could see it from here. But his mohawk was the first thing that popped into my head whenever I heard his voice.

"Me? No, not really. You?"

"All the time, baby. All the time. Never seen anything quite like this of course. Guess it helps that we're on a different planet." He went to the one of the crystalline walls and ran a hand across the surface. "External scans say its Geronium-275 mixed with impurities like calcium oxide, magnesium oxide, silica, aluminum oxide. Right here's the oxygen for your terraforming."

"Look sharp, mates," Facehopper said. "No time for sightseeing."

We continued down the cavern. We came across an HS3 waiting beside a formation, acting as a sentry, and the Chief had TJ send it closer to the entrance shaft to act as an intermediary with the ship, so that Hummingbird wouldn't have to travel as far back for the check-ins.

Bomb sent a message direct to my helmet. "Thanks for the kind words in the hangar, by the way. Trying to get me the mech and all. A bit misguided, but I do appreciate it."

"Sure thing," I said.

The cavern narrowed again, and we entered another unnaturally circular tunnel roughly five meters in diameter. The Centurions continued on about twenty meters ahead of us, scouting the way. The green dots that represented them on my HUD map winked out occasionally, then returned moments later as their signals waxed and waned within the tunnels.

"Sir," TJ said. "Lucky, Lucy, and Larry have reached a fork."

"Have them hold there," the Chief said. "How's the signal degradation?"

"I'm getting pixelization and frame freezes out the yin-yang."

We reached the fork. Five tunnels of equal size branched off in different directions.

TJ reported that three of the forks had not been explored yet: the middle one and the two on the right.

The Chief had him send the robot scouts down the middle fork while we stayed behind, waiting to see if it was worth exploring.

I watched the map on my HUD expand as the robots went deeper.

The dots abruptly winked out.

I glanced at TJ urgently.

The three green dots came back.

"That's about as far as I can send them without losing contact," TJ said. "But if I split them up, I can string out the signal for all its worth."

"Do it," Chief Bourbonjack said.

I watched two of the green dots proceed while one stayed behind and acted as a signal booster for the other two. Eventually, TJ had another robot halt, and he sent the last forward.

"You think Bravo Platoon still has any O_2 left?" Trace said, while we waited.

No one answered. We all knew how dire Bravo Platoon's O_2 situation was. Let alone their radiation situation.

They were okay.

They had to be.

Hang in there, Bravo, I told myself.

"Lucy's almost out of signal range," TJ said. "Have to halt her."

"All right, time to move forward, MOTHs," Lieutenant Commander Braggs said.

Hummingbird returned behind me, and Braggs had TJ send the HS3 straight back to check in with the ship again.

In single file we proceeded down the middle passageway of the fork.

We reached the first Centurion, Larry, and TJ sent the robot hurrying ahead to leapfrog Lucy.

A few minutes later:

"Larry just entered a new cavern," TJ reported. "There's some kind of metal object embedded in the floor."

"UC make?" Chief Bourbonjack said.

"No sir. Not SK either. Larry's scanning it, but he's not sending anything intelligible back. Must be the signal degradation. But that's not all. There are charred objects on the ground. Seem to be organic. Human."

"Pick up the pace, people!" Chief Bourbonjack said. "TJ, have the Centurions gather around Larry."

We all hurried forward, assuming the worst.

The passageway enlarged into a natural cavern, not as big as the previous one we'd come across, though. Soon enough we found the three Centurions, standing beside about five charred objects on the ground. The outline of each one was vaguely human. I couldn't tell if they were UC or SK.

Snakeoil knelt and touched one. A thread of black goo followed his gloved finger as he removed his hand. "It's mostly a superheated mass of carbon. Definitely organic."

"Human?"

"I am reading some ribonucleics, but no full DNA strands. But yes, the RNA does appear to be human."

"Look at this." Alejandro pointed out shrapnel embedded in the rock wall, and bullet marks.

Ghost knelt and picked up a shell casing. "UC design. Bravo." His voice choked up.

I know I felt my own eyes moisten. Members of Bravo had made some kind of stand here. I couldn't pretend they were all right anymore.

"Toughen up, MOTHs," Lieutenant Commander Braggs said. "We don't know that these are their bodies. We—" He had to stop. He was taking this pretty hard, like the rest of us. "Whatever happened to Bravo Platoon, there's going to be hell to pay, I can tell you that. I swear to you. No one touches my boys. No one."

It was a small speech, but it was enough. Those words hardened us.

"Here's the metal object TJ was talking about." Snakeoil crouched beside a small, metallic box set into the bottom of the cave. Lucy, the Centurion, was standing guard beside it.

"And what in the hell is that supposed to be?" Chief Bourbonjack said.

I came closer, and saw swirls reminiscent of Fibonacci spirals engraved all over the metal surface. Also known as golden spirals, because they recurred everywhere in nature, from the shells of mollusks to the spiral arms of galaxies.

"Seems to be some kind of communications device," Snakeoil said. "I'm getting a signal. Beamed straight up."

"I can confirm that," TJ said. "Lucy just picked up the signal. Seems to have activated with Snakeoil's approach."

"We tripped some kind of alarm?" Lieutenant Commander Braggs said.

"I don't know," TJ said. "Have a listen."

A garbled, robotic sound filled our hearing.

"Sounds like gibberish," Chief Bourbonjack said.

TJ nodded, then cut the noise.

"Anything else to add, Snakeoil?" the Lieutenant Commander said.

"There is. And you're not going to like it." Snakeoil ran a gloved finger away from the artifact, up into the air. "The signal comes out of the device but then seems to vanish about a meter up. I'm actually detecting a Slipstream signature. *In here.*"

I stepped back in alarm. I wasn't the only one.

"What the hell are you saying?" Chief Bourbonjack said. "A Slipstream? In here?"

"A quantum-sized one, yes. I think . . . I think this is some kind of trans-space antenna, for communicating over vast distances. Sort of like one of our InterPlaNet nodes, except with zero lag between it and the destination node."

"I didn't know the SKs had technology like that," Trace said.

"No one has technology like that," Snakeoil stated, rather ominously.

Right then I heard what sounded like a distant rustling, similar to leaves stirring on a breeze in the woods. No one else seemed to have noticed, though, so I assumed my ears were playing tricks on me.

Mao stepped forward, panting, making frantic gestures with his fingers, as if he were trying to tell us something but was so afraid that his voice no longer worked. His wrists were still bound by fibroin, so he couldn't move his gloves very much. It was a disturbing thing to watch.

"Big Dog, your canary's firing again," Trace said.

Mao dropped and started pawing at the cave bottom with his bound hands, like he just wanted to get away. His gloves didn't even make a dent.

"He's going to depressurize his suit if he keeps that up," Trace said.

Big Dog shrugged.

Then I heard the rustling again. I glanced at Facehopper. I was about to say something but he forestalled me with a raised fist.

I boosted the volume in my face mask. Above Mao's frantic pawing I definitely heard something, a noise that brought me right back to one of my earliest childhood memories.

About a year before I met Alejandro on the streets, I was still living with my parents at the plantation. That one summer, an infestation of caterpillars had overrun everything. They were everywhere. The grass, the trees, the farmhouse, the machinery—every single square centimeter was covered. No blade of grass, no leaf, no branch was spared. You couldn't take a step without crushing a hundred of the things. You'd walk under the trees and the larvae would be falling down on you in clumps.

The thing I remembered most about that infestation was the noise. The eerie, spine-tingling chitter of a hundred million caterpillars chewing up a hundred million leaves. Chewing up anything and everything that had any shred of life in it, turning our plantation—our livelihood—to ruin.

I heard that very same sound now.

"TJ," Chief Bourbonjack said. "Send the Centurions in. Dark."

The recon lamps on the Centurions deactivated, and the robots moved lithely down the tunnel.

"Dim the lights, people," Chief said.

We did.

Mao stopped clawing. He just perched there, listening like the rest of us.

I stared straight down the passageway the Centurions had taken. I couldn't see a thing, even though I had the night vision on my face mask cranked up to max. I decided to stare at the three green dots of Lucky, Lucy, and Larry on my HUD map instead, watching them move slowly away.

The chittering grew louder.

I swung the Mark 12 down from my shoulder, slid the safety off, and held the rifle at the ready. Beside me, my platoon brothers were doing the same with their own weapons.

The three green dots halted.

Red dots started popping up on the map, positioned directly in front of the green ones.

More red dots appeared as the Centurions cataloged and transmitted enemy positions to our Implants.

More.

I glanced sharply at Facehopper.

"Hold," he said.

I heard shooting in the distance, and saw flashes of gunfire down the cavern as the robots fired at whatever was attacking them. I remembered that the cave was full of methane, and I almost expected an explosion to arise because of the gunfire, but of course the methane remained inert without oxygen.

"What do they see?" Facehopper said in a soft voice. "TJ?"

"Death," Mao gurgled from the floor. "Death!"

"Shut up!" Big Dog kicked him in the side.

There were so many red dots now I couldn't count them. There was just this big mass of red bearing down on the three green friendlies.

"TJ?" Facehopper said. "Turn on the Centurions' lamps."

"Already on, sir," TJ said.

"Then what the hell do you see? TJ?"

He didn't answer.

"TJ?" Still he said nothing. "TJ! Petty Officer Second Class Wilson!"

"I—I don't know what I see." TJ said.

"Then show us the damn feed!" Lieutenant Commander Braggs said.

Too late.

The green dots abruptly winked out and the gunfire stopped. The red dots froze as the Implants recorded the last known positions of the hostiles.

Mao clambered to his feet and took off at a run down the tunnel, back the way we had come.

The metal anklets he wore clattered at Big Dog's feet. Somehow the SK officer had managed to get them off.

Ghost swung his sniper rifle around, dropped to one knee, and aimed.

I rested a hand on his shoulder. "Let him go," I said.

The albino hesitated. He glanced at the Chief, who nodded. Ghost lowered the rifle.

Facehopper gripped TJ by the shoulders. "What did you see, Petty Officer?"

TJ shook his head. "I don't know, sir. Creatures. Thousands of them."

"The hyena things?"

"No," TJ said. "These were different. More like . . . like . . . just, this roomful of gnashing teeth and claws."

Facehopper glanced at Chief Bourbonjack. "Orders?"

That clattering, chittering sound had been growing in volume. It sounded much worse than the infestation on my plantation ever had.

Lieutenant Commander Braggs was the one who answered. "Our backs are exposed here, with that five-way fork behind us. Let's fall back to a more defensible position. And might as well turn on your helmet lamps. They know we're here!"

As we retreated, the clattering continued behind us, seeming more frantic than before.

Or maybe just more eager.

I switched off the night vision, then gladly turned my helmet lamp up to full intensity. I didn't think I could fight whatever was trailing us in the dark. Not physically. Not mentally. But in the light, I had a chance.

Alejandro wasn't too far ahead. I could see Tahoe beyond him. The strength-enhancers in our exoskeletons were operating at full bore, and we pushed the suits to the max, spurred on by the unseen threat.

Soon the platoon emptied into the forking section of tunnel. We continued on, arriving at the vast cavern with the beautiful crystalline structures. The clattering had faded somewhat behind me.

Lieutenant Commander Braggs called a halt. "Here," he said, turning toward the circular, five-meter-diameter tunnel we'd just evacuated. "We make our stand here. We can guard this entrance all day. It'll be like Thermop—"

Before he could finish, my vision exploded with digital snow. Ear-piercing, garbled static consumed my hearing.

I fell to my knees, reflexively trying to cover my ears with my palms, but there was no way my gloved hands could ever reach them, not through the helmet. I shut my eyes tight, but that randomized pattern of digital snow didn't go away. It looked like flickering black bugs crossing a white background.

The Implant was malfunctioning.

I concentrated on the command words that would shut the device down. Thinking proved difficult with my hearing and vision so sorely affected, but I managed to remember the words and I said them in my head.

Zulu Romeo Lima!

The Implant switched off.

I fell forward, panting, sight and sound restored.

The ominously beautiful cavern was back.

As was the clattering sound.

There was no way to reboot the Implant, not without returning to the *Royal Fortune*. I wasn't sure I wanted to turn it on again anyway.

Half the platoon was on their knees in front of me, their hands held to their helmets, their bodies rocking in distress. The other half was trying to help those who were down.

The clattering grew louder. At the edge of the glow cast by the helmet lamps, I could barely make out a milling crowd of black shapes piling into the circular tunnel beyond.

Most of my platoon mates had recovered now, including Alejandro and Tahoe. TJ was still struggling nearby, so I went to him and shouted on the comm. "Zulu Romeo Lima! *Zulu Romeo Lima*!"

TJ finally disabled his Implant, and Alejandro and I helped him to his feet. I definitely felt his weight, because with the Implant offline I couldn't uptick the power of my exoskeleton. That meant I wouldn't be able to boost my strength much further than my body's own natural muscle power—the exoskeleton would offset the weight of the jumpsuit and not much else.

I'd also lost the Heads-Up Display generated by the Implant.

I tried accessing the secondary HUD that was part of the aReal built into the face mask: "HUD, on."

Nothing.

Well, at least we still had suit-to-suit communications.

"Good thing we retreated," Big Dog said grimly. "If our Implants had burned out in the middle of combat, I doubt any of us would be here."

Lieutenant Commander Braggs nodded. He was staring at the circular tunnel. "As I was saying, before I was so rudely interrupted, we make our stand here. Standard wedge formation."

We spread out without question, and dropped. None of us wanted to run. It was time to get some payback for Bravo Platoon.

I looked through my scope and took aim.

Ahead, a stream of . . . *things* . . . crawled through the tunnel toward us. Hundreds of them. Sharp spikes covered the black carapace that was their bodies. They had eight pairs of legs, with pincers and crushing mandibles on all sides. No eyes that I could make out. About one meter tall by two meters wide. Black, semitranslucent skin, so that I could see the three red hearts beating inside.

They were like big, multiheaded black crabs.

"MOTHs!" Lieutenant Commander Braggs said from the head of the platoon. "Fire at will!"

Facehopper had his Carl Gustav over one shoulder and he launched a rocket. It struck, and I saw claws and pieces of shell splatter into the air. Ordinarily the pressure waves from firing such a powerful weapon in an enclosed space like this could get pretty intense, but I hardly felt a thing. The suits did an admirable job of protecting us. The crabs weren't so well protected, though, judging from the ruined, twitching bodies left behind.

Big Dog launched his own Gustav; almost half the platoon was firing rockets at the incoming targets, while the other half reloaded those rockets. The constant stream of sonic booms resounded across the cavern.

I didn't have a Gustav, and nobody nearby needed help reloading, so I stuck to my rifle. One of those crabs walked squarely into my sights, skittering right for me.

I fired.

The creature added its splat to the others.

"Goddamn aliens!" Alejandro said over the platoon comm. He was helping Tahoe reload his Gustav nearby.

Skullcracker and Big Dog were the first to run out of rockets.

They picked up their heavy guns and started mowing down the aliens like they were cutting grass.

A bus-sized black creature slithered forward, barely fitting the confines of the tunnel's five-meter diameter. Though I couldn't see most of its body, I had the impression it was oval-shaped. It had these long feeler things in front, with two smaller ones where a mouth should be.

A giant slug, for lack of a better term.

Skullcracker and the rest of the platoon just unloaded on it. The bigger creature seemed to be phasing in and out of existence, so that sometimes our gunfire passed right through it. Eight rockets and countless rounds of ammunition later, we finally brought it down. The nearest living crabs abruptly turned over and died right along with it—though we hadn't touched them. The lifeless slug faded entirely out of existence, leaving behind the dead crabs.

More alien crabs surged forward, crawling over and around the bodies of their brethren.

"There's too many!" someone shouted.

"TJ, Facehopper, see if you can bring the tunnel down on their heads," the Lieutenant Commander said.

Rockets struck the roof of the tunnel ahead, and succeeded in bringing down a lot of fragments, but didn't come close to sealing off the tunnel.

"Angle's no good," TJ said.

I was picking them off shot by shot. I ran out of ammo, swapped magazines. Fired again. Making every shot count. Ran out. Swapped.

Beside me, my teammates were delivering just as much damage, if not more, but there were too many of the things. For every twenty that fell, another twenty came forward to take their place. Our ammo supply was steadily diminishing. Already the Gustavs were silent.

I hadn't noticed this before, but as the crabs got closer, I picked out dark, slimy cords leading away from the carapaces. I followed the cords with my eyes. They led to another one of those bus-sized slugs, slithering along in the circular tunnel not far behind. As that slug phased in and out of our reality, its cords stayed in place, maintaining the connection to at least two hundred crabs.

Facehopper hurled a grenade at the slug, timing it so that the grenade exploded just as the creature phased in. The explosion rocked the chamber.

The slug continued forward, ignoring the gaping hole in its side, and emerged from the tunnel into the main cavern. Big Dog, Skullcracker, and Tahoe launched more grenades, while the others unloaded their rifles into it.

We were forced to back away as the onslaught became too intense. The crabs connected to the slug closed on our wedge, the nearest ones falling about ten meters away from the tip of the formation.

I concentrated on keeping the crabs at bay, as did the other snipers, while the rest of the platoon focused on the slug itself. The bullet-riddled creature, chunks of flesh sloughing from its body, finally succumbed, and collapsed in a lifeless mass on the floor. The remaining one hundred or so smaller crabs that had been connected to it abruptly turned over, legs crimping in death. The dead slug dematerialized.

But the onslaught didn't cease.

More crabs simply piled out of the tunnel.

And more slugs. Two, one after another.

We'd backed to the far side of the cavern now, and concentrated all our fire on those slugs. Grenades were hurled in force. Machine guns unloaded.

We brought down those two slugs, and the crabs connected to them died instantly.

But then the slugs got smart. When the next one emerged into the cavern, it stayed back, letting its crabs advance, stretching the cords that bound them to the limit.

The smaller creatures literally swarmed our position.

"Get the cords!" someone shouted on the comm.

I switched to full auto and fired at those semitransparent, organic umbilicals, severing entire swaths of crabs from the host slugs.

The disconnected creatures instantly turned over and died.

The rest of the platoon concentrated fire on the cords too, but when we'd severed most of the crabs, the slug merely retreated, phasing out of existence so that the next slug and its army of crabs could take over.

This was a war of attrition.

And we were on the losing side.

I switched back to semiautomatic mode, and peered through my scope, searching the enemy lines, trying to see if there was something we were missing. Something obvious that could turn the tide to our advantage.

A bullet ricocheted off the tunnel floor beside me, and rock chips exploded in my face.

"What the—"

Another bullet whizzed past.

"I'm taking fire!" I said into the comm.

"It's Lucy!" TJ said, not ceasing the attack. "She's turned on us!"

I looked through my scope again, through the churning ranks of crabs. Sure enough, I spotted a flash of metal in the midst of the creatures.

It was indeed one of the Centurions.

There was a strange, blue glowing mist around its upper chest. I'd never seen anything like it. "What's wrong with it?"

TJ didn't answer. He was occupied.

I turned toward Alejandro. "Ammo!"

Alejandro tossed me three magazines. I loaded one, pocketed the other two.

More bullets whizzed past just above me.

It didn't make sense. Those Centurions rarely missed. I should be dead three times over.

Abruptly my vision was blocked as a crab ran right up to me—

It exploded. I glanced to my right to see who'd taken the shot that saved me.

TJ. He nodded when I met his eyes, then he got right back to work.

I aimed through the scope, hunting the churning battlefield for the Centurion again. There, a flash of metal. I fired a few shots, clearing the crabs from my target, then aimed at the Centurion's center of mass and fired.

The robot flew backward.

It got right up again.

That's right, you had to take out the CPU.

I aimed slightly higher, at the upper chest, right into the heart of that glowing blue mist . . .

I fired.

The robot vanished from view.

A blue vapor rose from where the robot body had fallen. Black electricity sparked along the edges of the vapor. It had no definite form, but as it advanced, I thought at times it looked vaguely humanoid.

I fired at the electrical mist and my bullets poked holes right through it—the thing continued forward unhindered, the punctures vanishing as the vapor merely reformed.

More gunfire came at us now, from the other two Centurions. Again I should have been dead, but whatever had taken over those robots had no idea how to properly aim the rifles.

"Rage," Facehopper said over the platoon comm, while hosing down three crabs. "See if you can take down the Centurions!"

"What about the Phant?" That was my name for the encroaching blue mist.

Facehopper knew exactly what I was talking about. "Concentrate on what we *can* kill versus what we can't!"

I abandoned the Phant for now, hoping that one of my platoon mates would find a way to take it out. I searched the seething mob through my scope while the others around me kept the crabs at bay. The creatures were so close now that several made it right up to our wedge before being shot down.

I didn't have a chance to find the other two Centurions because Lieutenant Commander Braggs issued an overriding order.

"Fall back!" the Lieutenant Commander said. "Fall back!"

Big Dog stepped forward while the rest of the wedge pulled back. He just let loose, severing the cords linking those crabs to their host slug with his machine gun. "You think you're good, huh? You want some? How about you?" When his ammo ran out, he tossed the weapon and switched to his rifle.

"Big Dog," Facehopper said. "Fall back!"

Tahoe, Alejandro, Ghost, Facehopper, and I lingered, waiting for Big Dog. We fired at the tumultuous throng, severing those cords, taking down crabs, trying to cover him.

Finally Big Dog started to retreat, walking backward, loosing rounds the whole time. Crabs were just falling all around him. "Come on, motherfuckers, is that all you got? That all?"

Then a Centurion bullet struck him. I saw the blood spurt from the back of his suit.

Big Dog fell backward, then he got up on one knee and kept firing. His suit bulged in the chest region, both front and back. He needed to have that patched right away. Probably needed a chest seal too, on both sides. I heard a strange gurgling on the comm. It sounded like . . . like he was laughing.

I ran forward with Ghost and Facehopper to help him.

A crab rushed right up to Big Dog, and he mowed it down—

Revealing a Phant.

It had crept forward unseen, hidden among the throng.

"Don't let it touch you!" Facehopper said.

But it was too late.

The mist enveloped Big Dog. He spun around, and his gaze met mine. I saw the heartbreaking fear in his eyes. He mouthed a single word.

"Help."

One second he was there, then the next he was just gone. When the Phant moved away, all that was left of Big Dog was a charred, organic mess on the cave floor.

Big Dog, my friend, my brother, a man I had trained with in the Teams for the past two years, a man who had survived the same arduous Trial Week, a man who had called out to me for help in his dying moments in the belief that somehow I, his platoon brother, would find a way to rescue him, was dead.

It was my fault.

I'd let him get shot by a Centurion.

I'd let the Phant take him.

The Phant.

The glowing blue mist was coming straight at me.

I felt a hand on my shoulder.

It was Alejandro.

"Rade. We have to go."

The mist was coming. It seemed almost hypnotic. Beautiful.

"Rade!"

His voice snapped me out of the trance and I ran. "What about Big Dog's body?"

"There is no body!" Alejandro said.

We sprinted through the tunnel. Since I couldn't uptick the strength of the jumpsuit anymore, I considered manually firing my jetpack to give me an extra boost of speed. I decided against it in the end, because one small mistake and I'd go careening into a tunnel wall. Safer just to run. I didn't want any of my platoon mates to have to turn back for me. The others shared the same sentiment, I guess, because no one used their jumpjets.

All I really wanted was to get back to the ATLAS. Then I could even up the odds a bit.

Then I could avenge Big Dog.

More than avenge.

We'd be dining on crab legs tonight, all of us.

And we'd see how well that Phant dealt with my mech's Gatlings.

The platoon reached the entrance.

Except the entrance wasn't there anymore.

"What in the hell . . ." Lieutenant Commander Braggs knelt before the cave-in that sealed us off from the surface.

"Mao did this," Facehopper said.

Chief Bourbonjack nodded. "The bastard probably had the tunnel entrance rigged with micro-explosives. Little parting gift for us."

"Goddammit." Braggs kicked at the fallen rocks.

"I'm reading a slight draft," Snakeoil said. "Moving through the rocks, toward the other side. If we had time, we probably could dig our way out."

"Unfortunately, we don't have time," Braggs said.

"This is why you never show your enemy mercy," Ghost told me.

That relentless chittering was growing louder behind us.

"I don't suppose anyone has any rockets or grenades left?" Chief Bourbonjack said.

None of us did.

The first crabs appeared, far down the tunnel. A slug was behind them, phasing in and out, crowding out the tunnel with its bulk, barely fitting within the five-meter-wide confines.

"Never thought it would end like this," Snakeoil said. "Suppose I can't complain, though. At least I get to die fighting side by side with my platoon brothers. That's more than I could ever hope for. Or deserve."

I snapped in my last magazine. "Brothers to the end."

"To the end," Alejandro said.

"To the end," Tahoe repeated.

"Wooyah!" Skullcracker shouted.

I hadn't heard that word since BSD/M. It was good hearing it now. It made me think of a quote from Winston Churchill, one that got me through training. *Never give in—never, never, never, never. If you're going through hell, keep going.*

My brothers and I dropped, assuming a wedge formation.

We would fight.

And we would die.

Brothers to the end.

"For Big Dog," I said, and fired.

CHAPTER TWENTY-TWO

And so my valiant brothers fired, mowing down the enemy, as my platoon made its last stand.

I didn't feel any of that naive invincibility, not this time.

We were going to die.

We were barely holding back the main onslaught of crabs as it was, when the giant slug decided to close. Half of us were forced to concentrate our fire on it while the rest focused on the crabs that were swarming our position and making it impossible to shoot their connecting cords.

We had one small advantage at least: Because of their size, only one slug could fit into that tunnel at a time. They'd have to line up in single file to get us. Then again, maybe that wasn't an advantage, because this slug just kept plowing forward—maybe pushed on by its brethren from behind. For a second I thought it was just going to bowl us over, but I guess it didn't like the sting of our gunfire, because when it got to within five meters of us, it decided to dematerialize and retreat.

You'd think that would be a victory.

Wrong.

By becoming immaterial, the creature allowed the crabs connected to the next slug in line to surge forward. And those multiheaded creatures almost overwhelmed us.

I ran out of ammo on my rifle and switched to the lone pistol I had at my belt. I was able to sever the connecting cords of those crabs with a single shot, but barring that, I found that aiming at the place where the "eyestalks" joined the multiple heads was just as effective. (I called them eyestalks, because they were located on the heads in roughly the spot where you'd think to find eyes, but in reality I had no idea what those stalks were.) Still, it was tricky, what with the way those creatures moved, and if I couldn't shoot the connecting cord I'd have to let the crab come right up to my position before taking it out.

I was shooting away, taking out crabs, when a clean shot at a connecting cord presented itself. I took the shot, but my pistol clicked.

"I'm out," I said.

Someone tossed me a spare pistol magazine.

I wouldn't have to fight with my fists yet, then. I wasn't looking forward to that moment. Those sharp, serrated pincers looked like they could easily slice through our jumpsuits. A fistfight with these things would end badly.

I aimed my pistol, but the clean shot at the connecting cords was gone. It was back to shooting the bases of the eyestalks.

I fired, and my bullet ricocheted from the carapace of my target. It took three shots for me to make the killing blow—the thing was just moving too fast.

At the edge of my vision I saw Alejandro turn slightly beside me to retrieve a dropped magazine. When he did that, he basically shoved the canisters of his jetpack into the side of my helmet. If a ricocheting bullet happened to hit one of his fuel canisters, I'd get a controlled, superheated burst of steam right in the face mask. Then again, that was better than getting the actual bullet in the face.

Wait a second. A superheated burst of steam . . .

"Guys!" I said. "Take off your jetpacks!"

My platoon brothers ignored me and continued firing.

I holstered my pistol and unbuckled the belts that kept my jetpack in place. I shrugged the pack off and hurled it against the cave-in, then positioned the pack so that the fuel canister faced outward.

"Rage." Facehopper glanced over his shoulder between shots. "You do know the fuel canisters are designed not to explode when struck by a bullet, right? You'll get a burst of steam, maybe some flame, and that's about it."

"I'm going to need this for a sec, Alejandro." While Alejandro fired into the onrush, I removed his bailout O_2 canister.

The cave was full of methane. However, methane and oxygen would only react if the concentration of the fuel (methane) was within the flammability limit, or envelope. Since I couldn't control the amount of fuel (the methane), I had to tweak the oxidizer.

I mentioned that the secondary HUD built into my helmet had been disabled along with my Implant, but other processing units in the helmet aReal seemed functional, and I was able to compute the required flow rate of oxygen from the bailout canister, given the surrounding methane concentration. (Trying to check this crap while gunshots went off and alien entities howled in agony nearby wasn't easy, trust me.) I opened the valve on the canister slightly, and had the aReal overlay the current flow rate from the valve onto my vision in yellow, with the shape of the destination flow rate displayed in green. I opened the valve until the yellow overlay matched the green.

A dismembered claw flew past my vision. I ignored it and, using the overlay as a guide, I held the valve beneath the glove of my other hand. I had to cause a spark at the interface between the oxidizer and the fuel.

The surgical laser in my finger could only fire at the preset depth of one centimeter, because I didn't have the fine-tune control the Implant provided. That should be good enough. I could still control the burst time, thankfully.

"Laser pulse, 800t," I said. My helmet picked up the request, and the laser in my finger pulsed for eight hundred trillionths of a second, right into the boundary between the pure oxygen and the methane. The valve tip lit up like a match.

One minitorch, as desired. Good.

I lodged the torch in the loose stone beneath the jetpack, positioning the flame right beside the leftmost fuel canister.

I glanced at Facehopper. "If you heat it first, then shoot, you'll get more than a controlled burst of steam."

Facehopper and Chief Bourbonjack exchanged a look.

"Everyone!" Chief Bourbonjack said. "Take off your jetpacks in pairs, and line 'em up against the blockage. Grab your buddy's bailout O_2 and make yourselves a minitorch with your glove laser. Place the torch beneath one of the fuel canisters, following Rage's example. Clear as mud? We'll do it two at a time, starting with Facehopper and Tahoe. Go!"

Facehopper and Tahoe doffed their jetpacks and shoved them against the cave-in. Facehopper took off Tahoe's bailout oxygen canister, and vice versa. They lit them up as I had, and positioned the flames beneath their fuel canisters, then the two of them returned to their positions in the wedge and shouted, "Done!"

And so it continued down the line, with my platoon brothers depositing their jetpacks and torches in pairs against the collapsed rock while the others defended against the endless onrush. Snakeoil opted out: it was too much work to take off and replace the communications rucksack, which fit snugly over his jetpack.

TJ and Ghost were last. TJ didn't look too happy when he rejoined the wedge. "We need to cover it up a bit, man. Direct the explosion somehow. We want to blow up the blockage, not *ourselves*."

He was right. Not only that, but it was taking too long to heat up the fuel canisters with the torches spread out like that. The canister I'd originally placed was only now starting to turn red-hot on the bottom.

I hurried back to the blockage, and moved the minitorches, concentrating them beneath two of the jetpack fuel canisters: mine, and another one placed early on. I sliced open the fuel line leading from the unheated, rightmost canister on each one, somewhat worried that the jetpacks would blow up in my face. Propellant spilled out from the severed lines, instantly vaporizing. The draft should draw the gaseous fuel into the middle of the cave-in. Precisely where I wanted it.

I started rearranging some of the surrounding jetpacks, rocks, and crab body parts, covering up the jetpacks so that only a small portion of the two main fuel canisters was exposed. Hopefully that would help direct more of the explosion inward.

I stepped away.

It was done.

We now had our improvised explosive device.

"We need some space!" I said, knowing that much of the explosion would still be directed outward. "We're too close!"

"We don't have any space!" Facehopper yelled.

The current giant slug was making a charge.

"We'll make some," Chief said.

Most of the crabs connected to that slug had been severed or shot down at this point, and the slug itself was riddled with bullets. We must have inflicted too much pain, because this slug gave up too, fading into insubstantiality and backing away, making room for the next slug in line with its fresh horde of crabs.

We fought our way forward, wading through the bodies of the dead. Magazines were exhausted, then reloaded.

I was down to my last few rounds and didn't want to waste them, so I holstered the pistol and scooped up a torn pincer. I swung it like a scythe as one of those crabs came right at me, and I cut off both its front legs at the joint.

The injured crab pulled itself up, and those long mandibles opened to wrap around my chest—

I brought the sharp, pointed end of my improvised scythe down on the carapace, cracking it in two. The thing collapsed.

Damn, these pincers were sharp.

We couldn't really go any farther. Sure, we'd pushed back the enemy front, and were wading deep in crab body parts, but I think everyone was on their last magazines now, and the current slug wasn't giving in to our onslaught.

I glanced back. In the small gap between the rocks and body parts I'd piled against the cave-in, I could see the two jetpack fuel canisters I'd concentrated the minitorches on. They were both orange hot, edging toward the yellow spectrum, with the bottoms tinged white.

"We're good!" I shouted.

"MOTHs," Chief Bourbonjack said. "I'll count it out. On three we turn, drop, and shoot. Aim for the two hottest fuel canisters. Take your pick. Keep firing until they explode."

"What if they don't?" Ghost said.

"Then we're screwed."

Three Phants drifted past the edge of the giant slug. No matter how many times my brothers shot them, the malevolent glowing mists always reformed, floating inexorably closer.

"Don't waste your time on the mists!" Skullcracker said.

Facehopper tossed aside his spent standard-issue rifle, and withdrew his pistol. "Chief, now would be a good time . . ."

"One!" Chief said.

"Two!"

"Three!"

We turned.

We dropped.

I aimed my pistol at the white-hot portion of my jetpack fuel canister—

And fired my last three rounds.

Around me, I heard the rapid, repeated staccato of firing pins striking primers as my platoon brothers opened fire. It was a beautiful sound. An orchestra playing what could very well be its last symphony.

There were four possible outcomes to sending those bullets into the superheated jetpack fuel canisters.

Outcome number one: The initial bullets penetrated the canisters. The interiors steamed out. The subsequent shots caused sparks that ignited the liquid fuel in each, causing an explosion hopefully powerful enough to breach the heat-weakened canisters.

Outcome two: The successive bullets caused the superheated canisters to catastrophically lose containment integrity. Each canister contained liquid fuel at an extremely high temperature and pressure. Basic physics stated that if a pressurized vessel containing liquid at high temperature were to rupture catastrophically, then there would suddenly exist a large mass of liquid at a very high temperature and very low pressure. That liquid would of course boil instantaneously, and expand at an extremely fast rate, giving a Boiling Liquid Expanding Vapor Explosion, or BLEVE.

Outcome three: Both options one and two transpired. Maybe the oxygen from the bailout tanks contributed as well, if any of those vessels became punctured.

Outcome four: A whole lot of nothing.

Judging from the massive fireball of orange flames I saw, it looked like option three was in full effect.

I ducked my head.

The shockwave pulsed over me.

Rock fragments hit my suit. I felt stabs of pain all along my backside as some of those fragments really dug in. The shrapnel must have formed a seal, because I still had internal suit pressure.

The heat flared up inside my jumpsuit, and it felt like I was reentering the atmosphere in my ATLAS again. Visions of being trapped in a burning box filled my mind, but I fought down the panic. I had to.

Then it was over.

The heat receded.

The jumpsuit had protected me. For the most part. There was a throbbing pain in my right buttock, likely from a piece of shrapnel that would have to be surgically removed later.

I burrowed out of the fragments that had buried me. The heat flash had caused many of those rocks to fuse into something resembling glass.

My vision was obscured—I wiped the lens of my face mask with a blackened glove, clearing away the soot or whatever it was, and I did the same for my helmet lamp. Even so, I couldn't see all that much in any direction because of the airborne dust.

I climbed to my feet and turned around.

There were charred alien body parts strewed over the tunnel behind me, amid the fragments of glassy rock. I couldn't see much else beyond the bodies, not yet. The tunnel was eerily quiet. The slug was completely gone. Dead and phased out of existence, I guessed.

There was movement on the ground beside me, and I spun my 9-mil toward it.

Alejandro emerged from the fragments of glassy shale. His jumpsuit was coated in the same black soot. A molten slag from one of the canisters protruded from his right shoulder.

He wiped the black stuff from his face mask and glanced at me. "Looks like a bunch of seagulls decided to use you as target practice."

"Yeah? You too." I nodded at the molten slag. "Except you got hit by bigger turds. How's the suit pressure?"

"Remind me how you ever talked me into joining up."

"I guess that means the suit pressure's fine."

Around me, my platoon brothers were burrowing free. I made a mental head count. Looked like everyone was present, and uninjured.

The clattering started up anew and I saw, as the dust cleared, that the shockwave had pushed the enemy line back about ten meters. The three Phants had been shoved backward too—the stunned mists were only now re-coalescing.

"Ammo," I said distractedly.

"I'm almost out." Alejandro tossed me a 9-mil magazine anyway.

"Guys," Ghost said. "We did it."

I followed his gaze. The dust had settled enough to discern the blast site. The blockage had cleared, but only partially. Either more fragments had fallen from above or the blast hadn't been strong enough to move everything. Still, just half the tunnel was blocked now, with the fragments reaching about waist high. Beyond, I could see light pouring dimly from the shaft. The jetpacks were gone—those that hadn't exploded were probably buried in the rubble.

"Now's not the time for dawdling, boys!" Chief Bourbonjack said.

The platoon sprinted forward.

Alejandro and I got there first and started crawling through the gap. The rest of the squad followed in twos.

"Never thought I'd be so glad to see the light of day in my life," Ghost said, wriggling through the gap just behind me.

Tahoe laughed beside him. "Coming from an albino, that means a lot."

I got through, stumbled to my feet, and hurried the final distance to the shaft with Alejandro right behind me.

"At least Mao left the rope," I said, grabbing onto the cord that was still dangling down. The sun's rays, scintillating with motes of dust, pierced the darkness around me.

I started shimmying up the ten meters to the surface. Though Alejandro was right behind me, the whole time I had this creepy sensation that one of those crabs was just below, snapping at my feet. The feeling spurred me on.

I was glad I was leading the way out, and only partially because I wanted to get away from those things down there.

You see, I didn't want anyone to take Hornet. Protocol dictated that when under threat, and the designated ATLAS operator was not present, anyone could jump into the pilot seat.

No way in hell I was going to let that happen.

When I finally pulled my body over the lip and into the full light of day, it felt like a massive weight lifted from my chest. I was free of that hellhole.

And best of all, my ATLAS was waiting for me right where I left it.

The bullet-riddled jumpsuit of Mao lay beside it: the mech had mowed him down, as per my last order.

Quid pro quo, I guess.

I resisted the urge to run straight for the mech, and instead turned around to help Alejandro over the edge of the shaft. Just then Snakeoil roared out of the pit, carrying Bomb in one arm and Lui in the other, probably expending half his jetpack fuel in the process. Too bad he was the only one left who *had* a jetpack, having opted out because of his communications rucksack . . .

I glanced down. The rest of the platoon was on the rope. Lieutenant Commander Braggs brought up the bottom, right behind Chief Bourbonjack.

I could already see the multiheaded alien crabs snapping at the air below him. Alejandro let off some shots, taking out two of the things.

To my left, Snakeoil landed, releasing Bomb and Lui. The two of them glanced at the unoccupied mech.

That was my cue.

I hurried over to Hornet.

"Unlock!" I shouted. "Load weapon patterns seven and five!"

I leaped into the ATLAS as the cockpit opened and the limbs swapped out. The left hand became a serpent rocket launcher. The right a Gatling gun.

The cockpit's elastic inner material pressed into my body, and I flinched at the sudden pain in my backside: I'd forgotten about the shrapnel embedded in my butt. Ah well. I was a MOTH. Pain was a houseguest. Sometimes uninvited. Always tolerated.

The windowless cockpit sealed up. Without the Implant I couldn't interface with Hornet mentally—all weapons-related commands would have to be vocal. And control of the mech would be via the pressure sensors that lined the inner material of the cockpit rather than by intention, and that would feel like wading neck-deep in sludge until I acclimated. As for my vision, while the helmet HUD was still disabled, the sight-routing mechanism utilized a secondary processor, so Hornet was still able to route what it saw onto my jumpsuit's face mask instead of my Implant.

"Gun in hand!"

The weapons swiveled so that the triggers were directly above my fingers. I walked toward the shaft.

Yup, without the Implant it definitely felt like I was wading through a bog. I fought for every step, but after a while I got used to it and the hindrance didn't seem so bad.

At the shaft, half the platoon was firing down, picking off crabs, covering the other half that still climbed.

My platoon brothers immediately made way for me.

Lieutenant Commander Braggs reached the halfway mark. Below him, the crabs had formed a body ladder, and the closest one snapped at his feet.

I fired my Gatling at the alien ladder.

Ever heard the word, *mincemeat*?

More crabs kept appearing at the bottom of the shaft, feeding my meat grinder. I was happy to show them what oblivion looked like.

Eventually the crabs got smart and stopped coming.

I ceased firing.

Chief Bourbonjack was almost out of the shaft now, and the Lieutenant Commander was just behind him.

Two Phants appeared at the base of the shaft.

Feeling cocky, I fired off my Gatling. A hundred holes appeared in the mists, and in moments the things had dispersed entirely.

All too easy.

Then the creatures started reforming.

Damn.

I fired again, in bursts, not giving the Phants a chance to coalesce, and taking out the crabs that had decided to show themselves. So far there was no sign of the giant slug those crabs were connected to. I guess it hadn't burrowed a passage through the waist-high gap in the blockage yet. Then again, it could probably just phase itself right through.

Alejandro and Facehopper helped the Lieutenant Commander from the shaft. He was the last one out.

"You think you can seal that opening, Rage?" Chief Bourbonjack shouted.

"Absolutely."

I gave my brothers a couple of seconds to step back, then I unleashed hell into that shaft, expending rockets and ammo at the lower walls like there was no tomorrow. I switched my focus to the upper section, stepping back, slowly circling the shaft, glancing at my HUD map now and again to ensure I didn't step on anyone behind me.

The wooden frame that held the rope blew clean away under my assault, and the Geronium rocks around the rim fell inward. In moments all that was left of the shaft was a sunken crater sealed off from the rest of the world. Well, that and a plume of dust.

"Sealed!" I said.

I kept my Gats trained on the opening, half-expecting the blue mist to seep through. Or for the crabs to smash their way out. Or for one of those slugs to phase-shift through the opening and rematerialize in full view.

Beside me, my platoon brothers stood in a circle around the crater, weapons aimed at the former shaft.

"*Mierda*!" Alejandro said finally. He seemed so small, standing there on the ground beside Hornet. "*Puta madre! Me cago en todo lo que se menea!* I shit on everything that moves! Shit shit shit."

He lowered his 9-mil. Others started to stand down around him.

"Hold . . ." Chief Bourbonjack said.

Those weapons went right back up.

We waited, just staring at the crater where the shaft used to be, watching the dust settle.

"Hold . . ." Chief Bourbonjack said.

A fragment of rock broke away near the lip of the crater I had made, and rolled down to the bottom.

"Back away, very cautiously," Chief Bourbonjack said.

We did, keeping our eyes trained on the crater the whole time. We convened about ten meters away.

"Sir, I still can't reach the ship," Snakeoil said. Like everyone else, he hadn't lowered his weapon, hadn't looked away from where the shaft used to be. "And I've lost contact with the MDV."

"Rage, see if you can reach either asset," Chief Bourbonjack said.

The wireless adhoc network built into the ATLAS 5s was a little stronger than the one that came with the jumpsuits and Implants, but definitely not as powerful as the InterPlaNet node Snakeoil carried around on his back. I doubted it would reach the ship, but the MDV was only half a klick away and definitely in range.

"Ship comms," I said to Hornet.

Static.

"MDV comms."

Static.

Now I was getting worried.

"Chief. I get nothing on both lines."

"There's some kind of EM interference originating from orbit," Snakeoil said. "I can't place it."

"I don't remember those clouds being here on the way in," Tahoe said.

I followed Tahoe's gaze. Black clouds filled the sky behind us.

"Do you guys feel that?" Bomb said.

I couldn't feel anything, but I was up in a gyroscopically stabilized ATLAS.

I heard something, though. A distant rumbling.

We all turned our eyes toward the crater.

The rumbling became louder.

Now I could feel the ground shaking.

"Fall back!" the Lieutenant Commander said. "To the MDV!" He led the way.

"I'll hold them off," I said.

Chief Bourbonjack stepped in front of me. "Rage, I can't allow—"

"Go, Chief. Trust me. I got this. Go."

"All right, son. But you better be right behind us."

He joined my platoon brothers, who were sprinting up the excavation site. Everyone had gone now.

Wait, not everyone.

"Get out of here, Alejandro!" I said. "Go!"

"Rade. I can't let you stand alone. I've always been here for you. I can't—"

"I'm in an ATLAS 5! Go!"

He didn't move.

I softened my voice. "Alejandro. I promise you I'm not throwing my life away. I'll be right behind you. I swear I will. This isn't a last stand."

He seemed about to protest, but then he nodded and ran after the others. As the rumbling grew louder, I watched him weave his way between the mammoth dump trucks and hydraulic power shovels on his way to the top.

I swiveled back toward the crater—

The ground literally blew open in front of me.

Crabs exploded upward like a geyser, and fell down all around me.

The creatures started attacking immediately.

They didn't look much different in the full light of day, their dark hearts beating visibly beneath their black, semitranslucent carapaces. Their multiple heads twitched and jerked, mandibles swaying about, chomping at the air and the metallic skin of my mech.

I didn't use weapons to defend myself. There was no need. I simply splattered entire swaths of the things with every swing and downward thrust of my arms. I crunched two or three underfoot with each step. I was an alien-killing machine.

But for every one I killed, five more piled out of the shaft.

Relentlessly.

Endlessly.

An entire section of rock around the shaft collapsed then, and a slug rudely burrowed out, slamming its huge hunk of a body onto the ground just in front of me. This slug was not black like the others my platoon had encountered, but white-hot, with silver steam flowing from every exposed portion of its body. It was in rock-melting or "burrowing" mode, I guessed.

I still had a Gatling loaded on my right arm, and I let loose, just hammering that slug. I arrested its forward motion entirely.

I loaded the second Gatling into my other arm, and fired with both.

I walked forward, waling on the slug's body with my six-thousand-rounds-per-minute weaponry, devastating any crabs that dared cross my path. The white-hot slug was retreating, shrinking from my onslaught, pieces of its steaming body just breaking off. That white skin was quickly turning black where my bullets struck.

"You evil maggot from hell!" I yelled. "You stinking mass of white pus! Go back to the pit you came from!"

It started to phase out.

"Oh no you don't!"

I swiveled serpent rockets into my right hand.

I launched one.

Two.

Three.

Huge chunks of flesh broke away, and black steam (blood?) filled the air.

Finally, the slug fell, and its dead body dematerialized.

I heard a high-pitched whistle, and realized that the Gatling in my left hand was still rotating at six thousand rpm, but was not firing.

I'd used up the entire belt.

I took my finger off the trigger, and rotated the incendiary thrower into that hand.

Another slug piled out of the sinkhole.

I backed away.

Another slug emerged.

Another.

All three were colored black—I guessed they weren't in "burrowing" mode.

Two hundred crabs were connected to each of them.

I glanced at my platoon brothers.

They hadn't reached the lip of the excavation site quite yet.

They needed more time.

I spun toward the crabs.

They were already all over me.

Pincers clattered against external pistons and compressor joints. Mandibles chewed at exposed tubing and wiring. Inside my cockpit it sounded like hail on a tin roof.

Warning indicators were going off all over the cockpit. Servomotor fluids in my left elbow joint were low. My right leg joint was damaged. My right eye camera was destroyed.

I slammed the creatures off my body, swiveling about, unleashing a curl of flame. I ignited entire rows of the things.

One of the slugs was bearing down on me.

"Jumpjet mode!"

I activated my jumpjets using the manual controls that appeared on the inside of my palms, and I broke away from the mass of crabs. I reached the apex of my flight, and as I arced downward I positioned myself so that I'd land right on top of the slug.

It decided to phase out just then, and I fell right through it.

I followed the outline of the immaterial creature, beating away the crabs that swarmed in on me.

The slug started to rematerialize around me. The crabs instinctively fled, but I kept moving, staying within the borders of its flesh, tearing a path through the soft tissue that was appearing. I was a bit worried that the thing's molecules would join with mine or something, but that didn't happen, maybe because I kept moving, never staying in one place.

The thing had fully materialized into this reality now, and I couldn't see a thing. Nonetheless I burrowed farther inside, ripping and tearing and mashing. I let off Gatling rounds and incendiary thrower bursts whenever I got stuck. I was starting to get worried, because I couldn't really plot a trajectory in here.

Thankfully I erupted from the thing soon thereafter, emerging like an exploding, pus-filled boil squeezed too hard. In my wake I left behind one very dead slug, its black guts bulging and steaming from a jagged, gaping hole in its side.

The two hundred crabs connected to it turned over and died.

"Rage," the Chief transmitted on the platoon line. I could barely understand him for all the static. "Where the f—" His voice cut out. "Are you?"

"Coming, sir," I said.

I got a bearing on my team. Most of them had clambered over the lip of the excavation. All except Alejandro and Tahoe, who waited for me at the top of the excavation.

Damn it. "Get out of here!" I sent them, though I'm not sure if my words got through.

I made my way toward the pair, zigzagging between hydraulic power shovels and giant dump trucks, trying to do as much damage as I could along the way. The horde proved endless: more slugs had poured from the sinkhole while I was occupied with the disemboweling of the other. There were at least six more of its brethren out there now, along with a thousand crabs.

I was about to activate my mech's jumpjets to get the hell out when I noticed a metallic glint beneath the sun, to my left. That glint saved me.

I fired the Trench Coat just as the onboard AI sounded the homing missile beacon, and I activated my horizontal evasive thrusters.

My body twisted sideways as seventeen pieces of radar-guided metal fanned out in a peacock pattern to intercept the four serpent missiles trained on my mech.

Explosions off to my right sent Hornet careening to the side at an incredible speed. Cockpit alarms were going off all over the place.

I smashed into the ground.

It was sheer luck that none of the serpents had directly touched my ATLAS. The Trench Coat could usually take out one or two missiles at once, but four? Yes, I was a very lucky man. Quick reflexes helped too, I suppose.

I stood and got my bearings. The outer edge of the crab horde was roughly thirty meters behind me. I was about fifty meters from the top of the excavation. Alejandro and Tahoe were still waiting for me at the lip. They'd both dropped to one knee, though, and were staring into the sights of their 9-mils.

Alejandro's voice came on the comm. "Rade, look—" He cut out. "Dump—"

I followed his aim, swiveling toward the massive dump truck

that loomed to my left, twenty meters away, parked at an angle so that its right side faced my mech.

There.

At the base of the truck, I spotted two of the ATLAS 5s from Bravo Platoon. I recognized the black panthers spray-painted onto the chest pieces. The first mech stood near the front right wheel of the dump truck, while the second had taken up a position beside the rear wheel. Likely they'd been hiding there, behind the wheels, in ambush.

I zoomed in on each one. I couldn't see the blue glow that would have signified Phant possession.

But those serpents had to have launched from somewhere.

In fact, the mechs launched two more as I watched them.

I dropped, and reactivated the Trench Coat. I had time to launch it twice.

The thirty-four metal pieces had ample opportunity to take out those rockets, and the blasts didn't affect me.

The rocket launchers on the enemy mechs swiveled aside, replaced by Gatling guns.

The things were learning.

I was a big target, even lying down, but there was a hydraulic power shovel not far from here, which I could use for cover.

I stood up.

The Bravo Platoon ATLAS 5s opened fire.

I dived to the right and the bullets followed me. I activated the ballistic shield on my left arm, replacing the incendiary thrower. Just in time, too—those bullets carved deep pockmarks in the surface but the shield held, protecting me. For now. Those pocks were becoming deeper, though, and I knew it was only a matter of time before the bullets pierced and struck the hull of my mech.

I didn't want to activate my jumpjets again and expose myself, not when there were so many places for cover here in the excavation site. I raced away from the outer rank of alien crabs that were closing in on me, and barreled behind the hydraulic power shovel I had in mind.

I took a moment to compose myself.

Okay. I'd have to use some strategy to win this.

Taking down multiple ATLAS 5s was nothing new to me.

I'd practiced scenarios like this almost every day in the simulator. One against two, and sometimes one against three. True, that was the simulator, and this was real life. I didn't see how it was all that different.

Except for the fact that I could actually die.

Not to mention the horde of hungry aliens that bore down on my position from behind . . .

"Override friendly fire protection," I said. Just in case my mech wouldn't let me fire at the Bravo Platoon ATLAS 5s.

"Friendly fire protection disabled," Hornet answered.

I leaned out from cover and launched two serpents, aiming one at each ATLAS.

As expected, the mechs simply stepped behind the wheels of the dump truck and took cover.

They were no longer targeting me.

Now I could use Hornet's jumpjets.

I stepped out from the power shovel and activated the jetpack as my rockets exploded against the giant tires. The blast didn't even give the dump truck a flat. Powerful tires.

I landed on the hood of the dump truck, and jumped again, thrusting over the cab toward the dump body. I activated the rear vertical jets in bursts, wanting to maintain my altitude with the least fuel burn, and when I was halfway across the body I ceased all thrust. I plummeted in a reverse parabola across the dump body, clearing the tailgate with about two meters to spare.

I fired off lateral thrusters, aiming my mech for the ground beside the rearmost, left side tire. I pulsed the forward lats, spinning Hornet in midair so that I landed facing the dump truck.

Both targets were in my line of fire, crouching behind the tires on the opposite side of the dump truck. Both targets faced away from me.

I loosed my full complement of serpents, dividing them between the two targets. As my rockets sped away beneath the undercarriage, I stepped behind the tire for cover, in case the Bravo mechs managed to return fire.

I heard the explosions, waited a moment, then peered out.

The closest mech lay crumpled not far from the tire opposite mine.

I couldn't see the other mech.

I swiveled my ballistic shield back into place on my left hand, and since I was out of rockets, I rotated the Gatling gun into my right hand. Had about fifteen hundred rounds left.

I fired at the crumpled mech, aiming for the section that housed the brain case, and the body shook beneath my onslaught.

Blue mist started rising from the mech.

I heard a clang from above—

The other Bravo mech had climbed onto the dump truck's body, and was aiming down at me from the tailgate.

I swiftly dived beneath the giant dump truck's undercarriage, avoiding the onslaught of Gatling bullets.

The Phant from the fallen mech was floating toward me. I fired at it, dispersing it, but the constituent vapors continued to close.

I sprinted along beneath the undercarriage, looking to take cover behind one of the front tires.

But that route became unavailable as the first wave of crabs reached the dump truck, swarming the front section.

I spun around in time to block the gunfire from the Bravo mech. I crouched behind my ballistic shield, and returned fire, forcing the thing to take cover behind the rearmost tire. Either it didn't know how to use its own shield, or didn't want to.

"Rade," Alejandro transmitted. All I heard after that was static.

"Hey, Alejandro," I said. "Kinda busy now."

More Gatling gunfire came in. I ducked behind my shield. The metal was going to give out on me momentarily—already there were gaps where the shield had been shot clean away. I returned fire, but I was down to four hundred rounds now. At six thousand rounds per minute, that would last me for maybe six or seven more half-second bursts.

Meanwhile, the Phant from the other mech continued to approach, and behind me, the first wave of alien crabs had almost reached my position, their clattering mandibles echoing from the undercarriage.

So much for this not being a last stand.

CHAPTER TWENTY-THREE

The possessed ATLAS kept firing. Sometimes those bullets streamed right past, chewing into the crabs behind me.

Good.

Come on, run out of bullets. Come on!

Keeping my shield firmly in place, I fired a burst from my Gatling into the churning ranks behind me, cutting away a swath of the closest crabs, buying time.

More holes appeared in my ballistic shield, forcing me to duck lower.

The Phant was almost on me . . .

I turned back toward the alien crabs.

Maybe I could use them.

I stood up and started bashing my way into the alien ranks, keeping the ballistic shield angled behind me. I swerved to the left, in a hook motion, putting about five ranks of the things between me and the enemy Gatling. My helpful Bravo friend mowed them all down for me.

I spun around and did the same thing in the other direction, hooking back to the right. Got the enemy mech to take down another row of crabs for me.

I dived deeper into the horde.

Claws were just snapping at me from all sides, slowing me down.

It got so bad that in moments I could scarcely move under all that weight.

And I knew that the Phant was still closing on me.

I fired off my horizontal jets, hurling myself backward and sideways through the milling throng. I launched a couple more Gatling bursts, and swung my ballistic shield like a hammer.

I broke free from the enemy ranks, but I knew I was right back in the Bravo mech's line of fire.

I spun around and brought my shield up in time to block the bullet onslaught.

The blue mist came at me from the left. The crab horde, from behind and my right flank.

Pinned down on all sides . . .

The gargantuan dump truck abruptly rumbled to life.

The vehicle plowed backward, the giant rear wheel bouncing over the mech that crouched behind it.

That was my cue.

I thrust forward while breaking into a sprint, and tore away from the milling mass. Firing a Gatling burst, I swerved right and hurried out from the undercarriage, and once I was clear, I activated my jumpjets at full vertical burn. In midair, I sloughed off a bunch of crabs that still clung to me.

Glancing down, I saw that the mech had been thoroughly crushed by the giant wheel. A Phant was seeping from the crumpled metal that remained.

I landed on the roof of the dump truck's cab and clambered to the driver's side.

"It's me," I sent over the comm before peeking inside, just in case—I didn't want to be confused for a Bravo mech.

Alejandro saluted from behind the wheel. "I was getting a bit ticked that you were having all the fun down there."

He switched the dump truck out of reverse, and accelerated into the seething mass of crabs and slugs that waited ahead.

"This is going to be interesting," I said.

The whole vehicle bobbed up and down as the dump truck plowed through the army of alien crabs, leaving a trail of dismembered claws and broken mandibles and splattered carapaces.

But already there were a bunch of crabs climbing up the side of the truck.

"Time to go, Alejandro," I said, mowing down a bunch of the climbers with my Gatling. I was down to a hundred rounds now.

"Not yet."

He laughed maniacally as he drove around the excavation site, the dump truck bouncing and jolting along. Alejandro aimed at a slug and accelerated to full speed. Well, as fast as he could go with a bunch of dead crabs clogging the undercarriage, anyway.

The giant vehicle rammed into the slug. The whole front section of the dump truck lifted up, and the vehicle ground to a halt as the creature got jammed up underneath. Alejandro revved the engine, but that got us nowhere.

Alien crabs had climbed the opposite side of the truck's cab, and swarmed onto the roof now.

"Well, that was fun while it lasted." Alejandro leaped out of the stalled truck. "Can I get a lift?"

I held Alejandro to my chest and activated my jumpjets.

I landed about thirty meters from the rim of the excavation, right beside one of those hydraulic power shovels.

I could have fired my jumpjets again, and in retrospect, I should have, but I thought I'd save fuel, and cross the remaining distance to the rim on foot.

It was one of the biggest mistakes I ever made. Maybe if I'd activated the jets, what happened next would have never transpired. Maybe things would have turned out differently.

Because when I hurried around that power shovel I walked right into a Phant.

I dropped Alejandro as the mist enveloped Hornet.

"Run, Alejandro!"

I fired off a reverse burst with my jets, launching myself backward.

But it was too late.

The thing had already seeped inside.

"Inner shell, release!" I said. "Release!"

The vision feed from the mech winked out, and I saw only the red emergency lights illuminating the cockpit. The elastic shell that held me in place retracted and I fell forward against the inner hull.

"Cockpit, open!" I said.

But it didn't. I must have damaged the release mechanism during the fighting.

I fumbled with the manual release latch. I jerked my hands away as I saw blue mist flow right in front of my gloves, just inside the cockpit.

I waited for it to envelope me, waited for it to burn me to a crisp like the other Phant had done to Big Dog.

But the mist ignored me entirely, never wavering from its purpose. It wasn't concerned about me.

It just wanted my ATLAS.

The mist flowed into the CPU unit, just below my cockpit.

"Rade, are you all right in there?" Alejandro's deathly afraid voice came over the comm. "Rade?"

The mech's servomotors roared to life.

"Run, Alejandro! I've lost control of Hornet!"

I tried the manual release hatch again. No good.

I heard what sounded like bullets ricocheting from the outer hull now.

"Vision feed on!" I said.

The outside world as viewed from the mech immediately overlaid my face mask.

Hornet swiveled toward Alejandro, who had disobeyed me of course. He was firing at the ATLAS with his pistol. That was like trying to take down an elephant with a blowgun. Sure, you might get extremely lucky and hamstring the beast, but you were more likely to just provoke the thing. The 9-mil armor piercers just weren't powerful enough.

"Alejandro, get out of here!"

Alejandro retreated as he fired, but he lost his footing and tripped, falling backward to the ground. I could see Tahoe sprinting down the slope, trying to reach him.

"Alejandro, get up! Get up!" I punched the cockpit hull with my gloved fists.

Hornet swiveled the Gatling gun toward him.

I was going to watch him die.

Basically by my own hand.

I fumbled blindly for the manual release latch one last time.

It responded.

The mech's vision feed winked out as the cockpit hatch opened up.

The ATLAS didn't want me inside anymore. I was a parasite that it could do without.

Probably wanted to take me down right after Alejandro.

But the mech had made a mistake, you see, because by opening the cockpit, it gave me access to its innards. In a small crack just beneath the cockpit hatch, I could see the brain case surrounded by the blue glow of the Phant.

Without pause I shoved my pistol through the crack and fired, slamming five bullets into the unshielded CPU.

I leaped out as Hornet collapsed in a useless heap; I hit the ground rolling and scrambled to my feet.

Behind me, the Phant emerged from the now-useless ATLAS.

"Let's go," I said.

"*Caramba*," Alejandro said. "Don't ever do that to me again."

Tahoe had halted not far ahead of us, and he was firing his 9-mil at the Phant and whatever else pursued us.

We reached him, and the three of us hurried over the rim of the excavation site. The seething front ranks of the alien crab horde flowed onto the plateau ten meters behind us.

The MDV was three hundred meters due ahead. The rest of the platoon waited there for us.

"About goddamn time," the Chief transmitted. The static on the comm was a little better. "Next time—" His voice cut out.

"Hey, Chief," I sent back, then glanced at Alejandro and Tahoe. "Ever ran a one-minute klick?"

Alejandro looked at me, then shook his head in disbelief. "*Caramba*."

I let loose.

The wind was starting to pick up. I could hear it whistle past my helmet, feel it shove me slightly to the left with each step.

A storm was coming.

My eyes were drawn to the horizon to my right, to the dark roiling clouds that filled the sky. A monolithic black shape was just starting to protrude from those clouds. I had no idea what it was. Some kind of ship, maybe.

I didn't look overlong. Too much to worry about right here, right now.

At first I didn't notice that the ground was shaking. I was running too fast, and I thought the shaking was just from my own movements.

But then a sinkhole opened up about twenty meters ahead, just off to the right.

A slug bigger than any I had seen so far came launching out of the black rock. It was white-hot, in burrowing mode, with steam flowing from its body. It towered above me, just this giant, evil maggot, straight out of nightmares, the size of a dreadnought starship. Not even my ATLAS would have been able to handle this.

Folds opened up in its skin, and multiheaded alien crabs connected by dark cords leaped away from it, oddly reminding me of paratroopers making a jump.

They were really big crabs.

As in, ATLAS 5 big.

Their massive pincers snapped at the air.

Their giant mandibles chomped in anticipation.

The things cut us off from the MDV.

Alejandro, Tahoe, and I fired off some shots, but the 9-mm pistols we had left were useless against these bigger crabs.

We were forced to backtrack—

I tripped.

Alejandro was at my side instantly, helping me to my feet—

A crab slithered right up to him from behind, mandibles open wide—

Gatling fire from the MDV sawed the thing clean in half.

The turret spun, chewing up the other crabs that were bearing down on us.

Lieutenant Commander Braggs stood at the base of the MDV's ramp, waving Tahoe, Alejandro, and me on.

"Rade, gotta hustle!" Tahoe said, helping me up with Alejandro.

The MDV cleared us a path through the crabs, but hit a bit of a snag with the bigger slug, which wasn't slowed down in the least by the Gatling gun. Those bullets actually seemed to bounce off its slick, white-hot flanks.

We ran right by the slug, though, our smaller size giving us an advantage, speed-wise.

But as I passed the sinkhole, I saw a new type of Phant float out. It was a darker-colored purple Phant.

And it moved a hell of a lot faster than any of the alien mists I'd seen before.

The three of us continued toward the MDV. I glanced over my shoulder constantly. That purple mist was gaining.

I was the best sprinter in the platoon, and I started to pull away from Alejandro and Tahoe.

"We're not going to make it," Alejandro said over the comm.

I immediately checked my speed. I wasn't going to leave them behind. "We *are* going to make it."

But he was right. That mist was just moving too fast. Maybe if we still had our Implants, and our jetpacks, and could tap into the full speed of our suits. But not now.

"I never told you how I fixed my rebreather during Moonwalk Qualifications, when I had my hands bound, did I?" Alejandro said.

I glanced over my shoulder. "Alejandro. I need you to focus!"

"I did it by dislocating my shoulder," Alejandro continued. "And breaking one of my arms. When I passed the qualification, the instructors sent me straight to the Weavers. Some Houdini I was."

"Alejandro . . ." The MDV was only about a hundred meters away now.

"I guess there's not going to be any Weavers this time around, though, is there?"

"What are you doing!" Tahoe said.

I glanced over my shoulder.

Alejandro had decided to stop.

To stop.

I halted, turning back. "We can make it, Alejandro!"

"Time for Houdini's last trick." Alejandro smiled wanly, then he ran diagonally away, drawing the purple mist from me and Tahoe.

The Phant easily overtook him.

Alejandro's last words were filled with static. "Told you I'd pay you back."

And then he was gone.

Alejandro.

The man who had raised me like a brother.

The man who had joined the MOTHs, and come to war, for me.

Had just died.

For me.

Incinerated.

Burned to a crisp.

Eight thousand lightyears from home.

Tahoe sprinted to my side, wrapping his hand around my upper arm. "Rade! Let's go!"

The Phant accelerated toward us.

I blinked away the tears and forced myself on.

I was crying openly, hardly seeing anything in front of me. A stream of Gatling bullets shot past me from the MDV. Maybe directed at the Phant. Maybe trying to slow it down.

I don't know.

I ran.

My body was functioning on autopilot, but my mind was done.

Alejandro Alejandro Alejandro.

I joined the MOTHs because I wanted to see if I had what it took.

But I didn't. No.

Alejandro had what it took. Not me.

Never me.

Giant, multiheaded crabs tried to intercept us from the side.

I made no move to dodge them.

I just ran on.

I had no fight left in me.

I was vaguely aware as the Gatling mowed them down.

"Rage! Cyclone!" Lieutenant Commander Braggs sent over the

comm line. "That purple bastard is right behind you! Hurry it on up! Don't let his death be for nothing!"

That snapped me out of it.

I was definitely not going to let his death be for nothing.

Never.

I wrapped my arm tightly around Tahoe's, and poured everything I had into my legs, sprinting for all I was worth.

I ran harder than I ever had.

Harder even than in training.

I was going to put out. More than put out.

That's for damn sure.

I wasn't a quitter.

Alejandro had died saving me.

I would never forget that.

But I couldn't mourn now.

My platoon was waiting for me.

I wouldn't see anyone else get hurt for me.

We neared the MDV.

Skullcracker had remained outside with the Lieutenant Commander, and they both used machine guns from the MDV's stores to pick off the smaller crabs that had sneaked past the Gatling fire. Skullcracker and Braggs retreated onto the craft mere seconds before Tahoe and I got there, and the MDV started lifting off.

Tahoe and I leaped onto the ascending ramp, and hurried in as it closed behind us.

I didn't look back. Didn't know how close the purple Phant had come to reaching us.

Didn't want to know.

In a daze, I went to my designated drop spot, and Tahoe went to his. The clamps automatically folded around my shoulders and waist. The fit was a bit loose, because I didn't have the jetpack strapped on anymore.

Across from me were the empty spots where Alejandro and Big Dog would have clamped in. The emptiness felt like two gaping holes in my heart.

Two of my brothers, the best of us, were gone.

Everyone had their heads bowed around me. I saw the shoulders of Chief Bourbonjack bobbing up and down, and I knew he was bawling. Tahoe couldn't meet my eye. He was just clenching and unclenching his fists.

This was the worst feeling I'd ever had in my life.

The worst.

Alejandro had found me on the streets, raised me, taught me how to defend myself, taught me what honor, courage, and commitment meant long before the Navy ever had. He had taught me compassion. Humility.

And now he was gone.

I just wanted to kill all those Phants. Screw honor, courage, and commitment. Screw compassion and humility.

I wanted to nuke the planet from orbit.

I wanted to make the system's sun go nova.

I wanted to wipe this whole quadrant from the map.

It was only when I felt the sudden turbulence that I got out of the malevolence that was brewing in my head.

The MDV tossed back and forth, bouncing and jostling everyone. I was repeatedly slammed against the restraining clamps. I liked it. Suited my raging mood.

"Mordecai, what's going on up front?" Chief Bourbonjack bellowed.

"Just the usual bit of turbulence in the polar mesosphere, sir," Mordecai said. "Nothing I can't handle."

"Then handle it!"

"How are the comms?" Manic asked Snakeoil.

Snakeoil looked up. His eyes were red. "Still static. The InterPlaNet, it's completely down."

"We gotta get through to the ship sometime, don't we?" Manic said.

"You're assuming it's still there."

"It's still there," I said angrily. "I refuse to believe that Alejandro sacrificed himself just so that we'd die in the end, stranded here."

Besides, Shaw was on the ship.

Shaw.

I couldn't lose her too.

It would kill me.

The MDV cleared the atmosphere. Looking through the portal across from me, it was a relief to see the triangular shape of the *Royal Fortune*. The jury-rigged privateer seemed undamaged as far as I could tell, its navigation lights flashing in calm counterpoint to the turmoil I felt inside.

I heard Snakeoil gasp beside me. Had he received some message from the ship?

I noticed he was looking in the opposite direction, toward the rear portal of the MDV.

"What in the hell . . ." Manic said.

I followed both their gazes.

Remember that monolithic shape I'd seen emerging from the roiling clouds on the surface? The one I thought might be some kind of ship?

Well, now that I was in space, and above those clouds, I realized that what I'd seen planet-side was just the tip of the iceberg. A very, very big iceberg. Calling that starship out there "big" was a vast understatement—the vessel was about an eighth the size of the planet itself.

No ship was that big.

It was impossible.

The behemoth of a starship was vaguely cranial-shaped, with three hollow areas on the front giving the disturbing impression of a black, elongated skull. Not human. Maybe bull, or cow. There was a slight purple glow in the two upper hollows of the massive cranium where the eyes would have been. There wasn't a mouth or teeth or anything like that, but rather some kind of pyramidal protuberance.

The part of the ship I had seen while planet-side would have been the chin of that skull. Black clouds still roiled about that chin, near the surface, maybe because of the ship's sudden entry into the atmosphere. Or maybe the clouds were particles thrown up from some kind of impact with the planet's crust.

The ship's surface seemed to be covered in markings of some kind, but when I zoomed in to the maximum extent of the lens in my face mask I realized I was wrong. There were no markings: the ship was composed of metallic lattices overlaid one atop the other, ten thousand layers deep, giving the impression of a solid surface when viewed from afar. The best part? Inside that three-dimensional lattice were entire areas of glowing blue or purple.

Phants.

"At least we know why the SKs got the hell out in such a hurry," Trace said. "Someone else already owns this gas station."

"I've reached the *Fortune*!" Snakeoil announced. He shared his connection on the platoon line. "Black Cadillac, this is Golden Arrow. Request permission to dock immediately."

"Permission granted, Golden Arrow," a female voice calmly intoned. Wasn't Shaw. "Be advised that we are initiating deorbital pre-burn. ETA to escape velocity approximately thirty seconds. It's going to be a hot dock. Good luck."

A "hot dock" was one of the trickiest maneuvers for a pilot to pull off. He had to land the craft in a relatively small hole on a relatively small target whose speed and direction changed constantly. It was like trying to toss a coin into the back-end of a tiny origami boat that was racing downstream through rapids. The computers on both crafts swapped telemetry data and were supposed to calculate the best possible course, but I doubted Mordecai would be relying on the autopilot for this one. He wasn't that kind of pilot.

We hit fast and hard: I heard the screech of metal on metal as the MDV scraped the overhead of the hangar bay. The black void of space was replaced by metallic bulkheads, and I felt the Gs as Mordecai activated multiple thrusters, trying to get us into the *Royal Fortune*'s inertial frame of reference.

The MDV smashed into the deck. We were bumped and jostled in our clamps.

The grappling hooks activated and attempted to dig into the deck.

The rightmost one took.

The leftmost didn't.

I was thrown to the left and heard more obscene screeching as the MDV swung like a pendulum and smashed into the bulkhead on the far side of the hangar.

The vessel finally came to a halt.

"Christ," TJ said. "Nice driving, Mordecai. Next time I feel like practicing a helo dunk I know who to look up."

No one bothered to wait for the bay to repressurize. We hurried outside into the artificial gravity and decamped in the airlock. When the bioscans declared us free of contaminants, we entered the ship.

Outside the hatch we took off our helmets and met with a security detail. The officer-in-charge led the Lieutenant Commander and the Chief away—presumably to the bridge—while the rest of us were escorted to the berthing area. Bulkhead seals had to be opened and closed to let us pass, because the ship was operating under high alert. The security man told us we were lucky the Captain hadn't just left us in the airlock.

At the berthing quarters, I went to the desk and put on the aReal glasses, since my Implant was still out. I logged into my account and pinged Shaw. I wasn't blocked anymore. Good.

Rade! she sent in subvocal mode. *I was so worried. I'm sorry about before. Listen, we can talk later, I'm—*

I cut her off. "Just give me a feed to the bridge. Cochlear and retinal."

And so she did. I piped it onto the viewscreen on the far wall for my platoon mates. They all deserved to know what Alejandro and Big Dog had died for.

"You're just in time," Captain Drake said.

Shaw glanced back: Lieutenant Commander Braggs and Chief Bourbonjack had entered.

"Sit-rep?" Lieutenant Commander Braggs said. Situation Report. I was surprised he was being so calm about it. Myself, I would have used a slightly different turn of phrase involving the F-word.

"A moment, Commander," the Captain said.

Shaw glanced at the main viewscreen and at the cranial-shaped black ship that ate up the stars. Her eyes dropped to the complex network of astrogation controls as she did her job babysitting the navigational AI.

"That's right," the Captain said. "Nice and easy, astrogator."

"Nice and easy, sir," Shaw said.

The planet, and the cranial ship, slowly receded as the *Royal Fortune* backed away.

"Just where in the hell did that thing come from?" Lieutenant Commander Braggs said. Not as calm as he let on then.

"My words exactly," Captain Drake said. "It just materialized out of nowhere, about forty minutes after you entered the mine-shaft. One moment there was nothing but empty space in front of us, and the next thing we know this Skull Ship appears right on top of the planet. Nearly choked on my coffee when I saw it."

"They came in on a Slipstream?" the Lieutenant Commander said. I was certain he had been bawling beside me in the MDV along with the Chief, but you wouldn't know it now from his confident manner or the authority in his voice. That was why he was the Lieutenant Commander, I guess, and I was not. I was barely keeping it together as it was.

"We haven't detected the signature of a Slipstream, no," Captain Drake said. "Of course, we haven't picked up much of anything. Our Skull friend is sending out massive amounts of electromagnetic interference. The working theory is that these guys possess stealth capabilities far in advance of anything we've ever seen. They're not SK, that's for sure."

"Then what are they?"

"You tell me, Commander. You were down there. What did you see?"

"What did I see?" Braggs was quiet a moment. "*Hell*, Captain. I saw hell."

The planet and the cranial starship above it continued to recede.

"I look forward to your debriefing," the Captain said. "Bring us about, astrogator. Plot a course for the Gate. Emergency speed."

"Aye aye, sir." Shaw made the requested changes to the ship's course and acceleration.

"They've made no aggressive maneuvers?" Lieutenant Commander Braggs said.

"That's the thing." From the sound of it Captain Drake was nervously thrumming the handrest of his chair. "All this time, the ship has just been sitting there, driving its keel into the planet's crust like we don't even exist. Hasn't paid us the slightest bit of attention."

"They were damn well paying attention to us down there, I can tell you that," Lieutenant Commander Braggs said. "Any answer to comm attempts?"

"No." Captain Drake sounded weary. "Either they can't acknowledge our communications or they won't."

The planet and the ship were gone from the forward viewscreen now, leaving only stars.

Shaw spoke. "Speed one-third and rising, Captain. G dampeners are still at one hundred percent."

"Good," the Captain said.

"The enemy ship is making no attempt to pursue," someone behind Shaw said. "And I'm still not reading any weapons signatures."

"That doesn't mean a thing," Captain Drake said. "Who's to say their weapons aren't equipped with the same stealth tech as their ship? We could have ten enemy torpedoes on our six at this moment and we wouldn't even know it. No, ladies and gentlemen, I won't believe we're out of the woods, not yet. Not until we've passed through the Gate and blown it to hell behind us. So get yourselves buckled in, because when we cut to standard speed in a few hours, we still have forty days to the Gate, with that Skull Ship watching us the entire way. Anything can happen in those forty days. And I mean *anything*."

CHAPTER TWENTY-FOUR

I spent a day in the Convalescence Ward, recovering from shrapnel wounds and radiation exposure alongside my platoon mates. Doctor Banye installed subdermal implants in all of us, which would drip-feed the necessary substances to treat the radiation poisoning in our bodies over the next few weeks—a treatment commonly known as "the juice."

While we were in the ward, Navy techs took a look at our Implants. Nothing seemed to be wrong with the devices, and since the survivors of Bravo Platoon had experienced the same issues on their drop, the techs were at a loss to explain the malfunction. Snakeoil suspected the Slipstream communication device we found in the tunnel had something to do with it. Personally, I thought the Phants were to blame. After all, the Implants had backdoors that allowed the military to send audio and video directly into our brains during briefings and other important events, so it seemed plausible, to me anyway, that the Phants had found a way to exploit that.

Whatever the cause, the techs explained that the garbage effect was amplified because of the wireless adhoc network shared between Implants. Each device sent out garbage updates representing the location of enemy targets, and accepted these updates from other Implants. This garbage data propagated in a sort of feedback loop, causing upwards of one billion updates per second, inflicting massive bandwidth bottlenecks platoon-wide. The garbage updates were also sent to the secondary Heads-Up Display systems in the helmets, which tried to interpret that data to display the outlines and dots of a billion enemies that didn't exist. The HUD processors couldn't handle such a massive influx of data, resulting in the overheating of a key component and the termination of our secondary HUDs. As usual, this was a problem slated to be fixed in a future generation of helmet.

As for our Implants, nothing had overheated there (if it had, we would be dead), and all it took was a simple reboot and our brain devices were good as new.

I mentioned the survivors of Bravo Platoon. Yes, there were two of them. They had returned while we were planet-side, and recovered in the ward with us. Their callsigns were Kasper and Pyro.

Those two had quite the story to tell. Wasn't a good one.

Bravo Platoon had gone down the shaft, and taken the far right passageway at the five-way fork. They ended up in a cavern filled with hundreds of blue Phants that were just floating there, apparently hibernating. Their Chief sent the Centurions through first, and when the robots made it across without issue, he ordered the rest of the platoon forward in traveling overwatch formation. Squad one reached the far side of the room and then squad two began to cross.

At that point, the roomful of Phants woke up.

It was a massacre.

Most of Bravo Platoon died in the first ten seconds.

Kasper and Pyro, part of squad two, survived only because they were closest to the exit.

They'd retreated back to the surface, leaped into their ATLAS mechs, and raced off, ordering the AIs of the remaining two ATLAS mechs to follow. The alien hordes swarmed out of the shaft after them, forcing them away from the MDV and the booster rockets that would get them home. They were harried and pursued for several hours, and lost contact with the two AI-driven mechs. When the alien creatures finally gave up the chase, Kasper and Pyro made their way back to the booster payloads, and launched the ATLAS 5s.

Without a communications man to boost their InterPlaNet node signals, they hadn't been able to get in touch with the *Royal Fortune* until they were in orbit—at which point the limited range of the wireless adhoc network built into the ATLAS 5s took over. They arrived at the *Royal Fortune* just before the Skull Ship appeared, while we were in that same mineshaft they had vacated.

It was strange, because our follow-up robots landed about two hours after Bravo Platoon had stirred the pot, so to speak, and everything seemed calm to us. Tahoe theorized that the behavior was similar to the defense reaction of a disturbed anthill or beehive. The ants would switch en masse to defense mode via chemical markers and stridulation, and when the perceived threat was neutralized, the ants would clean up their dead and then the bulk of them would immediately return to zombie or hibernation mode. To me, comparing an alien species to a colony of ants or bees was a bit shortsighted, but I guess Tahoe raised some valid points.

Not that I cared all that much . . . my grief wouldn't let me.

The day after I was released from the Convalescence Ward, there was a funeral service on board for our fallen brothers, composed of the remaining members of Alfa and Bravo Platoon. There would be another burial when we arrived on Earth, of course, for the families. But this service was for us.

We gathered around an empty coffin, which would serve to honor Big Dog, Alejandro, and the rest of Bravo Platoon. Lieutenant Commander Braggs gave a speech, but I didn't really hear it, lost as I was in my own memories of the man I had loved as a brother. Everyone here was a brother by now, of course, but Alejandro had been closer to me than anybody else.

Lieutenant Commander Braggs wrapped up. "This is the part of my job I hate the most. Saying good-bye to my teammates, my fellow brothers. And I do so with a heavy, heavy heart. Farewell, brave members of Team Seven. You will not be forgotten." He observed a moment of silence. "Please, each of you step forward and tell us a little something about the men we all loved."

And so we all took a turn, saying a few words or relating a short vignette, thanking the fallen for making a difference in our lives. Facehopper's eulogy for Big Dog was particularly moving. And TJ had some surprisingly heartfelt words for Alejandro. After each man finished, he tossed his golden MOTH badge into the coffin. That was one of the biggest honors we could bestow, offering up those badges that meant so much to us, those badges we'd earned through sweat and blood. Still, to be honest, it felt somehow like we didn't deserve them anymore. That we'd let our teammates down.

At least, that's how I felt.

Tahoe came forward. "I remember when me, Alejandro, and Rade first joined Team Seven. We were so wide-eyed back then. We got hazed almost every day. And we got it good. One time, a couple of the senior members woke me up in the middle of the night, brought me out to the pool, and started 'drown-proofing' me. Alejandro had heard the commotion, and when he saw what was going on, he came right down to the pool and dived in with me to take the hazing. Can you believe that? He could've stayed warm in bed. Could've slept through it. Instead he got up and dived into the freezing cold and drowned right along with me." Tahoe gingerly lowered his badge inside. "I wish I could have been there for you when you needed me the most, my spirit brother. I wish I hadn't let you down."

Chief Bourbonjack laid a hand on Tahoe's shoulder. "It's not your fault, son."

It's not your fault . . .

I stepped forward and approached the coffin. Fifteen golden MOTH badges caught the light inside.

"Tahoe's words pretty much sum up everything you need to know about Alejandro: he would have drowned for any of us." I swallowed, fighting back the emotion. "And Big Dog, well, Facehopper's speech, can't top that." I kept my eyes on those badges. I didn't think I could look at anyone, not without choking up, surrounded as I was by the teary-eyed faces of men who never cried for anything. "I thought I was the one who'd have to shoulder the blame for both their deaths. I thought I was the one who'd have to suffer in my head for what happened. But I realize now that I'm not alone. We all feel it's our fault. We're all suffering in our heads."

I slammed my MOTH badge into the top of the coffin, and let the pin embed. "Big Dog and Alejandro were the best of us."

Shaw was waiting for me in the corridor outside, by a hull window. We'd patched things up since I got back, and she did her best to comfort me now. Not with words, but with her presence.

She smiled at me, holding back the tears, and gave me a hug.

"I don't know what I'm going to do without him," I told her.

I gazed out the window over her shoulder, at the myriad stars, and I knew Alejandro had attained a star of his own.

Time heals all wounds, they say.

It's true.

Painfully, and slowly, but true.

It took a whole seven days for me to make love to Shaw again, a whole seven days of regret and self-pity and guilt before I started to see a glimmer of light, of hope, and begin the long trek back to the world.

I was in a deep, dark place, but I made it because of her. I talked to her about what happened almost every day. And she listened.

That's all that really needs to be said on the subject. We've all known grief, some of us quite intensely. We cope. We have to. It's part of the human condition.

Twenty days into the return flight, TJ and Bender (plus a couple of AIs and Fleet cryptologists) finally cracked the decryption codes on the SK Implants, and pieced together what happened eight months before we arrived.

One week after the SKs had begun excavating the Geronium-275 from the site, the first attacks came. A sinkhole would appear, and alien crabs and slugs would start coming out. The SKs would beat them off, toss some plastic explosives into the sinkhole, and seal it up.

The attacks proved little more than a nuisance at first, easily handled by rockets and Gatling guns and the ample supply of SK bioweapons (which included, among other things, the hyena-bear creature we had encountered). There weren't any Phants in those early attacks.

Eventually, as the raids picked up, the SKs decided to go after the source of the lifeforms. They drilled a shaft into one of the plugged sinkholes, with a plan to send a team down to place a low-yield nuke. No one wanted to go. So they sent robots down with the nuke instead.

The robots didn't return.

Neither did the nuke.

The order came for another nuke to be placed, this time via human hands. The SK troops still refused to go down. Eventually, the officer-in-charge ordered the administration of scopolamine to an entire company, leaving the troops entirely helpless to his will.

About two hundred of the company were sent down with the nuke.

Not a single man came out.

The nuke did explode, though.

In addition to sending the radiation levels on the site through the roof, there was one unintended side effect.

They'd awakened something.

From the ashes emerged strange blue mists: the Phants (my name stuck, and seemed to be the official designation for these incorporeal aliens now). The alien beings assaulted the SK positions relentlessly. The mechs and other robotic defense units proved useless, and soon turned against their operators when the Phants possessed them.

The Implant logs end there.

We're not sure if the SKs encountered the Skull Ship or not, but it's not hard to guess what happened next.

The SKs fled the system, leaving behind half a company in their haste. They destroyed the Gates behind them, both the one in this system, and in Tau Ceti. They mined the natural Slipstream exit point and prayed that nothing ever came through.

Let's just say, I wouldn't want to be living in Tau Ceti right about now.

The weeks passed, and on the fortieth day the *Royal Fortune* slowed in preparation for Gate traversal. The Skull Ship had remained behind at the planet, Geronimo, the entire time.

That final day on this side of the galaxy found me sitting in the mess hall during some off time. ETA to the Gate was approximately forty-five minutes. I was reflecting on everything that had happened. The discoveries made. The battles fought. The friends lost.

I was about to return to the berthing area, not wanting to be trapped in the mess hall during the passage through the Gate, when Shaw pinged me.

"Hey, babe," she sent, audio only. She was on the bridge, where she was needed.

"Wassup?"

"Not much, just working." She sighed.

"Why sound so sad?" I sent. "I'm the one who's supposed to be depressed, remember?"

I treated the subject lightly, but I knew all too well how easy it was to plummet into the depths of despair. She wouldn't let me, of course. While Shaw was here, I'd never retreat to that deep, dark place I'd gone to after Alejandro died, that place of regret and guilt that not even meds could rouse me from.

At least I hoped I wouldn't.

"Do I really sound sad?" she sent.

"Yeah."

"Oh. Well, there's something I have to tell you, actually."

I laughed. "What? You're pregnant?"

"No, silly. Can't you be serious for once?"

I tapped out a staccato rhythm on the tabletop with my hands. She hated it when I did that. Probably a good thing she couldn't hear it. "Well, tell me what's on your mind. With your mind."

"Okay. Do you remember when—" She paused. She did that now and again when we communicated like this, because while she was on the bridge astrogating, if the Captain or another member of the crew said something to her, she'd have to give them her full attention.

I reclined in my chair, putting my hands behind my head, and watched the stars through the mess hall's main window. "So, less than forty-five minutes till we reach the Gate. You think we're going to make it? Or is that Skull Ship going to show up at the last moment and block our way?"

She didn't answer right away. "Of course we're going to make it. Most of us."

"Yeah. Most of us." My thoughts drifted back to the planet, and I relived Alejandro's death all over again. It was funny how a word, or a turn of phrase, could send me right back.

I remembered that purple Phant, coming on too fast. I remembered Alejandro leading it away to save Tahoe and me. I remember him . . .

I blinked away the death. Such a waste. Such a horrible way to go.

I wondered, as I often did, what made that purple Phant move so much faster than the blue ones. I wondered what I could have done to save him. If I hadn't let my mech get possessed . . .

Speaking of which, whenever I thought about those possessed mechs, especially the Bravo Platoon ones, something tugged at the back of my mind. Something about what Pyro had said about his escape. Something important. But for the life of me I could never quite figure out what it was.

"I don't know why I waited so long to tell you," Shaw was saying. "I should have said something last night, when we were together. It's so much better to deal with stuff like this in person. But, it's so hard, Rade, and—"

"What? Did you just say something important?" I sent, distracted. The possessed mechs . . .

"Uh. Rade. I—"

Then it hit me.

"Shaw," I interrupted her. "The Phants. I know why that Skull Ship left us alone."

"What? Why?"

"Because of the ATLAS mechs."

"I don't understand."

I ran from the mess hall. "Remember how I told you that you can't tell when a Phant has possessed a mech? Because the profiles of the ATLAS 5s are too big, and completely hide the things? Well, guess what we have on board right now? Two ATLAS 5s, courtesy of Bravo Platoon's survivors."

"But that doesn't mean there are Phants inside."

"Yes, but something Pyro said makes me think otherwise. Probably should sound General Quarters. Send my Chief to the launch hangar, would you?"

"Okay, Rade. But what are you going to do?"

"Just checking something. Send him, please."

A technician was running a diagnostic on Ladybug, Manic's ATLAS, when I got to the launch hangar. The repairmen had done a bang-up job on the thing—the mech looked like new, save for a few scratches and dents and a leg that seemed slightly off-kilter from the rest of the body.

I glanced at the storage alcoves beside Manic's mech, where the two ATLAS 5s brought up from the surface by the survivors of Bravo Platoon were moored.

All three mechs looked completely normal.

Yet any one of them could be housing a Phant.

Maybe all three of them.

I kept myself at a distance. "Shouldn't you be in your berthing area, preparing for the Gate jump?" I told the technician.

"Just getting in some last-minute fixes, sir," the technician said, with the usual respectful tone the crew displayed toward MOTHs. "Become a sort of obsession for me, fixing up Ladybug, it has."

"You make it sound like you're the only one who's worked on the mech."

"Well," he grinned sheepishly. "That's because I am, sir."

I pursed my lips, and regarded his work. "Not bad. What's Ladybug's operational status?" I noticed that the weapons had been detached from the mech's arms. That was standard safety procedure during diagnostics. You didn't want weapons going off while you were working on a mech. There wasn't even a deployable ballistic shield. The other two ATLAS 5s had their weapons and shields fully attached, however, but not in the "gun-on-hand" position.

"Except for the left leg, she's running almost perfectly, sir," the ATLAS technician said.

I started walking toward the far side of the hangar. I could see the dents and runnels torn into the deck from where we'd crash-landed the MDV on the return trip from the planet. "And what's the problem with the left leg?"

"Well, I'll need to put in a new hip servomotor eventually. I salvaged a lot of parts from Aphid, and 3D printed almost everything else. Unfortunately, we're low on printer material, and the Cap has ordered all nonessential print jobs placed on hold till we're back. For some reason repairing the ATLAS 5s is considered nonessential."

"Yeah, sometimes priorities are pretty whacked shipboard, aren't they?"

"Isn't that the truth. I—Excuse me, sir, what are you doing?"

I'd just opened up the jumpsuit closet.

"I hadn't received word about a spacewalk," the technician continued.

I didn't answer him. I put on the thermo-body undergarment, then slid on the lower torso assembly. I shrugged on the hard upper torso and twisted it into place with the lower torso.

The technician stood up. "Sorry, sir, I'm supposed to order you to stand down."

"Talking behind my back, are you?" I said.

Keeping my eyes on the technician, who looked more afraid than anything else, I put on the arm assembly of the suit, followed by the gloves and boots. Finally I strapped on the rebreather subsystem and secured a jetpack. I twisted the helmet on and activated the oxygen.

I was supposed to wait an hour for my body to adjust to the internal pressure of the suit. But there wasn't time. I could've tried to shoot out the brain cases of the ATLAS 5s instead of what I had planned, but that would have just caused the Phants to emerge.

Right in the ship.

Definitely not a good idea.

Chief Bourbonjack burst into the hangar with three other members of Alfa Platoon: Facehopper, Skullcracker, and Tahoe. A fire team. They all carried pistols.

General Quarters still hadn't sounded, I noticed.

"What's this about a Phant on board our ship?" the Chief said.

"I'll show you." I turned toward Ladybug and was about to activate my jumpjets when the fire team pointed their pistols at me.

"Stay where you are, Rage," Chief Bourbonjack said. "I want you to take off that jumpsuit. That's an order." His voice softened. "Look, I told the LC we would deal with this quietly. I know you've been distraught over Alejandro's death. So if you do as I say, and take that suit off right now, I'll let this slide. No one else has to know beyond this room. Come on, son, take it off and we'll go see the doc."

"The doc," I said, coldly. "You think I'm delusional."

Chief Bourbonjack shook his head sadly. "You've been a wreck since Alejandro and Big Dog died. And now with what Shaw's doing, you've snapped."

"What do you mean, what Shaw's doing?"

Chief Bourbonjack scrunched up his nose, like he was confused. He glanced at Facehopper, who shrugged.

I didn't have time for this. "Look, you've all fought at my side. You know me, and you know I'd never let you down. Believe me when I tell you that the ship is in danger. All of humanity is."

"Rade," Tahoe said. Like Alejandro before him, he'd never quite gotten used to calling me *Rage*. "Listen to the Chief. We're here to help you, not hurt you. Take the jumpsuit off. We'll go back to the berthing area and sit the Gate jump out. We can talk about—"

"There isn't anything to talk about. We have to keep those Phants where they belong, on this side of the galaxy. I'm not backing down on this."

"You think there are Phants in the ATLAS 5s, do you?" the Chief said. He walked toward the mechs while the rest of the fire team kept their 9-mils trained on me.

He reached Ladybug and rapped on the metallic leg piece with his knuckles. "Anyone home?" He glanced at me, eyes twinkling, then he turned toward the technician. "Open her up."

The technician obeyed, and the cockpit folded open. The Chief climbed the support rungs on the right leg, and peered inside. "You see? No mist."

"Look in the small gap beneath the open hatch and the hull. Is the brain case surrounded by blue, glowing mist?"

The Chief peered into the gap. "Nope. The brain case is just fine."

"What about the other two?"

Chief Bourbonjack nodded at the technician, who activated the cockpit releases on the two Bravo Platoon mechs. The Chief climbed the rungs of each ATLAS 5 in turn and peered into the cockpits.

"Nothing. No blue mists around the brain cases. There's a little condensation, but that's about it. Satisfied now?"

Well, that was certainly unexpected. But it didn't mean I was wrong. There were lots of places a Phant could hide inside a mech.

The Chief leaped down to the deck and nodded at the technician. "Close 'em up." The cockpits of all three ATLAS 5s sealed. "Now stand down, Rage."

I gazed at Facehopper, Skullcracker, and Tahoe. At the pistols they had aimed at me. I smiled sadly. "If you have to shoot me, then do it now. Because I won't stand down." I looked pleadingly at Tahoe. "You know me. You *know* me. I wouldn't do this if we weren't in danger. Something occurred to me about what Pyro said. When he ran into one of the mists during his escape, he thought he was a dead man, but he kept running, and got away.

"I believe he was wrong. He didn't get away. I believe the Phant stowed away in his mech without him noticing. When a Phant invaded Hornet, it went straight for the brain case and left me alone. If I hadn't had my eyes inside the cockpit, I would have never seen it do that. The problem is, the mechs are too big and hide the profiles of the Phants, unlike the smaller Centurions. I'm telling you, there's at least one stowaway Phant inside this hangar."

"What if you're wrong?" Tahoe said.

"Then court-martial me."

"You're already going to be court-martialed," the Chief growled.

"I can prove it."

"How, by tossing the mechs overboard?" Chief Bourbonjack said.

"Basically, yeah."

"You're crazy."

"As I said, shoot me." I held my arms wide. "Shoot me."

They didn't shoot.

I activated my jumpjets and flew across the hangar, issuing the command to open Ladybug's cockpit while I was still in the air. Manic's former mech was provisioned to respond to my Implant, while the other two, belonging to Bravo Platoon, were not. I landed in the pilot's seat but before I could seal the cockpit I found myself staring into the receiving end of the Chief's pistol—he had climbed the rungs of Ladybug's leg before I landed, and he held his 9-mil's barrel right up against my face mask.

His eyes blazed. His lips were pressed together so severely beneath his mustache that the skin had become a milky white.

"Can't let you toss three billion digicoins worth of equipment overboard, Rage," the Chief said. "If the others won't fire, then I will. You know I will, goddammit."

I stared at my Chief. Yes, he would.

I could try to close the cockpit, but he'd easily let off three or four bullets before I could. At this range, the armor piercing rounds would go right through my face mask and come out the back of my head. There would be some minor damage to the cockpit. Easily repairable.

"Chief, listen to me," I said carefully. "Is three billion digicoins worth the risk of transporting a malevolent alien being into our space? A potentially invulnerable alien that can dissolve human flesh at a touch, and possess our robot support troops, our ATLAS 5s, and use them against us? Do you really want to be known as the Chief who allowed this threat into our space?"

"And if you're wrong, I'll be known as the Chief who allowed billions of digicoins to be thrown overboard."

"I'm not wrong."

Chief Bourbonjack stared at me for the longest time. His eyes never stopped blazing, not for an instant. They drilled right into me, judging me, probably searching for any sign of doubt, or lack of conviction, or insanity.

"You're going to make me shoot you, aren't you?" the Chief said.

I didn't know if he expected an answer, so I didn't say anything. I just looked into his eyes, waiting for the shot, expecting it.

If I had to die for what I believed in, then so be it.

"Damn it." He pointed the pistol upward, away from my face, but still ready to bring it down at a moment's notice. "I've seen that look before, in the eyes of trainees during Trial Week, trainees who would rather die than give up their dream. You're not going to back down, are you? You really believe you're right?"

"I do. Look, if I'm wrong, I'll spacewalk out and retrieve the mechs."

"Okay, Rage. Okay. I'll humor you. Goddammit."

He lowered the weapon and then climbed down Ladybug's rungs, boots clanking with each step. "Clear the deck people. We're depressurizing this bunghole." He glanced at the Bravo Platoon ATLAS 5s. "Never liked those mechs anyway."

Seated there in the cockpit, I peered into the small crack beneath the open hatch and the hull of my mech, gazing into Ladybug's innards, and I noted that there was no mist surrounding the brain case. Though I supposed that didn't mean too much. As I said, there were many places a Phant could hide in these things.

I sealed the cockpit and the internal layer of the mech took hold of me, and its sight became my sight. I stood to my full stature, and Ladybug obeyed. I felt the usual sense of power and invincibility.

When the Chief shut the airlock behind him, I walked the mech over to the hangar control console, and interfaced with my Implant. Or I tried to, anyway. I'd been locked out of the controls.

I sent Chief Bourbonjack a message over my helmet comm. "Chief, can you—"

"Warning," a female voice echoed in the hangar. "Depressurization commencing. Hangar atmosphere venting overboard. Warning."

I glanced back at the airlock, and saw the Chief peering through the portal. He nodded when I caught his eye.

I walked Ladybug toward the mooring area of the Bravo ATLAS 5s. The technician had been right, the left servomotor pulled to the left so that I had to correct my path every few steps.

"Which mech did Pyro ride, do we know?" I sent over the comm.

"The one right in front of you," Chief Bourbonjack sent. "Wolf."

I went to the indicated ATLAS and paused in front of it. There was no sign of any Phant. Well, just because I couldn't see it . . .

I tore open the fuel lines that fed its jumpjets. Then I bent the barrels of the Gatling guns, the launch tubes of the serpent launchers, and the nozzles of the incendiary throwers attached under each arm.

Satisfied that the mech was properly disabled, I hooked my huge hands beneath the Bravo mech's elbows and lifted. The stress that heavy load placed on the individual joints and servomotors of Ladybug was mirrored in the resistance the internal actuators applied to my body, so that it felt like I was lifting a moderately heavy weight. The whole point of that resistance-mirroring was to prevent a pilot from overloading and damaging his ATLAS 5, so that if I tried to pick up an MDV, for example, I'd really feel it.

I reached the hangar doors. Which still hadn't opened, I might add. "Chief?"

For a second I thought the Chief had changed his mind about this.

And then:

"Warning, hangar doors opening," the female voice echoed. "Warning."

A flashing red light activated somewhere in the overhead as the hangar doors parted down the middle. Since the air in the hangar had already vented, there was no explosive decompression or anything. The artificial gravity remained constant.

I stepped forward until I stood right on the edge of the void.

I held Wolf outside the ship.

I pushed forward, releasing my grip.

The mech floated away.

I waited a few moments, wondering if the mist would make an appearance, or if the mech would try to fight back.

But Wolf made no movement. No Phant emerged from it.

The lifeless mech just floated away.

"Congratulations, Mr. Galaal, you just threw out three billion digicoins worth of UC military equipment," the Chief's voice came over my helmet speaker. It wasn't lost on me that he'd called me Mr. Galaal, instead of Rage. "Not to mention, both our enlistments."

"Sir, I—"

"You what? Made a mistake? Yeah. Big-time. I hope you're pleased, because now we'll get to attend each other's court-martials. I'm shutting the hangar doors, dumbass. Step back."

"Wait, Chief," I said. "What about the other—"

"Warning, hangar doors closing," the hangar voice intoned.

I activated my jumpjets and flew across the hangar, landing beside the second Bravo ATLAS 5.

"Look, Mr. Galaal," Chief said. "You've already thrown out one multibillion-digicoin mech. Let's cut our losses and end this while we're ahead. You never know, maybe the Navy will grant us some leniency. Make our jail sentences lighter. Mitigating circumstances and all that."

"I don't know why you're so worried," I said. "I've got jumpjets. I can retrieve the mechs—"

"Ah, I see. So I'll tell the Captain that we have to delay, because you threw some mechs overboard. Well I got news for you. He's not going to stop. Not now. You go out there, we're not waiting for you. And that means you're not going out. So stand down, goddammit. You're wrong. You just can't see it. You're blinded by grief."

I looked at the remaining ATLAS 5.

The Chief was probably right.

No Phant had stowed away on board.

I wanted so badly to avenge Alejandro and give his death some meaning.

But I was wrong.

And if I couldn't go out there and retrieve that mech, there was no way I was going to make things worse by tossing the other mech outside.

I was done.

The Chief was right.

"All right, Chief. I'm going to—" Then I realized something. "Wait a second. Which mech had condensation around its brain case?"

"Mr. Galaal, I've just about had it with—"

"Chief, humor me a while longer. Which mech did you see condensation in?"

"Tell me why you want to know."

"Because, a Phant would probably appear as a liquid in a human-friendly environment."

"Condensation." The Chief sounded stunned.

"Bingo. So which mech? Was it Pyro's, the one I just threw off the ship?"

There was a long pause.

"No," the Chief said. "I saw condensation in the mech right in front of you."

I glanced at the hangar doors.

They were three-quarters closed.

I still had time, if I was quick.

But what if I was wrong?

"Mr. Galaal, do not touch that mech. I say again, do not—"

I reached around the second ATLAS to tear open the jumpjet fuel lines—

The Bravo Platoon mech exploded into action. Its arms rammed into Ladybug's chest piece, sending me flying backward across the hangar.

I slid to a halt near the opposite bulkhead, my body scraping a long runnel in the deck.

"Holy shit." The Chief's voice was full of static in my helmet.

I started to get up—

My vision filled with digital snow, and white noise consumed my hearing.

I raised a hand in front of me as if to shield myself from the garbage patterns that wouldn't go away even when I closed my eyes.

Zulu Romeo Lima!

The command words shut down my Implant.

Sight and sound returned. I was staring at the inside of my cockpit. Emergency alarms were going off all around me.

So the Phants were the source of our Implant troubles after all. I guess that meant everyone aboard was experiencing sensory deprivation right about now. They'd just have to cope until they shut off their own Implants.

I hoped whatever the Phant was doing didn't wreak too much havoc on the other ship systems.

"Audio and visual feeds, route to helmet." The mech directed its sight and sound to my helmet so that I could interact with the outside world again. I noted that the backup HUD in my helmet was disabled again.

I stood up. I'd forgotten how heavy these mechs felt when controlled without the Implant. My body would adapt to the sensation soon enough.

General Quarters sounded.

"This is not a drill!" came the voice over the main circuit. "This is not a drill! General Quarters! General Quarters! All hands . . ."

The Bravo ATLAS hadn't made any other move. That pinched head merely stared at me, yellow eyes now active and glowing eerily. It was waiting for me to make my next move.

It could have easily taken me down while I recovered from the Implant overload.

Maybe it was trying to communicate with me. Or maybe it was trying to give me a chance, out of some alien sense of honor. I don't know. Either way, that was a mistake on its part. I sure wasn't going to show it the same mercy. And I sure didn't want to talk to it, not after what its kind had done to Alejandro and Big Dog.

The hangar doors thudded shut.

"Chief, get those doors open!" I said into the helmet comm. He'd have to get the Captain to authorize an override, now that General Quarters had sounded.

The possessed mech was still waiting, motionless.

It wanted me to make the first move, did it?

I turned on my jumpjets. Full forward thrust. I hurtled across the hangar.

The Bravo ATLAS swiveled a Gatling gun into its left hand.

My first instinct was to activate the ballistic shield built into my own mech, but then I remembered that all weapon and shield loadouts had been removed from Ladybug for the technician's diagnostic run.

I had no shield.

And no weapons.

I kept my forward thrust on at full.

Almost there—

The possessed ATLAS brought its Gatling to bear—

I collided with the mech.

The two of us smashed into the far bulkhead.

I clambered to my knees instantly. The possessed ATLAS, below me, steered its Gatling barrel toward my chest.

I wrapped my hand around the tip of the barrel and bent it.

The Bravo ATLAS stupidly fired. Strips of metal peeled back from the barrel and the feed tray exploded.

The enemy mech discarded the useless weapon and grabbed my left leg. Standing, it lifted me right off my feet and swung me around, ramming me headfirst into the bulkhead. It was still hanging on to my leg, and hoisted me up again, this time hurling me into the deck.

Then the overdeck.

Then the bulkhead again.

I was getting dizzy. Alarms were going off all over Ladybug's cockpit.

The possessed mech still hadn't let go of me, so the next time it lifted me I activated my jumpjets at full burn and launched the two of us toward the hangar doors.

Which hadn't opened.

"Chief!" I said into the helmet comm.

I applied braking thrust, and we dropped to the deck right in front of the doors.

"Warning, hangar doors opening." The female voice echoed. "Warning."

The Bravo ATLAS released me. Serpent rocket launchers swiveled into either hand. If those rockets struck at this range, both our mechs would be destroyed.

But I guessed the alien in command of the mech wouldn't know that.

I wrapped my hands around the legs of the Bravo mech and swung my body hard to the left, activating side thrusters for extra momentum, and released, hurling the mech across the hangar like an Olympic thrower launching his hammer.

The Bravo ATLAS was spinning wildly toward the far bulkhead when it decided to fire off both its serpents.

One unaimed rocket struck the overhead. The other struck the right wing of the MOTH Delivery Vehicle, which was moored in the center of the hangar.

The shockwave sent Ladybug hurtling backward. I rebounded from the far bulkhead, landing face-first.

I clambered to my feet (which was difficult, given the problems I had with my left leg servomotor), and I took a moment to survey the hangar. The entire right wing of the MDV was disintegrated, and above me, a gaping, sparking hole was blown in the overhead.

With a boost from my jumpjets, I launched myself across the hangar at the still-recovering Bravo ATLAS.

I smashed into the mech as it rose. The two of us toppled to the deck.

I got up on top of it and grabbed the tubes of the serpent launchers with both my hands and bent them out of shape. Satisfied that my opponent's rockets were disabled, I wrapped Ladybug's arms around the midsection of the Bravo ATLAS and lifted the thing into the air.

It slammed its arms down, trying to break free of my grip.

I swiveled around and fired my jumpjets, hurtling the two of us toward the now open hangar doors.

The possessed mech shot off its own thrusters, lowering our combined trajectory. The two of us struck the deck hard, and sparks flew as we skidded along the metallic surface.

I increased my thrust, compensating, and the two of us shot into space.

I ignored the sudden nausea and directionlessness, fixing my eyes on the enemy mech, using it as my reference point.

The Bravo ATLAS swung its arms down once again, and when it still couldn't loosen my grip, it decided on a different strategy.

It activated its lateral thrusters on full, spinning slowly at first, then faster and faster, bringing us to a dizzying speed. I tried to counter by firing my own jets in a stabilizing motion, but the ATLAS kept tweaking the angle of thrust.

The centrifugal G forces in my mech shot way up.

I was about to black out—

I released the mech, and went spinning away from it.

I steadied my motion, and shook my head, trying to clear the dizziness. Then I got my bearings. I wished the Phant hadn't burned out my Implant and the Heads-Up-Display map, because I had to keep pivoting in multiple directions until I finally spotted the mech.

It was thrusting back toward the ship.

I pursued.

The possessed mech shut off its rear jets, then fired its lateral thrusters, turning to face me while continuing toward the ship.

The remaining Gatling gun swiveled into its right hand and fired.

I released my own lateral burst of thrust, which added a sideways element to my forward motion, and I circled the target, giving a wide berth to the stream of superheated bullets.

I noticed that the mech hadn't learned how to dial down the recoil of its weapons—firing the Gat had sent the thing spinning away. It was forced to stop shooting, concentrating instead on stabilizing its motion.

I adjusted my own trajectory so that I came at the ATLAS in a 3D version of a Fibonacci Spiral. Imagine a steel ball descending in an elongated spiral down the surface of a funnel, and you had an idea of my flight path. It was an advanced maneuver, and I knew the enemy would have a hell of a time targeting me on an approach like that.

The enemy mech fired off its lateral jets, struggling to bring its Gatling to bear.

I tightened my orbit and, as expected, the bursts of Gatling bullets the thing launched weren't even on the same three-dimensional plane.

The gunfire sent the possessed ATLAS spinning away again.

I was forced to compensate, but sooner than I expected I came up behind the mech.

I wrapped my legs around its waist from behind. The possessed ATLAS bucked and thrusted. It felt like I was riding a bronco. In space.

I tore out the lines that ran between its fuel canisters and the jets.

I was about to release the possessed mech and give it a good kick, but at that moment it discarded its Gatling and clamped its arms tightly around my legs, securing me to its waist.

It was my turn to buck and thrust, but I couldn't get the possessed ATLAS to release me: it had realized I'd disabled its only form of locomotion, and there was no way it was letting go now.

The two of us were spinning on an odd axis, and the stars seemed to be orbiting around us in a helical pattern. I was feeling more nauseous than ever, and did my best to focus on the enemy mech below me.

That's when I saw the blue mist.

The Phant had decided to abandon the Bravo ATLAS. The mech still had its arms firmly clamped about my legs, and no matter how hard I tried to break loose, I couldn't budge.

The mist floated toward Ladybug, steadfast, single-minded.

I tried thrusting myself free. No use. I merely dragged the lifeless ATLAS, and the mist, along with me.

I was locked in.

The Phant was going to take Ladybug.

Well, if the damn thing wanted my mech so badly, it could have it.

I turned all thrusters to full burn, intending to exhaust Ladybug's fuel supply. Then I locked in the controls and opened the cockpit.

The vision feed from the mech winked out and the inner cocoon released me. What I would have given in that moment for a pistol to blow out the brain case . . .

The hatch, unaided by gravity, had opened just a crack. I pushed on it, but could only force it to a maximum of forty-five degrees, because the hatch lodged against the bulging jetpack of the other mech beneath me.

I squeezed through the opening, passing dangerously close to the blue mist as it transferred into Ladybug.

I was halfway through when I got stuck.

I retreated a handspan, and tried again.

No good.

There was only one way I was fitting through that half-open hatch.

I unbuckled my jetpack. I disconnected my life support subsystem. I slid both assemblies away from my jumpsuit, and into the cockpit.

I tried again. There, that did it.

I wiggled through the hatch and out into the void, being careful not to lose physical contact with the mech. I grabbed the hatch, and turned myself around to retrieve the items I would need to live—

The hatch abruptly sealed shut.

The Phant had taken over.

Ladybug batted me away, launching me into the void.

"Suit oxygen level fifty percent," the friendly voice in my helmet intoned.

Looking down between my feet, I watched Ladybug and the other mech recede. The fuel burn ceased. Ladybug's lateral thrusters activated, and the ATLAS turned slightly, aiming for a distant target I couldn't see from this angle. The *Royal Fortune*, probably.

Ladybug's fuel hadn't run out, then.

Damn.

"Suit oxygen level twenty-five percent," the voice in my helmet cheerily intoned.

A blur streamed past. It struck the mechs.

I was blinded by the flash. It had to be a torpedo from the *Royal Fortune.*

The shockwave from the expanding gases of the explosion sent me tumbling end over end.

Watching those stars spin by was just too dizzying. I closed my eyes.

"Black Cadillac, this is Rage," I sent on all frequencies. "Do you copy? Over."

Static.

"Black Cadillac, this is Rage. Requesting pickup. Over."

Nothing.

"Black Cadillac, this is Rage. Over."

So this was it. I remembered what the Chief had told me about the Captain not ordering the *Royal Fortune* back if I went outside now, this close to the Gate. "He's not going to stop," the Chief had said. "You go out there, we're not waiting for you." I hadn't really believed it. I was sure Tahoe, or someone, anyone, would come back for me. No MOTH ever left another MOTH behind.

But I was wrong, apparently.

If he were alive, Alejandro would have come back for me, regardless of his orders. I remember telling him that one day he wouldn't be able to protect me. Turned out I was right, for all the wrong reasons.

So this was how it was going to end. At least I'd gone out on a high.

"Suit oxygen level three percent," the voice in my helmet said.

I heard a thud behind me, and I opened my eyes. "Alejandro?"

My motion had stabilized, and my oxygen levels were in the green. The buckles of a jetpack were hanging from my waist. I fastened them, and applied lateral thrust to turn around.

Shaw was there, in a jumpsuit. Tethered to a shuttle. "Need some help?"

I was relieved and angry at the same time. "Why didn't you say anything all this time?"

"What, and ruin the surprise?"

We latched on to a small hook at the top of the shuttle's fuselage, and hitched a ride as the pilot brought us back to the *Royal Fortune*. I was too exhausted, emotionally and physically, for much talk. But I was curious about one thing.

"Who's piloting?" I asked her.

"The AI."

The shuttle steered toward the *Royal Fortune*'s secondary hangar bay because of the damage to the main, and then Shaw beckoned toward the open doors. "After you."

There wasn't much fuel in the pack she'd given me, and I used up the last of it jetting inside. The abrupt change in gravity caught me off guard and I ended up tumbling to the deck.

I climbed to my feet and turned around, expecting to find Shaw right behind me.

She wasn't.

Nor was she latched on to the shuttle anymore. The craft had turned around, and was drifting away.

I suppressed a sudden panic. Had the Phant gotten to her, and taken over the shuttle?

"Shaw, where are you?" I sent over the helmet comm.

"Everything's fine, Rade. I'm in the shuttle."

That's when I noticed the full complement of hellfire missiles underneath the shuttle's wings. That meant she was the one who had fired the missile that had taken out the mechs. That also meant . . .

"Rade," she said over the comm. "I have to stay behind. I tried telling you before—"

"What are you talking about? *Stay behind*?"

"It's my job to blow the Gate on this side."

I couldn't believe what I was hearing.

"No." I shook my head. "Why would the Captain order *you* to do this? Why not someone else? I can do it."

"The Captain didn't order me, Rade. I volunteered. Actually, we all did. The bridge crew, I mean. We drew straws. I got the short one. It makes the most sense, anyway. I'm the best pilot, and the best on the weapons systems. It should be me."

I slumped to the deck.

First Alejandro, and now her.

Why did I have to lose everyone I ever cared about?

I stared at the receding shuttle. I wasn't going to give up, not yet. If there was a chance I could convince her to turn around, I had to take it. Besides, I was due an explanation at least. "There are explosive charges set up all over the Gate. Ready to detonate, with timers that are remotely activated. Why do you have to stay?"

"So, here's the thing. Those EM pulses from the Skull Ship haven't let up, and they're traveling system-wide. The electronics in the timers were designed for cosmic background rad, not constant bombardment from EMPs. It just wasn't something we could plan for. The timers stopped working a few weeks ago."

Electromagnetic energy. When you sent current through a wire, that wire developed a magnetic field. When you moved a magnetic field across a wire, it induced a current in that wire. EMP weapons operated under the latter principle, inducing massive currents in remote electronics, burning them out. Such weapons were relatively commonplace in this day and age, which is why sensitive components like integrated circuits and transistors were protected with glass switches, solid-state devices that opened a path to ground in overvoltage scenarios. Unfortunately these otherwise unshielded switches could fail under constant EMP stress, especially the smaller, lower-rated ones that had smaller substrates available for current and heat dissipation.

"Why not just set some more charges, then?" I said.

"I wish we could. But we've run out of time."

"What are you talking about? That Skull Ship is way back at the planet. There are no weapons pursuing us. Of course we have time." No answer. "The Skull Ship *is* still at the planet, isn't it?"

"No." Shaw sounded weary. "The Captain didn't want to alarm the crew. The ship has been following us, mirroring our heading and speed, for the past few weeks."

"What? 'The Captain didn't want to alarm the crew.' Ridiculous. We're spec-ops, it takes a lot more than that to frighten us. I can't believe you kept us in the dark."

"Hey, take it up with the Captain."

So the Skull Ship had been following us the whole time, and she knew. Now that I thought about it, Shaw *had* seemed distracted these past few weeks, but I'd been too consumed by grief, locked in my own world of self-pity and guilt, to notice.

"The ship is about two hours behind us," Shaw continued. "And we have reason to believe they could easily close that gap. It's funny, but it's almost like the ship is escorting us, or egging us on. Like they want to see us through the Gate. I suppose they wanted their little spy to make it into our space. Or maybe they were following the Phant's signature. I really don't know. Anyway, now you understand why we can't delay. We have to do this, and we have to do it right now."

Still I refused to back down. “Let the shuttle's AI do the dirty work. There's no reason you have to stay behind and babysit it.”

“Isn't there? Would you really trust an AI under the circumstances? With that Phant floating out there, ready to take over the shuttle? The hellfire didn't destroy it, you know. Just the mechs. And what about that Skull Ship, ready to close the distance in a moment's notice? No, this is something that only a human being can do.”

I sighed. “I don't know. This is . . . it's just crazy. What happens if that ship closes the distance like you say? And attacks you when we're gone?”

“I'm trained in evasive maneuvers. I'll survive. Long enough to blow up the Gate, anyway.”

I swallowed. “What happened to never leaving anyone behind?”

“Sometimes it can't be helped; you know that,” she said. “Don't you remember in Basic, sometimes one of us would have to stay behind and manually seal a hatch to save the rest of the crew in a sinking ship? Well, I'm the one staying behind and sealing that hatch.”

I squeezed my eyes shut. *Just like Alejandro did for Tahoe and me.*

“Can't the *Royal Fortune* just launch a few torpedoes at the Gate?” I said. “I'm sure we can time it so that the torpedoes strike before we're through.”

“We could. But the timing has to be perfect. We'd put the whole crew at risk. Given the choice between sacrificing one person and one shuttle, or risking the whole ship, the Captain chose to sacrifice the one. Wouldn't you?”

I still wouldn't give in. “What about mines?” I was grasping at straws now. “Can't we launch some timer mines, and set them to destroy the Gate behind us? There's enough shielding in a mine to easily withstand EMPs.”

“If this was a Navy warship, maybe. But the *Royal Fortune* is a jury-rigged privateer. We're not carrying any mines, Rade.”

"What if—"

"Rade! We've considered every possibility!" I was stunned by the ferocity in her voice. When she spoke again, her tone was gentler. "Rade. I have to stay behind. It's up to me to destroy the Gate. I'm sorry."

"So am I. Because I'm coming with you." The hangar doors were still open, just as if the Chief had wanted to give me that very opportunity. "I'm just going to get some fuel for this jetpack, and—"

"Don't you dare," Shaw sent over the comm. "I'm launching my full complement of hellfires the instant the *Royal Fortune* is through the Gate. If you're out there in a jumpsuit, the shockwaves from the explosion will rip you apart." She paused, as if gathering her thoughts. "Look. I purposely drained most of the fuel from that pack. I want you to stay behind. One of us has to survive. One of us has to go on living. And that's you, Rade. It has to be you."

I suddenly felt extremely tired, like I was holding up the weight of the world, and I couldn't do it anymore. I lowered myself until I lay prostrate on the deck. I was still staring at the shuttle, which was about the size of my thumbnail now.

"You can do this, Rade," Shaw continued. There was a lot of static on the comm, and her words cut in and out, but it didn't matter because I understood everything—I knew her so well, and was so used to her voice and her every nuance of tone, that even when I missed part of a word, I knew exactly what she had meant to say. "You're strong. The strongest of us all. If anyone can get through this, it's you." She laughed then. A sad laugh. Full of regret. "Look at me, trying to comfort you, when I'm the one who's going to die alone, eight thousand lightyears from home. I'm scared, Rade. I'm going to miss you. Miss everything."

"Please, Shaw. Don't do this." But I knew she had to. For the ship. For humanity.

"Good-bye, Rade. It was good being with you. Really good."

"Shaw . . ."

"Remember me in the deepest, darkest hours, when you think you can't go on. Remember me in the storm, when—"

The comm filled with uninterrupted static.

The *Royal Fortune* had passed through the Gate.

CHAPTER TWENTY-FIVE

When I finally got back to Earth, the Brass tried to give me the Navy Cross.

What an insult.

I told them three of my friends had died because of me.

I didn't deserve a medal for that.

My friends were the ones who gave their lives for me.

My friends were the ones who deserved the Navy Cross.

I lived, and I wasn't about to dishonor their memory by accepting some cheap, political bauble for surviving them.

A piece of metal wasn't going to bring them back.

Nothing would.

Some months later reports began to trickle in from Tau Ceti: the fifty-thousand-megaton nuke payload that mined the natural exit point of the Geronium Slipstream had detonated.

Something had tried to pass through.

Foreign matter was detected amongst the debris in the aftermath of the explosion, and whatever had attempted entry was presumed destroyed.

The SKs quietly dispatched their imperial minelayers and the entire area was re-mined with fresh nukes. SK battlecruisers were deployed to provide a constant watch.

Nothing further attempted to pass through that Slipstream. The region remained silent.

The message was clear, however:

We know about you.

And we are coming.

It was difficult to keep a fifty-thousand-megaton explosion hidden, given the technology available to professional and armchair astronomers alike, and theories spread like wildfire across the Undernet. Eventually, word got out about our secret mission, and what we had seen. Pictures were shared of the black, skull-shaped ship, known as the Great Death. Stories were told of the armies of hideous beings, and the *Yaoguai*—demons from the underworld with a particular appetite for the souls of men.

Doomsayers spread the word: It was the end of humankind's glorious expansion to the stars. The end of life as we knew it.

We'd awakened something on the far side of the galaxy that we should've left well alone. We'd stepped too far. Aimed too high. And the Great Death was going to come for us. Eventually.

Maybe they were right. Maybe humankind was doomed.

Maybe not.

But if the invaders did come, I knew it was only a matter of time, months, maybe years, before the MOTHs were called in. But we *would* be summoned, in the end. It was inevitable.

I was ready.

I'm Rade Galaal.

I've come a long way from the barrio I grew up in.

And I'm a MOTH now.

I pilot ATLAS mechs.

Let the enemies of humanity come.

Because when they do, there'll be hell to pay.

EPILOGUE

I opened my eyes.

My fingers fumbled in the shadows, and I found the water canister.

I took a long sip, then checked the craft's power cells. Thirty percent.

I adjusted the window's opacity dial, letting the sunlight pour inside, then I went through the daily ritual of donning my jumpsuit. When I sealed the helmet and activated the oxygen supply, I took a long inhale of the iron-smelling air.

While my body acclimated to the internal environment, I went to the pile of thick pelts I'd collected and started securing them to the suit's outer layer. The jumpsuits could adapt in coloration to match any terrain, of course, but I wanted actual fur. It confused the hybears sometimes.

When the acclimation period was over, I depressurized the compartment and lowered the ramp. I walked from my metal prison to the bigger prison of the outside world.

I stood at the bottom of one of the deep valleys that carved through the planet's surface. This valley lay along the equator, and I had named it the Main Rift. One of the nice things about the location, other than the relatively balmy temperatures, was that the radiation levels were low.

The long Forma pipe in the distance belched oxygen into the air. Not that it helped. The atmosphere wasn't breathable, and wouldn't be for a long while yet. Nor was the atmospheric pressure anywhere near Earth's.

Ahh, terraforming.

Would that it were faster.

Still, the Forma pipe did have a more immediate use: whenever I needed to refill my oxygen tanks, that chimney was just half a day's hike away.

I stretched my arms. It felt good to step beyond the confines of the craft.

Queequeg came to my side almost immediately, walking on the knees of his forelegs in submission.

"Good morning Queequeg." I scratched the animal's head. "Beautiful day."

He groaned softly.

My friendship with Queequeg was the only thing that kept me sane. I talked, he listened. Queequeg made me feel needed, gave me a reason to go on with each day.

The animal was what I called a hybear. He had the elongated head of a hyena and the bulky torso of a bear. Thick black fur sheathed most of his body, and tufts of green hair tipped his knees, shoulders, and ears. SK bioengineering at its finest. I suspected Queequeg and his brethren contributed to the terraforming in some small way. Probably inhaled carbon dioxide and exhaled oxygen or something along those lines. But don't quote me on that. I'm no bio-engineer, plus I don't have proper bio-scanning equipment.

The main problem with the hybears was that there was no one left to feed them, now that the Sino-Koreans were gone.

And they were hungry. They'd eat the Beasts if they had to, or each other, but they much preferred human flesh, judging from the interest they always showed in me.

I didn't have to worry about Queequeg, though. He thought he was human. Still, I had to be wary around him: he existed in a state halfway between a savage animal and a domestic pet, like his namesake from *Moby Dick*. Sometimes, if I tried to approach him after the frenzy of the hunt, he would snap at me and I'd have to talk so very soothingly to him.

I watched the dark, roiling clouds in the distance. The sight gave me an uneasy feeling in my stomach.

"Storm's growing," I said distractedly.

Queequeg clacked his teeth in answer.

If the storm swept this way, we might have to take shelter in one of the abandoned sinkholes that were common to this area of the planet.

But they were never really abandoned, were they?

My stomach growled, thrusting my gloomy thoughts aside. I'd said that the hybears were hungry. Well, so was I.

"Come on, time to hunt."

Queequeg stood to his full height and whooped eagerly.

I hefted my spear—a standard-issue rifle with the long, sharp mandible of one of the Beasts secured to the end with utility tape and superglue. A crude weapon to be sure, but I'd run out of ammunition a long time ago.

I gave the campsite one last glance to make sure everything was in order. My gaze swept past the damaged shuttle, and not for the first time, I wished the AI had awakened me from stasis in orbit rather than trying to land on its own.

When my eyes passed over the intact cockpit glass, I saw a stranger in a furry jumpsuit peering back at me.

Startled, I actually jumped. And when the stranger jumped too, I realized I was looking at my own reflection.

I should have laughed at my own foolishness.

I should have turned around and walked away, shaking my head.

But I hadn't seen myself in weeks.

I'd been avoiding it.

But now that this reflection presented itself, I stared.

And stared.

Beyond that face mask, my features were so sunken, so gaunt, my hair such a stringy mess, that the person I once was proved unrecognizable.

Who had I been?

What had I become?

I didn't even know anymore.

No, that wasn't true.

I did know who I was.

Who I *am*.

I've gone to places I never dreamed I could go.

Scaled heights I never dreamed I could ascend.

Survived situations so dire and encounters so fierce it's mind-boggling I'm still alive.

I really should be dead.

But I'm not.

And you know what?

I will survive this.

I will endure.

I *will* see Earth again.

That's a promise.

You can hold me to that.

We all live our own lives in this galaxy.

It just so happens that I live mine on a planet eight thousand lightyears from everyone else. For now.

I have to go.

It's time to hunt.

Remember me in the dark nights, when all hope seems lost.

Remember me in the storm, when you think you can't go on.

Remember who I am and what I stood for.

This is Navy Astrogator Shaw Chopra, signing off.

POSTSCRIPT

You can keep in touch with me or my writing through one—or all—of the following means:

Twitter: @IsaacHooke
Facebook: fb.me/authorisaachooke
Goodreads: goodreads.com/isaachooke
My website: www.isaachooke.com
My e-mail: isaac@isaachooke.com

Don't be shy about e-mails, I love getting them, and try to respond to everyone!

Thanks again for reading.

ABOUT THE AUTHOR

Isaac Hooke's experimental novel, *The Forever Gate*, achieved Amazon #1 bestseller status in both the science fiction and fantasy categories when it was released in 2013, and was recognized as Indie Book of the Day.

He holds a degree in engineering physics, though his more unusual inventions remain fictive at this time.

He is an avid blogger, cyclist, and photographer who resides in Edmonton, Alberta.

You can reach him at www.isaachooke.com